WINNING MISS WINTHROP

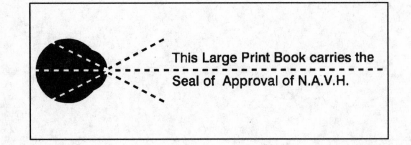

This Large Print Book carries the
Seal of Approval of N.A.V.H.

REGENCY BRIDES: A PROMISE OF HOPE

Winning Miss Winthrop

Carolyn Miller

THORNDIKE PRESS
A part of Gale, a Cengage Company

Farmington Hills, Mich • San Francisco • New York • Waterville, Maine
Meriden, Conn • Mason, Ohio • Chicago

Copyright © 2018 by Carolyn Miller.
Scripture quotations are from the King James Version.
Thorndike Press, a part of Gale, a Cengage Company.

**LIBRARY OF CONGRESS CIP DATA ON FILE.
CATALOGUING IN PUBLICATION FOR THIS BOOK
IS AVAILABLE FROM THE LIBRARY OF CONGRESS**

ISBN-13: 978-1-4328-4975-7 (hardcover)

Published in 2018 by arrangement with Kregel Publications

Printed in the United States of America
1 2 3 4 5 6 7 22 21 20 19 18

For my friend Jacqueline

Sister in Christ, encourager, &
beta reader extraordinaire

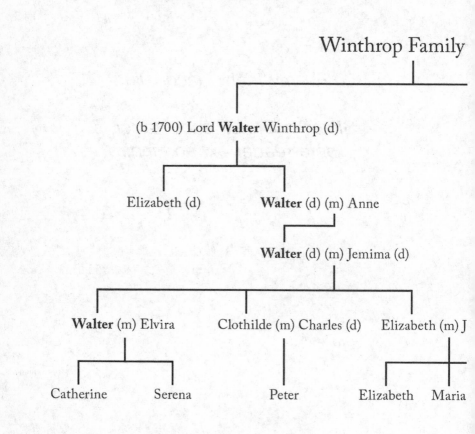

Winthrop Family

(b 1700) Lord **Walter** Winthrop (d)

Elizabeth (d)　　　**Walter** (d) (m) Anne

Walter (d) (m) Jemima (d)

Walter (m) Elvira　　　Clothilde (m) Charles (d)　　　Elizabeth (m) J

Catherine　　Serena　　　　Peter　　　　Elizabeth　Maria

Tree

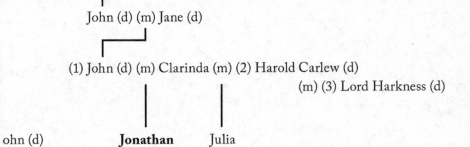

(b 1710) Jonathan Winthrop (d)

John (d) (m) Jane (d)

(1) John (d) (m) Clarinda (m) (2) Harold Carlew (d)

(m) (3) Lord Harkness (d)

ohn (d)   **Jonathan**   Julia

Jane

CHAPTER ONE

The deeply blue Gloucestershire sky brought comfort as Catherine Winthrop emerged from the tenant farmhouse. She drew in a deep breath of clover-scented air then turned to the farmer. "I am sure the doctor will be able to relieve poor Anne more than I. I'll have word sent as soon as I return."

"Thank ye, miss."

Catherine placed her basket on the seat of the gig then deftly climbed past the large spoked wheels. "I hope to be back in a few days to check on her. In the meantime, be sure that she does no unnecessary work as we both know she is wont to do."

Farmer Hassop touched his forehead in farewell.

Catherine snapped the reins and the gig jerked into motion. Soon Ginger had brought her to a fresh-mown meadow, the scent of which tickled her nose, and brought further ease to her heart. Over the brook, whose burble and swish recalled summer days of dipping her toes — when Mama was not looking, of course — willows arced gracefully, their twisting branches gilded in the late afternoon sun, contrasting beautifully with the green fields and the rich browns of furrowed earth.

The bright colors were a salve to the turbulence of the past hour. Poor Anne. Her cough had not improved any, despite Nurse's tonics, and she could not help suspect Farmer Hassop would not let his hardworking wife rest as much as she needed. Poor lady, married to a man who, while not a brute, was said to be one of the most selfish men in the neighborhood. Poor, misled Anne.

But then, Catherine knew only too well how easily a man could fool a woman.

The old ache in her heart panged again. But no good came of thinking like that. She shook her head at herself, and chose instead to fix her attention on the perfect patch of bluebells dancing in the light breeze. Early May was the perfect time to view the countryside in all its glory, and Nelly's Wood was the most spectacular locale. Bluebells, the delicate whites and pinks of wood anemones and yellow cowslips, even the last gold of daffodils could be appreciated anew amongst such a froth of color.

"Is it not lovely, Ginger?"

The chestnut mare tossed her head, as if in reply.

"Wait here."

Within a minute she had secured the reins, slipped from the gig, and was collecting great armfuls of the spring blossoms. She trekked back to the cart and placed the flowers on the seat next to her before climbing in and recommencing her journey.

"I'm sure Nelly, whoever she is, could never have appreciated such a fine sight as we. Do you not agree?"

Ginger nickered her concurrence and Catherine smiled.

The next farm was over a ridge. The Jeffcoat family had farmed this section of land for hundreds of years, their hard work evident in everything from the carefully maintained outbuildings to the precise capping atop the stonewalls. What a shame such heritage would be lost with the eventual demise of the current farmer, for without a capable son . . .

A tall form lumbered into view, broad face splitting into a smile. "Hello, Miss Cathy."

11

"Hello, Jack." She pulled to a stop outside the stone farmhouse. "How are you today?"

"Verra well, Miss Cathy. Is this your horse?"

"Yes, this is Ginger. You've met Ginger before, remember?"

Wide blue eyes stared at her, uncomprehendingly.

Catherine's heart panged. "Tell me, Jack, is your mother within?"

"Yes, Miss Cathy."

A somewhat squat form bustled from the farmhouse, wiping her hands on a floury apron. "Ah, Miss Winthrop. I thought it might be you. I hope Jack is behaving himself?"

"He always does, Mrs. Jeffcoat."

"Well, that be a relief to hear." She shot a narrow look at her son, towering over them both, before her gaze returned to Catherine. "And how be your mother and father?"

"Very well, thank you."

Although perhaps Papa was not *quite* as well as he could be. Since their recent return from London he'd seemed somewhat tense, closeting himself in his study these past days, snapping at whoever dared speak to him, barely acknowledging Mama, although Catherine could not really blame him for that. Any chance to escape her mother's zealous desire to know everything was something both Papa and Catherine eagerly seized upon, hence her longer than usual trip to the tenant farms today.

Catherine smiled. "They send their best." Well, they would if they thought to.

"I'm sure." Mrs. Jeffcoat smiled thinly. "Now, what can we be helping you with today?"

"Well, I told Cook that I thought a gooseberry fool would be just the thing for Father, and she said our gooseberries hadn't come on yet and, knowing yours are always early, I was hoping you might have some that you were willing to sell."

"Ah. Well, I had hoped to use them for my own man, but I suppose —"

"No, no, Mrs. Jeffcoat! I wouldn't dream of taking supplies destined for your husband. It was only if you had extra."

The older woman sighed. "Yes, but feeding my husband won't pay so good as selling to you, so I s'pose we can reach an arrangement."

"Oh, but —"

"No, let me not hear another word. I'm sure 'is lordship will get as much pleasure from them as my John would've." She shot Catherine a keen glance then waddled back inside the farmhouse.

Catherine shifted on the gig's leather seat, fighting the pangs of guilt her request had ignited. Yet Mrs. Jeffcoat *had* agreed, and she would be paid a fair price . . .

"Hello, Miss Cathy."

She turned to the gangling farmer's son and forced up her lips. "Hello, Jack."

"Is this your horse?"

"Yes." Her eyes blurred for a moment. Poor Mrs. Jeffcoat. How hard it must be, that the longed-for son be unable to carry the weight of their hopes and dreams. But Jack wasn't the moonling so many people thought. She'd often thought he'd make an excellent groom. He was very capable of caring for animals, and she'd seen his strength out in the fields. "Strong as an ox," Farmer Jeffcoat would say, desperate pride in his eyes . . .

But as Lavinia said, Mrs. Jeffcoat couldn't have known she would catch measles during her confinement. Jack's condition wasn't his fault, just as being sonless wasn't Papa's.

Her nose twitched as the scents of cows and dung grew with the lengthening shadows. When Jack wasn't murmuring to her horse he would stare at Catherine so steadily her skin would prickle. It was all she could do not to tell him to look away. She glanced elsewhere instead, thinking of her earlier visit to Lizzie, once a maid at Winthrop, whose excitement at her recent marriage was augmented with the news she was already increasing, and Jem, her farmer husband hopeful of a healthy boy by autumn. She knew she should be as shocked as Mama about the speed at which such things had occurred, but instead, could not help but feel a tad wistful, her envy mixed with a measure of anxiety. *Please, God, help Lizzie's babe be healthy . . .* And not as the boy-man who stood staring at her.

Relief unfurled within when Mrs. Jeffcoat finally reappeared. She placed a wooden pail half filled with the bright green fruit onto the seat next to the flowers.

"Oh, thank you, Mrs. Jeffcoat."

"They be a bit early, likely to be quite tart."

"I'm sure Papa will be very pleased."

The farmer's wife nodded. They worked out fair recompense then Catherine picked up the reins again.

"I'll be sure to fix you up tomorrow. Thank you again, Mrs. Jeffcoat, Jack."

"Goodbye, Miss Cathy."

And flashing a final guilt-laden smile, she encouraged Ginger to head for home.

She had no need for self-reproach, she thought, as the gig bumped over muddy

15

tracks. Just as Mrs. Jeffcoat was not responsible for her son's mental culpability, neither was Catherine responsible for her family's wealth and status. Papa couldn't help inheriting Grandfather's great fortune along with his title and lands, just as Cousin Peter would one day, too. Inheritance and good fortune were situations to thank God for, not feel guilt about, especially when she did whatever she could to help those less fortunate.

The road curved to the Winthrop gates. She lifted a hand as the gatehouse keeper's children waved, and encouraged Ginger to quicken her pace. As the trees met overhead across the drive, a chill passed over her. Evening was drawing near, and she wasn't used to being out quite so late. But still, her time had proved worthwhile. Papa was sure to love the berries, and the flowers *might* appease Mama . . .

Ahead, she caught a glimpse of lighted second-story windows, the curtains not yet drawn, despite the approaching dark. She frowned. Why hadn't the maids closed them? Why hadn't Mama scolded them into fulfilling their duties?

She passed the stone pillars marking entry to the Manor garden proper. At the *porte cochère* stood the doctor's carriage.

Her heart cantered with unease. Why was the doctor here? She pulled hard at the reins, the wheels skidding to a stop.

"Oh, Miss Winthrop! Everyone has been looking for you!" Geoffreys hurried toward her, his extreme fastidiousness not evident for once, as he condescended to hold the reins. "They're waiting for you inside."

"Who is waiting?" She climbed down, picked up her flowers, the fruit for her father.

"Your mother, and the doctor, and —" The butler swallowed.

Her neck prickled. Why did he refuse to look her in the eyes? She hurried inside. "Mama?"

She handed her spoils to William, who waited as she stripped off her hat and gloves before murmuring, "They're upstairs, miss."

She nodded and hastened up the enormous oak staircase that had cost her father thousands when he had remodeled five years ago. "Mama?"

A wail sounded. Heart racing, Catherine hurried past Serena's vacant room and entered her mother's bedchamber. Christie glanced up from where she was waving smelling salts under Mama's nose, her knit brow and nod to the adjoining room suggesting that whatever was amiss was very

17

serious indeed.

"His Lordship's in there, miss," she murmured. "The doctor's in with him, but . . ."

Catherine hurried into her father's room, the huge four-poster bed dominating the domain, its very size seeming to shrink her father as he lay, shrouded in the middle.

"Oh, Papa!"

Her father turned, gray-faced, gasping.

The doctor glanced up. "I'm sorry, Miss Winthrop, but there is nothing more I can do."

"No, no!" She hurried to the bed. "Father, Papa, please . . ." She glanced at Carrick, who had served Papa for years. "What can be done?"

He lifted his hands in a helpless gesture. "I am sorry, Miss Catherine, but he has been this way since clutching his arm nearly two hours ago now."

While she'd been off picking flowers! "No, no, Papa, I need you. Please don't —" She swallowed the word, as if hearing it aloud would bring it to fruition. "Lord God, have mercy!"

But it seemed God had none, as her father stiffened, then, with a final broken sigh, died.

■ ■ ■ ■

White's Gentlemen's Club, London

"I lay you ten guineas the next lady who walks past is a complete fright."

"Only ten? I wager five-and-twenty. What say you, Carlew?"

Jonathan Carlew looked up from his newspaper at his two companions. "I say a fool and his money are quickly parted."

"Well, nobody shall ever accuse you of being a fool, you stingy old man," Viscount Henry Carmichael said, tease in his eyes.

Jon hid his smile. Who would have thought one day's difference in their birth dates would lead to years of such jests? "What some call stingy others call wise."

"Your modesty overwhelms." Major Thomas Hale, the third member of the party, snorted. "Now, Carmichael, here comes our next contender. What say you, ugly or divine?"

"Must it be one or the other?" Jon asked.

"My dear fellow, a woman is either decidedly pretty or decidedly not."

"One simply has to decide which of the two?" Jon suggested.

"Exactly." The heir to the Earl of Bevington nodded.

19

"But surely that implies a degree of subjectivity, if, as the poets say, beauty does lie in the eye of the beholder."

The major lifted his glass to peer through the bow window. "Well, I behold a fright. Carmichael, you owe me a pony."

The viscount handed over twenty-five pounds, muttering about the audacity of such ladies to walk without consideration for the eyes of men.

"Can you imagine what the ladies must think of such ogling?"

"Ogling! Carlew, I resent the implication."

"My apologies, Hale, but I meant no implication."

Carmichael laughed. "You are a sly dog, Carlew. Next you will be saying a woman's appearance ought count for nothing."

Jon merely smiled.

"Well may it be for some to be fastidious about such things, but good heavens, if a man means to be leg-shackled then let it be to a lady whom he finds pleasing to gaze upon."

"Does that hold true for the lady in question also? Indeed, if this line of reasoning is so, there would be many of us destined to singlehood on account of our less than perfect looks."

The major gave a loud harrumph as Carmichael said, "You seem to forget the numbers of ladies at the ball last week who seemed very willing to overlook *your* ill-favored face."

The tips of Jon's ears grew hot. "I confess it had slipped my mind."

That evening in question had been one of the more excruciating of his life. Perhaps if he'd learned to flirt like Carmichael or Hale he might be more successful in ensuring the women who flocked to him knew not to expect anything more than a deftly turned compliment. But as Hale had commented that evening, Jon's more serious demeanor and deep voice lent a gravity to his words that only seemed to encourage the clinging young ladies with whom he had no desire to further his acquaintance.

"Next you'll be saying a woman should not be judged on her face."

"Should a man?"

His companions both stared at him before Hale gave another loud harrumph.

"Carlew, your observations are both unnecessary and unkind. Go back to your paper if you don't mind."

Jon chuckled, shook his head at his friends' antics, and retired once more behind the screen of *The Times*. His smile faded, the printed words before him meaningless. While he didn't begrudge them — they were his friends, who had helped keep him sane these past years when India had a way of hardening even the kindest of men — he couldn't help but wonder how these gentlemen would rate the woman who had once caught his eye. Not strictly pretty, let alone divine, he couldn't help but think she'd rate rather poorly on Hale's scale of attractiveness.

His fingers clenched. Relaxed. Not that he should care. These were foolish thoughts. He was unlikely to see her, and even if he did, she had long ago made her feelings abundantly clear.

No. Perhaps he was a fool after all. Surely two years of adventure and business should have been enough to rid him of these feelings.

Perhaps it was time to think on a lady who might not mind his connections to trade, at least until that far away day when he might assume the title. His earnings from his time on the Indian subcontinent should, correctly invested, hold out for quite a few more years, and the interest on his shares in his father's companies was steadily improving, so Trelling said. Perhaps there was a lady who might not mind being married to such a man. He could offer constancy, and quite a tidy fortune, if little else.

His spirits dipped.

Perhaps one day there might even be one prepared to overlook the haze concerning the legitimacy of his birth.

CHAPTER TWO

Winthrop Manor, Gloucestershire
"The Lord giveth, and the Lord taketh away."

The words circled Catherine's mind endlessly as she sat in her favorite chair, in her favorite room at Winthrop. She breathed in. Out. Hungrily soaked in rare stillness. She inhaled again, then exhaled, as if these simple actions might dim today's truth. The minister. The funeral. The mourners. The whispers and speculation-laden glances that shifted whenever her gaze met theirs. Most of all she was aware of a heavy numbness, a weight upon her spirit that no amount of assurances from the minister or her friend Lavinia could lift.

Her world had changed. Everything would be different. Everything would be . . . worse.

She drew further into the high-backed wingchair, placed her feet securely on the rich jeweled tones of the Axminster carpet,

24

clasped the red-striped fabric arms more firmly. She was not a fainting miss, no matter what example her mother might have set over the past week, barely moving from her bed. Someone had to comfort poor Serena, receive the visitors, attend to the grief-stricken staff, help make decisions about the words spoken at the funeral and what would be served afterwards. Someone had to be aware and take responsibility for whatever life might throw at them, now that Papa's anchoring presence was gone.

Rawness clogged her throat. Her eyes filled. She blinked. Blinked again.

"The Lord giveth, and the Lord taketh away."

She lifted her head, studying the cream wallpaper patterned with pale yellow roses. How pretty, how soothing this room had always been, with its lovely outlook to the rose gardens and the blue hills beyond. She breathed in, out, pushing past fresh pain. Soon Cousin Peter would live here, doubtless marry, and his wife would make decorating choices, placing their own stamp on Winthrop Manor. She and Mama would be forced to move to the Dower House, a grand title for a not-so-grand cottage tucked away on the far side of the estate.

Her lips twisted. She suspected it would

prove to be another of the projects Papa had not attended to in recent times. The discovery of several others — such as the unopened bills accumulating dust on his desk — had fueled further unease these past days. Her chest tightened. Breathe in. Breathe out. At least the Dower House was closer to Hampton Hall and Lavinia — whenever she and her husband, the Earl of Hawkesbury, were in — which was something. Even if it were farther away from the stables, and her gig, and the gardens, and . . .

Her eyes pricked again.

The door opened, admitting a cool draft as well as the hubbub she'd managed to avoid this past hour.

"Ah, here she is." Aunt Drusilla Villiers — tall, thin, her snapping black eyes and long Ashton nose reminiscent of a haughty witch — walked toward Catherine. "We were all wondering why the daughter of the house had made no appearance."

Catherine swallowed. Swallowed again. When could she put off this façade of hospitality and instead receive the comfort of others?

"I apologize, Aunt, but I was not hungry, and I feel a little tired —"

"Be that as it may, you still have an obligation, especially when your Mama is prostrate upstairs. That Lady Milton was at the tea table acting for all intents and purposes like *she* was the lady of the house. I ask you! She was rabbiting on about some Sally chit none of us had the slightest interest in."

She smiled faintly, imagining the scene. "Do you mean Sophy, ma'am?" Sophia Thornton, once a playmate of hers, had written a very pretty letter expressing her sorrow and regret that her latest confinement made travel impossible. It was kindly meant, but Catherine couldn't help feel the sting experienced with most of Sophy's correspondence, that her life was progressing nicely, while Catherine's life had felt stuck for years.

Her aunt shrugged. "Sophy, Sally, why should I care what her silly daughter is named?" Aunt Drusilla moved to sit on the gold and white striped settee near the marble fireplace. The door opened again, admitting Serena and their cousins.

Catherine eyed her sister objectively. Well she could understand those who accused the younger Winthrop girl of coldheartedness, with a countenance forever as calm as her name. Only Catherine knew the extent of Serena's grief, her sobbed regret at being away at school in Bath and missing a final goodbye had kept Catherine awake for much of the night, attempting to soothe away her sister's sorrow. Not that anyone could tell now. With her golden curls and ethereal complexion, Serena looked as unconcerned as though toddling off to a picnic with her cousins rather than mourning the loss of a father who adored her.

Her mouth pulled to one side. Perhaps Serena wore sadness better than Catherine ever could — oh, to be innocent seventeen again! — or perhaps she and her sister, in addition to inheriting Mama's Ashton nose, had also both inherited their father's unfortunate propensity for keeping trouble too close to their chests. She sighed. At least Serena could return to Bath and Miss Haverstock's seminary soon.

"Catherine!" A blur of copper-gold and concern rushed through the door, encasing Catherine in a warm hug. "Oh, my dear friend, I'm so glad to see you."

Lavinia Hawkesbury drew back, her slightly reddened eyes speaking of her distress. "I could not speak with you earlier as there was such a crush wishing to pay their respects."

Catherine nodded. The crush had made it easy for her to avoid both sympathetic comments and eyes, as she kept her own down.

28

Simple nods, simply expressed thanks, had been all she could manage. Members of both sides of Papa's and Mama's prodigious families, a few good neighbors, like Lavinia and the earl; others she either did not know or could scarcely recall. For a moment her heart beat faster. Would *he* have dared appear?

Lavinia's expensive black silk rustled as she dropped into the seat next to Catherine, the room filling with other guests awaiting the outcome of the reading of the will. Lavinia's middle was a little thicker these days.

Catherine cleared her throat. "I trust you are feeling well."

Lavinia smiled. "Better than last month, it is true. Nicholas seems determined to treat me as though I should be wrapped in cotton wool, but when we heard your sad news there was nothing that could stop me from being here as quickly as possible."

Catherine smiled for the first time in what felt like months. Lavinia's passion and care for her friends, coupled with a sometimes startling frankness, had appealed since they'd first met as young girls. Doubtless such unconventional behavior had been instrumental in winning the heart of the war hero earl who had moved to St. Hampton

Heath upon assuming the title three years ago. Yet Catherine knew Lavinia was not immune to challenge. The Lord giveth, and even for someone as good as Lavinia, the Lord had taken away.

Lady Milton, the squire's plump wife, now entered, her eager gaze running around the room until fixing upon Catherine. "You *poor* dear! How are you holding up? I notice you seem quite pale, and — you won't mind my saying, I'm sure, as our families have been acquainted for *so* long — perhaps a little sickly? But that may be simply the effect of that dress." Blue eyes flicked Catherine up and down. "Not everyone can wear black as well as my Sophy can. But then, she is one of us fortunate few who will appear to advantage regardless of what we wear." Her gaze slid to Lavinia's attire, hardening, before her attention returned to Catherine. "I'm *so* glad you are well, my dear, although I must say, I could not help but observe earlier that your Mama did not look at *all* well."

Breathe in. Breathe out. Perhaps the Lord might take Lady Milton away from their presence soon . . .

Lavinia met Catherine's gaze, nodded slightly, and turned to Lady Milton with a sweet smile. "Well, that is hardly to be expected, is it, Lady Milton? It would seem to me that a woman who looks well following the death of her husband displays a great lack of sensibility."

Lady Milton sniffed. "Far be it from me to disagree with *you,* Lady Hawkesbury —"

"If only that were true," murmured Lavinia.

"— I was only trying to express my condolences to poor Catherine here."

"Is that what it was?" said the irrepressible young countess.

Lady Milton glared, lifted her many chins, and moved to talk to another acquaintance, her nasal-inflected voice piercing enough for Catherine to catch something about the airs and graces a certain minister's daughter had assumed since hooking an earl.

Lavinia shrugged and rolled her eyes, eliciting another wry twist of lips from Catherine.

The room swelled with extended family, friends, forcing Catherine to adopt a more appropriate expression as the ladies of her acquaintance murmured sympathy and regret. Soon her mood slipped back to pain, as over and over their comments and questions reinforced the concern that had nibbled for days. This *was* a very sad time. What *would* she do now? How would her dear mother cope? How would Serena?

These questions, she knew, were subtle echoes of the more pressing inquisition: How would they afford to live? Some reduction in their circumstances must be expected, for even she had heard the whispers, of both servants and gentry alike, concerning Papa's profligate spending — and subsequent bills. But surely they would not be so terribly badly off?

Outside, through the tall French doors, she could see the wind tossing the leaves of the pines, their movement constant, yet uncertain, as the branches bent and swayed this way then that against unseen forces. Coldness seeped into her heart. Invisible, unknown forces, much like those in her life . . .

A stir through the room brought her attention to the door.

Catherine blinked. No. Surely not.

"Lady Harkness! Well, we certainly did not expect to see *you*." This, from Aunt Drusilla, whose blunt ways of speaking almost rivaled Lavinia's.

"Ah, Drusilla." The gloriously arrayed arrival gave a glittering smile. "Yes, we would have been here sooner but unfortunately we were held up at Swindon."

"By highwaymen?" asked Lady Milton,

protuberant eyes goggling.

"No, no. The horse had merely thrown a shoe." Lady Harkness glanced around. "Now, where is poor Elvira? I confess it's been such an age I do not know I should recognize her, but I did want to pay my respects."

Catherine rose. "Mama is indisposed."

"Ah." The ostrich feathers — far more appropriate for a London ballroom — trembled like the trees outside as the redhead nodded. "Miss Winthrop. Please accept my deepest sympathies."

But her green eyes were cold and hard, skimming over Catherine's dull garb as if searching for something — and finding her wanting. "I must confess to not recognizing you, either. You seem so much . . . older than the last time."

Catherine bit the inside of her bottom lip. If she understood Lady Milton's resentment to Lavinia, how much more did she understand this woman's antagonism toward herself. And it could not be denied, the past two years had not been kind.

A slender blonde, whom the previous arrival's flamboyant style had all but hidden, now moved into view. Lady Harkness glanced at her then waved a hand. "My daughter, Julia."

So this was the half sister she'd wondered over. Elegantly pretty, with blue eyes and even features, she seemed modest, unassuming. Catherine searched for a trace of his features —

But wait! Her heart thumped. If Lady Harkness and Julia were here, then surely *he* would be also.

The room tilted slightly as, for a moment, she really did feel faint.

Breathe in. Breathe out.

"Lady Harkness, is it? Please, allow me to offer you a seat here." Lady Milton, obviously impressed by the gleaming diamonds at the new arrival's throat, and oblivious to the hostility in the room, persuaded her to share her settee before launching into a series of questions about London that anyone with half an eye could see the newcomer was loath to answer.

Lavinia touched Catherine's hand and guided her to a quieter corner of the room. "Dear Catherine, you do not look at all well. What is it?"

How could she admit to her misgivings, or expose the secrets that had caused such pain? She could not. She drew in a deep breath. Attempted a smile. "I wish Mama were here."

"Of course you do. Shall I send someone

to see if she is feeling more the thing?"

"No, thank you, that is quite all right. I can do so."

But before she could ring for a servant, the door opened once more and Mama glided in. Her face was wan, her features strained, but the weariness of past days had not dulled her keen sense of drama. She glanced around the room, nodding to the expressions of sympathy, and then halted wide-eyed at the occupants of the settee. Her face blanched, before two red spots formed on her cheeks.

"*Dear* Lady Winthrop, we were just saying, weren't we, Lady Harkness, how we hoped to see you before much longer . . ."

Lady Milton prattled on, heedless of Mama's inattention, her gaze fixed on the woman seated beside her.

"Ah, Elvira. How are you?"

Catherine's fingers formed fists. Asking such a question as if this were a ball!

"As well as can be expected," Mama said stiffly. "I must admit to a certain degree of surprise at seeing *you* here, Clarinda."

"I do not see why. Surely as a concerned family member you might expect to see me here. Certainly I have more right to be here than some of these others." She cast a less-than-surreptitious glance at some of the neighbors, including Lady Milton, who seemed agog to see her friendly overtures so summarily dismissed.

"More right?"

"Certainly." The red head lifted proudly. "As the mother of the new baron, I believe I have more right to be here than anyone else."

"Surely you jest!"

This from Aunt Clothilde, whose son Peter was all but assured of the title.

Lady Harkness lifted an expensively draped shoulder. "I am only communicating what dear Mr. Whittington wrote in his letter to Jonathan."

Jonathan . . .

The world swam again.

Lavinia touched her shoulder, motioned her to a squat velvet chair. She sank into it gratefully as the raised voices from the older women continued.

"But my Peter is next in line. Mr. Whittington has confused matters."

"I do not believe so."

"But Peter has visited the estate for some time now, learning everything necessary from Lord Winthrop —"

"Has he really?"

Lady Harkness's catlike green eyes suddenly looked as sly as her words seemed.

Was she casting aspersions on Papa's training of Peter?

"Papa *has* taught Peter all about estate m-matters," Catherine disputed, wincing at the stammer whose appearance in front of intimidating individuals always made her feel even more foolish.

"I'm sure he has, but unless he is to become the next baron then it will all be for nothing. Surely it's time to let someone with a fresh eye come in for a change. The state of these carpets!"

Hot indignation burned in her soul, echoing the gasps of outrage filling the room. She opened her mouth but before she could speak Aunt Drusilla's voice came again.

"It seems a terrible thing for the title to go to someone with so few claims to it."

Lady Harkness's eyes flashed, her color rising. "How dare — ?"

"Ah, ladies."

The men, led by the Earl of Hawkesbury, poured through the open door. Catherine's insides clenched; her skin heated. *He* was here; would be in here any moment. She half rose, then resumed her seat, wishing she could edge back into the shadowed recesses of the room.

She studied the faces as they entered. Mr. Whittington looked rather tired and old, as if his efforts of the past hour had drained him. The earl moved straight to Lavinia's side, murmuring softly to her, which she replied to with a smile and a shake of her head. Catherine studied the door again. Peter entered, a sour expression on his face as he strode to his mother and whispered urgently to her.

Then *he* entered.

The world stopped. Her breath stilled.

She caught a glimpse of his tanned countenance and dark blond hair as he glanced around the room. She lowered her face quickly, anxious to avoid his notice, though a tiny part of her longed for his attention, craved to hear him say —

"Son, come sit here with me."

"Thank you, ma'am, but I prefer to stand."

The deep, deep voice drew her attention, just as it always had. As if unwilling to be there, he moved to the windows where he gazed outside, hands behind his back, his broad shoulders encased in black mourning clothes, the superior quality and fit showing him to advantage.

Not that she cared.

She breathed in. Out. *Lord God, help me . . .*

"What is this about? Whittington?"

The elderly man cleared his throat, apologized, then launched into a tangle of legal terminology. Eventually, after much mopping of brow, he said, "Now I know this will come as something of a surprise, but it appears that the estate is entailed to" — he swallowed — "Mr. Jonathan Carlew . . . er, I mean, Winthrop."

No.

The walls tilted.

"But Peter is dear Walter's nephew!" cried Aunt Clothilde. "Surely he stands a greater right than some illegitimate cousin —"

"How dare you?" Lady Harkness snapped.

Catherine glanced toward the window. Mr. Carlew's attention remained fixed outside. The only sign he'd noticed the slur and his mother's outrage was a lifting, a tensing of his shoulders, as though he'd suddenly drawn in air.

"While it is true that Mr. Carlew is a third cousin once removed, he still holds a greater claim as he is descended from Lord Winthrop's great-grandfather's younger brother —"

"If indeed he is," muttered Aunt Clothilde.

"And thus preserves the male lineage as required by law. It is true that Peter inherits the extra holdings, including the Avebury estate, but the title, the Manor, and tenant farms go to Mr. Carlew."

"But —"

"We shall see about that!" Aunt Clothilde snapped. "We shall have a *proper* solicitor look into this."

"As you wish." Mr. Whittington bowed his head.

"What *I* wish to know is how much the estate is worth," Lady Harkness said.

Mr. Carlew turned, frowning at his mother.

"Don't look at me like that, Jonathan. We all want to know. Well? What has he left you?"

He shook his head. "Mother, this is neither the time nor place."

"You mean because of these unknown persons?" The green gaze scanned the room. "I agree, it would be better if this could be kept in the family for the moment."

"Family?" Aunt Drusilla hissed. "That woman has a nerve —"

"I have a nerve and excellent hearing, also, Drusilla dear. Now, do wipe that expression off your face. I fear you'll start curdling the milk for my tea."

Someone tittered. Catherine's jaw sagged.

Was there anything this woman wouldn't say?

Catherine glanced across at Lavinia, whose arched brows no doubt matched her own. Next to her, the earl's expression mingled horror and amusement.

Lavinia shot her a sympathetic look and pushed to her feet. "I hope, Lady Winthrop, that you will be feeling better soon." She then murmured something to Serena before clasping Catherine lightly. "Send a message when you would like company. And remember, if there is anything we can do, please do not hesitate."

The earl reiterated his condolences from earlier and offered a grave smile. "I trust you will not hesitate?"

"Of c-course, my lord."

"Good." He nodded, as if satisfied, before moving to Mr. Carlew and extending his hand. Catherine watched the two men exchange a few words while the other ladies farewelled Lavinia. Other neighbors soon followed the Hawkesbury lead and made their departures as well, apart from Lady Milton, who sat complacently nibbling a small biscuit and studying the large Reynolds portrait hanging over the fireplace, as if hoping a lack of eye contact would render her invisible.

"Lady . . . Milton, is it?"

Mr. Carlew's deep voice drew the attention of everyone who remained in the room, including the avid appreciator of art, who swallowed her biscuit hurriedly. "Yes?"

"Pardon my ignorance, but are you so intimately connected with Lady Winthrop that you feel it your duty to stay?"

The squire's wife blinked rapidly. Catherine suppressed a smile. Never had she seen Lady Milton so disconcerted — save at the wedding of Lavinia to the earl. "I have known Elvira for years, so of *course* I consider it my duty —"

"Oh, take her away," Aunt Clothilde snapped. "Nobody wants her here."

Lady Milton drew herself up, chins in the air. "Well, I never!"

"About time you were," muttered Aunt Drusilla, as the nosy neighbor waddled from the room.

Catherine coughed to hide her snicker, the sound drawing Mr. Carlew's attention.

His blue-gray eyes widened, his cheeks paling under his healthy tan, like he saw a ghost. Her breakfast curdled within. She lowered her gaze to his dark waistcoat.

"Mr. Carlew, allow me to introduce Miss Winthrop."

He nodded to Mr. Whittington. "Thank

you, we are acquainted."

Mr. Carlew offered a small bow which she could only, politely, acknowledge with a nod.

He shifted away, leaving her feeling raw and hollowed. She exhaled with a shaky breath and forced her gloved fingers to relax. The worst was done. But oh . . . Her eyes burned.

"Now, shall we resume?" The lawyer glanced around the room.

Mama sat with Aunt Drusilla; Aunt Elizabeth, Papa's quiet sister who had raised three most unquiet girls, sat on the next settee, her red-rimmed eyes testifying to *her* sorrow at least. Churning emotion mingled with frustration. Did Mama's grief stem more from the loss of her position and house than any real sorrow at Papa's passing? Catherine stifled the uncharitable thought and moved from her position to sit beside her grieving aunt. Aunt Elizabeth clasped her hand.

Catherine glanced over at Aunt Clothilde and Peter, still wearing matching disgruntled expressions. On the other side of the fireplace sat Lady Harkness and her daughter, both wearing looks that could only be counted as expectant. Behind them, Mr. Carlew stood motionless, his expression as

43

grave as she remembered. Truly, the man did not look like he took pleasure in any of this.

Mr. Whittington began to speak, his dry voice and drier legal circumlocutions dulling her senses until she could hardly focus. Finally he turned to her mother. "Lady Winthrop, as you might be aware, your husband had quite large debts, and had heavily mortgaged the assets he did have. I deeply regret to inform you that you will have to live on a substantially smaller allowance than you have been accustomed to."

"What?"

"H-how much smaller?" Catherine ventured.

Mr. Whittington turned to her. "I'm very sorry, Miss Winthrop, but apart from the settlement monies put aside for you and your sister upon your eventual marriages, nearly everything else is gone."

She stilled. "How c-can they be almost gone?" She refused to look at Mr. Carlew, her cheeks burning in humiliation at his being privy to both her loss and her stammer.

"Do you mean to say we have no money?" Mama asked. "That . . . . that is impossible! Walter would never have left me without funds."

Mr. Whittington coughed. "I am afraid he

did, madam."

"No. No, I simply refuse to believe it. Walter would never —"

"Mama," Catherine murmured.

Lady Harkness glanced complacently at her offspring. "A lack of funds does not concern us, I'm relieved to say. *My* husband was an excellent provider."

"Her husbands," Aunt Drusilla muttered. "How many has she had? And all now dead. The Black Widow they say —"

"Aunt!" Mortification warmed Catherine's cheeks anew. How had Papa's death descended into such a sideshow of incivility?

"Lady Winthrop, you will have a small income, not more than eight or nine hundred a year —"

Mama groaned.

"And your daughters will receive a similar sum when they do eventually marry —"

Catherine wished she could groan as well. Why, why, why had *he* to be here to hear the doubt in the lawyer's voice? Like a spinster of twenty-five could hope to marry. Like anyone would want her. Hadn't his rejection proved it?

"And Peter? What about him?"

Mr. Whittington studied Aunt Clothilde with an expression bordering on dislike.

"Madam, while Peter is specifically mentioned in the will to receive the Avebury estate, I'm afraid there is nothing more provided for its running costs." He turned to Peter, whose mien had deflated at that last comment. "I trust you have other assets to assist?"

"I . . . er . . ." His pimpled face flushed, then he glanced at his mother.

She seemed to draw within herself before saying stiffly, "That is no concern of yours."

"Of course, madam."

Aunt Clothilde rose unsteadily to her feet, grasping Peter's arm. "This all smacks of gross incompetence! I cannot believe my Peter did not receive what is his proper due." She cast a venomous look at Mr. Carlew. "The title should at least go to someone with *real* Winthrop blood."

Murmurs of discontent and accusation filled the room, plunging Catherine's soul deeper into despair. How could they scrap over the title like stray dogs over a bone, snarling and biting at each other? Did nobody care Papa was gone?

The room eventually emptied of all save herself.

Her eyes filled with tears and she slumped into her favorite chair, burrowing deep into the cushions as though she could hide.

Breathe in. Breathe out.
The Lord giveth and the Lord taketh away.

CHAPTER THREE

Jonathan walked through the paneled Oak Room, thankful to be removed from the earlier tension, thankful for a moment of distraction to clear the turbulence of his heart and head. The Oak Room was a kind of long gallery — so he was informed by Geoffreys, the overly pompous butler — and was lined with paintings of long-dead ancestors he had never known.

Save for — yes. He stopped. Stared up at the large portrait. Blue-gray eyes scowled down from under heavy brows. This face he did recognize. His lips twitched. He would not thank his mother for the compliment of suggesting he took after his grandfather in more than just a certain shrewdness in financial matters. Yet he saw enough, remembered enough, for it to be true. The angle of jaw perhaps, the shape of the ears. But Jon hoped he never looked quite so displeased with life. Even if sometimes it felt true.

"Ah, dear boy. You're here."

He turned, sketched a bow. "As you see."

His mother smiled. Sparing a glance for the portraits, she shuddered theatrically. "The skeletons are as ghoulish as ever."

"Mother . . ."

"Why I ever married into this family I do not know. Look at them, so filled with pride it practically drips from their noses." She hooked a hand around his arm. "Your grandfather was the best of a bad lot."

"Even better than Father?"

She glanced at him with hooded eyes, as though she had words she dared not speak. Uncertainty rippled through him as it did every time she refused to speak of his natural father. He'd happily claimed Harold Carlew as his father for as long as he could remember, identifying so much he had taken on his name from a very young age. But had Harold been too eager to call him son? Were the Winthrops correct? Had there been a mistake after all?

"Do you remember visiting your grandfather?"

He nodded. How could he forget? It had been the start of a dream. An impossible dream.

"I was so glad you got the chance to make

his acquaintance before . . ."

Her words trailed away. He placed a hand on hers, gently squeezed. She sighed. "I suppose you'll want to move in soon?"

"Mother, I could not presume —"

"Why ever not? You are the rightful heir, after all."

Was he? He studied her, but her bright gaze admitted nothing. "I would hope Lady Winthrop would invite me, rather than impose myself upon them."

Her laughter trilled. "I'm afraid you would be waiting until kingdom come. Besides, you would not be imposing. How many times must I tell you that you rely too much upon such sensibilities? You belong here, not she, not they."

He shook his head gently. "Mother . . ."

She cast him a searching glance. "I noticed you seemed a little taken aback this afternoon."

His jaw clenched.

"I declare, I would not have recognized her again in a thousand years! She seemed altered beyond belief. Like a faded little brown mouse."

Faded. He forced himself to nod. Yes, faded was an appropriate term. And appropriate justice for what she had done.

"I do hope that woman won't cause any

trouble."

"Catherine?" Her name now tasted strange on his tongue.

His mother's lips pursed. "No, that ridiculous turbaned aunt of hers. Y'know, the mother of that poor child she thinks should inherit. Can you imagine — him, a pimply, gawky boy, running all this?" She waved a hand at the courtyard, one of two, Geoffreys had informed him on their brief tour of the Manor, after matters in the drawing room had descended into ignominy.

"I cannot see how he'll cope with running Avebury."

"Neither can I. One of Wiltshire's great estates? In those unproved hands? I'd sooner believe a sparrow can tame a lion. Or is it a tiger?" Her head tilted, she squeezed his arm. "It is so wonderful to have you home again, to know you are safe instead of in such a godforsaken place."

"God was with me there, Mother."

"Well, perhaps." She patted his hand. "But I am glad to have you near again."

She smiled up at him, and a burst of affection filled him, leading him to kiss her brow. They continued ambling, his mother's chatter drowning out the uncertainty from before. Whatever the questions surrounding his mother, he had never doubted her love

51

for him, or her total confidence in his abilities.

His smile slipped.

Unlike some.

"And sir, I have given you the blue bedchamber, which I trust you will find most comfortable." Geoffreys coughed apologetically. "I know it should be the master suite, but I'm afraid it is not yet ready."

Jon held up a hand. "Please, don't touch anything there on my account. I would rather leave things as they are for as long as possible."

"Oh." Geoffreys's hope-filled eyes dimmed a little. "Pardon my presumption, sir, but I thought you would want to change things."

"Perhaps in the future, but in these times of sadness, I'd prefer the family, indeed the Manor, to remain undisturbed as long as possible."

"Of course, my lord."

My lord? Jon blinked, before remembering.

The butler looked at him questioningly, but Jon shook his head.

"If that is all, sir?"

"Thank you."

Jon wandered slowly through a myriad of

corridors back to the main entrance hall, hesitating as he heard the whine of Peter's mother again. They had not been offered accommodation — unnecessary, Geoffreys had assured him, as their own home was only fifteen miles away. He stayed, rooted in the shadows, until their exit. His lips twisted. He might have faced a charging elephant once upon a time, but his courage faltered before the indomitable force of the Winthrop women and their sneered aspersions.

The door closed forcefully, as if the footman — William, perhaps? — was also relieved to see their departure. He stepped forward, caught the footman's shamefaced grin, then moved back past the enormous oak staircase — how much had the previous baron spent on *that*? — before footfalls on the stairs accompanied by a hasty enquiry of a servant led him to an exit into the gardens.

He hurried along the stone path dissecting the green expanse of lawn until he reached the relative safety of screening plants before an enormous hedge of yew. He turned. No whisk of a curtain hastily closed. No face peered from a window. For a moment he could pretend he was alone.

His shoulders sagged. Finally.

The past few days had proved a constant parade of people and appointments. He wandered along the weed-strewn path interspersed with urns seemingly forsaken by the gardening staff, judging by their shriveled occupants. A sigh escaped. How many other areas needed attention? The Manor's stonework needed repointing. From this position he could see at least two tilting chimneys and a great deal of peeling paintwork, unlike the neatly finished front façade. And this was only the most cursory of inspections. Then there was the matter of Avebury.

He scuffed the path with his boot. Anyone could see young Peter was without sufficient funds to assist in that matter. Whittington had spoken plain. The baron had lived on credit these past years, his gambling forcing him to sell the odd piece of unentailed land when necessary in order to make ends meet. If the baron had not spent money on upkeep here at the Manor, his primary residence, how much — how little — would have been spent there? Was this inheritance more noose than he'd first realized?

Tension knotted his shoulders again. What a difficult line he must walk, between appeasing the Winthrop family's concerns and doing what he could to salvage their fortunes. And this, without even taking into consideration the various personalities and expectations that would make this time so challenging.

The worries crowded in. Muscles bunched in his neck. He pressed deep into the base of his skull to massage them out. Forced himself to relax. To remember this wasn't the first time he'd faced difficult odds. India had been full of unexpected challenges. And each time, he — with God's help — had overcome.

The untrimmed yew hedge held a gate, propped open, with weathered palings. He walked through into a knot garden, its classical lines still evident despite the obvious lack of attention. The path led to an overgrown arbor, under which a stone seat was positioned, doubtless a lovely place in summer. The house loomed above the hedge, like a watchful giant, waiting for his move.

Who would have envisaged this? Six months ago, he was fending off disaster in Bombay; today, he held the keys to a future he'd never dared believe. And this house?

This house certainly possessed nothing of the modest proportions he was used to associating with manor houses. Geoffreys's tour had not included the upper floor, Jonathan not wanting to intrude any more than absolutely necessary, but he was reliably informed there were at least a dozen bed-chambers, for which the suite of rooms for entertaining made sense. Clearly Winthrop Manor was the primary residence of the head of the family, its age and importance everywhere seen, such as the heralds and coats of arms inscribed above the main entrance and stained in glass in the library's bay window.

But for all its magnificence, it held a homelike feel, far more than that of the Car-lew London residence where he'd grown up. Whilst large, indeed, somewhat showy — for as Harold Carlew always said, a suc-cessful businessman should be seen to be prosperous, for how else would people trust him with their money to invest? — the Port-man Square mansion was all sharp lines and angles, a little too new, a little too sterile.

The Manor, on the other hand, possessed a gracious charm, like Carmichael's paternal grandmother, whom he'd once visited dur-ing the Long Vacation whilst at Oxford. The dowager countess possessed beauty, faded perhaps, but her generosity and whimsical humor had smoothed away any awkward-ness Jonathan, a merchant's son, had felt upon meeting such a lady. This house held a similar appeal, as though she had known her worth for many a generation, and did not need any of the fancy trinkets and furbelows a less beautiful version might require.

A tiny sparrow danced by, as if celebrating Jon's good fortune. His heart lifted fractionally, and he smiled at his foolishness. But one thing he could be sure. Even Carmichael, whose family's grand estate in Derbyshire Jon had visited more than once, would be impressed and pleased for him. He could imagine the viscount's words: "Well, you've certainly fallen on your feet, old man."

Yes. Or more precisely, God had placed his feet here.

Jon wandered through the hedge again, veering left, to where a stained stone fountain sat silent at the end of another rose-lined path that led to the house. He studied the three French doors facing the garden. The drawing room perhaps? He assessed his bearings, nodded, and walked back. Sweetness lifted as he brushed past a few peach-colored roses.

He peered through the glass. The room was dim, but he recognized the position of settees. And it was unoccupied. He tried the handle. It moved easily, silently. So the servants at least oiled doors — clearly his predecessor had odd notions about prioritizing the manor's maintenance. As he entered, the drawing room's gentle ambiance rose to meet him, and he stopped behind a high settee, once again feeling the deep peace permeate his soul.

He glanced around the room. The Reynolds above the fireplace was perhaps not the artist's finest work, but its tones of gold and amber suited the room's mellow feel. How long had it been in Winthrop possession? Or was it an asset for which he could gain a return that would benefit more than just the casual visitor to this room?

Lord, give me wisdom . . .

His prayer, one uttered many times over the past few years, floated up, past the plaster fruits and — he squinted — angels that adorned the painted ceiling.

"Oh, Papa . . ."

He froze. Glanced around. Down. Saw the mass of black huddled on the settee directly before him. Positioned as she was, sprawled most unladylike with her hands covering her face, she had not seen him. And the high backs of the other sofas hid her from view of the door that stood ajar, through which came the murmur and bustle of servants. Amid the afternoon shadows he saw the black-edged handkerchief. A sigh fluttered, closing in a sob.

Compassion propelled him forward.

Resentment halted his step.

His fingers clenched. While part of his heart tugged at her pain, he could not help feel she would not want him to see her. Wasn't she the young lady whose actions ran counter to her claims? Her gentility but a mask . . .

Yet he could not help contrast this sad, faded picture with the young, vibrant creature he had once known. And be irrationally relieved that the man who'd destroyed his life had at least one person who mourned him.

The weeping continued, a rawness so deep his skin tingled.

Despite his misgivings, his heart twisted. He took another step toward her then paused. Would she welcome his sympathy? Sympathy born from an event that by its very nature led to his social promotion? She would not appreciate his words, however heartfelt. She had not before.

Better to leave. Better to keep from unnecessary intrusion. He had no desire to dine with the Winthrop clan tonight, though he must, for everything felt like he was stepping unwelcome into pain. Perhaps it would be best if he could prevent further distress by removing himself without her notice.

Perhaps if he found a maid, or her sister — he rather doubted her mother would be of any use — someone who could comfort her . . . Yes, that would suffice.

He stepped back. Onto a creaking floorboard.

Cursing himself inwardly, he hurried to the French doors —

"Who's there?"

The figure sat up, smeared hands down her face. Glanced around.

He could hide no more. He stepped forward. "Excuse me."

And with a bow, and a glimpse of her shocked face, he exited into the garden again.

Calling himself every kind of fool. For feeling. For caring. For wishing the past could be undone again.

His jaw hardened. But that was exactly the point. The past had passed. It could never be revisited again.

CHAPTER FOUR

Dower House
One month later

Catherine's gaze tracked up to the web of cracks radiating from the upper corner of the sitting room doorway. Her nose wrinkled. Clearly Papa had not given much thought to the future of his wife and daughters upon his demise. This truth had become appallingly clear over the past weeks, as the flurry of activity had eventually given way to desperate reality once Catherine and Mama had moved into the Dower House and realized just how different life would be now.

She shook her head and returned an unseeing gaze to the wall. Poor Papa, always living in the moment . . .

The horror and humiliation following Papa's funeral had soon succumbed to the weight of a thousand other worries. Mr. Carlew — for forever he would remain so, according to Mama, none of the Lord Winthrop for the likes of him, thank you very much! — had graciously given them three weeks to move, which was something, at least, despite Mama's protestations to the contrary. As the new baron, Mr. Carlew could have insisted they move immediately to enable his swift possession. But permitting the extra weeks had allowed time to sort what they could take, time to receive calls, time to conclude aspects of estate life they had always known — which Catherine had foolishly thought she would always know — in order to begin the new chapter elsewhere.

A shudder wracked her body in remembrance. Poor Papa's bills were so extensive she doubted they would be welcome among the village tradespeople. Mr. Whittington had gone over matters with her again, once everyone had left, giving her to realize just how dire their financial situation was. She was relieved to discover enough coin in her reticule to pay Mrs. Jeffcoat for the berries, but the others . . . A fresh wave of shame washed over her. How could Papa forgo paying the very people who depended on him? As it was, Mr. Carlew had promised to settle whatever bills remained, so Mr. Whittington assured her, a gesture as magnanimous as it was humbling — and shaming.

Her vision blurred, then sharpened as she gazed out the window of the cramped room. Instead of a peaceful vista to distant hills, this window — complete with broken shutter — looked out onto an unkempt hedge, beyond which lay the hay pastures, soon destined for cutting.

She should be counting her blessings that they had a place to stay, and did not need to live with someone else, like Aunt Elizabeth and Aunt Clothilde, who, upon the demise of their respective husbands, had been allowed to live at Avebury, under Papa's good grace. She should be thanking God that at least they had food to eat, that their meals were adequate, if not exactly tasty. She should be thankful that at least Serena was away at school, and away from circumstances so straightened and unfamiliar. She *should* . . .

But couldn't.

Gone was the sense of freedom that living in a thirty-room manor provided. Now they resided in just six rooms, where every footfall above loudly creaked its owner's trail. Gone too were the things with which she'd filled her days: the well-stocked library, the pianoforte, the gardens, the opportunity to ride out in her gig whenever she felt the need.

Yet worse than this was Mama's despondency. Nothing seemed to satisfy, her complaints about everything from the food to the loss of her paintings and furniture. Mama had insisted her favorite pieces move with her to the cottage, where now everything looked too crowded and cramped. Mr. Carlew had not protested, although Catherine was sure that his own mother's presence would have prevented a single stick of furniture from leaving the Manor.

"I should not have to ask that man for anything!" was Mama's most recited cry.

That man could only be Mr. Carlew, and truth be told, when she wasn't worrying about when the drips in the roof could be fixed or what was happening at the Manor she, too, would like to dismiss *that man* from all thought. She would like to.

But couldn't.

Her thoughts traced back to that awful moment following the fiasco after Papa's funeral. She'd thought she was in a safe space, thought nobody would dare intrude upon her grief.

Yet he had.

She cringed again at the memory. Clenched her fists about her embarrassment. Why should she care what he thought? So her crying bout had left her with blotched cheeks, a red nose, and tiny eyes — why did she care if he'd possibly noticed? Why should this *still* concern her so many weeks on?

Yet it did.

He'd tried to visit yesterday. As soon as she'd seen his big gray gallop up the lane she had hurried inside, leaving him to her mother. Her lips flickered. Mama had put him in no doubt about *her* feelings, at least, ensuring he rode off without chance to dismount, then entering the cottage with a look of satisfaction, crowing about her skill in refusing the interloper admittance. "For why should we want the likes of *him* here?"

Catherine had nodded, though a tiny part regretted such harsh measures. After all, he had been quite gracious in giving them extra time to move.

She groaned as her traitorous heart, her foolish thoughts, refused him absence. And even if she had been successful in refraining from conjecture, everywhere she went the neighborhood was rife with speculation. Would the new baron pay the tradesmen bills? Would he attend services? Would he — or more likely his mother and sister — begin "improvements" at Winthrop Manor?

It was this last one that remained trouble-some. She was glad — for the tradesmen's sakes — that Mr. Carlew had paid their bills so promptly. She hoped that he still held faith of such importance that he had attended services, even though she would doubtless feel discomfort at seeing his blond head in the pew where she had always sat. But for her heritage, her home, the memories of a lifetime to be cast aside, painted and papered over, this she could scarce abide.

"Miss? Are you ready?" Tilly, the one maid they could afford now, came forward with Catherine's cloak and Bible. "Madam will be down in a moment."

"Thank you, Tilly."

Probably the chief reason why Mama had elected Tilly to stay was because she always addressed Mama as Madam, without a hint of awareness of any lost status. Of course, it helped that Tilly had no near relatives to take her in, and that she was a compliant girl, willing to do far more than her previous duties had demanded. So amid the sadness in leaving Winthrop and the servants who had proved so faithful for so many years had come a small ray of light that they weren't so completely poor that they could not afford any servants. Their domestic staff had reduced to three: Tilly, Mrs. Jones, their cook and Lizzie's sister, and Frank, who acted as their general outdoorsman, and very occasionally as their groom.

Moments later they were on their way to St. Hampton Heath. Their new abode made the church far nearer than before. Attending services meant they would be able to connect with some of their older acquaintances — and hopefully avoid some of the new.

The gig pulled up outside the square-towered church, its gardens a mass of fading bluebells.

There was a rustle of expectation as Mama and Catherine moved down the aisle. She kept her chin up, looking straight ahead at the trio of stained glass windows above the altar.

The minister nodded, waiting for her mother's slow progress to finally attain their pew. Catherine almost stumbled when Mama stopped and loudly sniffed.

The occupants of the front pew glanced up, their expressions ones of complacency, triumph, and concern. Mr. Carlew rose. "Pardon me, madam, we seem to be in your place."

Catherine's cheeks flamed and she refused to meet his gaze, though she approved his actions. Mama's pride needed salving these days, rubbed raw as it was through the whispers and speculation concerning the mounting debts Papa had left.

"You are," was Mama's ungracious reply as she lifted her chin. "We shall sit elsewhere."

"There is room here, Lady Winthrop." His hand reached out, a gesture of conciliation.

Mama ignored it, only tipping her chin higher as she moved to the pew across the aisle.

Catherine tilted her gaze to glimpse Mr. Carlew's tightened lips before she turned after Mama.

The service could have been conducted in Chinese for all she was aware, so concerned was she with Mama's stiff, unbending posture beside her. The reverend's words floated past her, the songs and prayer, too, for nothing seemed to settle, nothing felt real anymore.

How many humiliations must Mama endure? Wasn't the loss of her house and money enough? And how much did God want Catherine to suffer? She'd long ago reconciled that she would not marry for love, but had not been quite at her last prayers, had held out a thin sliver of hope that some man might marry her, even if it were only for the dowry Papa would bestow. Which he would not now. Her eyes pricked. She blinked until tears no longer threatened.

God felt so remote, so unkind, and so disinterested in her life.

Eventually the sermon concluded, the prayers were prayed, and the doxology sung. She followed Mama outside into the sunlight, their progress slowed by the villagers' murmurs of condolence, to which Mama replied far more graciously than she had to Mr. Carlew earlier.

Lady Milton bustled forward, her penetrating voice drowning out the soft sympathy offered by Eliza Hatton, one of Lavinia's protégées, now the wife of the blacksmith's son and mother of two.

"Ah, poor Lady Winthrop. How *are* you?"

"I confess, Cornelia, it has been very hard. Walter was such a good husband. I miss him so." Mama dabbed at her eyes with a lace handkerchief.

Catherine's eyes narrowed. Surely Mama wasn't *enjoying* playing the grieving widow? She caught her mother's eye; Mama looked away, began talking rapidly.

She turned, feelings of nausea at her mother's duplicity crawling up her throat.

"Ah, Miss Winthrop. How are you finding your new accommodations?" Lady Harkness smiled, her gaze trickling over Catherine's sober attire.

"It is" — horrible, antiquated, musty, she wanted to say, but such things would only reflect badly on Papa — "adequate."

"I'm so glad. You must come visit when you get a chance. I'd be delighted to show you the samples for the new wallpaper in the drawing room."

Heat splintered across her chest. Catherine swallowed, drew in a deep breath. "Lady Harkness, do you intend to live at Winthrop?"

She raised an elegant burgundy-draped shoulder — no black for her. "For the moment, until Jonathan is properly settled. And until then, I want to bring the tired place to join us in the nineteenth century."

Properly settled? Catherine stared at her. Did she mean until he . . . found a wife?

"Dear child, there is no need to look like that. Surely one must expect a young man possessed of good fortune and title — humble though it may be, a mere baron, after all — to desire a wife? Yes?"

Catherine nodded.

"Yet I sense some hesitation. How very interesting." Lady Harkness turned, and gestured to her son and daughter, who drew near. "Come. I fear we have disconcerted

70

the locals quite long enough." With a small smile and smaller curtsy, echoed by Julia, she moved away.

Mr. Carlew nodded stiffly, his gaze half meeting hers, but not touching, before he too joined his sister and mother at the carriage, the *Winthrop* carriage, for the journey home to Winthrop Manor.

Pain twisted like a knife. Winthrop Manor was *his* home. Not hers. Not anymore.

Winthrop Manor

"Of course, Lord Winthrop. I'm happy to oblige." Geoffreys inclined his head and moved through the door that led to the servants' hall.

Jonathan swallowed a smile. Geoffreys's continued eagerness to oblige led him to suppose that the former Lord Winthrop had been either a tyrant or so lackadaisical in his manner that the servants were happy to have someone finally give orders. The paltry state of affairs around the estate made such truth plainly evident.

The only quibble he had with his staff was their insistence on addressing him as Lord Winthrop which, while saying much of their respect, also served as a constant reminder of the loss of the old name. Harold Carlew had been the father Jonathan had always

known, his marriage to the newly widowed
Lady Winthrop when Jon was only a babe
the most fortuitous occurrence of his life,
even if it had led to speculation as to why
the marriage had taken place so quickly.

His mood dipped, and he strode to the
oak-paneled study, closing the door behind
him with a firm click. He moved behind the
desk, the initial mess now cleared away,
thanks to Mr. Whittington's efforts, and
those of the Winthrop steward, Mr. Clipshom.

He sharpened the nib of his quill, looked
up and met the imposing stare of his grandfather's portrait. His hands clenched. Yes,
he'd heard the whispers, rumors he was
powerless to quell, especially as he'd grown
older and taller, and, some said, looked
more like old Carlew than any Winthrop
before him. But a man could scarcely ask
his mother if she had been unfaithful. And
in truth it never had seemed a problem, his
chance at the Winthrop title so remote he
had never bothered to attend any but one
Winthrop event in his nine-and-twenty
years. His knuckles turned white. Well he
knew the reason Mama had not been invited
to any more, those Winthrops proving quick
to judge and quicker to believe hearsay.

And Harold Carlew, though untitled with

a wealth derived from trade, had taught his stepson the values he still adhered to today. Faith. Honesty. Honor. It had served Jon well abroad and at home. Still, it felt like a betrayal to the man he'd respected to lose his last name and revert to the one he'd never really known.

He spent the next hour dealing with correspondence before a knock on the door prefaced William. "Excuse me, Lord Winthrop, but Lady Harkness wishes to have a word."

"Tell her I shall be with her directly — no, I will come now. Where?"

"In the drawing room, my lord."

He nodded, following the footman, refusing his offer to open the door. Why the previous baron had kept on so many servants he was quite unable to understand, especially for such trivial matters one could easily do for oneself. He was fast coming to the conclusion his predecessor cared more for appearances than economies.

His mother looked up from where she sat with Julia. "Ah, Jonathan. I hope I did not disturb you from your duties?"

"I was happy to be disturbed, ma'am."

A smile crossed her face. "I won't keep you long. It's simply I must have your opinion on the wallpaper."

"I beg your pardon?"

"The wallpaper. Does it not cry hideous to you?"

"I confess I had not noticed."

"Then I suppose you won't notice when I put something new up."

"But why should you do that?"

She sighed, shrugging at Julia. "Spoken just like a man." Her attention returned to him. "Next you'll be telling me you have not noticed the state of these chairs."

"Why? Is something the matter with them?"

"Dear boy, they are fraying! I have ordered new fabric —"

"Mother, no."

"Why, Jonathan!" she pouted. "Surely you do not wish to spoil my fun."

"I have no wish to spoil your fun, but would prefer you to enjoy such things elsewhere, not here."

"Why ever not?" Her eyes rounded in astonishment. "You must admit the furnishings are sadly outdated. How anyone could live in such a hideous mausoleum I don't know."

He half listened, waiting patiently until her familiar litany of complaints had run dry and she was more prepared to hear. This was important. "Mother, as you have a multitude of houses to choose from, I would rather you redecorate one of those. I am not prepared to spend money on Winthrop until I am certain it needs spending."

"Oh, Jonathan! I declare, sometimes you are just as much a clutch-fist as your poor papa."

His eyebrows rose.

"Of course," she continued hurriedly, "Harold was a good-hearted man, as you are, too. And you can certainly afford to refurbish, as your papa left you so well provided for."

"He wanted the money spent to benefit people, not for redecorating for the sake of it."

"For the sake of it? Jonathan, anyone would think you have gone mad! Can you not see just how much work needs doing around here?"

"No."

She made a moue of protest. "Your hesitation leads me to wonder if there is another reason you refuse to allow me to assist you." Now her eyebrows rose.

Like what? That she suspected he would prefer such things be attended to by his future wife? Jon refused to bite. "I have no desire to change things. I thank you for your kind offer but I am quite content."

"I don't know how you can say such things! The furnishings are so passé."

"Thank you for your observations. I hesitate to mention this, but it has crossed my mind that you may perhaps feel more comfortable elsewhere."

She stared at him. "Surely you are not implying you want me to leave?"

"I appreciate your support, Mother, but not the questions about my reasons and motives."

"Why, Jonathan! I don't know what you mean."

He gazed at her steadily until pink stained her cheeks.

"Can you blame a mother for hoping for her son's happiness?"

"I *am* happy, Mother."

"If you say so. But I couldn't help but wonder just what you ever saw in —"

"Mother," he said warningly.

"She's nothing like what I remembered."

No, she was not. He swallowed the bitterness as his mother's diatribe continued. The faded woman he'd seen yesterday at services was a million miles from the bright, vivacious girl he had first come to know. Indeed, he could have easily passed her on the street without a hint of recognition. But then, grief was a heavy weight to carry, enough to alter anyone, and black had never suited her.

"I assure you, any feeling is quite gone, and I shall *not* be making the same mistake again."

She sighed, smiled. "I am relieved to hear it. That family has always given themselves airs. You need to find a bride, and now, with the title as well as your income, you can aim as high as you wish."

He nodded as if he cared.

But inside, the raw hurt pounced again, like a savage animal, as the memories arose of her rejection. Perhaps his mother's advice was finally worth heeding. Perhaps he should — no, *would* — show Miss Winthrop just what she had missed out on.

CHAPTER FIVE

Dower House

"A little more to the left," Mama called.

Catherine nodded, wielding the garden shears even as she gritted her teeth, and wished for the hundredth time since breakfast that Frank had not decided to sicken with a bad back on the very morning Mama had decided the garden needed attention. Not one for patience, Mama had not allowed the loss of the groundsman to prove a hindrance to her plans, as she had enlisted Catherine's assistance instead. Catherine would pray for him, except she rather doubted the legitimacy of his claims of ill health. It had come on quite suddenly, as it did on many occasions when something demanding more than a nominal effort was required. Catherine snipped more vigorously. Perhaps she would pray for the mending of his honesty instead.

"Even great ladies must take an interest in

gardening," Mama's voice continued behind her. "Why, I have heard that the earl's mother herself takes a great deal of interest in the garden at Hawkesbury House. And remember our visit to Saltings and its lovely gardens? All the work of the dowager viscountess. So one can afford to take an interest in one's garden, even get one's hand's dirty, and not lose any dignity in doing so."

Except it wasn't Mama's hands that were getting dirty, Catherine noted wryly, as she snipped off the final protruding twigs. "Better?"

"What?"

Catherine glanced over her shoulder. Mama had stiffened and was glancing down the lane.

"What on earth does he want now?"

She stepped down from the small stool, shifted the gardening shears from one hand to the other. But before she could remove either her dirty apron or herself, the gray horse was huffing at the gate, his owner dismounted, reins tied to the gatepost. Frozen by embarrassment, she studied the clippings strewn at her feet.

"Good day, Lady Winthrop, Miss Winthrop," Mr. Carlew said in his deep voice. "How are you today?"

"Busy, as you can doubtless see."

Catherine swallowed, and dared look up.

He wore a frown, his gaze not meeting hers. "Do you not have a groundsman to take care of such matters?"

"We do," Mother continued, "but he has been quite exhausted in attending to a myriad of other tasks." Catherine shifted slightly to study the hedge, wishing herself invisible as her mother began listing some of the said tasks. If only she could hide away. If only she never had to see him again. If only she wasn't wearing such an ugly shapeless gown and had thought to fix her hair . . .

"Indeed."

His flat voice made Catherine steal another peek. His frown deepened as he looked around. "I will send someone over —"

"Thank you, but that is not necessary."

His face stiffened, before turning slowly to her. Catherine lowered her gaze to his neckcloth, wishing her cheeks did not heat at his notice. "Is there anything you would wish me to do to make your accommodations more comfortable?"

Besides move out? Catherine bit her tongue. One acerbic Winthrop woman was probably enough.

Her mother drew herself up. "We are to

be much obliged, I'm sure, but require nothing from you, sir."

"Mama," she whispered.

"Are you sure, ma'am?" he said, his attention returned to her mother. "I know the accommodations aren't quite what you are used to." His tone sounded almost apologetic.

Mama gave a loud sniff. "Are you implying I am unable to cope, or merely that my husband was not assiduous in all his duties in ensuring this cottage be adequate for my needs?"

Were his cheeks reddening? His reply was smooth, "Neither, ma'am. It is simply a desire to know that you and your daughter are comfortable."

"We are. Extremely."

He inclined his head. "If you are sure." He moved to untie his horse, his posture stiff, his countenance still determinedly averted.

Her heart panged. How long would this display of indifference continue? Unless he really was indifferent to her . . . She returned her attention to the hacked hedge, her eyes blurring.

"Do you doubt my word?"

Her mother's clipped reply made her blink, look up, catch his face veering away as he mounted.

"Ma'am, I believe you. But please believe me when I say if ever I can be of assistance, you need only say the word and it will be done."

"That will not be necessary."

"Of course." He tipped his hat, wheeled around, and nudged his horse away.

"The nerve!"

"Mama," Catherine murmured, "he will hear you."

"I do not care. How dare he presume to come here?"

"He dares because he is the new baron." She winced as soon as the words left her mouth, as Mama began another tirade on the injustice of it all, and the presumption of one such as he to assume such airs.

But to be fair, she had witnessed neither airs nor presumption. "Perhaps his motive is pure, and he merely wishes to be of service," she ventured.

"Do not let me hear such things." Her mother's eyes narrowed. "We know that man and his family play false."

Memories arose of the gossip surrounding Lady Harkness — she a widow of too many husbands — and others close to Mr. Jonathan Carlew. Papa had on more than one occasion dismissed Mr. Carlew's questionable antecedents and links to trade, openly deriding his friendships with Henry Carmichael, an earl's son and cardster who had sent more than one good fellow close to bankruptcy, and Major Thomas Hale, who had left a string of broken hearts as one of the more notorious rakes in town. Jonathan Carlew, so far as she was aware, was guilty of nothing but association with these two men, but as far as her parents were concerned, that was enough, especially considering the doubt over his true paternity.

"I never want to see that man here again!" Mama declared.

Catherine nodded, stooping to pick up the broken branches, conscious of a niggling sense of injustice.

Despite his actions in the past, despite the mortification she felt whenever she was in his presence that forbade her to meet his gaze, she couldn't help but have noted his persistent consideration today, despite her mother's rudeness.

Such consideration that plowed up the old questions she'd thought long buried, forcing her to wonder about her parents' fixed antipathy, and why they'd stayed so well informed about the man they professed to despise.

■ ■ ■ ■

White's Gentlemen Club, London
One week later

"Good afternoon, my lord."

Jonathan nodded at the doorman's acknowledgment of his newly acquired title. Of course he would know. It was his job to know. No doubt Jon's recent elevation to the Peerage would have caused a frenzy of conversation and wager of bets within the club's plush surrounds.

He bit back a wry smile as he walked through to the dining room. To think London's most exclusive club had started out as an immigrant's tea shop, its humble roots in trade conveniently concealed under decades of pretensions. Now White's was a gentlemen's club for the rich and aristocratic, where questions of birth could be forgiven by the heritage of Carlew wealth. He was quickly seated and ordered a late lunch, savoring the time alone as much as his boiled turbot dressed in a rich anchovy sauce. Yesterday and this morning had been a whirlwind of activity as he'd met solicitors, bankers, board members, and investors to run over figures, receipts, and accounts, using every ounce of his persuasive powers to convince shareholders that invest-ing in the new venture of steam locomotion would be worthwhile.

He felt drained. Yet somehow invigorated, as though the battles had reminded him of his purpose. And for the first time, he sensed a nudge of anticipation in returning to the peace of Winthrop.

"Carlew!"

He glanced up. Smiled. "Hale. How are you?"

They shook hands. "Tell me, when am I to see this new place of yours?"

"Whenever you come."

The major snorted. "As full of wit as ever."

"As you can see." Jon grinned. "So when would you like to come? I must warn you, the house is not quite up to my mother's standards. She is in attendance, you know."

"Oh. She has never really approved of me, has she?"

"I think it's more your liberties with the opposite sex of which she does not approve. And the way you talk with Julia."

Hale's cheeks reddened. "Julia knows I mean nothing by it."

"But my mother does not, so you might want to steer clear of her during your stay."

"Hmm. Your sister is remarkably pretty —"

"But not for you." Mother intended her daughter for someone much higher socially than a mere major in His Majesty's Armed Forces, even if that major had performed admirable service in Calcutta.

"I suppose not, no."

"However, I know Mother is amenable to a house party soon, so perhaps we can arrange something for then."

"I would be much obliged. Now, I best be off to see my old brigadier. He wants to chat about India, and you know me, I can never say no."

"Of course not. Good day."

Hale nodded, offered a mock salute, and moved away.

Upon concluding his meal, Jon rose from the table and proceeded to the saloon. In one corner he could see the major's dark head bent near a gray one, the general's loud voice leading to Jon's decision to sit farthermost away. He picked up a newspaper and sank into a brown velvet settee, and was soon lost in the news of a world so much bigger than his new estate.

"Lord Winthrop?"

He lowered the newspaper. "Lord Hawkesbury! Good afternoon."

"I trust I'm not interrupting anything important."

"Not at all." Jon gestured to the seat opposite, then folded the newspaper and placed it aside. "What brings you to London?"

"A quick visit for parliament. I do not like to be away longer than necessary."

"Of course not. I trust the countess is well."

"Thank you, yes. Although inclined to become a little bored at times, I believe. She is thankful for the kind attentions of friends such as Miss Winthrop."

"I'm glad." He schooled his face to a mask of polite indifference.

"And you? I imagine you have much to garner your attention these days."

Jon filled him in on a little of his meetings, noting that here, at least, was an aristocrat who did not seem to deride Jon as a "cit" nor despise him for his business affairs.

"You have been very busy. And now I have interrupted your moment of peace."

"No. I am happy for the chance to talk with you."

"And I you. I admit I have wanted to hear more about your time abroad."

He must have looked his surprise, for the earl chuckled. "I would much rather spend my time here learning about my new neighbor than trying to fend off wagers from the desperate." He leaned back in his chair. "Please."

So Jon told something of the story of a lowly clerk working for the East India Company promoted through both hard work and his director uncle's connections to being senior administration writer for the governor of Bombay.

"And you enjoyed your time there?"

"Yes. It was a time I needed to be away." He drained his glass, looking up to see the earl's lift of brow.

Jon kept his mouth shut, thankful for the other man's good breeding when he refrained from asking questions. Perhaps one day he might feel free to share more, but not now.

"I cannot help but envy you. My uncle, the fourth earl, was an intrepid traveler, and collected many curios from his adventures." Lord Hawkesbury's lips twisted. "In my time abroad I only collected a bullet wound, which does not impress my wife very much."

Jon chuckled. "It does not hold the same cachet as a tiger skin or ruby necklet, perhaps."

"Perhaps," the earl agreed. "And how are you finding Gloucestershire?"

"It is a little cooler than Bombay."

Sometimes he longed for the heat of India, to smell the spice-laden air, to feel the warmth soak into his bones. Here, everything felt overly chilly, people's attitudes seemingly reflected in the rain and cooler temperatures, most unlike the English summers he recalled. Or perhaps these feelings were simply the product of the cold shoulder he continued to receive from his predecessor's relatives.

What would it take for his offers of assistance to be accepted? For him to be accepted? Each morning he read his Bible and received nothing more than the sense he should forgive as Jesus taught, seventy times seven. He could understand their pain, even some of their misapprehension — didn't fear do that to people? Yet their slights and offense grew wearisome, and he was becoming tired of having to check his heart to root out each new seed of bitterness that interaction with the Winthrop women seemed to sprout.

"I suspect that frown tells me it is more than heat you miss." The earl leaned back in his seat, hazel eyes glinting.

"I admit the reception of some has been a little lukewarm."

"It takes time to be accepted in a new place. Trust must be earned, respect given, not assumed." His smile grew wry. "Especially in certain parts of the West Country."

"I have always been a Londoner, so country ways are not my forte."

"Country ways are much the same as any, based on truth and honest dealings with one's neighbor. I understand some may appear a little more forthright than certain elements of society might deem acceptable."

"Forthright is one word for it," Jon muttered.

"Keep on doing what you're doing. I have only heard good things, although there is one thing I find greatly concerning."

At his frown, Jonathan's stomach filled with unease and he searched his conscience. What had he done?

"I do not understand how somebody so new could have gained my wife's approval so quickly. You seemed very friendly after services last week."

"The countess is very charming."

"And more than a little discerning. I was not so quick to gain her approval, I assure you."

"Perhaps it was simply the subject matter she approved."

"She has always been keen to see the establishment of a proper school." The earl smiled. "Education in the village is something I wholeheartedly endorse."

"Due to my hearty funding?" Jonathan asked, cocking a brow.

"Seeing as God has blessed you to bless others in this way, you have my full support."

The earl soon made his exit, and Jonathan was left warmed with the impression that the earl not only approved of the project but also, it seemed, approved of him.

He sipped his water, his mood slipping. If only others agreed.

CHAPTER SIX

July

"Can you believe it? Now he wants to hold a harvest dinner for all the tenants. I declare I am growing heartily sick of hearing of all the wonders of this imposter."

Catherine looked up from her needlepoint. Her mother's constant slander scraped against the peace she strove to find each morning as she read the devotional Lavinia had recently given her. "Surely it is a good thing he is so assiduous in his duties to the tenants."

"Well your poor father never felt it necessary!" Mama placed the letter down. "I do not know what he is about filling their heads with stuff and nonsense. What was good enough when Walter was in charge should be good enough now."

Except it had become increasingly apparent just how far short of good enough Papa's care for the estate had been. In the two months since his arrival Mr. Carlew had funded the fixing of all fencing, mediated a successful truce in a long-standing feud between the menfolk of the Snaiths and Gillespies, and introduced a scheme to employ some of the older men to repair farming equipment, thus reducing costs for the tenant farmers.

The accusatory stares and murmurs of the villagers Catherine had experienced had changed to praise of Mr. Carlew's latest good deeds. This, despite the continued unseasonal cooler temperatures and increased rainfall that likely meant diminished yields this harvest. Her lips twisted. Truly, Mr. Carlew must be something of a miracle worker for the locals to speak so well of him amidst the uncertainties of the harvest.

"Why Clarinda feels it necessary to tell of every little thing he does I do not know. I feel sure she wants to rub my face in it!"

"In what, Mama? I'm sure she is not so mean-spirited."

"No?" Her mother eyed her narrowly. "If you knew what that woman was capable of —" Her lips clamped.

Catherine fought a flicker of curiosity. She would not give in to idle speculation. "Mama, perhaps we could go for a walk today. The sun is brighter —"

"The wind is too chilly."

"Then perhaps we could read outside in the garden, where it is more protected."

Her mother sighed heavily. "You can, my dear. I cannot look at that sad excuse for a garden without remembering what we had before."

She inhaled deeply. Exhaled. How long would Mama cling to what she could never have again? "Mama, I'm sorry you still feel so —"

"I don't want your pity, child!"

Catherine flinched. Heat filled her eyes.

"There, there. Don't look like that. I don't mean to snap." Mama sighed again. "It is hard, that is all."

"It is hard for me also," she said in a small voice.

Mama placed a hand to her head and groaned. "I think I need a rest."

"Then may I go visit Lavinia?"

"Oh, if you must."

Catherine nodded and rushed to change into riding clothes before Mama changed her mind. If she must? She certainly must get out of this poky house, otherwise she might burst!

Tea with the Countess of Hawkesbury was never anything short of enjoyable. Unlike

Mama, Lavinia took pleasure in unexpected visitors, and never produced a less than lavish spread, which often seemed more hearty meal than mere nuncheon. Perhaps this extravagance was because she'd spent much time of late confined to home, only engaging in short excursions in the neighboring village.

"Oh, it is good of you to take pity on me," Lavinia said with a smile. "I have had visits from Lady Milton, but it is not the same as a visit from someone who truly cares for me, and for whom I truly care!"

Catherine laughed, the sound pushing past the weight of emotion clogging her chest, making her feel lighter, somehow.

"So, you have heard enough about me. Tell me, Catherine, how are you?"

The words so kindly meant welled emotion in her eyes, and it was a moment before she could clear her throat to speak. "I am coping."

Lavinia reached across the sofa to clasp her hand. "I can imagine with so many changes there would be moments of pain."

"Mama has not been . . . easy," she said carefully.

"Of course not." Lavinia opened her mouth then seemed to think better of it, and closed her lips again.

"I do not know what to do. It seems anywhere we go we hear of what Lady Harkness is doing, or how Mr. Carlew is improving this thing or that." Catherine picked up her teacup and sipped her tea. "I am glad the estate is doing better, but at the same time I find such things so difficult to listen to."

"You do not want to be disloyal to your father."

"That's right! And yet, I cannot but be aware that Papa is not — was not — the man I thought him to be."

"He was not infallible."

"Exactly. I . . . I just wish he made better choices that did not so adversely affect so many people we have known for so long. Does this make me a disloyal daughter?"

"It makes you an honest one."

Catherine sighed. "I wish we could be elsewhere. I feel such guilt whenever I see the tenants and know Papa left so much undone. And though it pains me to say this, I am growing increasingly tired of having to listen to Mama's complaints about the cottage and its deprivations. Why, to listen to her, anyone would think we lived in a poor London slum rather than be fortunate enough to have as much as we do. But she does not see things that way. And I confess

I share her apprehension about what will happen to the Manor, especially under such a woman."

Lavinia settled back in her seat, hands clasped over her midsection. "I did not think Lady Harkness's visit would be *quite* so long."

"I suppose she wants to be with her family."

"Yes."

Catherine took another sip of tea.

"You know we invited them for dinner last week?"

She nodded, working again to overcome the stab of bitterness news of the invitation had wrought.

"Nicholas said our social obligations warranted it. And once you get past her abrasiveness, Lady Harkness is quite a stimulating dinner companion." Lavinia shook her head. "But I could not help but feel a sense of curiosity about how she fits into the whole Winthrop saga."

Catherine shared what she knew, sticking as closely to the facts as she knew them to be.

"So really it is nothing more than speculation regarding Mr. Carlew's birth?"

Catherine nodded stiffly.

"Well, I don't mind admitting that I do

like him. I suppose he cannot be blamed for having an unfortunate mother — he's certainly not the first." Her brow wrinkled. "So let me think this through. As your great-great grandfather's younger brother's great grandson, that would make Mr. Carlew your . . . your third cousin, once removed, correct?"

"I believe so."

"Hmm." Lavinia sipped her tea. "There was something about him — a gravity, a sense of purpose — that I found quite refreshing. He seems determined to make a mark, and from all accounts, has enough money from his father's estate to do so."

"His father's estate?"

"Mr. Harold Carlew's, I mean. Not that he said anything, you understand. Nicholas told me. Mr. Carlew seems quite modest."

"He is," she agreed unthinkingly.

Lavinia's gray eyes lit. "You know him."

Her cheeks grew hot. "Of course. A little, perhaps, anyway. H-he is my cousin after all."

"Your *third* cousin, whom until recently you've seen once in your life, or so I was informed by Lady Harkness the other evening."

Rather more than once, if truth be told. Catherine kept her lips clamped.

98

"She does seem to take something of an interest in you." Lavinia's head tilted. "Why is that, I wonder?"

Catherine shrugged, aiming for nonchalance. This conversation was making her feel hot and itchy. "I'm sure I do not know. Now, how is the dowager countess?"

Lavinia laughed. "That is unkind, asking me something like that when I'm finally learning something interesting. Because I cannot but feel that it is more a matter of you *choosing* not to tell me about Mr. Carlew's mother's interest in you, rather than being unable to."

"I've heard pregnancy affects ladies in different ways, so perhaps this feeling is just another symptom," Catherine said with a smile.

"Oh, you are cruel! Well, if there be something I need to know about Mr. Carlew, I do hope you will tell me, your *friend*. Because I really think him a most interesting man. Handsome, too."

"Miss Winthrop," a deep voice drawled, "perhaps you would enlighten me as to whom my wife is referring to as being handsome?"

Catherine blushed more deeply as the earl entered the room. His sardonic gaze and comments always left her feeling several seconds too slow in comprehending his meaning, trying to ascertain whether he was serious, or jesting, as he appeared now.

"I . . . we, ah —"

"We were talking of Mr. Carlew, dearest," Lavinia said, with a cheeky expression. "He is quite a handsome man, don't you think?"

A glimmer of a smile appeared in the earl's eyes. "I make it my policy never to discuss a gentleman's appearance. Appearances can be deceptive, can they not, Miss Winthrop?"

"Y-yes, my lord."

"More important is a man's character, and from my observations and what I've heard from London, Mr. Carlew seems a fair, kindhearted man." He sat on the seat next to Lavinia, stretching long legs before him. "I recently met him at my London club, and gather he had quite a time of it in India. He served in the office of Lord Nepean, the governor of Bombay. I was particularly impressed to hear of his help for the Company's widows, both English and native."

Catherine swallowed the bubble of pain-tinged gladness at such news. Now *this* fit with the man she'd once known; of course Jonathan would do something like that.

The earl glanced across at his wife. "It

took me a number of years to finally be able to afford to assist all the families left behind in my regiment."

"I imagine it helps when one has interests in several flourishing corporations," Lavinia said.

"It seems the Carlew business enterprises are being blessed to be a blessing," the earl continued, glancing at Catherine with a half smile. "And isn't that what our Lord has called us all to do?"

Catherine nodded, but inside her heart demurred. How could she bless others when God had removed all blessings from her?

Avebury, Wiltshire

"And this, Mr. Car— I mean, Lord Winthrop, is the baronial hall. See the wooden trusses? It is said they date from the fourteen hundreds."

Jonathan nodded. "Very nice."

The invitation to tea at Avebury had been forwarded by mail coach from Winthrop; unexpected, but he welcomed the change. There remained much to do, but stopping here on his return from London was a good way to break his journey, whilst also getting to know these distant relatives — without the disconcerting distraction of his mother lending further weight to their antipathy towards him.

Clothilde, technically of his generation, though he was younger by nearly two decades, kept casting him glances varying between dislike and hope. He forced his own resentment down and turned his focus to their yet-unspoken plea.

If Winthrop Manor did not exactly live down to its name, then Avebury was more palace than mere house, complete with Elizabethan red brick, a multitude of gables, baronial dining hall, and several turret-topped wings. Avebury possessed a myriad of treasures, such as a Rococo-inspired ballroom finished with Chinese silk-lined walls and several crystal-dropped chandeliers. He rather doubted it received as much recent use as in its glory days half a century ago.

This guided tour, led by Peter, Peter's mother, and Elizabeth, who together with Elizabeth's daughters had lived there for years under the former baron's largesse, was no doubt designed to show off the ancient pile to best advantage, but while he could appreciate the building's historic elements, it was apparent the amount needed to fund necessary repairs would be sizeable, far exceeding what he estimated Winthrop required. He was also keenly aware he was being tolerated simply because of his fortune; indeed had heard the words "but a merchant's son" before he'd first been admitted to the drawing room earlier.

"And this is the priest's hole." Peter motioned to a stairway before bending to remove a timber from one of the steps.

"For the tiny priests?"

"Well, not everyone was as big as you." Clothilde eyed him with a frown.

"Something to be thankful for, if one were a priest," he suggested.

Elizabeth offered a slight chuckle, and he found his heart warming to her.

A quiet woman, both in manner and appearance, she nevertheless had a shrewd look in her eyes, her lips pursing whenever her sister or nephew made one of their slightly witless comments. Which was fairly often.

"Perhaps you might be so good as to show me any plans of the estate."

"Of course! We must return to the study for that. We might have tea there, too."

"I would not wish to discommode you."

"Not at all," Elizabeth said. "I will see to it at once."

She hurried off, leaving the mother and son to lead him back to the study whilst conducting a whispered conversation he pretended not to overhear.

"Ask him now," hissed the older woman.

"C-cousin Jonathan?"

Jon smothered a smile. So it was cousin now? "Yes, Cousin Peter?"

"I . . . that is, we —" he shot a terrified look at his mother.

"Oh, go on! He will not eat you."

"Rest assured," Jon said, "I find the eating of cousins beneath even my admittedly low standards."

Clothilde gave a nervous titter, but looked at him askance. Peter just looked confused.

"Never mind, Peter. I think we both can admit to finding one's cousins unpalatable at times, would you not agree?"

"Sir, I . . . I do not . . ." Peter stuttered to a halt.

"What he means to say —"

"Thank you, Clothilde. I'm sure Peter can say whatever he means to say."

She shot him a scathing look but kept her lips tightly compressed as Peter's scarlet face turned to him.

"Sir, I do not want you thinking, that is, we do not think you . . ."

Jon's heart twisted. Poor lad. Was it any wonder he'd turned out so awkward with such a termagant as a mother?

"Clothilde, would you excuse us? Peter

and I need to have a talk."

"But —"

"A gentleman's conversation, you understand." He guided her to the study door then closed it firmly.

"How did you do that?" Peter breathed wide-eyed.

"Practice," Jon said wryly. "Now spit it out, lad. I haven't got all day."

"I . . ." Peter swallowed.

"Yes?"

"I want to apologize for . . . for remarks my mo— that is, that we might have made that do you disservice."

"Manfully shouldered, lad."

Peter blushed. "You do not seem —"

"Completely beneath you? Oh, I probably am. But I've been around some people who know how to get on and perhaps some of their polish has rubbed off on me." He motioned to the decanter of cut glass. "Shall we?"

Peter's eyes rounded. "Mother does not let me."

"Let you?" Jonathan's brow rose. "How old are you?"

"One-and-twenty."

"So you have reached your majority."

The chin rose proudly. "Of course."

"Then why are you letting your mother

dictate what you can and cannot do?"

Peter looked at him as if he'd spoken Hindustani.

Jon bit back a sigh and poured a finger of whiskey in two glasses. He handed one to the boy and resumed his seat, noting Peter's swallow and wince. Perhaps such a commonplace ritual of manhood was still a step too far for this young man.

He eyed his cousin. "Why do you let your mother control you?"

"She . . . she has my best interests at heart."

Jon merely studied him until the boy flushed again.

"She does! I know it may not seem so at times, but she wants me to be happy."

"I'm sure she does. But are you?" Jon nodded to the Avebury plans stretched out across the table between them. "Is this what you want? To be master of this?"

The boy was silent for a long moment. "Mother always said it would come to me."

"That was not my question. I repeat, is this what you want?"

"Of course."

Jon raised a brow and waited.

A multitude of expressions crossed Peter's face before he eventually sighed. "No."

"And what do you want?"

"I . . . I want to study rocks, and shells, and fossils, and see if I can find ancient specimens like that Mary Anning girl did."

Jon nodded. "She has found some remarkable treasures, hasn't she?"

For the next fifteen minutes he watched the boy's face light as he expounded upon recent discoveries of dinosaur bones and other artifacts. Now here was passion.

"Does your mother know any of this?"

The light faded, the boy's posture drooped. "She thinks such things fanciful."

"She does not understand you, perhaps."

Peter shrugged.

"Perhaps you could take a trip to the coast to see some of these things."

"Really? Oh, sir, I'd give anything to go!"

Jon's smile turned wry. "But I gather this is not what your mother is expecting you to say?"

"No." Peter's face fell. "She wants money for Avebury."

"I thought as much. And after all, I am a rich merchant's son, aren't I?"

"Are you?" Peter asked, ingenuously.

That was the crux of the matter, wasn't it? Though not a question that could be answered here.

Jon took a sip of whiskey, taking care not to show *his* wince against the burn. "Regardless of what my relations believe, I still have the means to help you. Which is what I want to do."

"You'll give us money for Avebury?"

Jon smiled. "Let's call your mother and aunt in, shall we?"

Moments later, the door opened, and Clothilde followed the footman in, wearing a slightly disgruntled expression.

"Is Elizabeth joining us too? I rather hoped she would."

Clothilde issued the footman instructions then turned as he left the room. "Now, what has been decided?" She looked expectantly between them.

"Let us wait a moment until — ah, Elizabeth. Thank you for joining us." Jon waited until both ladies had settled themselves before resuming his seat and steepling his fingers. "Forgive my frankness, ladies, but after all, I am merely a rich merchant's son . . ."

Elizabeth's lips twitched. Peter blushed. Clothilde's mouth turned down.

"Although apparently not *quite* so below notice, seeing as I now head the family," he continued in a thoughtful tone. Then he said in a louder voice, "Regardless, I'm well aware that your invitation for me today was for no other reason than you thought I'd be a soft touch, and you would perhaps somehow try to shame me into giving you money to restore this house to its former glory."

Clothilde's mouth fell open. Then closed. Then, "Sir, I dislike such insinuations!"

"Forgive me, madam. I thought I spoke plainly enough."

Elizabeth shot him a glance that mingled amusement and approval.

"Come now, Clothilde. Now is not the time for prevarication. Let us hear Cousin Jonathan's ideas."

He inclined his head to her, before eyeing the other woman. "I'm well aware, madam, that you neither like me nor think me most suitable for my new role, but I ask you, would your son here suit?"

"Of course he would!" She sat straighter in her chair. "Peter was born for the role."

"Really?"

"He . . . he would suit most admirably."

"He would suit some things most admirably, but steering a grand estate from near bankruptcy is not one of them. Do you know how much capital this house would require to bring it up to a satisfactory standard?"

She named a sum.

"Try tripling that, and you're halfway there. Over the past few months I have spent a considerable amount of time on Winthrop and am well aware of what is required, as my solicitors in London can attest. Clothilde, Elizabeth, I regret most heartily but I will not be investing my capital into Avebury."

"What? No, you cannot be serious. You must!"

"Why? Because this is your pet project? It certainly isn't your son's."

"Peter?" Frowning, she turned to her son, who shrank in his chair. "What have you been saying?"

"The truth," Jon continued, "which is something you do not appear to want to hear. So let me make it abundantly clear: I will not be investing in refurbishing Avebury. I *will* endeavor to seek other ways to ensure Avebury's long-term future, and I will support Peter in some other venture, but giving him management over such an estate I believe — well frankly, I believe it would kill him."

"No!"

"Yes. And I know I must seem a black-hearted villain, clutch-fisted as the rest, but it is for your son's sake that I do this. He does not want this responsibility, nor does he seem to have the capacity for it."

"But he has worked hard —"

"He's done nothing of the sort. He has followed others' instructions, mostly yours, if I'm not mistaken, but Peter clearly possesses little inclination for making this work."

"What would you know? I am his mother! And you are nothing but —"

"A merchant's son, I know. But surely that qualifies me to speak? I have worked with enough business-minded men to know what is a good investment and what is doomed to fail, and I'm afraid that unless drastic measures are put in place, Avebury will need to be sold."

"But you are rich! You should help us!"

"Why?"

"You . . . you are our cousin!" she sputtered.

"You now think I am?"

She stared at him, terror edging her eyes. "But we need you."

"You do, that is true. And so this is what I propose we should do."

For the next hour he laid out a plan, which met with fierce resistance from one lady and quietly spoken approval from the other. Peter was silent, obviously afraid any word might further incur his mother's wrath.

"I will need to have my solicitor look into

this," Clothilde eventually conceded.

The same who was to look into his legitimacy to the barony? He suppressed the retort, concentrated on conciliation. "I would expect nothing less. Now, have we time to look at the gardens? They must be most attractive in this late afternoon light."

His hostess agreed, grudgingly, and he spent the next hour or so working to appease his relatives' ruffled sensibilities. So successful was he, the evening meal even managed to be surprisingly pleasant, in spite of the attendance of Aunt Elizabeth's giggling girls, who gazed upon him with a mix of coquetry and alarm. Better still was the time afterward, when he and Peter lingered in the dining room after the dessert course was cleared away and the ladies had withdrawn, and Jonathan saw beneath the stammering nerves to the educated young man below. Clearly something would need to be arranged for him, preferably away from his mother.

And clearly Jon's new role was one that, if others truly knew the responsibilities involved, few would envy.

CHAPTER SEVEN

"No!"

Catherine glanced up from her knitting as her mother continued scanning the letter clutched in her hand. "What is it, Mama?"

"Clothilde says he refused to help save Avebury!"

"Really?"

"Yes! No, wait . . ."

Catherine placed the yarn and needles aside as she waited for her mother to finish reading. Words arose from the devotional Lavinia had lent her, words from the Gospel of Matthew about honoring one's parents. She drew in a quiet breath and released.

"Well, it seems he *will* provide assistance, but only on the condition that Peter accepts a new estate manager! The nerve of him! Thinking he knows best all the time."

"It *is* his money, Mama."

"Be that as it may, he should have more respect for what is due the family, and treat us accordingly."

"It is probably a good thing he does not."

"I beg your pardon?"

"If you remember Aunt Clothilde's comments after the funeral, I think it shows a great deal of forbearance from him that he would even go to Avebury, let alone offer to help."

"Well! I can see I'll have to be very careful what I say around here from now on."

Catherine bit her lip as her mother sniffed loudly. She said in a quiet voice, "Mother, I do not believe him to be quite the villain so many make him out to be."

"But —"

"And don't you find this constant resentment tiring? I know I do."

Mama sniffed again. "I do not understand you. At all!"

No. Catherine stared sadly at her parent. It was obvious she did not.

Her mother picked up the letter again, and held it high, screening her face, her stance and pout suggesting deep offense had taken root.

Catherine swallowed a sigh and glanced at the small table between them, where Lavinia's latest epistle lay awaiting reply. Each stroke of ink had sung Mr. Carlew's praises, listing his various accomplishments before noting his provision of sufficient funds to provide a teacher. Of course, by supporting Lavinia's long-held dream of establishing a village school, in the countess's eyes Mr. Carlew could now do no wrong.

The past few evenings had seen Catherine composing then rejecting several replies, for while she wanted to rejoice with the news of his good works, still she felt a tugging sense of disloyalty in admitting these were in fact good things. And how could she reconcile these good things with the man she knew capable of such betrayal?

Mama placed her embroidery in her lap. "I've a good mind to write to Drusilla and see if she is amenable for a visit."

Hope flickered in Catherine's heart. "A visit to Bath would be wonderful."

"I refuse to be chased away from our rightful sphere of influence, but I believe it would be beneficial for us to get away from here, at least for a little while. I do not think I can stand any more of that man or his insufferable relations' presence in our community."

Outside a horse's neighing preceded a knock at the door. Seconds later Tilly opened the door to the sitting room. "Excuse me, madam. Miss Carlew is here."

"*Miss* Carlew?" Mama glanced at Catherine before saying to the maid, "You may admit her when I ring."

Mama put away her workbasket then patted her hair, gesturing to Catherine to remove her apron and tuck it under the cushion on the settee. She then sat quietly, her posture one of ease, whilst avoiding Catherine's gaze as the seconds ticked by.

"Mama," Catherine whispered, after nearly a minute had passed. "Miss Carlew is waiting."

"Yes."

Catherine blinked. "Do you not mean to ring for Tilly to admit her?"

Her mother shook her head, her gaze sliding away. When sufficient time had passed for their unexpected visitor to grow cool waiting in the drafty hall she finally rang for Tilly to grant admittance.

The door opened and Julia Carlew entered.

"Miss Carlew!" Mama, all graciousness, gestured to a seat. "*Such* an unexpected pleasure for you to condescend to visit us."

"Good morning, Lady Winthrop, Miss Winthrop." The pretty blonde with perfect doll-like features smiled, albeit seeming a trifle nervously. "I do hope I am not interrupting anything of great importance."

"No, no, not at all," Mama said, as if forcing their visitor to wait unnecessarily was not part of her plan. "I trust your dear mama and brother are in good health?"

"Yes. That is, I believe so."

"You do not know so?" Mama's brows rose.

"Well, my brother tends to leave early in the morning to visit the tenants, so I often do not see him when I go downstairs to breakfast."

Mama's expression hardened slightly. "He seems very dedicated."

"Oh, yes! He always has been, when he has put his mind to something."

Except when it came to the one thing that could have ensured Catherine's happiness. A new pang of regret formed, kneaded by Julia's words. He had obviously not "put his mind" to pursuing her.

"And your Mama?"

"She is well, thank you. It is a message from her that I came to give." She glanced shyly at Catherine. "You may be aware that Mama has invited several of my friends to come and stay for a time, and they arrive later today. She is hopeful Jon will be drawn to one and make her his bride."

Her insides fisted. Her smile froze. No, she had not been aware. She barely heard the murmured invitation to dinner that night, or her mother's regrets.

Julia seemed to shrink. "Oh. I'm terribly sorry."

She was terribly sorry? How would Catherine cope? What would she do? Oh, if only they could leave . . . Somehow, amid the welter of conflicting emotions, Catherine became aware of Julia's gaze, a gaze that demanded she school her features to neutrality, and tamp down her pain. For despite everything, she found herself liking the young woman. Julia, with her mix of shyness and girlish confidences, seemed to hold an almost pleading look in her blue eyes, as if hoping Catherine might be her friend.

Her heart thawed a little. "Perhaps another time."

When no visitors remained. For while she had no desire to mingle with the young ladies deemed suitable as his prospective bride, she did possess some curiosity to visit again.

To see Winthrop *Manor* again.

That was all.

The next morning, having stayed up late reading one of Mrs. Radcliffe's ridiculous tales in an effort to ignore the agony of wondering what Winthrop's guests were like, Catherine returned from her now daily walk to the end of the lane to find the gleaming coach bearing the Hawkesbury crest near their door. Her heart lifted, her steps hurried. Surely a visit from Lavinia and the earl would be a highlight for the day. Her lips twisted. A highlight for the week, even.

"Livvie! Oh, and Lord Hawkesbury" — she hastened to offer a slight curtsy — "how do you do?"

Tilly brought in tea during which they exchanged social niceties about the weather. Upon the maid's exit, the earl's gaze lifted to the ceiling where the large crack splitting the plaster seemed to have doubled after recent rain. "And how do you find your new accommodations?"

Thus began a familiar litany of complaint from Mama. Catherine drew in a restorative breath, lowering her eyes to her teacup to avoid exchanging a too-speaking glance with Lavinia.

"Lady Winthrop, I am indeed saddened to hear such things. But have you not spoken to your cousin? He seems quite a decent-hearted man, whom I'm sure would be grieved to know you feel so."

"Carlew?" Mama snorted inelegantly. "He would do nothing save what would serve his own interest. And as for that woman, his mother, she is an abomination!"

"Really, Mama, that is taking things too far. Lady Harkness is —"

"Oh, what would you know, child!"

Catherine clutched the teacup until she thought it might break, mortification blooming across her chest, quite unable to meet anyone's gaze.

"I cannot for the life of me ask anyone from that family for assistance. They have made their lack of interest well known, which has decided me upon removing as soon as possible." Mama waved a hand. "I cannot stay here. You can see it is barely tolerable for a servant, let alone the wife of a baron —"

"I think it holds a certain charm," Lavinia offered.

"Because you need not live here," Mama sniffed.

"I'm sure if you only spoke to him —"

"No, I'm sorry, Lord Hawkesbury, but that is not possible. Did you know he refused to help my poor nephew at Avebury? Refused! When he's as rich as Croesus. That man has no conscience."

"I'm sure there is some misunderstanding."

"There is not, I assure you! I cannot tell you what it is like to be forced from your home, only to have to endure the likes of *him* living there, having parties we should be invited to —"

"But Mama —"

"And dinners, at which we should be included. Now nobody invites us anywhere. Nobody!"

Catherine chewed her lip as Lavinia offered soothing words of placation. Was it their mourning that had isolated them from the social doings of the neighborhood, or was it Mama's bitterness? Was the little news that came their way simply because people did not want to run the risk of offending Mama even further?

"And I cannot but admit to a certain degree of resentment at being issued last-minute invitations, as though I'm of no greater importance than someone just to make up the numbers!"

Lavinia and the earl glanced at each other, then rose as one. "I fear we have outstayed our welcome."

No! Catherine wanted to cry out.

Lavinia caught her look and smiled. "Lady Winthrop, I do hope you'll condescend to allow Catherine to continue her visits. I confess I'd be quite lonesome without her."

"Of course she may," Mama said, pettishly.

Lavinia clasped Catherine's hand in farewell. "Come tomorrow?"

"With pleasure."

Anything to escape this house of distress, and distract her from the inhabitants of the much bigger house a mile away.

The next day she escaped early, glad to be freed from the cottage's confines, glad to flee Frank's grumbles about preparing Ginger for her ride to Hampton Hall. Her heart lifted at the thought of spending the bulk of the day with Lavinia. How long it had seemed since she had not felt trapped by misery.

She found the countess practicing in the music room, and sank into a seat, listening to the matched voice and pianoforte fill the room. When she finished, Catherine clapped appreciatively.

"Now it is your turn," Lavinia motioned to the piano stool.

"No, no. I cannot do justice. Besides it has been too long since I played at home."

"It will be even longer if you don't take the opportunity now. And who knows when you will be asked to perform?"

"And who will be asking? We hardly have a surfeit of opportunities being offered."

"What about at Mr. Carlew's?" Lavinia

smiled mischievously.

"What about it?"

"There might be cause for performing there one day."

"Not by me," Catherine said firmly. "Besides, Julia tells me there are any number of young ladies in attendance at the moment. My absence will not be noted."

She thought she'd managed to sound noncommittal, but Lavinia's tilted head and assessing eyes gave her pause.

"Well, how about we try a duet?" Lavinia pulled down a music sheet from atop the gleaming grand piano. "This is not especially difficult, so you should be able to pick it up quickly."

"Your faith in my ability is appreciated," Catherine murmured.

"Silly! I know you take less pleasure in music than I, but some social niceties are worth maintaining, even if we find them unpleasant."

Catherine nodded, and allowed Lavinia to guide her through the piece. An hour later, after many false starts and much laughter, she had perfected her part to such a degree that when the earl visited, she was able to play her part creditably well.

"Bravo, ladies."

Catherine curtsied, and he escorted his

wife to a seat.

"I think you played that quite as well as Julia did last week."

Julia had visited? Her heart twisted. But wasn't Catherine supposed to be Lavinia's friend? She followed Lavinia to the settee, swallowing the feelings of envy and rejection, forcing her brittle smile to stay in place.

"Julia seems a nice, sweet girl."

"Although perhaps a little diffident," Catherine ventured, before adding quickly, "I quite like her."

"I'm glad," Lavinia said. "She strikes me as someone who could do with a friend, especially with her mother and brother so busy."

"I understand she has quite a few friends visiting at the moment."

"At the moment, perhaps, but when they are gone, she would do well to keep company with someone of good sense and character."

Was that a hint? "She invited Mama and me to dinner the other day."

"And you went? Oh, I'm so glad for —"

"We did not."

"Oh."

"Part of me wanted to go, but Mama felt it would be wrong. She might complain about not being invited, but she believes our mourning means we should remain quietly at home." Catherine offered a ghost of a smile. "Heaven forbid my reputation be sullied."

"Indeed!" Lavinia chuckled.

"And I confess, visiting with such a group of strangers does seem a little intimidating."

Lavinia shot the earl a quick look. "I wonder . . . do you think Lady Winthrop would consent to Catherine attending a dinner here? Just a quiet dinner, among friends — and perhaps some new acquaintances."

"Lavinia, my dear —"

"Nicholas, Catherine needs to have the chance to socialize. And how often is there such a group of young people nearby? Just think of the eligible young men!"

"I'd rather not," he said drily.

A giggle pushed past Catherine's misgivings. "Lavinia, I cannot ask you to do such a thing."

"You are not asking. I am offering, which is entirely different." She turned to her husband. "Nicholas, you know how dull things can be. And I'd like to make the most of our time before coming events make such parties impossible."

He sighed. "I suppose you would want my attendance, too."

"Of course! Someone has to talk to the

gentlemen."

He turned to Catherine, a half smile on his face. "Miss Winthrop, I hope you know I hold you fully responsible for this."

She blinked. What was the correct response? "I . . . um . . ."

"Don't tease her, Nicholas. Now, Catherine, you may be assured that we will send an invitation soon. Please do not worry. I'll word things in such a way your mother will be quite unable to refuse."

Catherine blinked back the moisture lining her eyes. How grateful she was to have such a friend! "I . . . I don't know what to say."

"That's easy. Say you will come. Now, I best consult with Mrs. Florrick and Giles to make sure all can be arranged."

Catherine made her departure, loaded with their good wishes and some fresh peaches from the earl's glasshouse. She left Hampton Hall, riding along the back way, having refused the earl's offer of his groom's escort.

"Th-thank you, sir, but it is not far."

"Such independence leads me to suspect my wife's influence at work here."

"I would hope to be as valiant as she."

He smiled, and that giddy sensation had gripped her insides as it did any time a handsome man smiled in her direction. Lucky Lavinia, indeed.

She nudged Ginger into a canter along the back lanes. The mare flew, as though glad to be released from the usual sedate pace propriety dictated. Her spirits lifted, and for a moment she almost touched happiness, expectation of pleasant things in her future lending wings to hope.

They came to a closed gate. Catherine looked around, saw no one to cast judgment, then urged Ginger over. Laughter escaped. "Good girl."

She glanced up. On the crest of the hill she saw a lone rider. From this distance she could not recognize him, save that his horse was big.

Ginger stumbled, jerking Catherine forward.

"What's the matter, girl?"

The horse began limping. She tried to gauge the distance they had come. Surely they had to be closer to the Dower House than Hampton Hall. "Come, girl. We're not too far from home."

Home. The word soured in her mouth. The cottage could never truly be home, not like Winthrop Manor would always be.

Ginger tossed her head, whinnying in discomfort. Catherine sighed. Carefully descended. She would need to walk back now; she could not remount without assistance. Why hadn't she accepted the earl's offer of his groom?

She picked up Ginger's front right hoof. The shoe had come loose, and she very much doubted Frank's ability — let alone willingness — to attend to such a matter. "Wonderful." She released the hoof and gathered the reins. "I suppose we both get to walk home now."

They had not gone more than twenty yards when she noticed a group of horse riders descending from the rise toward her. Why, *why* hadn't she accepted the earl's offer? She studied the horses, their riders. "Oh, no."

Surely that could be none but the new Lord Winthrop's house party.

She had nowhere to turn, nowhere to hide. She gritted her teeth as one by one they approached, slowed, and stopped, eyeing her — or her old black habit — askance.

"Ah, Miss Winthrop," came a silky voice. "We did not expect to see you here."

Catherine glanced up at Lady Harkness, dressed in a most becoming dark blue habit cut in the military style. "Good afternoon, ma'am."

She stilled as peripheral vision ascertained

the tall figure of Mr. Carlew dismount. She would not look at him. She *would* not!

The older woman completed a round of introductions, Catherine blind to all but the extreme youth and prettiness of Julia's friends. She muttered a "how do you do" as Julia nudged her horse closer. "Have you stopped to pick flowers? This part of the country seems filled with them."

"I . . . er, no, that is —"

"It appears the horse has thrown a shoe," said a dark-haired man who had joined Mr. Carlew on the ground.

"Have you far to go?" asked one of the pretty girls, whose name she'd already forgotten.

"N-no." From the edge of her eye she noticed Mr. Carlew pick up Ginger's foreleg. "Please, I do not mean to hold you up."

"I, for one, am happy for a rest," said Julia. "Jonathan likes to believe we are all as good equestrians as he."

"He is an excellent horseman," said Lady Harkness smoothly, green eyes watchful under her scarf-swathed hat. "Would you not agree, Miss Beauchamp?"

The prettiest of the young ladies murmured acquiescence, her look of open admiration at Mr. Carlew stabbing pain through Catherine's heart.

The other riders eyed Catherine dismissively before nudging their animals away. She was conscious of her somber black garb, the curious stares, the lack of sympathy from all but Julia.

"She should not be ridden."

Mr. Carlew's deep voice and conclusion she'd already reached drew heat from within. "Of c-course not. Which is why I am walking her home."

He glanced at her then, his eyes unreadable, not quite touching hers, his mouth one hard flat line.

Shame filled her at her outburst. "I am s-sor—"

"Carmichael, help me unsaddle Gulliver."

The dark man murmured, "You're not going to let her ride him, are you?"

"I'm not going to let a lady return home on foot."

"But Gulliver is a great brute."

"Miss Winthrop is a good rider."

So *he* had been the rider on the ridge who'd witnessed her jump earlier. Despite the sunshine, she shivered.

"You can manage him, can't you?" His eyes still didn't quite meet hers.

"Y-yes." She inwardly winced. Did he realize she now stuttered because of him, her confidence gone when he'd left? Oh, that she could assume such confidence now.

"How do you know this, Jonathan?"

He ignored his mother's question as he strapped Catherine's sidesaddle around the stallion. Before she knew it, his strong hands were around her waist, hoisting her into the saddle.

Breath caught, his touch the first since that unfortunate evening so long ago. "Th-thank you, Mr. Carlew," she murmured.

He nodded, still refusing to meet her eyes. He turned to Julia and Lord Carmichael. "Would you be so kind as to escort Miss Winthrop home? Julia will show you the way."

"Certainly."

He turned to her, his gaze settling somewhere past her left shoulder. "Shall I take Ginger to Winthrop to be reshod or would you prefer to have her home?"

He knew the name of her horse? She swallowed her surprise and thought through his offer. As much as she hated the obligation involved with his seeing to her horse at Winthrop, the alternative would mean him coming to the cottage, and Mama potentially seeing him, and having to listen to renewed moaning about her loss of status —

"Miss Winthrop?"

Could his voice be any colder? "I am

m-much obliged if you would see to it at Winthrop, sir." She murmured her thanks once more, but he seemed to ignore her.

She pressed her lips together to control the quiver, working to control Gulliver's restless manner. Gulliver — so much bigger, so much higher than poor Ginger — bent his head then shied, trying to toss her off. Heart racing, she ignored the gasps of the onlookers and spoke quietly, experiencing a profound sense of satisfaction as she stayed upright. A glance at Mr. Carlew saw him give a barely discernible nod before he looked away again. He had not expected her to fall; that much was certain.

Ten minutes later, she was back at the cottage, the ride on Gulliver one of the most exhilarating experienced in years. "Th-thank you, sir, for your assistance," she murmured as Lord Carmichael helped her down.

"No trouble at all. I must confess to a mite of envy. Carlew doesn't let just anyone ride that beast. Although I must say you seem to know your way around a horse."

"Thank you."

The dryness of her tone seemed to catch him by surprise as he chuckled, his smile widening. "Well, I best deal with this." He swiftly removed her saddle, depositing it on the hitching rail. Frank was — unsurpris-

ingly — nowhere to be seen. "Now, I daresay Carlew will return your nag once she is
seen to properly. However, if you'd prefer
to collect her, then I'm more than happy to
pass on that message."

"I . . ." Again indecision struck, as the
benefits of one course of action were
weighed against the disadvantages of the
other. She had no wish to see him with his
guests at Winthrop; neither did she wish him
to visit here, thus risking her mother's
displeasure. What to do, what to do . . .

Julia glanced between them, her brow
knotted. "Perhaps we could visit tomorrow
and return Ginger then."

A burst of gratitude filled her. "Thank
you, Miss Carlew. That would be very kind."

"Good day to you."

"G-good day." Catherine nodded as Lord
Carmichael swiftly remounted, he and Julia
raising hands in farewell, leading Gulliver as
they rode away.

Leaving her alone, feeling the bite of
humiliation, while much, much deeper, a
secret, twisted part of her wished she could
blithely spend the afternoon riding with Mr.
Carlew, too.

He was tired by the time he'd finally
tramped home. After days of rain and

133

clouded skies and unseasonably cool temperatures, the sun had certainly sung today, and now a fine layer of perspiration lined his shirt.

He handed Ginger off to the surprised grooms. "I expect Gulliver will return with Lord Carmichael shortly. If you can attend to the mare's shoe, I'd be much obliged."

"Of course, my lord."

He trudged up the hill to the Manor, glad the others had already entered and he did not need to wear his smiling host mask. Disappointment curled within. She still refused to meet his gaze. How long — ?

"Jonathan, dear, when you have a moment?"

He nodded to his mother. Gestured to his mud-spattered clothes. "I'll be with you presently."

Jon walked up the stairs slowly, not keen to hurry to this interview, sure his mother would only continue her speculation that his unwitting remarks about Miss Winthrop's horsemanship had evoked. He'd endured enough on the way home, between her comments and Hale's.

"She does not call you Winthrop," Hale had observed.

"She is not the only one." Neither did Carmichael.

"I suppose such things take time to adjust to."

"Yes." And doubtless she would still reserve that appellation for her father.

"Hmm. She seems quite a modest, mouse-like little thing."

He'd nodded. Too modest in looks to garner Hale's attention. Why that instilled relief, he did not care to examine.

"A mouse but with a tiger's growl," his mother had said. "Oh, don't look at me like that, Jon. You heard her before, almost biting off your head when you were only trying to help."

"Ungrateful, I call it," murmured one of Julia's friends.

"Ginger *is* her horse," he'd said mildly.

And he could understand a person not wanting to feel yet more obligation to someone they had no wish to further connections with.

"Perhaps she objects to high-handedness."

"Or simply your mode of delivery."

"Perhaps." He'd managed a smile without humor. Regret at her fixed aversion gnawed at him, and yet . . .

Jon placed a hand on the windowpane and stared at the knot garden below.

And yet . . .

He'd heard the soft inhale of breath when

he'd lifted her onto his horse. Felt her stiffen beneath his touch. Felt the moment take on significance beyond the seconds she was in his arms.

Was he mistaken in thinking it a sign that she also felt the tug of latent attraction?

CHAPTER EIGHT

The next afternoon saw Ginger's return, accompanied by Major Hale, Lord Carmichael, and Miss Carlew. Catherine's hastily offered invitation to tea was declined by the gentlemen, who expressed a desire to ride into St. Hampton Heath. Miss Carlew accepted happily, their conversation proceeding nicely until Catherine noticed her guest eyeing the invitation from Lavinia for the following evening's dinner party.

"Did you receive one, too? Lavinia said she hoped your guests would be amenable."

"You are going?" Miss Carlew's brow creased, as if confused.

"Lavinia has been my closest friend for years."

Her forehead cleared. "Oh. Well, I should like to be friends with a countess. Imagine getting to wear a coronet, and attending all those royal functions."

"From what Lavinia has told me she does

not enjoy those functions overly. As for wearing the coronet, she has not attended many such ceremonies this year, due to her upcoming confinement." A swift prayer arose that all would be well with this babe, and Lavinia would finally have the child she longed for.

"Of course." Julia bit her bottom lip.

"Miss Carlew?"

"Julia, please."

"Very well, Julia. Forgive me, but is something the matter?"

"I . . . I'm sorry you do not want to attend dinner with us."

Perhaps honesty was best. "Julia, please understand, Mama has only agreed to my acceptance because of our longstanding relationship with Lavinia. A quiet evening meal with old friends is quite a different matter to an evening with people one scarcely knows. After all, it is not the done thing to attend functions when one is in mourning."

"So Jonathan tells Mama and me."

"I beg your pardon?"

"He has asked us to not keep pestering you and your mama with invitations to dinner."

Oh. Her heart twisted. Of course he did

not want her around. He did not want her at all.

"I believe he thinks it might only add to the strain you must be feeling, seeing your former home, and all."

She swallowed. Prayed for her voice to remain steady. "He is all solicitude."

"Yes, he's quite sensitive that way."

Catherine glanced away, unable to meet her guest's innocent blue eyes.

"Miss Winthrop? Are you quite well?"

"Thank you, Julia, I am."

"Then we shall see you at the dinner tomorrow night?"

"Pardon?"

"The dinner at the Hawkesburys'. You said you were going?"

"Oh. Of course."

Julia's pretty smile flashed. "Wonderful. We shall see you then."

Catherine nodded. Wonderful.

Winthrop Manor
Next evening
"Well, that went well."

Jonathan nodded as Hale poured another brandy. The ladies had retired, leaving his two friends and himself to watch the flames burn down. Dinner at Hampton Hall had gone well, had proved surprising, in more

139

ways than one.

The earl and countess had welcomed his guests as sincerely as if they'd known them for years. But it was their other guests who had proved most interesting. Miss Winthrop had finally made a social appearance, her first in public apart from services. He knew she and the countess possessed some level of friendship, but hadn't realized how close they were until they'd performed a duet on the pianoforte, with remarkable skill.

He frowned. He didn't remember that about her. Neither did he recall seeing a certain Milton fellow hanging around before. Somehow Milton — the local squire's son, it appeared — had managed to sit beside her at dinner, then later whilst the other ladies performed. He'd often whispered in her ear, and she'd murmured back, clearly comfortable with the young man in a way she never relaxed in Jon's presence. His fingers tightened around the glass.

"You're awfully quiet, old man," Carmichael said from his position on the sofa.

Jon forced his lips upward. "I *was* enjoying the quiet."

"I will say this, that though ladies are very pleasant company, they are inclined to screech."

"I beg your pardon?"

"Perhaps you were too enchanted by the charming Miss Beauchamp," Hale said. "Did you not notice that every one of the ladies tonight either talked or sang in a very loud voice? Apart from the countess, of course. And your Miss Beauchamp."

"She's not my Miss Beauchamp."

"She's not?" Hale grinned. "Then you don't mind if I see if she prefers my Indian stories to yours?"

Jon's brows rose.

"You do? And here was I wondering if someone else had caught your eye."

He refused to bite.

"Miss Winthrop doesn't have a loud voice," Carmichael noted, slightly slurring his words. "She's qu-quite a quiet thing . . ."

Jon frowned. Was he making fun of her slight stammer? His brow knit further. Since when did she stammer anyway? He did not recall —

"Y'know, with her long face and nose Miss Winthrop rather puts me in mind of a horse I once had, a nag with the sweetest nature —"

Jon cleared his throat, eyed his friend steadily.

"Oh, beg pardon. I forgot for a moment . . ." Hale tilted his head back, the amber liquid from his glass disappearing swiftly in the practiced action. "She seemed to be having a good chat with that Milton fellow. D'you know him?"

"No." Nor did he have any intention to. The man appeared little more than a wind-sucking popinjay. He was content to limit his interactions with the fellow to the merest civility.

Jon took another sip, forcing his thoughts to more pleasant things as he studied the crackling fire. He liked this room, liked the mellow quiet of the old bricks, the history of its thick, sixteenth-century walls. The legacy of countless Winthrops who had gone before, building, establishing, growing — until his predecessor had almost gambled it away.

He shook his head. Was it better to let everyone think the previous Lord Winthrop was merely a poor manager, rather than the poor gambler he really was? Thank God nobody had said anything to Miss Winthrop tonight, but then, he didn't expect any of the guests — save Carmichael — to have much experience with gambling dens, and the viscount was too much of a gentleman to expose another's weakness and cause a woman pain.

He looked up, caught Carmichael glance away, smoothing away a smile. "Yes?"

"You seem troubled, dear fellow. Still can't make up your mind which of the young ladies it should be?"

"You are being absurd."

Hale chuckled. "Not absurd. It is why you invited us down, isn't it? To approve your choice and all that? Tell you what, I rather like the Henery girl. She seems a lively sort, and is quite pretty."

She also didn't have a word to say that wasn't linked in some way to dogs.

"I thought Miss Winterbottom to be more your thing," Carmichael mused. "She seems quite pious. I even overheard her asking the countess about the services here. I ask you!"

"Yes, but she's more good than good-looking," Hale drawled. "I don't think I would find her much fun."

"Tell you who I don't think would be fun is that Miss Winthrop! Barely said a word all night —"

"And looked a perfect fright," interrupted Hale.

"— until she made that comment, right at the end. To Lady Henery, no less!"

Jon's lips twitched. Another moment that had surprised as well as disconcerted. He pretended to sip his wine as the scene arose in his mind. After the meal, the ladies had performed an impromptu concert in the music room. Miss Winthrop's surprisingly lovely duet with the countess had engendered requests for more, which Miss Winthrop had agreed to reluctantly, playing with indifference and a few slipped notes.

Lady Henery had said loudly, "I have always held that when one does not bother practicing it is but a sure sign of an indolent nature."

Quick as a flash, Miss Winthrop had murmured, "Or a sign that they are simply in want of a pianoforte."

His eyes narrowed again, remembering the titter that filled the room. Did she mean to imply they were without? Surely the Dower House was equipped with such things.

"There is that look again." Carmichael glanced at Hale. "Perhaps we should be more circumspect in our observations about Miss Winthrop."

"You are being ridiculous," Jon said.

"If you think that, then you did not see the way she glared in your direction when you were talking to the pretty Miss Beauchamp."

His heart leapt. Then dropped. She did not care for him. She did *not*. Didn't her avoidance confirm her aversion? He shook his head. Tried to assume a nonchalance he did not feel as he shrugged. "Miss Beauchamp is a little young, but she seems quite amiable."

"Quite amiable *and* a tidy armful," Hale nodded before draining his glass.

"Exactly how young is too young, old man?" Carmichael's brows rose. "Would I be right in assuming a lady of six-and-twenty more suitable?"

"Five-and-twenty," he muttered, unthinkingly.

"I knew it!" Carmichael crowed. "Miss Winthrop wins!"

Jonathan thunked his glass on the table. "Perhaps you should attend to yourself and be a little more prudent in your observations. I assure you, Miss Winthrop and I do not suit —"

"So she will not be attending the ball next week?"

His heart flickered in memory of another ball. He suppressed the sting and groaned, "Why did I ever agree to hold a ball?"

"Because you are a wonderful host?" suggested Hale.

Jon heaved out a breath. "Because I am a glutton for punishment."

"So will she attend?" Carmichael persisted.

"I don't think ladies in mourning attend balls, do you? Rest assured, I have no interest in Miss Winthrop, and can safely promise you that we will *never* be anything more than mere neighbors."

He leaned back in his seat, daring his friends to question his assertion.

God help him.

CHAPTER NINE

The following Monday, Catherine was back at Hampton Hall, having assumed a look of polite indifference as Lavinia continued to chat about Mr. Carlew and his visitors. She gritted her teeth. Wasn't it enough to constantly hear his praises being sung? Why must her dearest friend do the same? If only she knew. And as for all the young ladies deemed suitable prospects . . .

Her smile grew even more brittle as Lavinia moved on to praising Miss Beauchamp.

"Miss Beauchamp seems a very nice sort of girl, although she is quite young." With a grin, Lavinia added, "But I suppose that is the problem with superior young men. They make it hard to approve even the most suitable of candidates."

"I . . . I suppose so."

"I am sure we will hear news of a match soon."

Catherine stilled. It seemed as though her entire being rose up in protest. She swallowed the bile as Lavinia studied her curiously. "Are you not the least bit interested in these things? Are we not supposed to care about our neighbors?"

"By gossiping about them?" Catherine raised a brow.

"Such a harsh indictment!"

"Such a true one," Catherine murmured.

"Such comments put me in mind of Lord Winthrop." Catherine stiffened as Lavinia eyed her. "He shares your dry sense of humor."

She forced her smile to stay fixed.

Lavinia placed a hand on her swollen belly. "Nicholas has mocked my lack of observation these days, but Catherine, I have sensed for some time now that you are one of the few who do not approve of our new neighbor. Please forgive me, but I did not think you as prejudiced as other members of your family."

Her gaze fell, unable to meet the honest love in her friend's eyes.

"You must excuse me if I have said something distressful, yet I cannot but be concerned. Has Lord Winthrop done something to upset you?"

"N-no." She peeked up to see Lavinia's

148

brows rise. "Of course he has not. Why would he?"

"Why indeed." Her friend's gray gaze grew penetrating. "So he has not upset you."

"No!" Catherine swallowed a bubble of panic. "That is . . ."

"That is, yes?"

She shook her head, lowered her gaze again. "It was a long time ago."

"But not long enough if he still has the power to discomfit my friend. Would it perhaps help if you shared?"

No, it would only expose her stupidity and weakness.

"Dearest Catherine, I feel that this is something you have carried for quite some time, and I know how wearying such a burden can be."

"I — no. Thank you. I do not wish to impugn anyone."

"And I don't wish for my friend to be so heavy laden. We are at a crossroads, are we not?"

Catherine nodded, glancing up to find Lavinia steadily watching her. "It is only . . ."

"Only?"

And, like a pond whose walls were breached, so it tumbled out.

"I . . . I first met Mr. Carlew during the

season, just after you were married. It was Grandpapa's birthday, and all the cousins were in London to celebrate. Grandpapa had been unwell, and not expected to reach such a milestone. The first night of celebrations, I m-met Mr. Carlew and his mother. She was still Mrs. Carlew then, but as the wife of Grandpapa's cousin she had been invited. Of course, Mama and Papa were horrified that people with such connections in trade had been invited and were quite blatant in their disdain. I remember feeling so s-sorry for Jonathan that I made a point of speaking with him as much as possible, especially as it seemed few others were. And in doing so, I discovered just how much we had in common."

She paused, remembering that first night. Feeling prettier than ever before in her new pale yellow silk and diamond necklet. Feeling sure that this would be the season when she would finally meet the man of whom she had always vaguely dreamed. Her surprise at finding such a kindred soul in Mr. Carlew, despite his questionable antecedents. His blue-gray eyes, softening with admiration each time she stole from the ballroom to speak with him.

"H-he was very kind, and handsome, and gentlemanly, and not at all like my parents had implied."

"Speaking from my own observations he does indeed appear so." Lavinia's eyes twinkled. "Especially the handsome part."

Fire rushed along Catherine's cheeks. She returned her attention to her hands. "I learned we shared an interest in horses, and poetry, and God. I knew my parents did not approve of him, so when he suggested we meet again I happened to mention what time I usually rode in Hyde Park." She managed a smile. "Imagine my surprise to find him there the next day."

"Imagine," Lavinia murmured.

"Again we talked. Russell, our groom, didn't mind. I was never out of his sight, and Mr. Carlew was so obviously a gentleman. And he was: gentle, and so good-hearted. We k-kept finding opportunities to meet, sometimes while riding, but also at church or the park or the museum. Eventually he said he wanted to talk with my father, but I dissuaded him. I did not want our lovely times together to stop. He said he would write . . ."

And he had. Twice. The first time with such pretty words from John Donne's "The Good Morrow" she had memorized them immediately: "If ever any beauty I did see which I desir'd, and got, 'twas but a dream of thee."

Her chest, her throat grew tight. Time had shown how illusionary such sentiment had been, that dream long ago fading into nothing, just like her pretensions to any kind of beauty. At Lavinia's sympathetic look, she pushed past the ache to continue her story.

"H-he talked of his father — I mean Mr. Harold Carlew's business, the success he was making of it, his plans for expansion. He had ties to the East India Company but wanted to see the natives prosper, not just the Europeans. He had such a *good* heart, which is why I don't understand —"

"What happened?"

Catherine swallowed. The pain rose up again. "One day he didn't appear in the park for our ride together. I supposed he might be sick and thought nothing of it. But the following day, and the next, when he still did not show and sent no word, I began to wonder if something was wrong. Eventually I wrote him a letter, asking what had happened, assuring him of my affection, and he sent back the stiffest little note saying —" Fresh hurt clogged her throat, filled her eyes. "S-saying that he was very sorry but it had all been a terrible misunderstanding."

"Oh, Catherine!"

"I gave him my heart, but he didn't

w-want it." Her voice broke on a sob.

"Oh, my dear." Lavinia shifted close, pulling Catherine's head to her shoulder.

Tears dripped down. She swiped them away. "I do not know what I did wrong. Should we have been honest from the start? Did I say something to offend him? Should I have encouraged him to speak to Papa?"

"Your father said nothing?"

"Never. Neither Papa nor Mama ever spoke of him in any terms except disparaging his birth, so I do not think they knew. Mama was always so busy with plans for me to meet other men, she never knew I had already met the one I wanted."

"And Mr. Carlew has given you no word since returning?"

"Nothing. He is kind, it is true, but distant, like I am a mere acquaintance he has no desire to further know. I cannot reconcile this to the man who —"

She stopped, shame quivering inside and around her.

"Who what?"

Catherine studied her calfskin half boots. Lavinia was married, and increasing. Surely she would understand, would not judge. "He kissed me." She rushed on past Lavinia's intake of breath. Better to get this out now, once and for all. "It was our final

153

meeting, although I didn't know it at the time. We were at a ball, a masquerade at Lady Sefton's, but we knew each other's disguise as we'd discussed them previously. Mama had wanted me to dance with Lord Harville, but I slipped out to the garden with Mr. Carlew. I knew it was wrong, but I l-loved him and wanted to be with him. He was begging me once again to let him speak with Papa, so to stop him fussing I . . . I kissed him."

She peeked up to see Lavinia's look of half horror, half admiration. "Catherine!"

"And he kissed me back."

And that was the thing she had found so difficult to comprehend. If he had been shocked by her actions surely he wouldn't have responded. Yes, she'd noticed his hesitation at first, but then his arms had stolen around her, and he'd drawn her close, his lips warmly possessing hers in the loveliest, most wonderful moment of her life.

Her eyes filled anew. Such sweet, sweet memories! To have known such tenderness, to have felt so beautiful, so cherished, so desired. Had she been mistaken? Was she such a fool? Or had she magnified such feelings beyond what truly happened, misjudging things by the events that followed, events that ripped away all certainty, leading to the numbness that remained deep within?

"I thought he loved me." She winced at the plaintive note in her voice, but could not deny the truth. His kiss *had* said so. His repulsion had obviously set in later.

Lavinia clasped Catherine's hand once more. "And you are certain he did not speak to your father?"

"How could he without my knowing?"

Lavinia bit her lip.

"I kept half expecting him to visit, despite my pleas not to, because he was so concerned that it might appear underhand, and he is — he was — honorable."

Lavinia sighed. "I'm so sorry. I see now why it is hard for you to hear talk of any new attachment."

"It is hard simply for him to live in the same vicinity."

"Of course." Lavinia squeezed her hands then released them. "Thank you for sharing. You can be sure I will be praying most earnestly for God to direct your path. And Mr. Carlew's, too."

Catherine's eyes blurred. "Th-thank you."

A short while later she was riding home, feeling an awkward mix of relief at finally having shared her burden, and renewed hopelessness, that the precious memories stirred up today would oh-so-quickly turn to dust again.

Avebury, Wiltshire
Jonathan studied his cousin as his estate manager continued speaking. Was he such a fool as to hope the lad would truly hear, and not just listen?

"You can see the fields are less productive than they would be if they were joined together." Peter frowned as Mr. Clipshom continued. "I recommend removing the hedging and enlarging the field to allow for greater planting."

"And greater profits," Jon murmured.

He eyed his young cousin as Winthrop's estate manager continued espousing other cost-saving measures. Jon's brain might work for financial matters, but the ins and outs of farming were beyond him. They seemed beyond Peter, too, but the boy had at last realized the need to at least be aware, even if he might never plow in himself.

After extensive discussions between Avebury's most interested stakeholders, a three-pronged solution had been offered to save the historic estate: to sell what could be sold, rent out available land and encourage greater productivity amongst the tenant farmers, and open the house and grounds for tours. Such plans were approved wholeheartedly by Mr. Whittington and Mr. Trelling, and more reluctantly by Clothilde's solicitor, Mr. Bantry. Peter, whom Jonathan had urged — no, demanded — be privy to the discussions, had been forced to see the magnitude of Avebury's problems, his wideeyed silence as figures and the naming of huge sums of capital were tossed around, proving just how much he was out of his depth. So Jon had begun Peter's education the way he had learned to survive in India: in deep waters.

"Thank you, Clipshom. I'm sure Peter is feeling not a little overwhelmed by now."

"Well, it's a right shame nobody did open your eyes to seeing how badly managed this property was." Clipshom eyed Peter firmly. "Anyone would think you'd never seen it before."

"Lord Winthrop — that is, Uncle Walter — he used to show me around . . ." His voice trailed away uncertainly.

"There be a world of difference between being shown around and caring enough to know when your steward is being lazy." Mr. Clipshom sighed, and shook his head. "To think no one from the big house has visited these fields in years!"

"Any successful business requires thorough knowledge of a multitude of factors," Jon said. "And the ability and diligence of one's workers is a mightily important one."

Peter nodded, his expression could only be described as glum.

"So really, it depends on you," Jon continued. "How much do you want Avebury to succeed? Because if you, Clothilde, and Elizabeth are prepared to invest a great deal of hard work, then I believe that the estate can be saved. If not, then it will prove to be an elephant-sized burden on your shoulders, one under which you may well collapse."

"I still don't understand why you can't give us a lump sum," Peter muttered.

"Because it will never be simply one lump sum. Unless you become cognizant of the details of running such an estate, you will be requesting a similar sized lump sum on a regular basis, and I would much rather invest in things that will prove of greater benefit than simply propping up an old edifice."

Peter's eyes widened. "Mother will think you don't care for Avebury."

"She may, and frankly, it would be true."

His cousin's jaw dropped.

Jon worked to soften his tone. "Perhaps if I had been brought up here I would care more. The house possesses a certain charm, and with its unique history, I do think it could prove quite a draw for visitors, especially given its location so close to London. As I said to your mother and aunt, many of the big houses, like Derbyshire's Chatsworth, are open to the public upon occasion. With some inexpensive attention and tidying up of gardens, there is no reason why people would not choose to visit Avebury as well."

"You really think so?"

"I do. But I repeat: I remain unwilling to prop up bad debt with good."

The hope filling his cousin's face faded, his features twisting in a frown.

"His lordship has the way of it," said Clipshom. "And if your tenant farmers improve their farming practices, it will see increased yields, which means increased income from rents."

"And if you are not responsible for the upkeep of small holdings you do not care for, then your energies can be devoted to ensuring this house survives for future generations," Jon reiterated.

As they continued to ride around the property Jon was reminded again of the importance of wise investments, of planning for the future, of ensuring assets were properly maintained. To reverse such damage could prove ruinous to a man's finances. Things left undone for too long only demanded a price too high to pay in the future. Avebury was testament to that.

By the time he was headed back to Winthrop he'd reached some other decisions.

Propping up the past was a fool's game. He should have listened to those misgivings he'd had that first evening at Winthrop. The past had passed. It was best to move on with the future. With *his* future.

Jon squared his shoulders.

He would see if Miss Beauchamp's parents were amenable to return for a longer stay.

CHAPTER TEN

July passed. August saw the return of slightly warmer weather coupled with further rain showers, weather that made Catherine and her mother feel increasingly fractious and ever more aware of the small confines of the cottage. Back at Winthrop they had escaped heat within the spacious rooms, or better, by traveling to the seaside, even occasionally to one of the large estates in cooler climes, where parties and the company of others distracted from weather and forced thoughts away from oneself. Now, it seemed as if all their thoughts had turned inward, brooding, leading to short tempers and cold indignations.

But perhaps, in Catherine's case at least, this was also reinforced by the return of Miss Beauchamp and her mother, a return that seemed to prove Lavinia's suspicions about Mr. Carlew's intentions. Catherine tried to tell herself she did not care. She did not! But she could not prevent a few tears from falling onto her pillow at night, even as she despised her weakness.

She shook her head at her foolishness as she stepped around mud puddles on the lane. Why spoil her daily walk with thoughts of him? Why not be glad for the chance to escape for a few minutes, to escape both the cottage and Mama's offended silence, her current pique stemming from Catherine's audacity to disagree about the state of the meal last night, asserting it was fully cooked when Mama said otherwise. Time alone should be sweet distraction.

She squinted, her heart dropping in recognition of the riders at the end of the lane, and she had to force her steps forward, rather than veering off and hiding away, as she'd prefer.

"Miss Winthrop!" Julia reined in her horse. "I was just saying to Lydia that I was hopeful of meeting you again."

Catherine glanced up at Julia's golden-haired guest and dredged up a smile. "Good day, Miss Beauchamp."

"Oh, call me Lydia, please."

The ingenuous smile went some way to thawing her heart. She could not yet return the exchange of first names, though still sought to be polite. "Are you enjoying your stay?"

"Very much. I do like this part of Gloucestershire."

Catherine lifted a hand, shading her eyes. "And where are your people from?"

"A little town in Wiltshire, although we stay in London quite often, which is where we met Julia and her family."

Was that a slight blush on the girl's cheeks? No wonder Mr. Carlew was so enamored. She fought the envy. Lost. Nodded, smiled stiffly, and turned as if to walk away.

"Would you care to go riding with us, Miss Winthrop? I'm sure being such a local you would know all of the cooler spots to visit."

"Oh, yes, Miss Winthrop, please do," said Lydia. "I'm sure Julia would love to have someone else to listen to, rather than my prattle."

The newcomer wasn't making it any easier for Catherine to dislike her, not with such self-deprecation. "I don't know . . ."

"Please?"

It would be churlish to refuse. And it would keep her away from the cottage for a little longer. "If Mama does not mind."

Any hopes of refusal were dashed by

Mama being asleep, and Frank's unlooked-for speed in enabling Ginger to be ready to ride. She joined the ladies upon their return from further exploration, half wondering if the man she wished to avoid would also suddenly appear.

The next hour proved strange respite, as relief at Mr. Carlew's absence wrestled with wariness and not a little curiosity. She would much prefer to ride alone, perhaps even dip her toes in the stream near Nelly's Wood, but such practices might not meet the approval of her companions. She glanced across at the younger girls, both so fresh and innocent, impropriety and scandal so foreign to them both. If only . . .

Catherine forced regret aside, and focused on the pleasure of riding Ginger once more. Julia and Miss Beauchamp's innocent chatter proved strange balm to Catherine's twisted emotions.

They cantered down a small hill until Julia stopped under a copse of trees. "Well! I think the sunshine is begging us to break for a while."

"You may be right," Miss Beauchamp agreed, before glancing across at Catherine. "Miss Winthrop, might I say you are quite a horsewoman."

"You may," Catherine murmured, to her

companion's gurgle of amusement.

"Oh, I do like your sense of humor," Julia said. "It reminds me of Jon."

Catherine stiffened, her hard-won ease dissipating.

"Miss Winthrop, may I be so bold as to ask a personal question?" Miss Beauchamp said.

"It depends on the question."

Miss Beauchamp laughed prettily. Catherine covertly studied her. Was that why he liked her? Tinkly laughter? Happiness unfettered by past mistakes? Such pure and lovely looks?

Aware her companions were awaiting further response, Catherine summoned up a smile. "I believe you had a question, Miss Beauchamp?"

"Oh! I just wondered how you learned to ride so well."

"I grew up with horses." Such as the ones we're sitting on, she almost added.

"Ah. Of course."

Ginger nickered. Catherine stroked her glossy mane.

"That's right. I forgot you're Lord Winthrop's cousin."

Because addressing her as Miss Winthrop did not give that away? Perhaps he liked her because she was unlikely to challenge his intellect, Catherine thought nastily.

"If you don't mind my asking, why do you call him Carlew and not Lord Winthrop?"

"Lydia . . ."

"Thank you, Julia. I don't mind answering." Catherine eyed Julia's guest. "I f-first knew him as Mr. Carlew's ward."

"Ah."

Catherine noted Miss Beauchamp was taking on her soon-to-be mother-in-law's manner of curiosity as well as her expressions. "I had wondered, you see . . ."

It was clearly an invitation to enquire. Which Catherine refused to fulfill.

Julia nudged her horse farther into the shade, but Lydia remained singular in her focus. "It is only that your manner towards him seems a little peculiar at times."

Catherine gritted her teeth.

"I see you do not ask for elaboration. Very well. Let me just say that Mama and I have often wondered at your avoidance of him . . ." Lydia allowed her horse to move closer, away from Julia's hearing. "It is just I cannot help but wonder if there is something of which to be aware."

Dismay at the effects of her actions coiled shame within. "He is all that is good," she replied stiffly.

"I'm so glad!" Miss Beauchamp smiled,

166

her eyes lowering modestly. "I should not want to align myself with someone if that were not so."

An icy bar lodged directly behind her chest, contracting then expanding with every breath she took. Each painful throb welled water in her eyes. She blinked. Told herself not to be so foolish. He was nothing to her. Nothing!

She nudged Ginger's sides, shifting away from her tormentor. Really, she could scarcely blame Miss Beauchamp for such questions. She seemed sweet and innocent — which was problematic, because it offered Catherine no justifiable grounds to dislike her.

Wheeling Ginger around, she hastened up the ridge, away, alone, for a few precious seconds. But the thunder of hooves close behind sent the solace of solitude to flight. She forced another smile, nodded, acted all politeness. *Lord God, help me . . .*

As they neared the Jeffcoat farm she saw a figure straighten, wave. She waved back.

"Who is that?" enquired Miss Beauchamp.

"That is Jack, the son of farmer Jeffcoat."

"Is he a beau of yours?" she asked slyly.

Catherine ignored her, rode up beside him. "Hello, Jack."

"Hello, Miss Cathy." His cheery countenance was salve to her fractured feelings. "Is this your horse?"

"Yes, Jack. This is Ginger."

His wide eyes turned to her companions whose expressions grew equally slack-jawed. "Miss Carlew, Miss Beauchamp, this is Jack Jeffcoat."

Julia nodded, Lydia frowned, both moving away without further acknowledgment. Catherine's smile grew tight as she over-heard comments about a "moonling" and she desperately asked after Jack's mother and father. His replies were ever slow, but she forced her attention to remain fixed on him, redoubling her attempt to make the farmer's son feel her acceptance.

"I think it's time we return," Julia soon called.

Catherine stifled a sigh, said goodbye, and rejoined the others. Soon they were trotting closer to the Manor.

"Would you care to join us for lunch?" Julia asked. "Or will you remain forever adverse to dining with us?"

Was that pique in her friend's voice? "It is not that."

"If it makes any difference, I believe my brother to be out." Julia sent her a search-ing look. "I know you do not like him very much."

What could she say that was true — and still polite? "I . . . I do not dislike him."

"I know on occasion he can seem a little too principled, which bothers Mama at times, but he is also very considerate when he wants to be. But you need not fear his company. I believe I heard him tell Mama he would be out until late this afternoon, so really, it is the perfect time for you to come."

For some perverse reason she wanted to. She felt almost reckless today, or maybe just braver, like the changes at Winthrop she was sure to see would not hurt her as much as they might have previously. "Are . . . are you sure I would not be intruding?"

"Positive!" Julia grinned. "I'll race you both back to the stables."

Half an hour later, Catherine was seated again in the dining room, eating something delectable, surprised into admiration about the new drapes. The girls were in the middle of lighthearted conversation — such a contrast to Mama's diet of complaint — when the door opened and Lady Harkness entered, followed by Lydia's mother. The former glanced around, her brows rising when she spotted Catherine. "This is a surprise, Miss Winthrop."

"Julia invited me, ma'am."

"Oh, I do not doubt that. You hardly seem

the sort to just appear."

Catherine blushed, her taste for luncheon gone. Perhaps she should make her excuses and leave —

"Don't look like that, child. You are welcome."

"Th-thank you."

She swallowed the remaining syllabub without tasting it, half listening to the conversation between the ladies when the door opened again.

"Here you all are!" The deep-voiced, tall figure moved into the room.

Catherine froze, wishing she could sink beneath the table.

"I'm pleased you're feeling better, Mother." Mr. Carlew nodded to Julia. "Mrs. Beauchamp, Miss Beauchamp, a pleasure." His eyes widened a fraction. "Miss Winthrop." He offered a small nod, before glancing away to the other occupants of the table. "My business concluded far earlier than I envisaged, so I thought to join you. I hope you don't mind."

"Of course not," his mother said.

"We always enjoy your company," Miss Beauchamp cooed, smiling coyly at him.

The conversation picked up again, a cacophony of loud, high-pitched female voices, underscored by those deep, dark tones. Catherine tightened her hands in her lap, eyes on the table centerpiece, conscious of Lady Harkness's scrutiny; conscious he refused to look at her. Pressure increased in her head.

"We came across a funny fellow on our ride today," Julia said.

"Oh, yes. A moonling," said Miss Beauchamp.

"A tall young man, near the west fields," continued Julia. "Miss Winthrop and he were having quite the chat."

"Poppet," warned the deep voice.

"I thought at first he was Miss Winthrop's beau." Miss Beauchamp giggled. "Silly me."

The indignation at Lydia's earlier comment melded into mortification. Perhaps Miss Beauchamp wasn't so ingenuous as Catherine had believed.

"A moonling?" said Lady Harkness. "I was not aware any such persons lived on the estate."

Mrs. Beauchamp frowned. "Moonlings are dangerous, are they not? I cannot like knowing one lives so near."

Tension rekindled within. How could they say this? How could she let them? "Jack is n-not a moonling," Catherine said. "His m-mother became ill before his birth. He

171

c-cannot be blamed for any mental deficiency."

The room fell silent; five pairs of eyes stared; the heat searing her chest seemingly to have set fire to her entire body.

"I beg your pardon," Julia said in a subdued tone.

"You seem to take a great interest in the tenants, Miss Winthrop," Miss Beauchamp said in a kindly — patronizing? — manner. "For a moment you sounded just like our host."

Her warm smile at Mr. Carlew sent a prickle of pain through Catherine's heart.

"I do think it quite wonderful how keenly you involve yourself with your tenants," the blonde continued. "Many landlords would be interested only in the rents they receive."

Catherine studied the lace tablecloth. How true . . .

Thoughts of her father's lack of interest in his tenants were banished at Mr. Carlew's deep voice. "Jack seems to have such a way with animals. I believe he'd make a fine groom."

"Yes," Catherine whispered, stealing a glance at the head of the table. He did not look at her, but was smiling at Miss Beauchamp. Miss Beauchamp, whom he would soon make his bride.

172

A fist clutched her chest. She glanced away. Studied the collection of pineapples lining the silver salver in the center of the dining table. They blurred.

"Miss Winthrop?"

She blinked. "Pardon?"

"You seem a little pale. Are you quite well?"

No. "Yes, thank you, Julia."

She pasted on a smile, glanced across to encounter Lady Harkness, eyeing her with a frown. "Are you sure?"

"I . . . I have something of the headache."

"I expect it's this heat," said Miss Beauchamp. "After all the recent rain it's enough to make us all feel out of sorts."

A gnawing feeling filled her heart. She would only ever be a visitor here. Her house would become less and less familiar as it became more and more strange. And when *dear* sweet Lydia became his wife, how would she ever find enough excuses to stay away?

Oh Lord, help me . . .

Catherine pushed away from the table. "Please excuse me." She hurried past the astonished guests and rushed blindly from the room, turned to go up the stairs, then paused. Placed a hand to her head. This was not her house. Her bedchamber no longer hers.

"Miss Winthrop?" Lady Harkness had followed her, the green eyes troubled. "Please, allow me." She guided Catherine to the yellow drawing room, leading her to a sofa. "I have a maid collecting smelling salts," she said, gently pressing her to be seated.

Catherine sat, agitation pumping furiously through her limbs. Breathe in. Breathe out.

Christie — Mama's maid! — returned, smelling salts in hand. Lady Harkness waved them under her nose. The pungent scent sharpened her brain, speared fresh awareness . . . fresh pain. "Th-thank you."

"Would you care to lie down?"

"No, ma'am, thank you, but I would prefer to return home."

"Send for the carriage," Lady Harkness tossed over her shoulder.

"Of course, ma'am." Christie shot Catherine a worried look.

Lady Harkness continued her odd perusal. "Tell me, what do you think of our sweet Lydia? She is a charming little thing. Will make a charming hostess, do you not agree?"

Catherine's hand clenched. "Y-yes, she will."

The soft voice continued. "I am pleased

she has made your acquaintance, Miss Winthrop. It always helps to have a local's knowledge when one is to move into a new area, do you not agree?"

How long until the carriage would be ready? She pressed fingers deep into her forehead. "I . . . I suppose."

"And she is quite pretty . . ."

"Very pretty," she agreed desperately.

"Jonathan seems to think so. I overheard him say so just the other day. But then, he has always admired that type." The green eyes watched her carefully, as if begging her to disagree.

"I . . . I am sure you are right."

She must be. For had he not rejected Catherine and her far more plain looks? Pain slivered her heart anew.

"Excuse me, ma'am, the carriage is ready."

"Thank you. Miss Winthrop? Shall we go? I shall make your farewells if you prefer."

"Th-thank you."

A minute later and William had handed Catherine into the carriage. She had a moment's sweet relief before Lady Harkness reappeared and climbed inside also.

"Oh, p-please do not feel you need to accompany me," Catherine said. Mama would have a fit.

"Nonsense. I cannot permit my guests to

go home so poor in spirits. Besides, it gives opportunity to feel I have accomplished something on this otherwise dull and dreary day."

Catherine conceded, having had years of experience in recognizing a formidable woman's will. Somehow she managed a semblance of polite conversation until the carriage reached the lane.

"Thank you, Lady Harkness. Your kindness is m-much appreciated."

"Is it?" Her lips curled, momentarily reminding Catherine of a cat. "Never mind. I'll confess to a greater degree of curiosity than solicitude. I leave that to my son." Her smile faded, her features melding into a frown as the carriage stopped outside the cottage. "*This* is where you live?"

"This is the Dower House."

"Oh."

"Th-thank you." Catherine stepped outside, turned. Gritted out a smile. "Good day."

"Good day."

As she entered the cold, dim cottage, the image of Lady Harkness's frown remained, while the questions pricked her silent sorrow, leaving Catherine longing to hide in her room before —

"Catherine? Is that you?"

She closed her eyes, bit back a sigh. "Yes, Mama."

And spent the next half hour fighting desperately for composure, wishing she could be anywhere else.

Jonathan sat in the study, correspondence unattended, his thoughts unable to divert from the unsettling incident at lunch. He supposed it was his fault; if he'd not finished matters so quickly he would not have returned, would not have been cast into this quandary of mixed emotion. He'd glanced at Miss Winthrop, but her gaze remained averted, as it had been nearly every time they had met. She seemed pale, wan, the black of her clothes, not nearly as fashionable as Julia's, made her seem much older, like the spinster she was, the spinster she might always be.

A pang of pity was chased by heat as his heart hardened. What sort of presumptuous person sought entrée to a lunch hosted by people they deemed beneath them, then refused to engage in civil conversation? Although . . . The anvil striking his chest reduced its ferocity. Although judging from the varying expressions on his sister's face, perhaps it was *her* presumption that had invited one of Winthrop Manor's previous inhabitants. Still — the old injustice flared again, refusing compassion. Miss Winthrop could have declined —

Knock, knock.

"It is open."

The door pushed open, followed by his mother. "Jon, dear, may I interrupt you a moment?"

"Of course." He shoved his worries to one side. Watched her move to study a picture on the wall.

"How are you enjoying our little visitor?"

He strove for noncommittal. "Miss Beauchamp is quite amiable."

"I think she will make someone an excellent wife one day."

"Mother —"

"You cannot deny, Jonathan, that is why you brought her back to stay. It *is* best to know as much as one can about a prospective partner."

"You make it seem like I'm inspecting a horse."

"Marriages that are rushed into, well, we both know that can be a mistake."

Jon nodded, aware his mother referred to that of her brief marriage to Lord Harkness, whose tyrannical and jealous nature had reinforced Jon's decision to leave the country — and left few mourning the peer's sud-

den death from apoplexy only two months after the exchange of vows.

Her eyes seemed troubled. She moved restlessly around the room, picking up then replacing one item after another. "May I ask a question?"

"Of course."

"I could not help but realize today at luncheon that you never look at Miss Winthrop." Her gaze narrowed. "Why is that?"

The old bitterness surged again, chased by an ember of long-buried emotion that refused to give satisfaction to his mother's curiosity. He could say nothing.

"How exactly did things end in London?"

"Mother." His hands grew clammy. "I do not wish —"

"Was it possible a mistake was made?"

He forced his face to remain impassive. "Her father made it very clear."

"And you never spoke to her?"

Jon shook his head. She'd tried once to speak to him, but his hurt was so immense he could not bear to look at her, let alone hear her voice. "It was over two years ago, Mother."

"Two years ago, and you still cannot look at her." She moved from her perch on the armchair to the door, pausing to look over her shoulder. "Why is that, I wonder."

She exited, and he slumped in his chair, asking himself the very same question.

CHAPTER ELEVEN

Catherine placed the needle down and glanced out the drawing room windows. Rain sheeted incessantly. Everything within her yearned to leave the house, but she could not. The past week's wet weather had turned paths to sludge, fields to mud. Neither she nor anyone else would be so foolhardy to travel, let alone visit, in such conditions.

So she was forced to endure Mama's company and needlework. The mending basket was now empty, leaving her to embroidery. She bit back a sigh and carefully drew the needle through the white cambric in a tiny, perfect stitch. If only she could similarly wield such control over her stupid emotions.

"I declare if this rain does not soon cease we shall be fit for nothing," Mama sighed.

"Or be forced onto an ark." Catherine tried a smile.

Mama stared at her blankly. She had never understood Catherine's levity.

The brass clock ticked patiently on the mantelpiece. Ticking away the seconds, the minutes, the insignificance of her life. Outside, the relentless rain eased to a patter, echoing the equally stultifying conversation within. Mama's world had shrunk to herself, her personal aches and pains, her miseries, her misfortune. Complaints about the weather, the poor condition of the house, and the injustice of it all were occasionally interspersed with commentary about the quality of Catherine's needlework and how black did not become her, and sighing over reminiscences of bygone days.

Mama placed her embroidery hoop aside and rose. "My lumbago kept me awake for most of last night. I think I'll return to bed. There's nothing for me here, anyway."

Wasn't her daughter enough reason, insipid as their conversation might be? Catherine swallowed the hurt. "Shall I get Tilly to find your medicine?"

"If you would."

As Tilly hunted amongst Mama's various tonics and vinaigrettes, Catherine escorted Mama upstairs to the bedchamber, ensuring the fire was lit, the curtains closed, and her mother made as comfortable as could be.

The door rasped as she pulled it to. Perhaps Frank could do something about that. Or — her lips twisted — perhaps not.

Catherine returned to the damp coolness of the sitting room and picked up her needlework. Day after day of cold, miserable rain. Without functions to attend, without visitors to receive, without her gig, she was forced to remain inside, where the rooms only seemed to grow smaller. The only advantage was she could pretend last week's events at the Manor had never happened. Thinking over her humiliation only increased the headache that had kept her awake for more than one night. Wondering, wishing . . .

If only they could get away.

If only they could be somewhere that did not forever remind of bereavement, of the past, of lost futures.

Verses from this morning's Bible reading flickered into memory. She winced. Sighed. Prayed. *Lord, give me patience. Help me honor Mama. Help me be a blessing to others . . .*

She refocused on her needlework, dutifully stitching until the clock struck noon, then wrapped the needle in paper and placed it away in her wooden sewing box. Stitching was the merest distraction. The lack of physical activity had induced a lethargy that grew by the day. No walking. No riding. Nothing more strenuous than climbing the too-steep flight of stairs several times each day. Restlessness writhed, as though a dozen adders resided within. If she did nothing for too much longer, she might shatter.

Her stomach groaned — yet another sign she lacked the ladylike qualities Mama was so insistent upon — admitting to hunger pangs. Although perhaps this desire for sustenance was borne from needing something to do, rather than genuine hunger. She moved to the kitchen, peering out the low window to note the rain had finally ceased.

Mrs. Jones glanced up. Shadows underscored deep lines of fatigue. "Yes, Miss?"

"Mrs. Jones, you do not look at all well."

"I am well as can be." Her face hardened, then she resumed kneading dough. "I'm a wee bit tired, that is all."

"Pardon me, but is something the matter?" Catherine stepped closer.

The cook sighed, clapped flour from her hands then wiped them on her apron. "It's my sister, Miss."

"You mean Lizzie?"

"She's been a mite unwell, and her new-born is fractious. I've been that worried about her." She shifted a tray of raspberry tarts on the large oak table centering the kitchen. "Jem has been sick, too, but can't leave the cows in this weather, so I've been puzzling over what to do."

"But that is obvious."

"Miss?"

"You must assist your sister until the family is better. Surely we do not require your assistance as much as they."

"I . . . I cannot just leave."

"You can if I come with you."

"But Lady Winthrop —"

"Is in bed, and hardly likely to know if you and I are here or not."

"Miss, sure and you would not — that is, you do not need to feel obliged —"

"I feel the same sense of obligation anyone who is a Christian must. Please do not worry about your work here. If the evening meal is prepared, then Tilly can serve it, I'm sure. Now, what remains to be done?"

A quarter hour later, having informed a startled Tilly of their plans and written a note of explanation for Mama, Catherine rejoined Mrs. Jones in the kitchen, both now dressed in clothes more appropriate for a

185

journey through mud.

"Miss, I do appreciate this, really I do, but I cannot help but wonder —"

"Mrs. Jones, I know I've not had much experience in nursing, but if nothing else, I can hold the baby while you attend your sister."

"Very well." The cook eyed her shoes. "But you'll want to wear your sturdiest boots, miss. The mud out there is fit to swallow those slippers."

Catherine dutifully exchanged her shoes, reappearing holding the slippers in one hand. "Thank goodness it has stopped raining. Now, have you got some food packed? Can I carry a basket?"

"But we should not —"

"Why? We have an excess of food, and I'm sure your sister's family would be appreciative. Pack that fresh loaf, the cake, and those tarts. Mama will be glad to see them being put to good use."

Well, she would if she knew about it. And even if she wasn't, she *should* be.

Minutes later, they were squelching through mud, Catherine tasting something close to happiness at finally being freed from the cottage. The sun remained behind heavy clouds, giving the day a muted feel. Dampness from the morning's showers clung to the leaves and grass, sprinkling them with moisture as they passed beneath each tree. The wind shivered through the hedges and oaks, skimming over the muddy ground, which — as promised — threatened to suck away her balance. The journey to Lizzie's farmhouse was not long, but Catherine felt close to exhaustion by the time they arrived.

She divested herself of mud-encrusted boots at the door and wobbled into her slippers as Mrs. Jones pushed open the door with an ample hip and a call. "Lizzie!"

The red-cheeked young housewife looked up. Blinked. "Maggie! And Miss Winthrop! I" — she turned, coughed — "I did not expect you here."

"And when I woke this morning, neither did I," Catherine said with a smile. "I understand you've not been well."

Lizzie coughed again. "It's Mary that worries me. She won't stop screaming."

"Where — ?"

Before she could finish, the baby signaled her whereabouts with a lusty yell. Catherine glanced at Lizzie's crumpling features and said briskly, "Your sister is here to care for you whilst I care for Mary. Now rest."

"But Miss —"

"Rest," Catherine repeated firmly, then

hurried up the creaking stairs to the ever-louder cry. She pushed open the door to an earsplitting wail coming from the wooden cot.

"Poor darling."

At her words, the babe silenced, staring at her with wide blue eyes.

And promptly resumed her forceful cry, as she realized the stranger was not her mother.

"There, there, dearest. I know I'm not your pretty mama, but you do not need to act *quite* so disappointed."

Catherine picked up the tiny blanket-swathed girl, lifting her to her shoulder. Within seconds, a loud burp and wet feeling on her sleeve indicated what the previous problem had been. She wrinkled her nose at the sour milk smell, noting traces of baby sick now laced her hair. Wonderful.

For the next three hours she did all she could to placate the child, singing to her, holding her close, changing her sodden clothes. Poor Lizzie. How challenging to care for a restless child when ill herself. A bubble of gladness rose within. How satisfying to know Catherine's time was finally being put to good use.

When the babe started nuzzling her chest she felt a moment's blush before carrying

Mary downstairs to her mother, then she returned to tidy the room. Once completed, she sat in the aged rocking chair, tracing the carved handles with her fingers. Obviously handmade, passed from one generation to the next, the chair displayed such workmanship, the pride of a husband and father-to-be. How many dreams had been spun as women rocked their children in this very seat?

An acute yearning took hold. She wanted a baby. Her own. But that would take a miracle, hemmed in as she was by her mother's expectations, and the lack of any suitors. Her eyes burned. *Lord?*

Silence, save for chair's slight wheeze and *ker-thunk.*

Wheeze and *ker-thunk.*

Catherine drew in a deep breath. Exhaled. Swallowed the rawness in her throat. Pushed to her feet. Stirring up dreams that could never be fulfilled was a fool's game. She pushed out a tight smile. And the ladies of Winthrop were never foolish, were they?

She returned downstairs to be greeted by the heady scents of yeast and beef stew. The place looked transformed. She complimented Mrs. Jones on her hard work, which was met by a shrug but pink cheeks.

Lizzie smiled from her corner of the room.

189

"You've been a godsend."

"I'm glad you're looking a little more refreshed."

"I haven't rested during the day for ever so long. There is always so much to do."

Catherine nodded, feeling like a hypocrite. If only she had *something* to do. "Well, I suppose I should leave you. Mama might be getting a little worried. I left a note, but . . ."

The two women nodded, and Catherine winced inside. Probably half the county knew of Mama's reputation for anxiety.

"I trust you'll be feeling much better soon," Catherine said, stroking the sleeping babe's downy head, before glancing up. "And Mrs. Jones, if you wish to stay, I will convey appropriate excuses to Mama."

"But, Miss, you cannot walk back by yourself."

"Why ever not?" She removed her slippers, shoved her stockinged feet into the muddy boots. "I don't imagine I will meet anyone on my return. It is less than a mile, after all."

"But your mother —"

"Is probably still abed, and as such, need not be concerned. Which is probably how it should remain, would you not agree? Now, Mrs. Jones, regarding tomorrow. Shall I tell Mama you cannot come tomorrow, as you are caring for a sick relative?"

"Oh, Miss, I could never do that."

"I think you could, if you so desired. I know I've never been a particularly adept student in the kitchen, but I don't think I've completely forgotten all the instructions you and Cook were so patient in teaching me back at the Manor."

After a moment's hesitation, Mrs. Jones said, "Thank you, Miss. I'd be much obliged."

"Good." She turned to Lizzie. "I hope to see you all looking better next time."

"Next time?"

"If you'll permit me to visit again. After all, young Mary and I need to become better acquainted."

Gratitude flashed in the former maid's eyes and was echoed in her words.

Catherine made her adieus then traipsed back along the path to the cottage. As she'd suspected, she encountered no other travelers on such a dire day, though once she glimpsed a horseman on the ridge. She blinked, but he remained fuzzy and indistinguishable. Did she now need eyeglasses? Wonderful. Surely such a thing would complete her transformation into an old maid.

She entered the cottage quietly, was met

by Tilly who informed her that Mama had not stirred, and thus remained unaware of Catherine's absence, so after bidding Tilly to silence she crumpled up her earlier note and hurried into clean clothes.

That night at dinner, having heated the stew from earlier, she mentioned Mrs. Jones's dilemma.

"But who will cook for us?"

"Mama, you have scarcely eaten a bite in two weeks." She eyed her mother's barely tasted bowl of lamb and vegetables.

"But if I feel hungry tomorrow, I would want something more substantial than this." She waved a dismissive hand.

Catherine swallowed a tender chunk of lamb along with her exasperation. "Mama, surely we should extend a helping hand to those less fortunate. Lizzie is not well, neither is her husband, and their newborn does not allow much rest."

"They should have thought of that before deciding to have a child."

"Mother!"

"Don't 'Mother' me, my girl. I am still mistress of this house, and I do not give a by-your-leave for any of my servants running off to do whatever they will, simply because a relative has had the bad management to have a child when they cannot take care of it."

"They are sick, Mama! And this is Lizzie, whom we both know to be —"

"Be that as it may, I do not see why we should be forced to suffer just because they took a notion to be unwell."

"Took a notion? Mama —" She bit back the uncomplimentary comment about her mother's inclination for invalidism. "Some people *are* actually unwell. If you could've heard her —"

Mama's eyes rounded. "She was here?"

"No." She winced internally at her slip. "Of course not."

"You went there?"

"Mama, she was ill. Surely we must care for our neighbors in such situations."

"Never tell me that you walked?" Mama looked aghast.

She kept her lips sealed.

"I hope you were properly attended!"

"Mrs. Jones was with me." She refrained from mentioning her lack of escort for the return journey. Prudence did not invite sure condemnation.

"Well! I cannot approve, although I suppose it does show we are still concerned with the well-being of our tenants."

We are? She bit down the acidic comment.

"But I still do not like the thought of being forced to eat warmed over food simply because you took a notion to be kinder to your neighbors than to your own mother."

"Think of how positively the neighbors will view such kindness," Catherine said tiredly.

"That *is* something, I suppose."

A little something, she thought. A sop to her mother's sensibilities, if nothing else.

The sun felt warmer today, drying the mud into thin slivers that cracked and crackled under Gulliver's hooves. Jonathan breathed in the scents of hay and soft sweetness from the blossoms, glad to be back, glad to be outside.

His recent trip to London had left him weary of mind and body. The recent dividends were not to be derided, but he wished to do without the mercenary talk of the stockholders committee meeting. Rich men who desired greater riches without investing into socially beneficial schemes disappointed him as much as it had Harold Carlew. The foremost benefit of his time in the capital had been meeting Hawkesbury at White's.

Despite their different social upbringings, it seemed their acquaintanceship was ripening into friendship, faith yet another trait they shared. When Jon had wandered into White's dining room, the earl had invited him to join his table. Over a delicious meal of steak and kidney Jon had shared something of his frustration, until Hawkesbury reminded him of Jesus and the rich young ruler. "Some people count the cost of things of eternal significance as too high, whilst others are simply blind." He gave a wry smile. "I know, because until I met my Lavinia, I was very blind, indeed."

"You were very fortunate to meet her."

"Fortunate, or was it God's perfect timing? I think we both know the answer to that."

"God made the way for you." Unlike him. Miss Beauchamp was lovely, and the more he grew to know her, the more he agreed with his mother that the girl would make a very good wife. But . . . a wife for him?

"Yes." The earl eyed him. "You must excuse what will seem an impertinence, but do I detect something of frustration concerning your own situation?"

Jon stilled. "My own situation?"

"Forgive me if I'm being obtuse, but is it not Miss Beauchamp whom you intend to wed?"

"Nothing has been settled."

"I see."

Something in the hazel eyes suggested the earl did understand. Gratitude bloomed in his chest when no further questions came, and they both finished their meals.

The plates were cleared swiftly, both men refusing the port offered by the waiter, Jon excusing himself on account of his need to return home.

"Winthrop, before you go, may I offer you words once said to me when I was in a similar quandary?"

"Of course."

"What do you think your heavenly Father is saying about the matter?"

Jon glanced away to study the paneled walls. The room continued its gentle buzz of conversation, but within the question whirred loudly.

But that question was the problem. Whenever he tried to pray he only heard silence. Was that confirmation or a negative? Or were his head and heart too confused for him to hear anything at all?

He shook his head and said aloud, "I will trust for the Lord to direct my paths."

"Amen." The earl had nodded, before making his departure.

That prayer rose from Jon's heart again as he nudged Gulliver to the southern farm, determined to think on less troubling things. Mr. Clipshom, his estate manager, kept him informed about his tenants, which had necessitated today's visit. James Foley was a fifth generation tenant on the Winthrop estate, his dedication and forbearance evidenced by his willingness to listen to Clipshom's suggestions about new farming techniques, despite his rich farming heritage.

Jonathan liked the blunt-spoken young man as much for his humility as for his common sense, his patience in answering his new landlord's questions showing a deference some of the older farmers were yet to offer.

He crested the ridge and rode through neat yet muddied fields, evoking memories of the monsoon-ravaged fields of India. As he dismounted outside the farmhouse, a thin wail came from the top window. He half smiled. Knocked on the door. It swiftly opened, revealing the young farmer, a partially eaten meal on the table. Clearly Jon's visit had been badly timed.

"Good day, Foley."

"Lord Winthrop! We weren't expecting you, not with all this mud."

"I suspect if we ceased our duties every time a little weather made things difficult there would be few tasks completed."

"Aye, that be the way of things 'ere."

The crying from upstairs ceased. "I seem to have interrupted your meal." Jon indicated the table.

" 'Tis no bother."

They chatted briefly about the recent rains, and the sad potential of the future harvest, when a creak on the stairs prefaced the appearance of the farmer's young wife, holding the now-quiet baby. Her eyes seemed worried.

Jon smiled to relieve her fears. "Good day, Mrs. Foley."

"M'lord." She dipped a curtsy. "Has Jem offered you something to drink?"

"Thank you, but I've come to enquire as to your health. Clipshom tells me you've been unwell."

"Aye. The missus and I have been quite sick this past fortnight. If it weren't for Lizzie's Maggie —"

"My sister," the young wife said, shifting the babe in her arms.

"— we might have been done for." Foley continued as though he hadn't been interrupted. "She was here most days —"

"And nights."

"— cooking, or cleaning, or just taking care of the wee one."

"You are blessed to have such a sister," Jon said to the farmer's wife.

"And blessed she works for Lady Winthrop."

"Oh? I do not recall a Maggie working at the Manor."

"Oh no, sir. Maggie — Mrs. Jones she be now — still works for the Lady Winthrop, at the Dower House. Although, she hasn't done much working there of late. I do hope she won't get into trouble —"

"Now, love, remember Miss Catherine said she would see to things."

Jon's heart skipped a beat. "Miss Catherine?"

"Yes, m'lord. Miss Winthrop's a right good one. She's been here, too."

"Whenever she can get away," Mrs. Foley added. "Her ladyship can get awful anxious and gets these moods, you see."

He nodded as if he did see. "And Miss Winthrop?"

"Comes to care for the wee one. She's always apologetic for not doing more, but I tell her every pair of hands helps. You know how it is with babes, sir."

"I don't," he replied, "but I can imagine."

"Well, so could she. In fact, she was here earlier. I'm surprised you didn't pass her on the way."

He frowned. "She walks here?"

"Well, she certainly doesn't fly, I know that much." Foley grinned.

"Sir, you look surprised," the farmer's wife said.

He felt surprise. And a degree of admiration steal past his defenses. He hadn't thought on her overmuch these past weeks; hadn't dared —

"Lizzie here doesn't like how she comes alone."

"She walks without an escort?"

"Well, she don't have a bunch of footmen now, does she?"

Alarm rose within. This part of Gloucestershire was hardly the back streets of London, but still, anything could happen. Anger at himself for feeling concern made him say, "I thought she knew better."

"Well, and I think she does!" Mrs. Foley bristled. "But how else is she to get here?"

"But she should not walk alone."

"That is what I tell her, sir, but she says it's only a short distance."

"I'm surprised her mother permits such a thing."

Mrs. Foley glanced at her husband before looking at Jon. "I don't know if her ladyship is always aware, sir."

He nodded, his lips thinning. So her

independent streak had not completely gone, then. "And you say she's recently left."

"Aye, sir. Not more than twenty minutes ago."

Which should allow plenty of time for him to find her, then to wring her pretty neck.

He spotted her halfway to the cottage, arms filled with yellow cowslips, shoulders slumped. "Miss Winthrop."

She turned. Mud spattered her rosy cheeks, drenched her hem. Her dark eyes widened.

Something twisted deep within, as for a moment, he was lost in their depths, in his memories. He forced his thoughts away, forced himself to focus on the mess, on the mud. "What are you doing?"

"Picking flowers."

His brows rose.

"As you have just come from the direction of the Foley farm, I suspect you know what I've been doing." She lifted her chin. "We take care of Winthrop's people."

Perhaps she did, but his conversations with many of the farmers revealed her father's decided lack of care. He tempered his tone. "That is most admirable."

She shot him a look as if disbelieving then glanced away.

His heart panged. She did not believe him? "Please allow me to escort you home."

Half a dozen emotions crossed her face. "There is no need, sir."

"But you should not be walking alone."

"Perhaps. But there are many things in this world that are not as they should be."

Was this a veiled reference to his assumption of the title? He forced down the spurt of resentment, forced himself to repeat his offer.

Her fists clenched, then relaxed. Her thank-you sounded like it came through gritted teeth.

Without a sidesaddle, and dressed as she was in her simple gown, he couldn't very well lift her onto his horse, so he slid down and accompanied her, wondering what his mother and guests would say when he returned in such mud-spattered condition.

Miss Winthrop did not speak, which suited him well, as he had no words to say which might not sound condemning. So he walked alongside her, taking the moment to enjoy the crisp breeze on his face, the tang of wet grass and damp earth, the soft swish of her skirts. Gulliver nickered, seeming to object to the thick mud squelching and sucking beneath them.

While wrestling with the reins he caught

her sidelong glance. She glanced away.

"It seems Gulliver is more precious than some and dislikes being dressed in mud."

"Do you mean to imply something, sir?" She stopped, eyebrows lifting.

"Of course not."

Now her eyes narrowed, chin rose. She marched on.

Bemused, he hurried after her. The thick hedge came into view, behind which huddled the yellow-gray stone of the Dower House. "The Foleys mentioned your good deeds."

"I have no wish for them to be advertised, sir."

And with a mother inclined to worry he could well understand why. "I think you most magnanimous. Except, I do not like you visiting alone."

She sighed, slanted him an upward look. "Do you plan to accompany me each time I visit?"

"I . . . no. Of course not."

Her lips tightened, so he couldn't tell if she was relieved or disappointed.

"But I do not want you walking alone."

"Well, we do not always get what we want, do we?" Her eyes flashed, and she hurried up the path to disappear inside the cottage.

Leaving him torn between resentment and

reluctant admiration, and conscious that this conversation was the most they had exchanged in over two years.

The nerve of him! Spoiling her happiness at finally feeling useful. Acting so concerned, like he cared for her well-being, when past actions made it obvious he did not. She huffed her way inside. Shut the door so she needn't glimpse his concern and feel that twinge of regret again.

"Catherine? Is that you?"

She sighed. "Yes, Mama." She removed her cloak, hung it on a peg beside the door, then moved to the sitting room to meet her mother's frown.

"Where have you been?"

"Walking in the lane." It was the truth. Mostly.

"Was that Mr. Carlew I saw outside?"

"Yes, Mama."

Her mother's brows pushed together. "What was he doing?"

"Walking, Mama?"

"Don't take that tone with me! I could see that he wasn't riding. Was he walking with you?"

"Yes."

"Was he talking with you?"

"Why? Are you worried he is going to

proposition me?"

"Catherine!"

"Mama, I do not understand why you would object to his escorting me home."

Mama sniffed. "Home from where? And why would you need his escort? Surely you were not walking alone?"

Catherine swallowed.

"I do not like you being so thoughtlessly independent! Who knows what might happen?"

"Lavinia always did," she muttered.

"You are not to compare your conduct with hers. And I daresay that now she has a little more knowledge of the ways of the world, she does not do so any longer. Can you see the earl countenancing such behavior?"

"Actually —"

"Catherine!"

"But Mama, who is there to accost me?"

"That is enough! I do not want you visiting anywhere alone anymore. Do I make myself clear?"

"Yes, Mama."

She bit her lip, willing the tears away, as her heart bowed to the inevitable, and her precious glimpse of freedom was snatched away.

CHAPTER TWELVE

"Oh, Lord Winthrop! Look what Julia and I found!" Miss Beauchamp pointed to an antiquated gig. "Would you mind if I drive around in this little contraption? I requested your groom to make it ready, but he seemed a trifle reluctant."

Jonathan nodded to the older man. "Wilson, please assist our guest."

He turned away, avoiding the reproach in the stableman's eyes, as Carmichael and Miss Beauchamp exchanged pleasantries about the day's fine weather. Well he knew his decisions were sometimes less than pleasing to his staff, but few dared question the new baron openly.

Was there something wrong in his request? His fingers clenched. How he hated to second-guess. Hale's and Carmichael's return this morning had coincided with the confusion that had steadily risen in the night. Miss Winthrop's obvious aversion yesterday had fueled memories, fueled regrets. He had thought himself in hand . . .

Miss Beauchamp's laughter tinkled. He met her open, warm gaze with a small smile.

She beamed at him, turning aside to answer Carmichael once again.

Daily interactions with his visitors had done what house parties were doubtless supposed to do: encouraged new appreciation and understanding of his guests, particularly this pretty, unaffected, sweet-tempered guest. Would she accept his suit?

He knew from the way Mrs. Beauchamp eyed the artwork and expensive furnishings what she would recommend to her daughter. There seemed no hesitation over his possible disreputable antecedents for *that* lady. And yet . . .

Something still did not sit well. His prayers on the subject seemed to meet with neither a yes nor a no. Which meant — what, exactly? God wanted to bless him, so his Bible told him. Surely finding a wife was simply more of the blessing.

Shaking off his thoughts, he soon joined Hale and Carmichael in riding alongside the ladies, Julia having joined Miss Beauchamp in the little carriage.

Miss Beauchamp was soon swiftly passing along, smiling hugely as she gently snapped the reins. "Look at us! I feel like a grand-mother, driving this odd little thing."

"We must look like grandmothers, too," said Julia with a laugh.

Jon smiled indulgently, ensuring their excursion would not traverse too many awkward hills for the gig to pass over. They rode along the back lane to St. Hampton Heath. Near the top of a rise he could see two figures. He nudged Gulliver to a slower pace as Carmichael raised a hand against the glare of the sun.

"Old man, is that Miss Winthrop ahead?"

Jonathan nodded, before realizing Carmichael could not see him. "I believe so, yes."

"Why the deuce is she walking about without a maid?"

He swallowed the reply: Doubtless because she could no longer afford one.

"Who is that?"

"I believe . . . young Jack."

"Young Jack? He looks a trifle too tall to be termed 'young' Jack," Carmichael muttered with a sidelong glance.

"He is young of mind," Jon murmured.

"You mean — wait, why is he standing so close to her?"

Jon squinted. Saw the young man lift a hand. Lean closer.

208

Tightness banded his chest. Was Mrs. Beauchamp correct? Was Jack a threat to others?

He prodded the stallion into a canter, a gallop, his pulse racing faster than Gulliver's hooves. He nudged Gulliver closer, closer, his gaze pinned on them.

Miss Winthrop took a step back, but Jack moved too close again. She held out her hands, saw Jack hold them —

"Miss Winthrop!" He pulled up short, slid from Gulliver's back, hurried to her, eyes, thoughts, only for her. "Are you quite well?"

She glanced up, shading her eyes, her mouth pulled down, as if displeased by his intrusion. "I beg your pardon?"

"Is anything the matter?"

"No."

"You are not harmed in any way?" He glanced at the gangling youth, holding a covered plate, his slack-jawed face devoid of comprehension.

"Jack? Harm me? Have you lost your senses?"

"I thought —"

"Jack would no more harm me than would a butterfly!"

Her quelling look forced his step back. "I beg your pardon."

"It is Jack who is owed the apology."

"I, er, I am sorry, young Jack." He eyed the plate dubiously. "But I suspect your offerings to Miss Winthrop are not always appreciated."

Jack looked vacantly at him. Jon turned to Miss Winthrop, whose face held two bright spots of color.

"I do not know what gives you the right to presume to know my feelings upon *any* matter —"

His lips twitched. It would not be off the mark to presume she was angry.

"— But I resent your interference, sir, and wish you would refrain!"

His amusement faded, as the icy contempt in her eyes and voice sent a shiver across his soul. He bowed. Stepped back. Fiddled with Gulliver's reins, pretending not to watch as she turned to the gangling youth and smiled.

"Now, Jack, please tell your mother I hope she enjoys the pie." She lowered her voice. "I trust she will find it palatable."

"Palatable?" Jack said in his not-so-quiet voice.

She encouraged him on his way, before her attention returned to Jon. The warmth in her expression drained away. "Thank you for your concern, Mr. Carlew. Good day."

She moved to leave but he stepped in her way. "Are you quite sure, Miss Winthrop?"

"Sure about your concern or that it is a good day?"

"I wish you would know my concern is real. I would not like for y— for anybody to be in danger."

"Jack? Dangerous?" She stared at him. "I have known him all my life. Perhaps he is not as clever as some, but neither is he cruel. He is, in fact, as gentle as a lamb. I assure you, I am as safe with him as I am with anybody in Winthrop Manor. Now, please excuse me."

She stepped around him, just as Miss Beauchamp drove toward them. Miss Winthrop stilled, paled. Her hand fluttered to her mouth.

"Catherine!" Julia called, a big smile lighting her face. "Do you not agree we look like perfect little grandmothers in this contraption?"

"No."

The broken whisper caused a strange pang to strike his chest.

"Miss Winthrop? Is something the matter?" Miss Beauchamp asked. "I'm afraid you do not look at all well."

The dark eyes so fixated on his guest swept to him then back again. "I . . ." She swallowed. "W-where did you get the gig?"

"This old-fashioned thing? We found it in

the corner of the stables, didn't we, Julia?"

Something like a wince crossed Miss Winthrop's features.

"I thought it looked quite quaint and vastly amusing. It looks like it hasn't been touched in years! Would you like to have a turn?" Miss Beauchamp added kindly, "The seat is not very wide, but then neither are you, so I can move —"

"That will not be necessary, thank you," Miss Winthrop said stiffly, before murmuring an excuse and hurrying away, barely acknowledging Carmichael's offer to escort her home.

He watched her departure, conscious of his rising irritation. Why was she always so rude to his guests? Why did she always treat him with disdain? It was almost like she held him at fault for their estrangement.

He continued to ponder her strange reaction on their return to Winthrop Manor, responding with single syllables to Carmichael's commentary on the countryside as Hale danced attendance on the ladies.

When they rounded the drive, Wilson hurried out to help the ladies from the gig, and the small party drifted toward the house ahead of him.

Jon nodded to the head groom. "The reins appear to need repair."

"Yes, sir." Wilson, usually so affable and obliging, refused to look at him.

"Is there a problem?"

"No, my lord."

He frowned. "Miss Beauchamp said you were reluctant to fulfill her request this morning."

The groom's cheeks flushed. "If I might speak candidly, sir?"

"I always prefer that."

"Y'see, I did not feel quite right about her using it, seeing as the gig was a gift from his lordship and all."

"The former Lord Winthrop?"

"Aye, sir."

He had a queasy feeling he already knew the answer, but asked the question anyway. "A gift for whom?"

The man's weatherbeaten face lifted to his. "Miss Catherine. He gave it to her nigh on two years ago. Picked it up in London."

His heart twisted. Two years ago. Had the gift been reward for rejecting him? Regardless, it was little wonder she had seemed distressed.

"She loved it, would use it all the time, old fashioned though it be. Some days she'd be out for hours, visiting the tenants, or Miss Lavinia — pardon me, I mean the countess, up at the Hall. And while it hasn't been used for months, I still did not imagine anyone but she using it."

"I see."

"But I'll get right on it, sir, and have those reins fixed up in no time."

"No hurry," he surprised himself as well as the groom by saying. "Should anyone request its use, say it is in storage for its rightful owner."

Wilson blinked before a wide smile split his weathered face. "Well, that I can do, sir. Although I don't quite see how Miss Winthrop could use it, seeing it needs a horse, and the stables at the cottage are none too big —"

"A gift is a gift, and I would be loathe to impair someone's pleasure through my ignorance. Tell me, are there other items of which I should be made aware?"

The man shuffled his feet. "If I may be so bold, sir, I suggest you speak to Mr. Geoffreys."

"You may."

A smile twisted the man's face and he muttered something about getting back to cleaning the tack room before he swiftly disappeared, leaving Jon alone with his thoughts, his memories, those gnawing regrets as he made his way back to the Manor.

"Carlew!" Hale called from atop the stone steps leading to the terrace. "Beg pardon" — he chuckled as if he'd uttered a witticism — "your *lordship*! Wanted to see if you were free for a game of billiards."

"Billiards?" Jon forced his thoughts to disentangle, forced himself to act the good host. "Of course."

"Good."

Jon nodded. Perhaps it would be good. Distraction through a game or two might counter some of the turmoil he'd felt in the last few hours. Focusing on the here, the now, the certain had to be better than dredging up the past.

"I need to know if you're as good as you were back in India."

Jon pushed out a smile. "Now I've established a billiards room here" — one of the few changes he'd made at Winthrop — "I'm sure to be much better."

It wasn't until much later, several wins later, that he finally got the chance to speak to Geoffreys privately in the study. "I need your help in a sensitive matter."

"I am at your service, my lord." The impeccably groomed man bowed.

In the months since Jon's arrival he'd found the butler required a delicacy of manner in order for him to unbend a little. He obviously preened himself on his knowledge, and seemed to believe Jon's own knowledge was severely handicapped by his unfortunate connections in trade.

"It's recently come to my attention that certain things which belonged particularly to the family of his late lordship have not been passed on to their rightful owners. I cannot help but wonder if there are other elements in the house which might also be thus affected."

"If I may say, sir, your sensitivity shows a great deal of consideration." Geoffreys gave a thin smile. "There are, you understand, certain difficulties in ensuring everything was distributed appropriately, given the" — he coughed — "given the circumstances, as it were."

The near bankruptcy. Jon nodded. "I understand. I just wished to know if anything personally belonging to either Lady Winthrop, Miss Winthrop, or Miss Serena still remained in the house. If so, I wish to ensure it is either given to them, or protected, as the case may be."

Thus followed a conversation that left him by turns unsettled and relieved, though concerned that several of his mother's plans would need to be halted immediately. It even left him wondering whether his trip to

London on the morrow should be post-poned.

And that night, surrounded by his guests at the dinner table, dressed in their finery, laughing, enjoying spirited conversations and mild flirtations, a tiny part of him again wondered about the girl who had lost almost all.

CHAPTER THIRTEEN

September

Catherine frowned as she studied the waving fields outside her bedchamber window. Shorter than previous years, she hoped — she prayed — the harvest would provide sufficiently for the farmers. Every so often the village encountered a family straggling from the north or from as far away as Wales. She had heard of hardship and famine due to the crop shortages caused by the unseasonably low temperatures, such news causing many prayers to rise from her heart. Such perspective also alleviated her feelings about her own situation — she had much for which to be thankful. Even if at times she struggled to remember to be grateful.

A visit from Serena in celebration of her birthday had been small comfort this past fortnight, her delight at their reunion tempered by her younger sister's obvious shock at their new accommodations. Now forced to share a bedchamber, Serena's whispered dismay had further disheartened Catherine. "This place is so small and cramped. I feel like I can barely breathe, let alone paint anything!"

Her artistic sister's relief upon leaving to go visit another friend was apparent to anyone who truly knew her, her placid countenance effective disguise to the less observant. But though she was glad Serena did not have to suffer boredom also, her departure only reinforced Catherine's own loneliness.

"Catherine!"

She sighed. Sometimes it *was* hard to be thankful. Mama was not easy, her attitudes grating against the peace Catherine strove to find in her morning devotions. And she did not want to impose on Lavinia's friendship too much, especially as time drew near for the babe's arrival. And she could *not* bring herself to return Julia's occasional visits; she did not dare kindle the heartache of seeing Mr. Carlew with his younger, much prettier —

"Catherine!" her mother called again. "Where are you?"

She gritted her teeth as verses she had read that morning about honoring parents arose in her memory. *Lord, help me honor*

Mama. It is not always easy —

"Here you are." Mama burst into Catherine's bedchamber without knocking. She held a white paper, thickly scrawled, dotted with a blob of red sealing wax. "Drusilla has replied at last. She wishes our arrival for next week."

Catherine blinked. "Next week?"

"Drusilla says she would welcome my company — and yours, too, I suppose — especially as society is a trifle thin at the moment."

"But . . ." A hundred thoughts cramped her brain, crammed in her throat. She swallowed. "How would we get ready to leave in time?"

"We shall not need much, some clothes, that is all. Most of what we have is so outdated we shall have to buy more."

"But we cannot afford it. Mama, you know we must economize —"

"Do not say such dreadful things! If I need new gowns, I shall have more. Who are you to say no?"

Only her daughter, whose marriage settlement was fast being spent on unsustainable living expenses. "*I* need nothing more. We shall remain in black, shall we not?"

"I will wear black my remaining days. You, however . . ." She paused, frowning. "Black has never become you, Catherine. It makes you look sallow."

"Thank you, Mama," she replied, unable to hide the hurt in her voice.

Her mother harrumphed. "As you are approaching half mourning, I think you may wear gray. We do not want any young men thinking you are ineligible."

"Mama! I cannot, that is, I do not want —"

"To make a suitable match? Nonsense, my dear. You are still a Winthrop, even if that name doesn't count for as much as it once did. And though you might not bring a dowry quite as large as before, you will have something."

A very little something, she thought, if Mama's spendthrift ways continued.

"Now, do not spoil my anticipation of the future with reminders of the past." Mama glanced out the small window, her expression one of discontent. "The sooner we can leave this place the better."

And Catherine, heart filled with misery, agreed.

The sound of carriage wheels outside drew Mama's loud sigh and snapped, "Oh, for goodness' sake! Who is it now?"

She joined her mother in peering out the window, saw the crest on the coach.

"Well! The earl condescends to visit us again," Mama said in a tone that managed to sound both plaintive and smug. "It is good to see *some* still recognize what I am due."

Hurrying downstairs, Catherine informed Mrs. Jones of the need for tea, whilst Mama, her woebegone ways vanished, stood at the door as though heading the receiving line of a grand London ball.

Mama's voice carried down the short hallway. "My lord, how *kind* of you to condescend to call on us again."

The earl murmured something as Catherine hurried to meet them. After greeting the earl, she clasped Lavinia's hands. "I did not think to see you visiting at this stage."

"We had hoped to see Serena," Lavinia said. "It's been an age and I wondered how she was finding school in Bath, and how her art studies were progressing."

"Oh, but she is not here. She is —"

"The Aynsley girls collected her yesterday," Mama said, the note of pride in her voice unmistakable. "Serena will be in Somerset until classes resume. I *do* like how she has the good sense to cultivate those sorts of friendships. And the viscount's daughters are quite charming. But it is good of you to visit. Especially as we are quitting the neighborhood."

"You are leaving?" Lavinia's brows arched. "This is a surprise."

"We are to visit my aunt —"

"We shall visit my sister in Bath," Mama interrupted, as if Catherine hadn't been speaking. "I find I simply cannot abide staying here."

Lavinia and the earl exchanged glances. The door opened and Tilly entered with the tea and a plate of tiny currant cakes. Tilly poured as Catherine handed around plates, ensuring everyone had something to eat.

Mama spread a cake with clotted cream and took a bite.

"Will there be anything else?" Tilly asked, glancing between Catherine and Mama.

"Thank you, no."

Tilly offered a small curtsy and left the room.

Mama delicately wiped her mouth. "This place makes me feel positively ill! For months now we have suffered, have we not, Catherine? She with headaches, whilst I have suffered with my wretched back."

Lavinia murmured something suitably sympathetic.

"Then that man had the nerve to let that silly young creature go about in Catherine's gig! I ask you!"

"Really, Catherine? Is this so?" At her nod the earl's brows furrowed. "I am surprised."

Surprise had filled her the day following the incident, when a short note of apology had arrived from Mr. Carlew, a note doubtless meant for conciliation, but sighted as it had been by her mother, had instead proved to be cause for yet further complaint. Catherine bit back a sigh.

"It quite decided me," continued Mama. "I have had a letter from my sister positively demanding my staying with her in Bath as soon as possible."

"Bath *is* quite lovely." God bless Lavinia for her propensity to find the positive.

The earl nodded. "My cousin seems well pleased with it. There are many things to occupy one's time."

"Of course, *I* could not attend any functions, and Catherine could not attend any grand assemblies, but a few concerts, perhaps."

The misery grew within. Well might Mama have acquaintances but, except for her aunt, Catherine had none. Even Serena would be in school. How would she cope without a true friend to confide in? And without Lavinia's comfort and perspective . . . Catherine swallowed the pain.

As if sensing this, the earl said, "Miss Winthrop? How do you find the proposed re-moval?"

Conscious of her mother's scrutiny, she forced a smile to her lips. "I think it neces-sary for peace of mind." Whose peace of mind she would not say.

"Well, I hope by that comment you don't mean to imply I've been anything less than satisfied with our arrangements here!" Mama snapped.

"Of course not, Mama." She lifted her gaze to encounter Lavinia's, soft with sympathy. "I think perhaps it would be to everyone's benefit if we were not here, wondering over every change, feeling . . ." Resentment. Constraint. Frustration.

"I see." The earl glanced at his wife before his attention returned to her. "So, Miss Winthrop, you are amenable to staying in Bath."

"Y-yes."

"The sooner the better," Mama added, before sighing loudly. "Oh, if we could only leave today, I would be wondrously pleased."

"But that is the problem, you see," Cath-erine said in a low voice. "Constrained as we are by such limited means —"

"Catherine!"

"It is true, Mama. We lack the traveling

coach we would once have used, and must wait for the mail."

"The mail?" Lavinia frowned. "I would hate for you to travel by such means."

"Surely you could ask Lord Winthrop," the earl countered.

"Carlew? I'd sooner ask an adder to bite me!" Mama snapped. "When I think of how kindly we have always treated him, and this is how he repays us!"

"But if you only asked for his help —"

"I should not have to ask. He should be aware!"

"Lady Winthrop, I understand him to be quite fair-minded, but that is a long way from being a mind reader. I'm sure he would not wish for you to feel this way."

"Did you know the first time we met him, over two years ago in London, Catherine took pity on him?" Mama carried on as if the earl had not spoken. "She condescended to speak with him. He should be grateful for such attention!"

Catherine squirmed internally, refusing to meet the knowingness she knew would be in Lavinia's gaze.

"I recall now he has traveled to London for business," the earl said.

"The curse of the merchant class," Mama sniffed. "So you see, I could not ask for his assistance even if I wanted to, which I don't. Oh, I don't think I can bear another week in such confines!"

Catherine met Lavinia's gaze, the sparkle eliciting a reluctant smile at Mama's contradictions and histrionics.

Lavinia shifted awkwardly to place her cup of tea on the small side table, before addressing Mama. "Would you perhaps like to use the Hawkesbury traveling coach?"

"I would never dream of such presumption!"

The earl's brows rose. "Are you sure, madam?"

Mama's cheeks grew scarlet. "If by that remark you mean to accuse me of impertinence —"

"Not at all. I merely mean to suggest that it would be my pleasure to offer the use of our traveling carriage, should you require such a thing."

After a great show of reluctance, Mama allowed herself to be persuaded, and a date was fixed in two days.

"For we cannot make calls, you understand, and indeed, there are very few in the neighborhood for whom we are obligated to make farewell calls."

Lavinia looked faintly horrified. "But surely your cousin —"

"Deserves no such civility. You'll note he did not feel obliged to inform us of his departure."

"Because he will only be in London for a few days, as he does each month." The earl frowned. "You will doubtless be in Bath much longer."

"I certainly hope so."

Lavinia exchanged glances with her husband before saying to Catherine, "So if this is to be our farewell, then I wish you to have a most pleasant time in Bath."

"And I hope your new arrival to be everything that is a blessing. I am exceedingly sorry I will miss seeing the little one."

"Yes, of course. We *do* wish you a safe time of it," Mama oozed.

"Would it help to house Ginger at the Hall?" the earl asked. "McHendricks would relish another animal to care for, especially as we are not here as often as I'd like."

"Th-thank you, sir. I don't believe we would have the . . ." means, Catherine swallowed, "the opportunity to house Ginger appropriately in Bath." And she could scarcely trust Frank to tend Ginger as he ought.

"Very good. I'll send McHendricks around tomorrow." He stood, supported his wife to rise.

"We will write." Lavinia hugged her. "Take care to send your direction."

"And I shall write to my cousin to be sure to let her know to call upon you."

"Thank you, sir. I should be glad to enlarge our circle of acquaintances there. And thank you for the use of your traveling coach. It is excessively generous."

"Of course." He dipped his head in farewell before assisting Lavinia inside the coach. "Doubtless you will have much to do in the coming days. I wish you well."

"Thank you," Mama said most graciously.

They waved, and Catherine pasted on a smile as they watched the coach disappear down the lane.

Soon the news of their departure was conveyed to Mrs. Jones and Tilly, which inspired a great deal of packing, much to Catherine's dismay. Surely Aunt Drusilla would not welcome guests with *quite* so many trunks. "We need not take everything, Mama. It is not like we shall be doing anything much in the way of entertaining."

"But we should investigate getting some new gowns for you, my dear. Bath is so popular you know. We may find a gentleman there who takes a fancy to you."

"Mama!"

"Don't Mama me! You know as well as I

do that you are not getting any younger. The time to find a husband is now, before you put on even more weight and grow tired and frumpy looking."

Catherine's heart stung, her eyes burned. But as she fumbled to formulate a reply, Mama's conversation veered to other matters, allowing Catherine to keep her mouth shut.

Yet despite the challenges of leaving, their guests' words about Bath's many diversions caused an ember of hope to flicker within.

Perhaps the busyness would distract them long enough to find peace.

Perhaps this would be a time when the past could finally be left behind.

Perhaps in Bath she would finally find her future.

CHAPTER FOURTEEN

Bath
December

The wind whistled sharply, rippling past Catherine's cloak and hood as she walked along Barton Street on the way to the circulating library. She huddled into the sparse warmth offered by her gray pelisse, conscious the air's cool bite would redden her cheeks and nose, but glad to be on her errand anyway. Thankfulness bubbled up that her aunts had agreed with Mama that Catherine could now wear half mourning. Not only did this allow her to wear the grays and soft lavenders that became her so much better than strict black, but half mourning also gave permission to circulate more publicly. She glanced up, admiring once again the squared stone buildings of symmetry and grace lining the cobblestoned street. To her left, the greenery of Queen's Square beckoned, evoking memories of the countryside around Winthrop.

Breath escaped in a chilly cloud. For the first time in a long time she felt almost happy. Happiness had for so long remained elusive, swelling within then slipping away, escaping like a hot air balloon she'd seen long ago in Hyde Park. But now, here, where their circle was gradually expanding, and with easily accessible interesting shops, libraries, and tea shops, there was enough of the new to see and do to distract from what had been, and to somehow remind her of who she used to be: lively, without a stammer, brimming with energy and expectancy. It was amazing how the constraints of others' expectations no longer weighed her down; to not have her disappointments and failures constantly flaunted seemed to have set her free.

She smiled to herself as she rounded the corner onto Wood Street. Thank God for Bath. Thank God that Aunt Drusilla lived in such a well-positioned locale on Gay Street, Catherine was able to walk to her destination — sometimes even unaccompanied by a maid! Thank God for Aunt Drusilla's hospitality, even if she had been less than enamored of their premature arrival.

Mama had soon dismissed such dismay — "But what did you expect me to do? The earl was begging me to use his coach, simply begging me. I could not very well refuse now, could I?" — and Aunt Drusilla had been forced to accede to her elder sister's reasoning.

Catherine's smile widened. She wasn't the only one forced to bend to Mama's domineering ways.

"Good day, Miss Winthrop."

The gravelly voice stole her attention from her musings. "General Whitby! Hello."

The general, an acquaintance of her aunt's, had soon become one of the few favored by Mama to escort Catherine when she attended the occasional evening concert. Due to his age — fifty if he were a day — and gentlemanly manners, Mama saw no harm in him.

"I had hoped to bump into you, my dear. Will you and your good aunt be attending the Mitford dinner next week?"

"I am not sure, sir."

"Well then I shall put off my reply until you are sure. Heaven forbid I go and find there be nothing but old biddies."

"Heaven forbid, indeed!" Catherine chuckled.

He took out his pocket watch and checked the time. "I best be off to taste some of those foul waters again. May I accompany you, Miss Winthrop?"

"Thank you, but I am going in the opposite direction." She showed the book she held. "Mama has asked for the next by this author."

"And how is your dear Mama?"

"Quite well, thank you, sir."

"Good, good. Well, I must say that lilac becomes you very well. Very well, indeed. Well, good day to you."

"Good day, sir."

Catherine continued her journey, thinking over the general's remarks. How glad she was to be able to honestly say Mama was well. For Bath agreed with her. The instant she'd walked through Aunt Drusilla's door it was as though years had erased from her face. She seemed happier, too. Mama might not attend any public events, and would wear black for the year and a day deemed respectable, but Catherine rather suspected Mama liked her status, with all its social benefits. For here in Bath Mama's rank, although not as high as some, was still high enough for her to be deemed one of the more important ladies, her name would be heralded by the masters of the assemblies should she ever, one day, condescend to attend.

Catherine rounded the corner, bumped

into a tall figure. "Oh! I beg your pardon."

"No, the fault is mine." The dark chestnut-haired man reached to steady her, before peering more closely. "Miss Winthrop? Is that you?"

"Last time I checked, Major Hale." She smiled.

Eyes the color of coffee stared at her until her cheeks heated. "Oh, I'm sorry. Excuse my poor manners. I did not expect to see you here. Especially looking . . ."

She raised a hand to her hair. Was it falling out? Did she look a fright?

"Looking so well." He smiled, eliciting a curl in her heart. Suddenly she could see why Julia had once whispered of his reputation with the ladies. The man possessed charm. "It seems Bath agrees with you, Miss Winthrop."

"I believe that is supposed to be its chief recommendation."

He chuckled, glanced around. "I see people looking our way. Might I be so bold as to enquire your direction? I would like to pay a call, if I may."

"Why?" The word slipped out before she could stop it. "I . . . I beg your pardon."

He smiled, apparently unbothered by her rudeness. "I see one must keep one's wits when talking with you, Miss Winthrop."

"I should prefer that to talking to the wit-less."

His grin grew. "May I speak with you again? I would here, but the wind carries a bite on these streets and I would not have you catch cold. When might I have the pleasure?"

She thought quickly. Mama would scarcely countenance his visit to the house, and meeting unchaperoned in public was un-wise. While Bath was a genteel kind of place, both Aunt Drusilla and the earl's cousin, a Miss Pettigrew, had dropped warnings about the speculation that occurred amongst so many of the idle. But to have a handsome man wish to meet her . . . Per-haps she was not at her last prayers, after all.

"Perhaps I might see you at the abbey tomorrow morning around eleven."

"The abbey? I will be there. Good day, Miss Winthrop."

"Good day, sir."

He doffed his hat, and she was struck with the ridiculous notion that his face carried a trace of admiration.

The following morning, Catherine ac-companied Mama on her now daily walk to the Pump Room to take the waters. As

236

usual, the waters were drunk with a pinched face, and mutterings about the vile taste, but as Mama believed they had healed her lumbago she was loathe to miss an appointment and thereby risk the return of the dreaded complaint.

Later, as Mama listened to some new acquaintances gossip, Catherine leaned close to murmur, "Mama, would you mind if I visit the abbey for a moment?"

"Whatever for, child?"

"I . . . I wish to sketch one of the images I saw on a memorial stone." Which she would, as soon as she'd had her conversation with Major Hale.

Mama frowned.

Catherine's heart sank. Perhaps this wasn't the best excuse, after all. Mama had never really appreciated art, despite Serena's giftedness for taking a person's likeness. "It is only a short walk from here. I'm sure nobody could object. I would not be long."

One of the ladies Mama was listening to, a Mrs. Gulbrandssen, said something in a hushed voice, forcing her listeners to lean in. Mama glanced at Catherine. "Oh, very well then, go. But don't get distracted like your sister does." She turned to the other ladies. "My younger daughter likes to think she's an artist. She's at Haverstock's, you understand."

"Haverstock's!" The ladies murmured with approving nods. Only the best families could afford to send their daughters to such an auspicious seminary.

Thankfulness curled within again that Serena's fees had been paid upfront. "Thank you, Mama."

Before her mother could change her mind, Catherine hurried from the room, down the stairs, and out the main entrance, crossing the square's thirty yards or so to the abbey's heavily carved wooden doors. Inside was hushed, festooned with evergreens for the Christmas services next week, only a few people wandering about, gazing up at the huge glass windows rising dozens of feet to the arched ceiling. She hastened across the stone-flagged vestibule, past the baptismal font, over to the northern wing. There she found the major, ostensibly examining a memorial stone, his face easing into a smile at her approach.

"You came."

"Of course." She glanced around. It would do well to find a suitable stone for sketching, to not look like this was a clandestine meeting. "What brings you to Bath, sir?"

"I am here to visit my old general, by name of Whitby."

"General Whitby?" He nodded. "How remarkable. He is good friends with my aunt."

"Then perhaps we will see more of each other." He smiled, and her heart gave a silly flutter.

She spoke sternly to herself as they wandered to the abbey's southern transept. How shallow was she to allow a young man's smile to muddle her emotions? Especially a young man who had not behaved in the most courteous way back at Winthrop. As memories panged, her mood sobered. She eyed a series of sneering gargoyles carved into a stone pillar.

"I suppose you have been keeping abreast of the news from Winthrop?"

A strange thudding began in her heart. She kept her face impassive, inclining her head as if assuming interest in the design of a memorial stone. "Julia writes regularly."

After their surprise evacuation from the Dower House, Catherine had penned a letter of apology to Julia, her friend's reply somehow expressing through the polite nothings something of their hurt at not being informed as to their absence. Since then, the tone of Julia's letters had gradually become more conciliatory.

"Then you'll know that cousin of yours

has finally decided to be leg-shackled."

No. No! Her heart dropped as the silent scream protested within. She grasped the carved end of a wooden pew, her knuckles whitening in her effort to remain upright.

"Took him long enough. I don't know why he dithered so long. He's like a smitten schoolboy. They'll do well, I imagine."

"M-Miss Beauchamp, I suppose?" Her voice sounded hollow in her ears.

"Who else? She's a pretty little thing, I'll give her that, but not quite in the style I imagined should suit the running of such a grand place."

This homage to her former home she imagined to be his way of recommending himself to her. He was wrong. She cared not for his opinion anymore, wanting only to be away, so she could hide the inner rawness threatening to spill from her eyes.

"Miss Winthrop? I thought you'd be better pleased. It must be good news surely to know the estate will be looked after for future generations."

Future generations? Nausea slid through her middle. Mr. Carlew's children — with Miss Beauchamp?

She sank into the pew, pretending interest in the stone vaulting high above. "I wish them every happiness." Had felicitations ever sounded so empty? "She will make" — she swallowed — "a good wife."

"I hope so, though she seems a little young. But I suppose time will change that, eh?"

"It has a tendency to do so," she murmured. Look how much time had changed her.

She blinked away the burn. Forced herself to rise, to assume interest in yet another memorial stone.

Anne Lambert
Beloved wife and mother
Died 1728

She studied the intricately carved angels, forever guarding poor Anne's memory. Wistfulness stole across her heart. Anne might be long dead, but she'd once been loved, she'd once experienced life, and birth, and dreams. Oh, Anne might be long gone, but she had lived!

Catherine swallowed. Time certainly changed things. And perhaps it would even change this ache. Even if two and a half years had not managed to eradicate it.

She drew in a deep breath, conscious of the major's perusal. She fixed a smile to her face. "So, Major, how long will you be in Bath?"

"Just another two days, then I must return to London. I am stopping at Winthrop on the way, if you would like me to carry any messages."

"Thank you, but apart from carrying our good wishes I have no other message to give."

"Very well, then." He bowed, turned, then pivoted back. "Will you attend the concert this evening?"

Her smile was growing brittle, fading fast. "I do not think so." Not anymore. She had an important engagement with her pillow, which would probably result in red eyes.

"Tomorrow?"

"I cannot be certain what plans my mother and aunt have made."

"I see. May I escort you somewhere now?"

And possibly be seen with him by Mama? "Thank you, sir, but I shall remain a little longer."

He looked disappointed. "Then may I wish you the joy of the season and the hope that you will accept my best wishes for your good health and happiness."

"Thank you. And for you, sir."

He nodded and after ensuring once more

she did not require his escort home, departed.

Leaving her slumped in a pew, wondering if she could don her mourning clothes again, and why, in the midst of such a beautiful cathedral, God felt so very far away.

Winthrop

The click of the white ball against the eight was followed by a thunk as the ball dropped into the corner netting. Jonathan moved to the opposite side of the green baize table, steadied the cue, and hit again. Smiled at his success.

A gentle tapping at the door was followed by Geoffreys's murmured, "Excuse me, sir, but Major Hale has arrived."

"At this time of night?"

He'd become used to quiet days and quieter nights. With Mother and Julia in London these past weeks, he'd become accustomed to filling his evenings with account work and, on odd occasions, improving his billiards game. Jon balanced his cue on the table. Hale was sure to welcome a game or three. He hurried into the hall.

"Hale! Good to see you." They shook hands. "Have you eaten?"

"I ate at the White Hart, on the way. But I

won't say no if you still have some of that delicious Scottish brew you had last time."

"Of course." Jon led the way to the smoking room and the whiskey Hale had taken a liking to. After pouring his guest a drink, he settled into the overstuffed chair across from him.

After a general exchange of information about the past weeks, Hale leaned back in his chair. "The place seems rather quiet. I don't suppose Miss Beauchamp is here?"

"Of course not." At his friend's upraised brow Jon hurried on. "My mother and Julia are in London. I could scarcely have houseguests without them."

"Of course not," Hale agreed, taking another sip. "I just wondered . . ."

"Wondered what?"

"Nothing. Please accept my felicitations."

Jon frowned. "I have no news."

"What? I thought you had decided."

"I have neared a decision."

Hale blinked, as though startled. Jon hurried on. "There is still much to consider to ensure such an undertaking be mutually beneficial."

"You speak as though this is another of your business ventures."

"And as far as her father is concerned, it would be," he said. Fifty thousand in shares

in Carlew investments would not be glossed over by any parent seeking their daughter's material happiness. He need not guess what Mr. Beauchamp would encourage his daughter's answer to be when Jon finally proposed.

"Yes, well, perhaps for him it is, but for you, Carlew, is it nothing more? Surely you love the girl."

"I — of course." His conscience panged. He ignored it.

"Then what is the delay? For goodness' sake, man, how long will you keep that girl waiting?"

The very question Mother had asked on his most recent visit to London. Doubtless the very first question she would ask when they arrived tomorrow for Christmas.

"I — oh, well."

"Oh well what?"

"I may have been a little presumptuous." Hale's cheeks reddened.

"What do you mean?"

"I, er, may have told someone that you were betrothed."

"You may?" Jon lifted a brow, his stomach filling with unease. "And who might this person be?"

"Well, you'll never guess whom I saw in Bath. Quite took me aback, she did. I

245

declare she seemed almost pretty."

No . . . His heart stuttered. "Not — ?"

"Miss Winthrop, that's right! She was quite different, smiling and witty, well, she was at first, anyway. Until I, er, told her about you and the Beauchamp girl." He glanced guiltily at Jonathan. "Sorry, Carlew."

"No matter," he said shortly. How could it matter? She'd long ago made her feelings plain. And hadn't he long ago forsaken any hope of reconciliation?

"Truly, Carlew, I didn't know you had an interest there."

He unclenched his fingers. Breathed out. Breathed out some more. "I don't."

"No?"

"No."

"Well, that is good news." Hale glanced up, an almost shy expression on his face. "Fact is, I rather wondered at having a crack myself."

"What?" Jon blinked. Was the world going zany or was it just him?

"I suppose I should talk to you, seeing as she doesn't have a father. And now you're the new Lord Winthrop and all, I suppose you would stand in his place."

Jon shoved a hand through his hair, wishing he could order his thoughts. "I did not think you believed her pretty enough."

"Perhaps I am learning to appreciate that a woman's face can't hold attention as long as her words can, and" — he smiled — "she's got a surprising tongue on her."

Something hard and cold clenched his chest. "I'm surprised you stopped long enough to find out. I remember you once described her as a perfect fright."

"Yes, but that was when she was here. In Bath she seems, I don't know, to have bloomed. But perhaps that's the effect of being away from her wasp-tongued mother."

"Lady Winthrop is not there?"

"Oh, she's there all right, but" — his smile grew sly — "not when I was speaking to Miss Winthrop."

Nausea rumbled through his stomach. He'd be hanged to see Hale interfere with her. "You are aware she has little dowry."

"What does that matter? I have enough. Just think" — and now Hale had the audacity to grin — "we could be cousins-in-law."

"Third cousins once removed-in-law," he growled.

"Carlew, you don't seem a bit pleased for me. Here I am for the first time in my life possibly willing to consider settling down, and well, I call it ungentlemanly not to encourage me in such an endeavor."

"Ungentlemanly? You?" Jonathan fought to keep the sneer from his voice. "I cannot conceive why you'd wonder at a man's hesitation in wanting to recommend someone in his care to your protection."

"I beg your pardon?"

"Come," Jon uttered with a grating laugh. "We both know you can have no honorable interest in Miss Winthrop."

Hale stared at him, two white spots high on his cheeks. "I'm going to pretend I did not hear you say that," he said softly.

"You can pretend all you like, but denial won't change your past."

Hale's eyes flashed. "Perhaps it won't. But I'm not the only one hoping my past won't dictate my future."

Jon sucked in air. "What do you mean by that?"

"Precisely that. Do you not believe a person can change? Or are you so utterly straitlaced you judge a man forever on his history? Yes, perhaps I'm not worthy of a lady like Miss Winthrop, but I'm beginning to suspect you would not approve of anyone. And that, along with your reluctance to offer for Miss Beauchamp, only makes me wonder why!" He pushed to his feet. "No, don't get up, I'll see myself out. You might have the Midas touch when it comes to business, but you treat your friends worse than any poor beggar I ever saw on a Calcutta street."

"Hale, I apolo—"

The door slammed.

When Jon finally followed him outside, it was in time to see a gig being driven smartly away. Leaving him wondering if he'd fractured a friendship forever.

And wondering just how much of Hale's words were true.

Chapter Fifteen

Bath
January 1817

Bath seemed very gray in winter. Perhaps that was the effect of leaden clouds and spitting skies; perhaps it was simply the state of her heart. Catherine trudged up the street, clasping her hood at the throat to protect from the icy wind. She was a ghost, walking, talking, even occasionally smiling, drifting through her days. Inside she was dead. All hope snuffed out. Nothing touched her; nothing *could* touch her. The tiny flame of hope she'd foolishly, so *foolishly* nurtured had died with Major Hale's words three weeks ago. Somehow she maintained a calm demeanor; somehow she went through the motions demanded by society, but the joy of Bath, the freedom she'd drunk so thirstily, all that seemed wasted now.

Her mother's grumbles and complaints beside her seemed a distant drone. Catherine paid little heed, forcing herself to adopt the semblance of polite interest propriety deemed acceptable. Christmas had passed, the pain of her father's absence adding greater sorrow, which was only slightly alleviated by a church service reminder as to its true meaning, a small exchange of gifts, and a special meal. New Year passed. Epiphany.

Aunt Drusilla had looked askance at her several times, but Mama remained oblivious. Despite the cold, Catherine maintained her church and library visits, the occasional concert engagement. People of shallow acquaintance might see nothing wrong, but Serena had been able to tell, sharing her concern at Christmas, which Catherine had managed to fob off with a forced smile. Lavinia, too, would know, but she was far away, her delight in new motherhood all she should be focused on. So Catherine kept her letters bright and cheery; nothing of her making would cause shadows in Lavinia's happiness.

The drizzling conditions had intensified by the time they finally reached the front steps of the residence on Gay Street, Mother's complaints about the taste of the waters from their daily walk from the Pump Room unabated. "And I do wish Bath was not so steep. Nor so rainy!"

"Perhaps you might find a nap beneficial, Mama."

Her mother sighed, murmured accord, and moved upstairs, groans accompanying every step. Catherine went to the drawing room, tried to read her Bible, but as seemed usual these days, the words were simply black marks on the page.

"Excuse me, Catherine?"

She looked up.

Aunt Drusilla motioned to the Bible. "I hope I'm not disturbing you?"

"No, not at all." She closed the heavy covers.

Her aunt perched on the settee opposite, brow wrinkled. "I was hoping to have a word with you."

Oh. Dread lined her stomach.

"How are you?"

Catherine hitched her lips into a smile she hoped looked believable. "I am well."

"Hmm. May I make an observation?" At Catherine's nod her aunt continued. "When you and your mother first came to Bath, I knew you both to be ill. You were so dispirited, and your mother has always been inclined to be sickly. Such things are hardly surprising, if the descriptions of your house are to be believed." She smoothed her skirts.

"I had high hopes to see you recover, and for a time you seemed to improve, but lately . . ."

Catherine stilled. What had Aunt Drusilla seen?

"There's no need to look like that. I may never have been blessed with a child of my own, but I like to think of you as the daughter I never had. And it seems to me that of late you have felt burdened. Of course, a girl should go to her mother, but your mama, shall we say, has never been able to show much interest in things that do not directly affect her own happiness."

"Aunt Drusilla —"

"Come now. We both know it is true. She's been that way since a child, always carrying on with her imagined tragedies, and at her age is unlikely to change. But I am not concerned about my sister. I *am* concerned about you."

She could not move. Her aunt's keen-eyed gaze pinned her to her seat like a moth to specimen paper.

"What has happened? You are not the young lady I knew as always laughing, riding about like a madcap."

Catherine cleared her throat. "I've grown up."

"Well, yes, you have, but this burden isn't

253

a maturity I would wish on anyone."

What could she say? She wouldn't wish these feelings on her worst enemy.

"What has happened?"

Her eyes pricked. Emotion swelled, refusing speech. She swallowed. Eventually managed to croak, "Papa."

Her aunt's gaze softened. "Of course. But that does not account for why you grew morose again. Has something else happened? Have you received disappointing news?"

"Please, Aunt, I would rather not —"

"Not tell me, I know. But it does not please me to see you so lifeless." Aunt Drusilla sighed. "My dear, I am known for my blunt ways, so you'll have to excuse me when I ask, is it a man?"

Catherine's heart thumped.

"I gather from *that* look the answer is yes. So what is the problem? He has disappointed your hopes?"

She dragged her gaze away to look out the library windows. It was raining more heavily now. Of course it was. Wintry bitterness outside to match the bleakness within.

"Who is this man?"

Her eyes narrowed as she returned her attention to her aunt, fighting to control her breathing. Did Aunt Drusilla possess no scruples?

"Do not look at me like I'm about to snap off your head. I am not your mother, and you are not a simpleton, so I gather he is worthy enough to secure your affection."

Well, if she insisted on knowing . . .

Catherine lifted her chin. Swallowed. Then told her.

"Well!" Aunt Drusilla blinked. "Good heavens! Well."

Hollow amusement clanged within. Rarely had she seen her aunt so flabbergasted.

"I suppose it could be worse. Elizabeth writes to say Carlew has been most circumspect in his dealings with Avebury. She seems to think him a sensible man, especially in dealing with that fool Clothilde and her ridiculous son. I cannot help but appreciate Elizabeth's good sense, though she's always been too meek for my liking." She nodded. "And it speaks well of his character that he did not insist on your immediate removal from the Manor. If only it wasn't for his unfortunate mother!" Aunt Drusilla peered at her sharply. "So, when did this happen?"

"In London, at Grandfather's birthday."

"Nearly three years ago?"

She nodded.

"All this time! Well, I'll say this for you,

my girl, you owe nothing of your reticence to my side of the family."

That was certainly true.

"And Mr. Carlew wrote to you?"

Her eyes blurred. "Only to say h-his affections had changed."

"And your parents did not know?"

"Oh, please, Aunt Drusilla, I could not bear it if Mama were to know."

"Of course." Her aunt sighed, her sympathetic gaze sharpening again. "You're sure your father did not? I'm sorry to speak ill of the dead, but your father was not the most scrupulous of men."

But everything about Mr. Carlew's behavior had changed afterward. It *had* to be true. "It does not matter now."

"But it must, otherwise you would not be carrying on like this."

She said stiffly, "I do not believe I have carried on —"

"Oh, don't get all missish with me! Tell me. What has happened to cast you into despondency now?"

"H-he is engaged."

"Well!"

"To a Miss Beauchamp. She is quite kind —"

"I do not care if she is a saint!" Her aunt's eyes flashed. Was it disappointment to be

the tenants had reduced to weekly. He felt as though he was slowly earning their trust, like that of the Hassops, whose farm he had visited before this stop at the Foleys'.

He nodded to Mrs. Foley. "I am glad to see you looking better."

"It helps to be getting more sleep, sir."

"I have heard that."

Hawkesbury had mentioned something similar during a brief conversation at White's, when Jon had enquired after the countess and their new daughter. The earl's joy at becoming a father in early November did not seem diminished either by the fact he remained heirless or that his sleep was now much disrupted. Jon had fought envy, fought the what-ifs. And he fought envy again now in the cozy farmhouse kitchen.

"I will leave you to it then." He gathered his overcoat and beaver, shook hands with the farmer, and nodded to his wife.

"Oh, sir, I be wondering if you've heard anything from Miss Winthrop?"

He stilled, chest banding tight. "No."

Mrs. Foley sighed. "I would be liking her to know how well the babe be doing now, seeing as she took such an interest early on, and all."

"I believe my sister has written to her. I

shall endeavor to see the message passed on."

"Oh, that be right kind of you, sir."

"Not at all."

He bowed, exited, and hurried through the frosty air to the barn, where Gulliver kept warm under blankets. Minutes later he was riding up the lane.

Memories rose, shifting between those from years ago and those more recent. Her antagonism. Her insistence on being away from him. Her shock. Her disappointment.

If only . . .

He shook his head — the cold must be affecting his brain! — and rode up the snowy lane.

Jon nudged Gulliver closer to the Dower House. His mother's return from London over Christmas had prompted this visit. The day after their meal of celebration, a wretched day like this, as they relaxed before the crackling fire she'd said, "Oh, I've been meaning to ask what you intend to do about the cottage."

"The cottage?"

"Yes. I would certainly not like to stay there."

He'd smiled. "I think we can both rest assured you need never live in a cottage, Mother."

She laughed, but then grew serious. "I might not, thank God. However, the same cannot be said for others. And since it's vacant at present, I think it timely for you to spend money on something closer to home."

Only then had he realized that she referred to the Dower House.

"It won't require anything of the expense required by Avebury."

"Thank goodness," he muttered.

"Thank *your* goodness, rather. I still do not believe that woman has any idea what you have done for her. And her son."

He shrugged. "It does not matter."

"Does not matter? If only we could all be so cavalier when it comes to spending thousands on a derelict old ruin."

"It is not quite *that* bad."

"Not anymore, thanks to you. Regardless, I do think it important to treat family members with respect, even when they refuse to show us proper consideration. I still cannot understand how they could be so discourteous as to not inform us of their departure."

"Mother, that was months ago."

"And still no word!"

"I've had word," Julia piped up from the corner settee, curled up in front of the fire, reading a book. "Catherine and I have exchanged several letters."

Several letters? Jon eyed his sister. What else did he not know?

"Yes, well, that is hardly the same," Mother said, studying her beringed fingers with a frown. "It is simply courtesy to inform one's neighbors of one's proposed movements."

"Mother, they hardly require my permission to leave," Jon said.

"You were away in London, anyway."

"Thank you, Julia. This conversation need not involve you," said their mother.

"But if it involves fixing up the cottage, then I think it should," she said, sitting upright with lifted chin. "I've been inside and it's simply horrid."

"I beg your pardon?"

She coughed, then shivered, as if remembering. "It's terribly nasty, and dark, and cold. I'm glad they're not there now. It must be unbearable in winter."

"Why did you not say something before, poppet?"

"I did not think of it." Julia shrugged. "And besides, sometimes it doesn't seem to matter what I say, you both don't seem to want to listen."

"Now, Julia . . ."

Their protestations had met with another shrug. "Anyway, I always had the impression they were too proud to ask for your help."

"But I am responsible for such things." Shame slithered through his soul. "I wish I had known."

His mother sniffed. "It was your predecessor's role to ensure the Dower House remained fit for his family's habitation. You cannot hold yourself accountable for another man's failings."

"But —"

"But nothing. You could not very well barge in without their leave, but as they are no longer there and by all accounts have no fixed return, now is the perfect time for you to see just what needs to be done." Her eyes had grown sober. "And if what Julia says is correct, there is a great deal to be done."

His stomach clenched anew in uneasy expectation. Just how much needed to be done he was about to find out.

Gulliver slowed, the thick snowdrifts near impassable. Jon slid off, walked the final yards to the dense hedge behind which the cottage huddled. Smoke curling from the chimney suggested someone resided within. He opened the gate, and tugged Gulliver through to the empty stable. After covering the stallion with a blanket, he moved to the back door and knocked.

"Hello?"

The door opened before he could knock again. A woman, plump-cheeked, brown haired, and flour-dusted stood there, eyes rounding. "Good heavens! It's his lordship!"

"Good day, Mrs. — ?"

"Mrs. Jones, sir." She dropped a curtsy.

"I hope you don't mind the intrusion, but I have come to inspect the cottage."

"The mistress still be away."

"I know. It shan't take a moment."

After a brief hesitation, she stepped back. He entered, and quickly acknowledged the concerns of his mother and sister. Darkness permeated the building that not even the hastily opened curtains could help. And it was cold. Bitterly cold. Wind whistled round the windows, drafts of icy air stealing through cracks as long as a man's arm. Why, why, *why* hadn't anyone told him conditions were so miserable?

"Sir, I 'pologize for the state of things. We weren't expectin' any company."

He traced a finger through the dust lining a shelf of books. "I hope you keep house better when your mistress is in."

"Oh yes, of course, sir."

"I would not keep someone in my employ

if they only worked when I was watching."

"Oh, but sir —"

"Tell me, do you wish to keep your job?"

"Of course, sir!"

"Then there are a few things I wish to know."

Half an hour later, he retrieved a snorting Gulliver, gave him a quick rubdown before heading for home. Icy wind chattered, stealing underneath his turned-up collar, biting his ears and cheeks.

How could he have not noticed the dire state of affairs? What kind of kinsman was he?

Fresh weight settled on his shoulders, his mind churning apace with Gulliver's hooves.

No wonder they hated him. No wonder she hated him. Right now, he hated himself.

He groaned aloud.

Mistake upon mistake upon mistake.

CHAPTER SIXTEEN

Upper Assembly Rooms, Bath

The room filled with the hubbub of tonight's audience, the excitement almost palpable as the crowd escaped the confines of hearth and home to gather for an evening's entertainment. Catherine reveled in the chance to be out in society once again, to be free from Mama's overbearing presence and manner, to wear the pretty mauve dress Aunt Drusilla had made a present for her.

"Miss Winthrop!" General Whitby smiled at her. "May I say how lovely you look tonight?"

Catherine smiled over her fan as though she was as much of an accomplished flirt as Sophia Milton had been before her marriage. "You may."

He chortled, a sound not dissimilar to a braying horse. "You will outshine the other ladies tonight."

"I hope so," she replied, "especially as they tend to be my elder by at least two dozen years."

Another throaty chuckle made her smile all the more real. The banter was like donning a once-favorite gown she'd long ago discarded; it felt so familiar, so comfortable, she could wear it all the time.

"Not everyone has the constitution for cold evenings such as these," the general continued, looking around.

"I believe I've grown somewhat immune to the cold. I've become acclimatized, you see."

"Well, you are from a chillier part of the world, I suppose."

Well he might suppose, but that wasn't her true meaning. The coldness encasing her heart for so long had eased of late, partly due to her aunt's stern intervention, partly due to the challenge she found in the Bible.

The strains of the musicians tuning, their notes clashing until harmony prevailed, seemed almost to mirror her own heart's recent tension. For too long she had lived with discord between heart and head, feeling and faith. God's abundant life awaited. No more would she allow her peace and hope to be stolen away. She was loved by

God; His presence empowered her in her weakness; His promises stirred hope for the future.

So the cloak of timidity was one she cast aside each day. Sometimes she struggled, the fears fueling her uncertainty needing to be combated with God's assurances. But regret was tasteless, a dry bone she had gnawed for way too long. She was putting her past behind her, and if people thought her behavior improper, such as spending time with dear, genial General Whitby, she at least had Aunt Drusilla's encouragement propelling her on. Which was why she was here, at the Upper Assembly Rooms, sitting next to the general, waiting for the famous soprano from the Continent, Madame Lavallier, to begin.

A gorgeously arrayed large-bosomed lady appeared, bowed, and soon began to sing. Her voice swelled, filling the room adorned with laurels, garlands, and wreaths of flowers. The string music lifted then fell, its rich tones the perfect accompaniment to the soprano's dulcet rendering, tugging listeners on an emotional journey, one Catherine was happy to get lost in. She smiled. Released breath. Now this, *this* was what made Bath enjoyable.

The Italian song soon gave way to an Irish

air, then a performance of *Robin Adair.* Catherine joined in the applause at the commencement of the interval.

"Quite magnificent, do you not agree?" the general murmured.

"Quite." Although she felt sure Lavinia's talent could surpass the professional's.

He tucked her hand under his arm, leading her to where the refreshments were served. "I hope you'll think of attending the ball next week."

"I'm afraid all I can do is *think* of attending." She smiled, gesturing to her clothes. "I do not think even my aunt would agree to my putting off all semblance of mourning just to attend a ball."

"I suppose you are right." He sighed. "You break my heart, child."

She laughed.

His eyes twinkled. "Now, I have a little matter to discuss with you. My friend Major Hale, have you seen anything of him of late?"

Major Hale. Her heart chilled. "No, I have not seen him since before Christmas."

"Hmm. He'd mentioned plans to be here in the new year and I rather thought I'd see him by now, but have heard nothing."

Her smile drooped. He was probably too busy with Mr. Carlew before his wedding, seeing as they were such friends.

"Well, I suppose there is nothing that can be done. Only I do wish for someone closer to your own age to accompany you to these things."

"I hope you are not feeling too tired, sir?"

"Too tired? No, although I rather suspect several of my acquaintances think me too old to be escorting such a pretty thing around town."

Catherine smiled, and squeezed his arm. "You do yourself a great disservice, sir."

"Whilst you do my old heart a world of good, my dear."

So despite her mother's pleas to not be *quite* so chummy with the general, Catherine reveled in the fact that strangely, against all odds, she had made a friend.

The general, contrary to her mother's fears, seemed to have no designs for matrimony, being instead happy to advise and criticize all prospects as they moved around the room. His eyeglass would lift, then be allowed to fall, as various candidates were dismissed as too plump, too tall, too thin, or too small.

"A man should be but the husband of one wife, so the Good Book tells us. Have you ever wondered why that might be?"

"Too many wives might spoil the man?"

He laughed. "Back when I was on the Indian subcontinent, we often dealt with rajahs who believed in polygamy. I cannot imagine anything worse. Imagine the constant screeching!"

She smiled wryly. She did not need to imagine. Growing up, she'd heard enough screeching from a man's only wife.

"I like that about you, my dear — you only speak when you have something to say. And usually what you've got to say is worth listening to."

"Why, thank you," she replied in her driest tone.

"And not quick to take offense — I admire that, too."

She laughed.

"There, that's more like it. Now, tell me, why should that foppish fellow be staring our direction? Do you think the color of my waistcoat too bland compared to his?"

She glanced over. Almost stumbled. "Perry?"

"Perry, is it? He looks more like a plumpish peacock to me." He gave a dismissive snort. "I wouldn't have anything to do with him, my dear, except it seems you already know him, and yes, he seems to be coming our way. How unfortunate."

"Hello, Mr. Milton," said Catherine,

extending her hand.

He took it, bowed. "Miss Winthrop, how are you?"

"Very well, thank you." Noting his look at her companion, she performed the introductions. "General, allow me to introduce Peregrine Milton, an old friend of the family's. Perry, this is General Whitby, a new friend of ours."

As the men bowed to each other, Catherine continued, "The general has been most anxious to make your acquaintance. He wondered whether the, er, handsomely dressed young man gazing in our direction was casting aspersions on his choice of waistcoat."

"You are a naughty puss," murmured the general.

"Not at all," Perry responded grandly. "It was simply I did not recognize you, Catherine. You look quite handsome."

As Catherine digested this, the general snorted. "Young man, a compliment presented in such a cack-handed way can scarce be considered complimentary. But if you meant to tell my young friend here that she is in very fine looks then I congratulate you on your powers of observation."

Perry's mouth dropped open. "I, er . . ."

"Mr. Milton" — Catherine shot the general a reproving look — "tell me what brings you to Bath."

"My new coach. It's slap up to the echo."

"I meant —"

"I think even ol' Hawkesbury would envy me."

As he continued espousing his new vehicle's virtues, she tried to ignore the general's chortle of "Peacock *and* peagoose."

"Is your father here in town with you?"

"No, just the *mater.*"

Her heart sunk. "Wonderful."

"She won't believe how well you're looking either."

"Now, lad," growled the general.

"I . . . er, I hope to see you soon again, Miss Winthrop." He bowed. "General Whitby."

As he threaded his way back through the crowd, the general muttered, "Useless popinjay."

"He is not useless, dear general, just perhaps a little enamored of his own importance. He is to be the squire at St. Hampton Heath one day."

"I hope he's learned some common sense by then."

That might be too much to hope for. "He lost his betrothed last year, you know."

"No, I didn't. Remarkably careless of him,

wouldn't you say?" His teeth glinted in a smile.

She stifled her amusement, schooling her features to appropriateness. Perry had not seemed to take the loss with any great display of grief; had instead begun pursuing a young heiress whose visit to the neighborhood was quickly cut short. It had proved enough to set tongues wagging —

"I daresay I'm too harsh on the boy, but I've never taken too well to such dandies. Millinery men. Would be much better sent off to the army to straighten them out."

"I believe there might be *some* men in this world who have attained sense without being forced into such measures."

"You're a saucy thing. Very well, I'll concede. A few men, not many." His brow creased. "Young Hale has a friend, I saw him once at the club in London. He wasn't military, but by all accounts seems a good sort of chap. Hale met him out in India."

Pulse racing, feigning disinterest, she nodded to an elderly couple as the general rattled off several names. Well his eagle eyes might spot a dandy, but she feared he would spot her distress if she spoke.

"Carrington? Castle? Carlew, that's it. A merchant, connected to the Company, I believe, but as sensible a man as I've met. A man of such good principles one cannot but be impressed. Miss Winthrop?" He turned to her. "Your grip has tightened. Are you quite well?"

"Q-quite well."

"Shall I return you to your aunt? I note the gossiping old tabbies are having something of a field day. I hate to think it's at your expense, my dear."

"It is quite all right."

She smiled, the general returned her to Aunt Drusilla, and after the concert they departed back to Six Gay Street. And she fought to keep her attention on the pleasant evening, on the diverting entertainment — and not on the man, the mere mention of whom dipped her spirits and made her wonder whether living on a street with such a name was yet another one of life's absurd ironies.

Whites, London

The streets of London in mid January owned a bleakness even the wintry wilds of Gloucestershire did not share. Jonathan forced his attention away from the Bond Street view to the men standing before him. The monthly business meetings over, he'd sought solace in his club, where he had the dubious pleasure of meeting certain shareholders who took exception to the recent downturn in the price of cotton, and were enquiring — none too softly — as to why their profits were not as good as last month.

Mr. Meade, heavy gray-tinged brows jutting out like a shop awning, clenched the chair back, knuckles whitening. "I simply do not understand!"

Jon glanced wistfully at his rapidly cooling meal. Why had the man waited until now to ask his questions? He strove for patience in his voice. "As I said earlier, business has its ebbs and flows. One cannot expect to garner a twelve percent profit every time."

"Hmph," grunted the other man, a portly owner of several Midlands mills. "I don't suppose you've seen any great loss in your takings?"

Heat surged in his chest. Jon stared at him, jaw clenched to prevent answer, until the first wave of anger passed. "I assure you, *gentlemen*" — he forced out the word — "I take no pleasure in seeing your shares devalue. But may I remind you that they are not worthless. In fact quite the opposite. Indeed, if you feel the need to sell I could recommend numbers of people only too willing to take them off your hands." He raised his brows. "Perhaps I should enquire —"

"Now, now there's no need for that," Meade interjected. "I may have been a tad hasty. I understand you to be an honest man."

"If that is so, then perhaps you'll refrain from making observations to the contrary."

The factory owner's cheeks mottled. "I said I am sorry."

Did you? Jon wanted to say, but refrained. Perhaps Meade thought he really had.

"I best be leaving you to your meal, now. See you next month."

Jon dipped his chin, waiting until the men disappeared through the glass doors before releasing his grip on the fork. It clattered to the table, drawing eyes that quickly withdrew. He pushed away his plate, the salmon half-eaten. The greed of some men sickened him; he had no appetite for more.

"Carlew! Or should I say, Lord Winthrop."

He glanced up. Found a smile. "Carmichael."

They gripped hands, and the viscount sank into the seat opposite. "Salmon not so good?"

"Try, the meeting not so good."

"Unhappy shareholders, eh? I saw Meade steaming out as I came in. He invested with your lot, didn't he?"

Jon managed a thin smile.

"Quite so, quite so. Well, let me order and then I'll tell you about these amazing few days I spent at Derbyshire House. You'll never believe who was there."

The tight coil in his chest gradually unwound as Carmichael shared tales of life amongst the gentry that by turns shocked, horrified, and amused him. According to Carmichael's stories, these people, this class Jon had stepped into, behaved worse at times than the heathen in far away countries to whom they sent mission monies. He shook his head.

"Too racy for you? You've always been a little straitlaced, as I recall. Never mind." Carmichael tucked into his steak with relish. "Tell me, how is that marvelous mother of yours?"

"She is well, thank you. Enjoying her time shopping, and catching up with old friends."

"Give her my best, won't you? And your sister? How is fair Julia?"

"She is also well, though prone to a ticklish cough." And occasional bouts of the sullens, but he didn't think his friend needed to know that.

The viscount spoke through a mouthful of steak, "Heard from Hale?"

"No." Guilt panged. Nor was he likely to. Jon drained his glass of wine.

278

"Hmm. He seems to have gone to ground again. I don't mind telling you that Hale has always been something of a puzzle to me. It's not as though he's swimming in lard — I think his father but a parson in Norfolk or some such place — and yet the ladies flock to him. Ah well, probably just found himself a new fancy bird."

As long as it wasn't Julia, or . . .

"Why the frown, Carlew? I would have thought you'd be glad he's not dangling after your sister."

"You truly think he would?"

"I think he might wish to, but I suspect a certain big brother might have something to say about that."

Jon forced his fists to unclench. "I cannot help but feel sorry for whomever is his next fancy."

"I shouldn't worry. Unlikely to be anyone you know."

"I suppose," he muttered.

But how could he be certain? And why did a little niggling suspicion demand he care?

Dinner that night was at the Beauchamps. Julia's friendship with Miss Beauchamp had cooled somewhat, a fact he was grateful for, as it lessened the need for him to find excuses to stay away. Jon forked in a mouthful of venison, confliction cramping within. Yes, she was pretty. Yes, she was all that was amiable and seemed to share his faith. Yes, he was aware of speculation that matched her name with his, but . . .

And that was the problem. He couldn't define the "but." And until he held no hesitation in his heart, he did not want to fully commit by uttering words that could not be undone.

But despite his reservations, some things could not be absented, such as tonight's meal that he attended with Julia and his mother. So he ate, made conversation, engaged in light banalities, all the while thinking, wondering, wishing —

"Lord Winthrop?"

Miss Beauchamp's smile regained his attention. What was the topic of conversation? Something about . . . "Silks?" he guessed.

"Precisely! See? I knew dear Lord Winthrop would know." She fluttered her eyelashes at him. "He has such an eye for fashion."

He smiled guiltily, catching Mr. Beauchamp's frown. "Please forgive my abstraction. My time in London is not all my own."

His host grunted. "I suppose a man like you would have much to occupy him."

A man like him? His dinner soured. Did Mr. Beauchamp mean a man of the merchant class? Jon might have secured the affections of the ladies Beauchamp, but his host was quite another matter.

As if sensing his discomfort, his hostess inclined towards him. "Tell me, how does your work at Avebury go on?"

He forced a smile. He suspected Mrs. Beauchamp's interest in the old estate had less to do with wanting to know his plans for refurbishment and more to do with showing her husband just what a prize catch he was. He kept the details short, to the point.

"And your friends who stayed? How are Major Hale and the Viscount Carmichael?" Miss Beauchamp's enquiry was offered with a sliding glance at her father, as if she, too, wanted to reinforce Jon's aristocratic connections.

"I saw Carmichael today. He is well, and sends you his greetings." This he offered to his mother, but doubtless his sociable friend would offer it to all.

"Henry is such a dear boy," his mother said. "Utterly charming."

"And the major?" Miss Beauchamp turned to her father. "You'd like him, Father. Can you believe he fought the natives in India?"

"Hmph."

"We do not see much of Major Hale anymore," said Julia. Was that accusation in her eyes?

"Really? Oh." Miss Beauchamp's smile dimmed, and the conversation soon turned to something else.

Later, in the carriage ride home to Portman Square, Julia turned to him. "Why do we not see Major Hale anymore?"

"I — that is we — had a slight difference of opinion."

"Difference of opinion?" Julia said, brows aloft. "So you and Hale argued? I know you, and something of the major, and rather suppose he objected to your highhanded ways."

"Oh, Julia, dear —"

"No, Mama. I want to know. I suspect Jon might have chased him away."

"I didn't chase him —"

"You did something to make him not want to stay. And all this time you have refused to answer." Julia crossed her arms. "What is it you're trying to hide?"

"Nothing."

"No?"

"Julia, that is enough."

"But Mama, men like the major don't run away. He has saved countless lives, and is a hero, and courageous, and —"

"Julia, how well do you know Hale?"

She stared at him, lamplight streaking across her face as the carriage turned the corner. "Well enough, I suppose."

"Has it ever occurred to you that I might not be the one with something to hide?" He pushed down the sliver of shame. His words did the former soldier no *great* disservice, but . . .

"What do you mean?"

"Jonathan, this is neither the time nor place."

"Mother, I believe it's time Julia learned something of his reputation."

"His reputation?" Julia's voice was small.

"He is not a man I want being friendly with my sister."

The sounds of London streets filled the carriage: the creak of timber and leather as they rounded another corner; the clip-clop of hooves on cobblestones; the huff of horses breathing in cold air; the call of working children, announcing their skills and wares.

Julia coughed. "But I thought he was your friend."

In the wash of darkness he caught his mother's raised eyebrows.

He swallowed and turned away, as the

questions, guilty questions, in his heart began again.

CHAPTER SEVENTEEN

Six Gay Street, Bath
February

Catherine smoothed her gloves, admiring the sheen of satin and the way they perfectly complemented her evening gown and pelisse. Tonight's musical performance at the Assembly Rooms would feature a selection of arias sung by a famous Italian soprano. Anticipation for the evening had had Bath's inhabitants humming for days.

"Now, Catherine," her mother said, "the general is quite respectable it is true, but perhaps you should not let him claim your attention *all* evening."

"Yes, Mama."

She glanced at Aunt Drusilla, caught her glance at the ceiling. Smiled.

"Now, Elvira, you are sure you do not wish to come?"

"I am content," Mama said, with the air of a martyr.

That might be a slight exaggeration, thought Catherine, but at least it made a change from Mama expressing her *dis*content.

"Now just be sure to not let the general monopolize you all night."

"Mama —"

"No, I do not like the gossip that comes my way."

"Perhaps if you did not indulge in it yourself, dear sister, you would be rather less likely to hear it."

Catherine swallowed a giggle at her mother's shocked expression, kissed her cheek, collected her cloak, and followed Aunt Drusilla outside to the carriage. A few minutes of travel and they came to a standstill, the crush of vehicles forcing their early exit and a hurried dash to the colonnades marking the entrance.

The air was sharp and cold, but the assembly rooms were warm and lively. After being welcomed by the host and handing off their cloaks to the attendants, they made their way to the site of tonight's musical performance.

The Octagonal Room, with its yellow painted walls, high windows, and four carved fireplaces was centered by a magnificent chandelier, with its sparkling drops of shimmery light highlighting the gleam of diamonds and the sheen of silks and satins. Multiple conversations pulsed with happy expectation, gossip, and mild flirtation, the clamor rising to the musicians' gallery above.

"There are so many people!" Catherine whispered to her aunt.

"I'll grant you that it is not as sparse as some winter nights, but I suppose that's the effect of having such a well-known musician perform."

"We were fortunate to get tickets."

"That was not good fortune, my dear, but good management."

Catherine chuckled, glancing around, looking for any familiar acquaintance.

The general caught her eye, his face brightening. She smiled as he drew near. No wonder Mama was concerned. For the casual observer, the general's marked attention, his singling them out above all other acquaintance, was almost enough to make a person believe him to have something of regard for Catherine — except he only ever treated her as he might a daughter. And she felt nothing but sincere affection for his kindness and willingness to share her wry humor.

"Good evening, General. It is good to see you."

"And you, sweet girl. How are we tonight, my dears?" He smiled at Aunt Drusilla, whose treatment of him — a mix of condescension and approbation — bore further witness to his good nature. "A pretty crowd indeed to hear the pretty *signorina.*"

"It certainly seems — oh."

At her aunt's disgruntled look, Catherine turned, and promptly felt a similar lowering of spirits. "Lady Milton." She offered a small curtsy to the plump figure, then an even smaller one to the figure standing alongside her, brushing invisible particles from his sleeve. "Perry."

"Mrs. Villiers, Catherine." The turbaned head bowed before a frankly curious gaze set upon the general.

He took out an eyeglass, his inspection of Lady Milton serving to grossly magnify his eye, whilst making the object of his attention obviously quite uncomfortable. He turned to Perry. "I presume this is your mother."

"Yes, of course." Perry performed the introductions, under the watchful eye of one personage and the outrage of the other.

The general bowed. "I should have known him as your son, madam, the moment I set eyes upon you."

"Oh?" Her face thawed from its frosty lines, clearly expecting a favorable response. "And how did you know? He is considered to have a certain air, I know, and is often thought quite handsome —"

"He has something of your figure."

And with another bow, and a muttered excuse, the general moved to the other side of the room and claimed a seat beside another gentleman of military persuasion.

"Well!" Lady Milton exclaimed. "I hope you've not had much to do with that man, Catherine. He is obviously not of our class."

"You may speak for yourself, Lady Milton," said Aunt Drusilla. "The general is connected to some of the finest families in England."

"Oh, but I —"

"Come, Catherine. Let us take our seats. Good evening, Lady Milton, Mr. Milton."

Catherine nodded and followed her aunt to the front row, next to the general and his companion, whom he introduced as Lieutenant Harrow. They spent a few minutes quietly conversing, until the musicians entered the room and tuned their violins.

The music was good, the program called it "excerpts from *commedia in musica*," but Catherine couldn't help but think that while

Italian arias were all very well, one's appreciation might be greater if one more fully comprehended Italian. Still, to be out, to be dressed in finery, to not be stuck moping at home, was such an improvement she could scarcely complain even if the songs be sung in some tribal language from the South Seas!

Afterwards, they reconvened in the Tea Room, their enjoyment fading as Lady Milton and Perry exchanged seats with their neighbors to sit beside them.

"Well, that was certainly interesting," Lady Milton said. "However I must say I did not understand very much of the shrieking. Perry did not understand a great deal, either, I'm afraid."

"Why are you afraid?" Aunt Drusilla asked.

"I beg your pardon?" Lady Milton's brow furrowed. "I do not quite take your meaning."

"I thought it was just Italian she did not understand," the general murmured. "I didn't realize she had a problem with English as well."

Catherine gave him a speaking look, and turned to Perry. "I gather you would prefer your opera to be in French."

"I think I'd prefer it to not be opera."

"Perry has never been very musical, unlike my sweet Sophia."

"And how is sweet Sophia?"

As soon as she asked the question, Catherine knew she shouldn't have. When Lady Milton finally paused in her litany of praise and drew breath, so did the rest of the table.

"Well, I am pleased for her." Catherine turned to Perry. "Tell me —"

"And how is your dear Mama?" This to Catherine. "I was hoping to see her here tonight." Lady Milton craned her neck and looked around, as though Catherine's mother might suddenly appear from behind a column.

"She is not hiding from you, if that is what you were expecting."

"Oh, no, no. Of course not." She gave a foolish titter.

"My sister is in mourning, Lady Milton," Aunt Drusilla said. "She does not attend evening routs."

"Of course not, no. I would not expect her to. That would be *most* improper."

Then why had she hoped to see her tonight? Catherine swallowed her retort.

"A remarkably foolish woman," the general growled.

"I was merely hoping she would be amenable to a visit from an old friend."

"Who?" the general asked in a louder voice.

"Why, myself, of course."

"Oh. I had to wonder when you said you expected to see her here. You appeared almost disappointed she was not, and further disappointed to find she had not broken society's rules. I had to wonder if such an attitude were indicative of friendship."

Lady Milton drew herself up. "I'm sure I don't know what you mean."

"I think you might have a fair idea." The general pushed to his feet, pinched Catherine's chin, and made a series of lavish bows. "I hope to see you good people on the morrow," he said to Catherine and her aunt. He turned to Perry and his mother. "Good evening."

Perry rose to return the bow, while his mother simply stared with an icy glare.

"What an odd man. Such extraordinary manners."

"We have found him most convivial company, have we not, Catherine?"

"The general is very pleasant," she agreed.

"Well, I don't know what your mother might say should she know he was taking such liberties with you."

Catherine winced, wishing Lady Milton's voice wasn't quite so carrying.

"He has taken no liberties with my niece, and I would thank you for keeping your voice down."

"Well!"

"Catherine, are you quite finished? I see dear Lady Northam over there, and find myself needing to speak with her at once."

"Oh, but before you go, Mrs. Villiers, might I impose on your good nature and call upon poor Elvira tomorrow? I'm sure she would welcome a visit from an old friend, would you not agree, dear Catherine?"

Manners forbade her initial response. She merely replied in the affirmative.

"Oh, good. Then I wish you good night."

This was said with a complacent smile, one that left Aunt Drusilla agitated. "I do wish you could have staved her off with an excuse. That type of woman insinuates herself into people's lives and then there is no getting rid of her. Next she'll be expecting an invitation to tea!"

Catherine said nothing. There was nothing to say, as she strongly suspected her aunt to be right. Coupled with this was a misgiving equally strong: that her time in Bath would be tainted the longer Lady Milton was around.

■ ■ ■ ■

Aunt Drusilla was sadly not mistaken. Lady Milton's threatened visit the next day somehow transmogrified into a dinner invitation, which, issued as it was by Mama, neither of them could prevent. The following evening's meal was not even leavened by the presence of the general, as Lady Milton's murmurs had snaked into Mama's misgivings, resulting in her declaration to not wish her daughter to have anything to do with "that man" until further notice.

Her aunt's objections were fierce, but Mama was adamant, leaving Catherine upset, and more determined than ever to not sit meekly by when Lady Milton made her outrageous comments, as she inevitably would.

Perry joined them, his absence at yesterday's visit due, so his mother had said, to her sudden need to secure the services of a Doctor Janus. Of course, her lack of immediate need — evidenced by her sitting placidly in Aunt Drusilla's drawing room — lent doubt to such assertions, only furthering suspicions that Perry's absence was merely a device to inveigle a return visit, during which the oh-so-helpful son would be produced.

Why such measures were necessary remained a mystery, until halfway through the meal, during the second course, when the beeswax candles had lowered an inch.

Catherine turned to Perry, seated on her right. "So, tell me how you have been these past months. I have rarely seen you since the Hawkesbury dinner."

"Perry has been most assiduous in his duties to the good people of St. Hampton Heath."

"Your duties?" Catherine asked.

"I assist Father with some village concerns."

When his talk on what such duties involved shifted to plans concerning his father's farm, and more particularly, breeds of cows, she nodded, returning her attention to the roasted capon. Aunt Drusilla might not always appreciate her guests, but she did know how to set a fine table.

"And the lodge, of course."

She glanced up. He was still talking to her? "I beg your pardon?"

"He said he means to soon move to Ivy Lodge," Lady Milton enunciated loudly, as though she might be talking to a deaf person.

Catherine glanced at her aunt amidst a

horrible suspicion. Aunt Drusilla's horrified expression suggested she shared similar distrust. Surely he wasn't . . .

Perry intoned something about doing her a great honor. "For when I marry —"

"Lady Milton, may I enquire about your daughter's youngest child?"

Desperation indeed, from her aunt whose loathing of Lady Milton's constant references to her daughter had led her to issue an edict to never introduce Sophia into conversation. "For that woman introduces her too often as it is."

Lady Milton, either oblivious to her son's precipitous advances or simply pleased at such interest in her beloved Sophia, proceeded to list dear little Lucien's various accomplishments, including — marvel of marvels — talking, at the age of seven months!

"I was not aware such prodigies existed in your family."

"Well, to be sure, the babe sounds more like a mewling kitten most of the time, but I declare, when he sees me, the first thing he does is cry 'Mam-mam.' "

"I'm sure many small children would cry for their mothers given such cause," murmured her aunt.

"He is *such* a delightful child, although

dear Sophia can find him a trial. He can be a handful, squalling from dawn 'til dusk. Fortunately, she has a bevy of nursemaids to assist her."

"How beneficial for her," Catherine said.

Lady Milton peered at her. "Well, yes. But then, she was lucky to have married so young, to *such* a handsome, well-connected young man. Some young ladies are so very fortunate," she said complacently.

The unspoken implication was that some were not. Catherine exhaled. "Lavinia is very blessed, isn't she?"

Her aunt's lips twitched.

Mama nodded. "Yes, indeed."

Lady Milton frowned. "*Dear* Catherine, I thought you seemed a little out of sorts the other night. I'd wondered if it was certain colors that did not become you, when I see it has been ill health all this time. I would have thought Bath had improved your looks by now."

"It is sad, is it not, Lady Milton, how some of us are so frequently doomed for disappointment?" Catherine smiled sweetly.

The older lady's brow creased.

The servants cleared the table for the next course. When that was set and they left, Catherine turned to Perry. "Now, enough about Sophia. How are your younger sisters?"

"But Sophy —" began Lady Milton.

"Perry? Your younger sisters?" Catherine said determinedly.

He glanced at her, then at his mother, his mouth opening then closing like a fish.

"Sophia —"

"I am not asking about Sophia, ma'am, but her sisters."

"Catherine," her mother interrupted. "I understood Sophia to be one of your closest friends. Surely you are interested in hearing more?"

"Mama, once upon a time I too thought Sophia one of my closest friends, but she has made little effort to keep in touch since her marriage, apart from one short note following Papa's passing."

"She has been very busy with her children —"

"For whom she has a bevy of nursemaids." Catherine's brows rose as she studied Lady Milton. "I wonder, how many times has she visited you in the past year?"

"Hmm. Three, no, four times, is it Perry?"

"At least," he agreed.

"And not once has she deigned to visit Mama and me. Not once."

"That *is* true," Mama murmured.

Lady Milton's chins rose. "I do not understand where this bitterness is coming from, Catherine."

"Do you not?" Aunt Drusilla murmured, gimlet-eyed.

"It is not bitterness, Lady Milton, simply honesty." Catherine continued, "It is hard to hold much interest in Sophia's affairs, especially when we do not seem to be of interest to her. I suspect it is a truth better left unsaid, but I do not wish to be inflicted for the rest of my days with information about someone who has made their indifference to our own affairs so plain."

"Well! You've certainly inherited your family's shrewish tongue."

"Perhaps."

"Or perhaps she's simply tired of listening to your gossipy, interfering one."

"Drusilla!"

Catherine's aunt placed her napkin on the table. "I do not know your antecedents, *Lady* Milton, but I have scarcely seen such a display of poor manners in all my years."

"Yes, well, your niece —"

"Has been insulted, and badgered, and lectured by you, *you,* a puffed-up nobody from goodness knows where —"

Gasps echoed around the table.

"Who wheedled her way into my house,

299

then proceeded to carry on boring the table with the unexciting exploits of her decidedly non-prodigious child, before having the temerity to accuse my niece of bitterness, when she merely speaks the truth."

Lady Milton's cheeks flushed magenta. "Such rudeness!"

"I do not invite you to visit again. I do not invite you to speak to me. In fact, I do not invite you to stay a moment longer."

Lady Milton rose, her over-full bosom heaving. "I have never been so insulted in all my life!"

"Good evening to you. Oh, and to you also, Mr. Milton."

Perry shot Catherine a look half affront and half apology, before escaping after his mother.

Aunt Drusilla sank back into her seat. "I am sorry, Elvira, if that woman truly thinks herself your friend."

"Well . . ."

"But I'd be sorrier for you if you thought she was."

Catherine chuckled. Even Mama smiled.

"Can you believe that young man? Was he really trying to make you an offer?"

A shudder ran through her. "I am so thankful you reclaimed the conversation." Catherine turned to her mother. "Mama, I know you wish to see me safely wed, but I could never abide living with that woman as my mother-in-law."

"And I could never permit you, either."

"*Such* a vulgar mushroom," said Aunt Drusilla.

The tension suddenly dropped as the room filled with quiet laughter.

"Come. I believe it is time for us to retire for the evening."

Catherine smiled to herself as she climbed the stairs to her bedchamber. Well there might be consequences to suffer tomorrow, but tonight she would enjoy her small victory for all its worth.

Meekness might be a virtue, but neither did it mean permitting oneself to be trampled upon.

A smile filled her face. She was a mouse no more.

CHAPTER EIGHTEEN

The consequences for such free and honest speaking quickly became apparent. By the end of the following day, two of Mama's anticipated visitors, a Mrs. Baxter and a Lady Hindmarsh, had sent notes of apology to say they were unexpectedly detained. By the end of the next day, they had had a harried visit from Lord Hawkesbury's cousin, Miss Pettigrew, who had informed them both of the substance of the gossip — that the general was angling for Miss Winthrop — and its source. By the end of the week, Catherine's visits to the Pump Room had seen such an increase in blatant speculation that it was nearly impossible to look anywhere without seeing an averted face or hearing her name whispered behind fluttering fans.

Catherine writhed within, yet — heeding a grim Aunt Drusilla's advice and the flustered instructions of her mother —

willed herself to smile, nod, and curtsy as society demanded.

The general, of course, thought it all a good joke, as evidenced by his unexpected arrival late on Saturday afternoon just when the ladies were about to dress for dinner. Instead of moving upstairs, they remained in the drawing room to hear the general recount stories from his week.

"And the old biddy barreled up to me and had the nerve to ask if it was true! I told her young Catherine was a bit young even for my tastes and still she tut-tutted!"

"Oh, what are we to do?" Mama moaned.

"What is there to do? Rumors cannot be quashed until truth is revealed, but people much prefer lies to the truth."

"Thank you, Drusilla, but I cannot think philosophy will help Catherine's reputation."

"I don't know why you are so concerned, Mama. It is not as though there are any real prospects here for us to be concerned about my reputation."

"She's right, Elvira," said the general, whose familiarity of address gave Mama no shortage of complaint when he was out of earshot. "Bath has a shocking lack of truly eligible gentlemen for my young friend this year. I don't know what the world is coming to."

"Unless of course one was to count Mr. Milton as an eligible?" suggested Aunt Drusilla.

"I believe he no longer labors under any such misapprehension," Catherine murmured, yesterday's events rising to mind.

He had met her yesterday morning whilst she was returning a book at the library. Her first thought had been to snub him, before the words from her morning devotional came to mind. So she'd turned the other cheek, permitted him to escort her to a quiet corner of a nearby park, and allowed him to assert his apologies for his mother's behavior, whilst she wondered how he could turn his neck, given the high points of his neckcloth were so stiff and starched.

"Must you stare at a fellow so?" He tugged at his cuffs. "I feel so wretched already."

"I cannot be responsible for the guilt you feel. But tell me, have you spoken to your mother about her wicked lies?"

"I . . . er . . ."

"I take it that's a no. Then I suppose you cannot have felt so terribly bad, after all."

"But —"

"I am sorry, Perry. Sorry for this situation

that escalated out of all proportion, merely from a kind elderly man taking pity on a poor fatherless girl. But I am sorrier for you."

He flushed. "That is a fine way to speak to someone who had wished to do you a great honor!"

"The great honor of becoming your wife?" His head jerked in a nod.

Her heart panged in sympathy. Poor Perry. Had he really thought she would be grateful? "I understand your desire to wed, especially after poor Amelia's passing, but I am sorry Perry, the only thing I will bestow upon you is my failure to accept your proposal. It was very well expressed, you understand, and I am fully cognizant to the fact it must have taken a great deal of effort to con such sweet sayings, but I feel it would be doing us both a great disservice to accept a man I cannot love."

"You cannot?" He seemed shocked at the notion.

"A man who does not, I think, love me."

He flushed. "Oh, but . . . but I do think you rather pretty."

"And yet marriage requires rather more than admiration of appearance, would you not agree? Come, Perry." She smiled gently. "Can you really think your mother would approve?"

His brow knit, as if considering this for the first time.

"Will you be friends with me?" She held out her hand. "For old times' sake?"

He grasped her hand reluctantly. "Very well."

"And perhaps escort me on my way home?"

"Of course," he muttered.

Their way home had necessitated a slow parade through the main streets, as Catherine "remembered" several items she needed to purchase. The advantages of such an exercise were twofold: firstly, to show that the general was not the only man willing to escort her around town; and secondly, that if people saw Peregrine Milton accompanying Catherine they might wonder at Lady Milton's claims and suspect them as the wicked slander they were.

Of course — her lips twisted as the drawing room's conversation swirled around her — she had not thought the consequences of such a promenade through to its entirety, as she'd learned just this morning that the Pump Room gossips now described her as fast. Fast? She smothered a wry chuckle. Perhaps once upon a dream. If only people truly knew how far from the truth that description held now.

"This is no smiling matter, Catherine!"

"Of course not, Mama. But I cannot see what is to be done. And I'm tired of acting like I should be ashamed of something, when we all know I am innocent."

"But —" Mama glanced nervously at the general.

"Yes, yes. I know what you were about to say, my good woman. Perhaps my attentions did appear a trifle marked. But I agree with your good daughter here. I have done nothing wrong, and I refuse to apologize for preferring her youth and humor to those hen-witted scarecrows people think I should prefer."

Mama's face crumpled. "Oh, what are we to do?"

"Now, now, Elvira." The general patted her on the shoulder. "Let us have a bite to eat then we can think some more."

"Are you dangling for an invitation for dinner, General Whitby?" asked Aunt Drusilla.

"Not dangling. Asking plainly."

Catherine chuckled.

"Oh, how can you laugh at a time like this?" Mama moaned.

"Because, Mama, words are but noise carried away on the wind."

"Hmph!"

They had to be. Gossip couldn't really hurt her. Could it?

Catherine's fine ideals about the power — or lack thereof — of words were sorely put to the test the following day at services. For despite the hymns and message on forgiveness, despite the gracious prayers and time shared in Holy Communion, still people eyed her askance as she returned from the Communion rail to her aunt's pew. And later, as the congregation gathered in the square to chat outside the church's huge wooden doors, she could not help but notice the friendly smiles of a week ago were no longer being returned. Instead the ladies looked through her, without acknowledgment, as though she was not even standing there, their snubs as cutting as a whip.

She forced herself to smile past the sting. To breathe in. Exhale. Pray. *Lord, give me wisdom. And grace. And vindication . . .*

As Mama and Aunt Drusilla spoke with some ladies, their brittle smiles doubtless designed to show their lack of concern for the insinuations whirling around Catherine, she noticed another lady standing nearby, a Mrs. Plume whom she'd met whilst visiting Serena at Miss Haverstock's seminary.

"Good day, Mrs. Plume." Catherine smiled her most winning smile. "How is your daughter? Is she enjoying her studies?"

"Oh, er, yes, I believe so."

"Our Serena writes to say how much she is enjoying learning art. We never had much opportunity to learn whilst growing up."

"Oh. I, er, believe the art master is considered to be quite handsome."

"I wouldn't know." Her stomach tensed; was this turn in the conversation veering into insinuation? She would *not* allow Serena's name to come into question. "Haverstock's is a fine institution, would you not agree? Which subject does" — she thought desperately to remember the daughter's name — "Victoria prefer?"

"I couldn't say."

The sun, weak though it was, pushed through the clouds to highlight the cross poking from her Bible.

"That is a lovely piece," Mrs. Plume said, motioning to the bookmark.

"Thank you. It was a gift."

"From the general?"

The words slammed into Catherine's hard-won peace. She stifled a gasp, feeling as though she'd been forced to run the curved length of the Royal Crescent and back. She drew in a deep breath. "Actually, it was a gift from the Countess of Hawkesbury."

"Oh!" The woman blinked. Stepped back. Looked around.

"Yes, Lavinia is a dear friend of mine," Catherine persisted. "She and the earl have often dined with us." Back when Papa was alive, but still . . .

"Oh. I didn't know."

"I imagine most people don't, but then, we don't like to advertise our connections with such eminent members of the Peerage." In a move Perry would have approved of, Catherine flicked an imaginary speck off her spencer.

"No. No, of course not."

"It would be considered vulgar, would you not agree?"

"Yes." The woman glanced away.

"I often find there is a great deal too many idle tongues at work in small towns. People say the most outlandish things, without having any true knowledge of the facts."

"Y-yes." Mrs. Plume's desperate gaze had secured the approach of a Mrs. Lampscombe, whose severe bearing belied the fact she was oft considered the most malicious gossipmonger in all Bath.

After an exchange of nods, Catherine smiled. "Mrs. Lampscombe, I was just telling Mrs. Plume about my dear friend Lavinia's marvelous stitchery." She pulled the bookmark free, held it up to the light. "Would you not agree?"

Mrs. Lampscombe eyed it before giving it a dismissive "Hmph."

"Lavinia, the Countess of Hawkesbury." The lady's eyes widened, Catherine noted with satisfaction. "I'm humbled that someone so grand would take time to stitch such a wonderful token of affection."

"It is a very fine piece," Mrs. Lampscombe said, now deigning to admire it properly. "She must be quite young, if she is your friend."

"We are of similar years, but I am not exclusive about the age of my friends. I believe it is important to show respect to and be friendly with all people. Even those old enough to be my grandfather," Catherine added daringly.

"So I have heard." Her look was disapproving. "I cannot imagine what a young person would have in common with such a man as General Whitby."

"With such a hero? To be sure I possess little of the heroic, but what he enjoys is something you could ask of him yourself."

Her eyes flashed. "Young woman —"

"Do you think me so young?" Catherine

asked. "I am nearly six-and-twenty. I'm sure most people would think that quite ancient." She leaned closer. "In fact, I believe some think I am at my last prayers."

"Whether you are at your last prayers or not does not interest me in the slightest."

"Then may I suggest you do not act as though you do?" Aunt Drusilla moved beside Catherine, her voice acerbic. "Gossipers do the devil's work."

Mrs. Lampscombe's brows lowered, her mouth opening to reveal pointed teeth.

Catherine's mind flicked to the verse about abundant life, the first part of which stated the devil came to steal, to lie, and to destroy. How true this proved of gossip.

"My niece is owed an apology," Aunt Drusilla continued. "I trust if you would prefer not to have all *your* indiscretions bandied about as common fodder, then you'll keep your tongue under control."

Mrs. Lampscombe blanched, stepped back, bowed stiffly, and walked away.

"Come." Aunt Drusilla grasped Catherine's hand. "Your mother cannot bear to be outside a moment longer."

At luncheon, Catherine's adrenaline at her battle had drained away, leaving her feeling flat and dispirited, as though this was the biggest blunder of her life. And she had brought Lavinia's name into things? The *earl's*? What would happen when they discovered this?

Mama's distress could not be hidden. "Mrs. Lampscombe is a person of influence!"

"Is that not what we are?" Aunt Drusilla's eyes flashed. "I must admit to a great deal of resentment that one woman's vicious tongue can sway opinion so quickly. How dare people attend to such a mushroom?"

The image ignited a brief smile.

But the weight of innuendo soon snuffed it out, and it was only by rereading David's trials in the Psalms that Catherine was able to sleep that night with any degree of peace.

Winthrop Manor

The guttural sound ricocheted round the drawing room.

"Julia! How many times have I told you? Please try to cough more discreetly."

"But Mother, sometimes one's cough cannot be contained."

"Be that as it may, you would be well served to learn to withhold it as a proper young lady should do."

"Does the same hold true for sneezes?"

Jonathan peered across his newspaper and met the amusement in Julia's eyes.

"Julia . . ."

"No, really, I want to know. For last night when we were dining with the Hawkesburys, I distinctly heard the countess sneeze. She was not at all embarrassed."

"But she is a countess, and need not worry what others think."

"But, Mama, why should we? She wasn't always a countess. She must have sneezed prior to marrying the earl."

Jon caught his mother's stony glare. He lowered his paper. "Julia, perhaps it would be better to forgo arguing the finer points of etiquette. I cannot think you will win."

"But I don't —"

"I believe complaining is not considered socially acceptable, either."

"Hmph!" Julia shot him a scathing look and a muttered "traitor" before flouncing out.

"And neither would stomping."

His mother's frosty gaze remained fixed on him, compelling Jon to pick up the newspaper.

Well he knew her concerns about etiquette, seeing as they stemmed from his refusal to act in the matter of Miss Beauchamp.

A twinge crossed his chest. Yes, he knew his own behavior to be rather less than what could be considered socially correct. He had led her on, so the gossips said. He'd overheard mutters in the club: as flighty as that mother of his. Even Julia's name was bandied about, linked in some ridiculous way to some military gentleman she'd danced with too many times at a recent ball. All in all it had hastened his decision to return to the wilds of Gloucestershire, where such rumors and innuendo did not exist or matter.

Except his worries chased him even here. What could he do? He could not, in all good conscience, continue to dance attendance upon a young miss of which he was not sure. But how was he to become sure?

His chest constricted again. He'd once been sure of a lady, but had so thoroughly misjudged the situation he could not help but be extra cautious now. He'd even hinted of his dilemma to Hawkesbury yesterday, as they'd shared a moment's quiet over port, but the earl could offer nothing more than ask what God wanted.

And that was where he stayed. He stared at the page blankly. God remained silent. His confusion thundered on.

"I gather from the fact that you have not turned a page in almost ten minutes, that either there is an article of immense value and worth, or you are wool-gathering."

He folded the paper, placed it on the table, and eyed his mother. "Was there something you wished to say?"

A tight look crossed her features. She exhaled. "I am concerned about Julia."

"Yes?"

"She has become quite obstreperous of late, and I cannot like it."

"Julia has not been herself."

"No. She doesn't mind me, but that's to be expected somewhat. But when she doesn't mind you . . ."

He nodded slowly. It had grieved him for Julia to ignore him lately, to lose his status of beloved big brother, the one she'd always turned to, especially after the passing of their father. But then Julia wasn't the girl she'd been when that happened six years ago.

"She is becoming a young lady," he began, "and —"

"She *should* be, but these hoydenish tendencies greatly concern me."

"Perhaps it is just a stage."

She shook her head. "I am not so terribly strict, am I? I have been, perhaps, even more liberal than some. I cannot think I have completely unrealistic expectations?"

His amusement at her "liberal" comment

died under the bite of remorse. It was so rare to see his mother stripped of her customary confidence. He moved beside her, grasped her hand. "Mother, you have been a rock."

Her eyes shimmered.

"A shining, extremely modish rock" — he squeezed her hand as she smiled — "but a rock nonetheless. You cannot hold yourself responsible for Julia's behavior all her life."

"But she is so young, so unaware of how easily a woman's reputation can be damaged."

He hid the grimace. That had been exactly the concern behind his recent plain speaking with his sister, as he'd warned her of just what her fast ways could lead to. How men like Hale could take advantage. And even if a man was innocent, he knew, only too well, how an innocent girl's ardor could kindle passion that could never truly be doused. His spirits sank. Was it his idealistic expectations that had turned Julia's heart away?

"I will speak with her again." His words sounded hollow in his ears.

"Would you?"

His mother's face, so pleading, sent another shaft of regret through his heart. "Of course." And he would continue to pray.

"I cannot feel that without companions she is acting more from boredom than anything else." She sighed. "But London was too full of distractions, and people I do not think appropriate for her well-being, I thought it best perhaps to remove her."

"And where do you think she might be better suited?"

He felt a prickling sensation as soon as he said it, and knew just what her answer would be.

"It was the cough that decided me." She smiled, an echo of her usual brilliance, yet her eyes remained watchful. "I think we should go to Bath."

CHAPTER NINETEEN

"Good morning, Miss."

"Good morning."

Bess drew open the curtains, tied them back with twin sashes of gold silk. "Looks to be another rainy day, I'm afraid."

"Thank God we don't have more snow."

The maid nodded politely and moved to kindle the fire.

Catherine drew the blanket closer. There was much to be thankful for, even if one had to be shut up due to inclement weather. Aunt Drusilla's house did not leak, nor was it drafty. And the servants here were so well versed in ensuring guests had their morning hot chocolate and had comfortable rooms that one could almost spend the entire day in bed, should one be so luxuriantly idly inclined.

"I believe the letters have arrived. Dobson said the mail coach was delayed due to yesterday's storm washing out a bridge. I will go and see if there be any for you."

"Thank you, Bess."

Another blessing was that Mama was no longer in any position to see, let alone open and read, Catherine's mail. Which was probably extremely fortunate, considering her recent correspondence.

She shifted up against the pillows, pulled her Bible close, and read through several psalms. These ancient songs had proved a lifeline this past week, the promises ones she had clung to amidst the storm of speculation that continued to rage. Her words to Mrs. Lampscombe and those of Aunt Drusilla had only ignited a fresh crisis. Little had they known she was Lady Milton's cousin by marriage, and the accusations had been carried back, causing a fresh wave of lies. This time, taking aim at her father. Lies — ridiculous lies — about his so-called gambling!

Such accusations were so patently untrue that the inhabitants of Six Gay Street had scarcely given it a second thought. But she wondered to what extent this would spread, and just what might be necessary to douse the speculation once and for all. Perhaps, as Aunt Drusilla hoped, Bath might soon feast on some other poor unfortunate's new scandal. Perhaps, as Catherine prayed, this recent spell of rain would keep the gossip-mongers away from each other.

"Excuse me, miss? A letter for you."

"Thank you."

She closed the Bible and placed it back on her bedside table. Saw the franked envelope, the direction, and opened it, her pulse loud in her ears. Had she been forgiven?

Dear Catherine,

To say your letter was a surprise is something of an understatement, seeing as I had only received one the day before, but upon reading it I completely understood. I cannot conceive how such a person as LM deigns to be so bitter. I shared my concern with Nicholas, and neither he nor I mind your claiming friendship; indeed I'm of a mind to pay you a visit, just to lay any concerns to rest, but N urges me to wait until these dreadful rains cease. But I encourage you, dear friend, to use my name and all that is associated with it as much as necessary to your best advantage. Surely those with such toplofty notions will find what they seek if you do so. As for me, I will be very happy to know any status gained upon marrying N will be well used.

Catherine sighed. God bless her friend, and the earl. A smile flitted across her face. How she longed to see the faces of the scandal-mongers when the crested carriage appeared — but only if it meant no distress for Lavinia. She resumed reading.

I trust and pray these trials are not weighing you down, but propelling you into faith and God's Word. These verses were quickened to me recently as I was reading Second Corinthians, and I thought of you, "We are troubled on every side, yet not distressed; we are perplexed, but not in despair; persecuted, but not forsaken; cast down, but not destroyed . . . For our light affliction, which is but for a moment, worketh for us a far more exceeding and eternal weight of glory." So I implore you to think on good things and be of good cheer. I hope you will be encouraged as I.

Catherine blinked away the moisture. Picked up her Bible, ruffling through the pages until she found the verse, read it, and read it once more. Her heart quickened; the hurt eased as hope renewed. God *was* using Catherine's trials for His purpose. She just needed to trust Him.

She marked the position with the stitched cross and picked up the letter again.

In other news, baby Grace has recently started to smile, revealing herself the proud possessor of two dimples, which N believes she owes to me, whilst I am equally positive he is responsible, as I have tried to show in the foolish little sketch I have enclosed.

Catherine pulled out the underlying paper, and her heart caught. A watercolor of a smiling baby with rosy cheeks. Oh, to have such sweetness in one's life. She swallowed the stab of envy. Lavinia deserved to be so blessed.

The letter continued.

We live in constant expectation of hearing that Winthrop is to have a new mistress, but as yet this is not the case.

Her heart stabbed again. Think on good things. Think on good things!

We are to have dinner with LH and LW on Saturday, before they depart.

Depart where? Her mouth dried. What if he returned to India? What if she never saw him again? Had Lavinia explained further?

We hope to also see J, but she does not always attend, and there are rumors she's grown a little wild. Of course, this does not trouble me greatly, as we know such things often stem from misunderstanding, and we both know a certain young lady who was also described in such a way. Nevertheless, I am sure LH and LW would appreciate your prayers, as no doubt would the young lady in question.

I remain, yours affectionately,
Lavinia Hawkesbury

Catherine drew in a deep breath. So much to digest; so much requiring reply.

She slipped from the bed, moved to the small table and chair, pulled out her writing paper, goose quill, and inkpot. After sharpening the nib she began to write:

Dear Lavinia,
I cannot begin to tell you of my great relief . . .

■ ■ ■ ■

London Road

"But I still don't understand. Why do we have to go to Bath?"

Jonathan drew breath and slowly exhaled, counting to ten. Ever since his mother had broached the idea Julia had transformed from mildly obstreperous to openly hostile. The carriage ride from Winthrop had been painful, his mother's efforts at placation as ineffective as his own. The more miles they traveled the more he felt his patience pulling thinner, like a string about to snap.

He glanced outside. Heavy skies brooded. The road carved into the hillside seemed more akin to a sloppy goat track, the recent rain responsible for the landslips that had delayed their journey thus far. Another movement of mud and earth now blocked the road, waiting for the grooms to clear the debris away, forcing him and his mother to dig even deeper for patience as Julia's lack thereof was on full display.

"I wish we were there."

He chuckled, relief at Julia's contradictory words making his laughter louder than usual. "I thought you did not want to go."

She shrugged. "Anything must be better

than this old and creaky coach."

Jon opened his mouth to respond when he caught his mother's glance. He settled back into his seat. At the next change of horses, he would make sure to exchange his seat inside for his saddle. He did not care how wet or dirty he'd become.

The house they rented was in Upper Camden Place, one of Bath's best addresses. A new house, three stories of golden Bath stone, it possessed the gracious perfect proportions of the town houses on either side, as well as a magnificent view across Hedgemead Park and the River Avon to Sydney Gardens and beyond. The interior held a grandeur that subtly hinted of his wealth without screaming vulgarity as some overdressed places were wont to do, so his mother said. She was well pleased with their situation, but Julia . . .

Jon looked across the drawing room to where his sister stared out the window, her mouth a sullen line. He would not stay for the entire duration of weeks his mother believed necessary for Julia's improved health — his business meetings in London and his work at Avebury and Winthrop still demanded attention — but he did not like his sister's brooding nature. She was too like him, he realized with a pang, too quick to hold on to things best left forgotten.

"I wonder if we'll see anyone we know," Mother said, with not a little desperation lining her voice. Jon mentally reviewed his list of acquaintances.

"I doubt it," Julia said. "Bath seems full of old biddies."

"But your friend is here," Mother replied, casting him a quick glance before fixing her attention on Julia, whose face had lit. "Remember? Lady Winthrop is here with Catherine."

His heart snagged.

Julia shrugged, her expression reverting to dejected defeat. "I doubt she'll be very amusing."

"Well, we won't know unless we see her." Mother's bright voice had dulled. She cast Jon a look that could be described as pleading.

"Julia, perhaps you could decide to think of others for a change? I understand you have not been well —"

"You don't understand anything!"

"Poppet" — he gritted out the pet name — "please try to remember we are trying to help you."

"I don't want your help. I just want to be with — oh!"

She turned and rushed from the room.

"Leave her," he murmured, as his mother moved to follow. "Give her time to calm down."

"Oh, Jon, have we done the right thing in coming here?" Her green eyes held the sheen of tears.

He squeezed her hand. "Let's pray so."

And she too left the room, leaving him feeling the renewed strain of what Bath might bring. His heart flickered. And not just in regards to managing Julia.

CHAPTER TWENTY

"My dear, I cannot tell you how glad I am your mother has consented to our little promenades again."

Catherine smiled, drawing closer to the general as one of the many people strolling through the Pump Room veered into her path. "It took not a small amount of cajolery on the part of Aunt Drusilla, I assure you."

"Well, I am thankful that sweet-talking has returned an old man his pleasure."

A gasp came behind them. She almost stumbled. Felt his hand cover hers. "Steady, Miss Winthrop, steady."

She nodded, lifting her chin a little higher, her smile tight as she walked arm in arm with the general and encountered the eyes that widened, the eyes that slid away. She was not responsible for other people's foolishness and sordid thinking. But how could people seriously consider she would marry anyone the age of the general? Did she truly appear so desperate?

A spurt of hysteria-laden laughter pushed past her shame. Poor Mama, who had spent her life always worrying over her eldest daughter. Only now had she truly something to worry about.

"I am glad to see the return of your sense of humor."

"It has been under heavy fire of late."

He chuckled. "But we do not surrender, do we, my girl?"

"No." Even if Mama's reservations about today's visit to the Pump Room had sadly proved correct. She glanced about at the well-dressed perambulators. Today she had nothing of which to be dismayed concerning her attire, her lilac silk with cream lace, an early birthday gift from Aunt Drusilla, sent from the mantua-maker only yesterday.

The general sighed. "I wish your dear mother would consent to another excursion. Perhaps you have heard of the Wakefield's ball?"

"I have heard of it." Envy streaked hot within. If only she could go . . .

"It is to be a masquerade. I so wish you could attend, but I suppose it is a stretch too far even for you."

"I believe so."

"Such a pity. Oh, well. I suppose I shall

have to find another pretty girl to dance with."

"And cause my reputation to be utterly lost? For shame! Would you have everyone say 'there goes poor Miss Winthrop, whose only conquest has quite given her up for younger, fresher fare'?"

He laughed. "You do yourself a great disservice, young lady. I cannot believe you think me your only conquest."

"Well, there is Perry, I suppose."

His great booming chuckle reverberated around the room, drawing eyes their way again. "But seriously, my dear. Has no other young man caught your eye?"

An image wavered, was smothered. "No."

"No? Your hesitation tells me otherwise." He smiled. "Now I know you do not speak truthfully."

The next minute was filled with teasing enquiry, so that she was very glad when a figure drew near and bowed. "Major Hale!"

"Miss Winthrop, General. How do you do?"

There was an exchange of pleasantries, then the general gave a broad wink. "I wonder if you, sir, might be the answer to my young friend's blushes."

Catherine fought to keep the frown from her brow. "The major and I are but acquaintances, sir." She turned to the younger man. "Forgive me, but we did not expect to see you in Bath again so soon."

"I . . . er, have reason to believe a . . . close friend of mine shall soon be in town."

She studied him, wondering at the flush darkening his cheeks, the way his eyes had brightened before becoming hooded, the way he deftly veered the conversation to some innocuous topic before offering his apologies and a bow and then departing.

Further contemplation of his odd behavior was cut short as the general's musings about possible suitors resumed, until she soon, most gratefully, returned to the company of her aunt and mother.

"Bath is so boring."

His mother closed her eyes. "Julia, we've only been here a day."

"And it's raining."

"Bath cannot be answerable for its weather, poppet."

Julia made a face at him. "I suppose we can blame God for that." She returned to her lookout by the window. "Oh, there is a coach!"

"Good heavens. Who on earth can that be?" Mother complained. "I cannot understand those who think it necessary to call uninvited, especially under such abysmal conditions."

"Oh. It is only Lady Milton. I don't like her very much. She always looks as though she smells something bad."

"Not everyone is so fortunate to have your sweet countenance, poppet."

Julia rolled her eyes at Jon and he grinned back, pleased as a reluctant smile crossed her lips. "I suppose I'll have to talk to her son as well."

"He is here, too?"

"Yes. He could quite possibly be the most boring man alive, even more boring than you, brother dear."

"Thank you," he said drily.

Her smile glimmered and was gone, her face settling into petulant lines again. "He never has a word to say that isn't about himself or his possessions. At least you don't do that."

"I'm glad to see my stock is rising."

"I never understand why he must talk of cows. Cows! I ask you!"

A knock prefaced the footman's entry. "My lord, ladies, Lady and Mr. Milton are here."

Jonathan nodded, caught his sister's look of disgust, and his mother's grimace. The door opened again, admitting a pungent cloud of something that smelled like stale roses and self-consequence.

Lady Milton stretched out her hands, for all intents and purposes as though she and Mother were long-lost sisters. "Dear Lady Harkness. How *good* of you to see us."

Mother stepped back from the light embrace, her features cool as she gestured to the hard-backed sofa. "We usually prefer our visitors to give some advance notice."

"Oh, but we are such close neighbors, I felt sure you would not want to deny me."

Julia made a noise, halfway between a snort and a chuckle.

Lady Milton turned to her, her smile dimming a little. "And *dear* Julia. How are you?"

"Very well, thank you."

"Julia is here for her cough," Mother's voice was icy.

"Quite so, quite so. Well, Bath is the place to be if one wishes to improve."

"Really?" murmured Julia, glancing between Lady Milton and her son. "I wonder how long it takes before one can expect to see improvement."

"Mr. Milton," said Jon, casting a stern look at his sister, "I wonder if you would be so kind as to oblige us in a little matter."

Mr. Milton glanced at Julia, his face

334

brightening. "Anything, anything at all."

"We were wondering just what attractions one might recommend to visitors new in town."

"Oh!" For a moment he looked taken aback, but soon began to list various entertainments, concerts, balls, and masquerades — this last said with a hopeful glance at Julia.

"That sounds good, does it not, Julia?" Jon's glance at his sister revealed a light in her blue eyes, light that shuttered when she noticed his gaze. She tilted her chin, and turned toward their younger guest.

"And how are your cows, Perry?" Julia asked solemnly.

The young man flushed. "I . . . er . . ."

"Really, I am most anxious to know." This was said with her hands clasped, eyelashes fluttering.

Jon's eyes narrowed. What game was she playing at now?

Perry's cheeks darkened to beetroot. "I am most gratified by your interest, Miss Carlew."

Judging from the look on Lady Milton's face, gratification was not what that lady was feeling, her confusion expressed a moment later.

"Oh, but Lady Milton, I was sure you'd

recall my fascination with bovine creatures. After all, you did just say we are close neighbors, did you not?"

"Julia," murmured Mother, before saying in a louder voice, "speaking of neighbors, I wonder, Lady Milton, if you might be so good as to tell us if you have seen Lady Winthrop recently. I wondered how she might be getting on."

The flash in Lady Milton's eyes rather undercut the noncommittal answer offered.

"And how is Catherine? Have you seen her of late?" Julia enquired.

"I beg your pardon?"

"Have . . . you . . . seen . . . her?" Julia spoke deliberately, as if speaking to a slowtop.

"Miss Julia, if I might be permitted to say, you do not seem at all well."

"*Moi?*" Julia placed a hand on her chest. "I am perfectly well, thank you, Lady Milton. I'm simply interested to learn whether dear Catherine finds Bath to be a place of improvement also."

A curious expression crossed their visitor's face. It was like that of a greedy child who had just stolen a sweet, like she knew something they did not. "Oh, yes. I would say Bath agrees with *that* young lady most considerably."

Mother frowned. "I'm afraid I do not take your meaning."

Lady Milton glanced from one to another, her smile swelling. "You have not been here long enough to hear the news."

"What news is that?"

"Miss Winthrop. After all this time she's finally found herself a fancy man."

His fingers curled on his knee. "A what?"

"She is engaged."

What? No . . .

"Mama, that is not —" Perry began.

"Well, perhaps not *quite* engaged, but the talk all over town is of her and her soldier."

His breath caught. Not — ?

"Catherine?" Julia quickly glanced at him then back to Lady Milton. "Well good for her."

"I beg your pardon?"

Julia lifted a shoulder. "I'm happy if she is happy. I should not want to see *all* young ladies made miserable." This was said with a scowl at their mother that their unwanted guest could not fail to notice.

"Have I come at a bad time?" Lady Milton glanced from one to another, eyes bulging with interest.

"Mother, perhaps we should leave," Perry said.

"Perhaps you should," muttered Julia *sotto voce.*

Jon rose, forced his lips up in what he hoped passed for a smile. "Thank you for coming, Lady Milton, Mr. Milton."

With a final significant look at her son that forced him to rise, Lady Milton creaked to her feet before they offered goodbyes that were returned only by himself, and the door was closed.

"Julia! I have never been so embarrassed!"

"You, Mother?" The look was insolence itself. "I only said the things we all wanted to."

"But that woman is a busybody, someone whose tongue is hung in the middle. You cannot act like that and expect her not to mention it all over town!"

"Like she spoke about poor Catherine?"

Something twinged in his chest. He swallowed. "I cannot think everything she says is true."

"No? You don't think Catherine has a military suitor? I'd like to know why she's allowed to be courted by such a man when I'm not." Julia's raised brows lowered to an expression more agitated. "I really hope the soldier isn't —"

She bit her lip, and hurried away. His mother, after various mutterings about their recently departed guests and the foolishness of the young, left too.

Leaving him, alone in the tumble of emotion, filled with misgivings about his sister's apparent fixation with his former friend, his anger and frustration melding with a simple truth that the mere mention of her name had been enough to confirm.

This was why he had hesitated.

Chapter Twenty-One

The concert music filled her senses but still could not drown the inner turmoil. A hundred thoughts clamored for attention, increasing the tension between appropriateness and her desire.

It was wrong of her, she knew, but since the general had first mentioned the Wakefield's masquerade ball she could not help but want to go. Ladies in mourning didn't attend balls, even if there was only a few short months until attending such an event would be deemed proper again. Perhaps there was something deeper, something twisted about such a longing. It would only serve to remind her of all that could never be. To remind her of that perfect evening three years ago. For while the general was all solicitude, she wished he was much younger, and taller, and blonder.

Such foolishness! She touched a hand to her cheek. It was so hot.

"Catherine? Are you well?"

"Yes, thank you, Mama," she whispered.

Aunt Drusilla leaned forward from her position beside the general, and murmured of her concern, forcing Catherine to reassure with a smile and return her attention to the front of the room.

The music swelled importantly then dropped away, a reflection of her own emotions. One moment she felt steady and sure, her renewed confidence at the fore; the next, it was as though she remained the little brown mouse, wanting to scamper away because someone looked at her oddly or murmured something behind a fan. She knew they could not all be talking about her, but still . . .

How on earth would she cope if she had true notoriety? Even Lavinia occasionally had her name in the newspapers, yet she never paid heed. How did she *do* that? Catherine was sure she could never not care what others thought of her.

She sucked in a breath, straightened her back, her eyes fixed on the musicians. The darkness was stealing in again, threatening to dampen her hard-won poise and assurance. Tonight had necessitated a fast removal from their carriage through the assembly room to gain their seats at the concert's front row. She sat on the extreme left, away from the aisle, and from this position could see only the musicians ahead and her mother and the general on either side.

Her lips twitched. Some days it felt as though she had all the shame with none of the gain. The gossips might all think she had the general at her feet, but she could not even imagine wanting to kiss him. And if, by some remote chance, the man of her lost dreams should make an appearance, how would she be able to convince him otherwise?

The shrill soprano continued to pierce her ears. She winced. Was she coming down with something? If so, these supposed health-giving waters were not doing their job very well.

"Catherine? You seem a little flushed."

"I am —" She swallowed dryness. "I'm a little thirsty."

"Allow me," the general said, moving to get up.

"No, no. Please stay and enjoy."

"I will go with you," Aunt Drusilla muttered. "I've had about enough of all this caterwauling."

Catherine nodded, and they rose, stealing down the side of the brightly lit room, trying to avoid the sea of curious faces with open mouths and wagging tongues that marked their progress. Her cheeks flamed. She thought she heard a "Miss Winthrop" and hurried faster, glad to reach the sanctuary of the ladies withdrawing room, to feel coolness touch her skin, to drink a glass of water.

"You do not seem at all well, my dear."

"I just need a minute." She tried out a smile. "I don't think that music agrees with me."

"I don't think it agrees with many people, judging from the amount of conversation I could hear. I certainly would not want my performance ignored like that."

"It would be challenging."

Aunt Drusilla motioned to a chair. "Now, do you wish to return? Or shall I ask the attendant to take us home?"

"Oh, but Mama —"

"Would be well looked after by the general, I'm sure. So, which should it be? Home, or staying here?"

"Could we visit the Tea Room? I wonder if my lightheadedness is due to not eating very much before."

"Yes, that fillet of sole was barely fit for human consumption. I do not know what Cook was thinking."

They retreated to the Tea Room and had

a glass of lemonade and some biscuits. Her spirits had improved considerably by the time the general and Mama appeared.

"Ah, my little friend. I am pleased to see you looking so much better."

"Thank you, General. I now feel much more the thing."

"Probably that woman's singing is what did it. I don't understand these Continental women sometimes. I'd rather hear a bunch of dogs howling at the moon."

Catherine laughed. "You are not enamored of such things."

"No. I can honestly say it will never be my real love."

He smiled close to her face.

Jon stilled. Breath lodged in his throat. That . . . that *man* had just said love. What was he doing? He was old enough to be her grandfather! And what was she doing, allowing him so close to her? Unless . . .

"Well! I never would've believed it!" Julia's whisper cut through the heat of vexation spreading within. "He's got dyed hair! Oh, this is good."

Her laughter twisted his insides, making him at once defensive and aggressive. "*She* might not care about a man's looks."

"I should say that's most apparent!" She

frowned. "Wait, are you accusing me of being so shallow?"

His eyes narrowed. "Why would I do that? Which men have you been looking at?"

Her hands clenched, and she opened her mouth to speak just as Mother rustled up to them.

"Well, this is a turn up! I would never have recognized her. She looks far from the country mouse we know."

He nodded, eyeing Miss Winthrop as she smiled up at the other man. His heart clenched.

"She looks very pretty," Julia said, turning to watch them, too. "The cut of that gown is extremely flattering. Don't you think she looks attractive, Jon?"

He swallowed.

"Not everyone can wear lilac . . ."

As his sister continued her commentary, Jon's heart pounded with a dozen emotions. Envy. Desire. Shame. Regret. He kept himself still, conscious of his mother's watchfulness, conscious one word could dispel the illusion he had fostered for so long.

". . . and her hair in that style makes her seem much younger."

His mother made a noncommittal noise, her gaze sifting the room. "I think you exaggerate a trifle, but I can understand now why Lady Milton said such things, and why such an attachment might cause a stir. Miss Winthrop makes everyone else look rather faded."

"You mean old, Mother," Julia said peevishly.

"I am somewhat surprised. I would never have picked her as being interested in *that* aged a man." Mother turned, eyeing Jon with a look akin to speculation.

He willed his expression to remain neutral and kept his voice low. "I am glad he is not a man we recognize."

Her eyes widened. "Yes. Oh, I hope *that* man does not learn of our arrival and suddenly appear."

His stomach clenched. Thank God it was not Hale. For Julia's sake, for Catherine's, for his.

Julia turned from where she'd been eyeing the unknown. "What are you two whispering about?"

"Nothing."

"Whenever somebody says that and wears the same expression as you do now, I do not believe them, brother dear."

"Well, shall we go and meet the paramour?" Mother said.

"I'm not sure she wants us to. She ignored

me when I called her name before."

"You didn't expect her to stop for a chat midway through an aria, did you, Julia? Come. Enough nonsense." Bracing internally, Jon marched his family to the table, around which sat Catherine, her admirer, her mother, and the aunt whom he vaguely remembered from the funeral.

Lady Winthrop was the first to notice, her jaw sagging inelegantly. "Mr. Carlew!"

He winced. How long since anyone had called him that name? He bowed. "Lady Winthrop." He turned, met the aunt's widened stare. "Madam."

Then he turned to the third member of their party. "Miss Winthrop."

He met her gaze.

For a long, delicious moment he was transported back to a simpler time, before titles, and estates, and death had confused and conflicted his life. He'd forgotten how long her lashes were, how steady her gaze could be, how the chocolate depths of her eyes held such sweetness, and joy, and trust.

Except they didn't see him like that anymore.

He blinked. Dragged his gaze away. To the man she did — for some reason — regard.

"General Whitby," Lady Winthrop's voice seemed to come from far away, "this is Mr.

— I mean, Lord Winthrop."

They exchanged slight bows, before Jonathan recollected himself and introduced his mother and sister.

Julia offered a small curtsy, acknowledged and dismissed the older women with one look, and turned to the younger. "I thought you did not want to see us."

Catherine's brow wrinkled. "Were you at the concert?"

"I called out to you! Did you not hear me?"

"That was you?" Miss Winthrop rose, smiled. "Oh, I'm so glad!"

Surprise shot through him as she hugged his sister, light filling her face like it did in his memories. Julia's stiff posture unbent as she lightly clasped her in return.

He glanced at his mother. She wore the slightly stupefied expression he was sure was on his own face. Soon the younger two ladies were talking, chatting as he used to hear Julia converse with her friends. Something in his heart eased and gratitude towards Miss Winthrop flowed at this reappearance of the sister he loved.

"Lord Winthrop," said the aunt — a Mrs. Villiers, he recalled, "I believe congratulations are in order?"

The air seemed suddenly sucked from the

room. He glanced from face to face, knowing he doubtless looked as ridiculous as young Milton, but was unable to formulate a reply. He stole a glance at Miss Winthrop, but her face was averted, her lashes splayed across her cheek. "I . . . we . . ."

Dear God, he was worse than Milton! He could barely speak *or* look at her.

"Jonathan and Miss Beauchamp have an understanding," his mother said, before frowning at him.

Jon swallowed, wishing away the fire in his cheeks, wishing he could loosen his tight neckcloth, wishing the general had not moved to stand quite so possessively behind Miss Winthrop.

"Disgusting, I call it."

He glanced at the large lady nearby, looking over at their group. Her cold eyes met his narrowed ones, her cheeks pinking before she turned and walked over to a hovering Lady Milton.

The Winthrop ladies glanced at each other then rose with one accord. "Please excuse us, Lady Harkness. We must leave. Catherine has not been terribly well."

He studied her; her cheeks had paled, her gaze still averted. Was that why she'd exited the concert?

The aunt exchanged glances with her

sister. "We would be pleased should you condescend to visit us." She gave the direction, an address in Gay Street.

"We'd be delighted," Mother said, all graciousness, her resentment at their hurried exit from the neighborhood seemingly all forgotten.

The ladies curtsied, the general nodded, and they walked away, their passage marked by a sea of faces turning to watch their procession. More interesting was the fact that not one of them turned to acknowledge Lady Milton, despite her standing nearby. Their gazes remained straight ahead.

By mutual unspoken assent, they soon followed, and did not speak of it again until they were safely ensconced back in the Camden Place parlor.

"Well!" Julia sank into the sofa. "*That* proved far more interesting than I expected."

"As I said before, I am very much surprised. Pleasantly so, I might add," said Mother.

"And you, brother dear? You looked like you'd seen a ghost when you saw Catherine."

"Perhaps he did," murmured their mother.

He glanced sharply at her, but her expression was all innocence.

"That general is far too old for her, though. Yet he seems nice enough."

He nodded, his heart writhing at such fiction, preventing further speech.

"Did you notice the way none of them spoke to Lady Milton?" Julia twirled her pearl necklace around her fingers. "I wonder why."

Mother snorted. "You do not have to wonder too hard, dear girl. I'm sure Lady Milton's wagging tongue can be held responsible."

"Really?"

"What do you imagine I was warning you about? That woman is like a disease, where you don't realize you've been infected with poison until you're half dead."

"How extremely poetic, Mother." Julia's amusement faded into contemplation. "Poor Catherine." She shook her head, glanced at him.

He managed a grave smile.

"What is *wrong* with you, Jonathan? I almost laughed out loud when Catherine's aunt mentioned your engagement. You were almost as bad as Mr. Milton. And that will never do, brother dear. I shall simply have to disown you."

"Yes, what was with you?" Diamonds flashed in his mother's hair as she looked

351

up at him. "I thought everything was settled."

He cleared his throat. "It is not."

Fatigue washed over his mother's face. "You have *still* not decided?"

He stood, for what felt like a very long time, feeling as though he swayed next to a precipice.

But it was done. She had decided. So must he. "I have."

And he told his decision, and fortified himself as they wrapped him in hugs of glee.

Chapter Twenty-Two

Catherine kept her eyes closed against the light, closed against the day, closed against life. Being awake meant speaking, speaking meant pretending, and she was so tired of pretending. Far better instead to be sick, to stay in bed, to avoid everyone's questions — and those that plagued her heart.

She never imagined anything could hurt as much as his rejection from nearly three years ago. She had thought she had coped with the constant murmurs surrounding his engagement, even the long, drawn out, endless speculation.

That was until she had known it was true.

That night, the tears couldn't come. Whether she had cried them out long ago or whether it was still too raw, too real for tears, Catherine did not know. She could barely think.

She was numb.

The morning after the horrid concert she

did not get up. She could not. The heat in her cheeks had spread through her body, leading to a heaviness that seemed to have soaked into her bones. Mama took one look at her and sent for the doctor, who believed she suffered from fatigue. It meant the visit from Lady Harkness was put off, a fact she only knew from Bess who'd murmured, when Catherine had asked in one of her lucid moments, that Dobson had informed Lady Harkness's coachman there was illness in the house.

A hothouse flower arrangement, accompanied by the general's surprisingly neat handwritten note, had momentarily lifted her spirits, as did a later one, sent from Julia, of pretty daffodils, but flowers could not minister to a shattered heart. She doubted even God could. So she slept.

Something clicked. She raised heavy eyelids. A shadow crept across the room. "Who is it?" Her voice sounded raspy, far away.

"It's only me, miss."

Bess?

There was a scraping sound. Then something fragrant filled the air, a perfume that tugged at her memories, begging her to recall spring days and sweet, sweet evenings . . .

She turned her head. Violets.

The tiny purple heart-shaped blooms blurred. "Who?"

"There was no message, miss. Dobson found them at the front door when he went to collect the post."

"Th-thank you."

She bit her lip. Closed her eyes. Amidst the swirling confusion something settled, sure.

Violets had always meant . . .

Him.

The next day the pain in her head had cleared sufficiently to enable perusal of the devotional once more. Catherine stared at the closely printed page. Today's reading came from James. "My brethren, count it all joy when ye fall into divers temptations; knowing this, that the trying of your faith worketh patience. But let patience have her perfect work, that ye may be perfect and entire, wanting nothing."

She frowned. Hadn't she had enough trials? How much did she have to persevere? How mature did God really need her to be? And why was patience described in feminine form?

A knock came at her bedchamber door. At her invitation, her aunt entered, her worry lines easing. "My dear, I am glad to finally see you sitting up." She glanced at the posy of violets peering from the earth-toned vase beside her bed.

Catherine felt her cheeks heat, but kept her eyes on her aunt. Did she know who had sent them?

Aunt Drusilla's lips pursed before she turned to Catherine, her dark eyes tinged with concern. "You've been ill for three days now, and had a number of people quite concerned. Your mother, the general." She moved to the window, fiddling with the curtains. "Even Miss Carlew called in, wishing to convey her mother's and brother's best wishes."

Her heart stuttered.

"So it is true. He *is* engaged." Her aunt turned, brows lifted, as if awaiting her response.

"Y-yes."

"It doesn't change what we already knew."

"No."

"So what will you do?"

The words from her reading taunted her. Count it as all joy? She met her aunt's frowning face. "I . . . I do not want t-to . . ." She swallowed. Her eyes filled with tears. "I do not want to be pitied."

"Of course not. But you do not have to be."

"But with this endless gossip I might as well move back home, for my prospects here are nonexistent."

"Do you want to be married?"

And have babies? A family of her own?

"Of course."

"Need it be now? Can you not just continue with the general until it becomes apparent you are nothing more than friendly acquaintances? Gossip will die eventually. All it takes is for a greater scandal to replace your news."

"I . . . I suppose." She swallowed. "I just . . . I just wish I could be somebody whom a man would choose to love, rather than be left feeling like I'm caught in the midst of someone's mistakes once again."

"I see." Her aunt was quiet for a long moment, before nodding. "I will speak with him."

"With Mr. Carlew?"

Her aunt started before giving a tiny shake of her head, her face softening for a moment, as if with sympathy. "No, the general. He is a man of honor. I feel sure he will support us." She gave a ghost of a smile. "Especially if we call it a campaign."

Catherine nodded, her thoughts, her emotions, too scattered to plainly grasp her aunt's meaning. What campaign did Aunt Drusilla speak of? Why could this not be resolved? Just how patient did God want her to be?

The following afternoon she felt sufficiently stronger to descend the stairs and meet the general in the drawing room. He rose upon her entry, his countenance lighting as he stretched his hands towards her, leading her to a seat. "Ah, my dear. I hope to see those roses in your cheeks again soon."

"Thank you for your flowers, sir." She sank gratefully into a cushioned settee.

" 'Tis the least I can do," he assured her, before regaling them with the news from the past few days.

Catherine half listened, her tiredness such she did not realize the subject matter had shifted until she heard her aunt mention her name.

"So, dear general, you can see we count on you to protect Catherine's good name."

Wait. Catherine looked between the general and her aunt. What had been said? Why was Mama nodding? Did this relate to yesterday's conversation?

"I do not like it." He sighed, turning to Catherine. "I understand the reasoning, my dear, but I cannot help but feel I will be playing you false."

What had she agreed to?

"You will not," her aunt stated. "We all know the truth. That will not change."

"But my dear," the general gave Catherine a fatherly smile, "what if you do meet someone who takes your fancy, or who takes a fancy to you? I would be in the way."

Catherine released a long breath, feeling as though she had finally been handed her script and now knew her lines. "But there *is* nobody." Nobody who wanted her, anyway. She fought the burn in her throat, her eyes. "And even if there were, he would never get the chance to know me, not with all these rumors flying around. People already couple us together, and this way" — she swallowed — "this way, I would not be considered a laughingstock."

He studied her a long moment before shaking his head and uttering a sigh. "Well, I suppose my actions have contributed to this sad state of affairs. I see my actions must get us out."

"Thank you," Catherine said, gratitude swelling within. What a good man. How right Aunt Drusilla had been to appeal to his honor. For a while anyway, she would be able to hold her head up, to stare the gossips in the eye, to pretend this man she regarded like a father was the one who had captured her affections, to perhaps even convince the man who had long ago stolen her heart that he possessed it no more.

Her conscience panged; she ignored it. It *wasn't* a matter of deception, but social survival.

"It is only for a short season," Aunt Drusilla assured. "Just long enough to protect Catherine's reputation in Bath, until you both return to your *own* abode."

This last was said with an upraised brow at Mama, which caused her to flush and look away.

"But I do not want to be the jilt," the general said with a small smile.

"And I have no wish to be jilted." Again.

"But what will we say about wedding dates?"

"We'll say that is something we'll consider once out of mourning," Mama declared.

Catherine forced a smile. "Whilst I remain in Bath we will pretend, and then when I return home, we will drift apart."

"But if a gentleman catches your eye, please let me know."

Her smile grew stiff. "I doubt I will have to."

Because the only man who ever had, had

pledged his life to another.

The news of an engagement did not seem to make much difference to the gossips, save for heads to nod in self-satisfaction, and a few bolder acquaintances to offer their congratulations, and enquire about the wedding. Mama's comments about observing mourning soon dealt with that.

Catherine almost felt reconciled to her new — assumed — status, when her sanguinity was put to the ultimate test a few days later, in the form of the previously postponed visit from Lady Harkness.

Lady Harkness swept into the drawing room as was her wont, her attire and manner flamboyant as ever, trailed by her daughter and son. After a general exchange of curtsies and bows, Lady Harkness took her seat and turned to Catherine. "Ah, Miss Winthrop, we are so pleased to see you have recovered."

"Thank you, Lady Harkness. And thank you for the lovely bouquet, Julia. That was very kind."

Catherine stole a glance at Mr. Carlew, but his face registered nothing when she mentioned the bouquet. She stifled the heart pang. As the older ladies commenced a discussion about the recent weather,

Catherine directed her attention to Julia, sitting languidly beside her on the settee. "I had a number of very kind well-wishers, and some lovely notes. But there was a mystery."

"Really?" Julia's eyes brightened. She sat up, her interest as obvious now as her previous ennui had been.

"A posy of violets was left on the front step, with only an initial, C."

"What? No message?"

"None." Her gaze lifted to him, but he had turned, was facing out into the street, hands clasped behind his back.

"How romantic!" cried Julia, drawing the other ladies' attention. "The C meant you, I suppose, and was not a hint of the giver?"

"Oh." Her heart sank. "I hadn't thought —"

"For heavens sake, child! Can you possibly imagine Elvira or myself receiving such a thing? We're far too old for such gestures."

"They are certainly beautiful," Catherine said. "I have always loved violets. They have such a sweet and subtle scent."

"It is a lovely notion, to be sure," said Mama with a sigh. "But I would much prefer to know the recipient. Flowers from an anonymous anyone might be simply that — from anyone. Why, it might be from a dustman!"

Julia glanced at Catherine, her eyes dancing. "But perhaps it was a soldier. Are you sure it wasn't the general?"

"He sent roses."

"Of course he did."

The low-voiced mutter drew their attention to the window.

"Did you say something, Jonathan?"

"Nothing of pertinence, Mother." He nodded, his gaze sliding past Catherine without acknowledgment.

Her insides chilled, she ducked her head. It was as if they had gone back to being strangers. Only they were not. And never could be. Would it always be thus between them?

"I seem to remember something about violets." Julia frowned. "It was a long time ago . . ."

As Julia's chatter continued — chatter which demanded neither acknowledgment nor reply — Catherine's gaze lifted. Mr. Carlew glanced away.

Had he?

No. It had to be coincidence. Why would he?

She stared at his averted face, noting a muscle twitching in his jaw. No! The thought was preposterous.

Catherine winced and rubbed her forehead, as if she could push her thoughts into order.

"Miss Winthrop?" The deep voice compelled her attention. Mr. Carlew surveyed her with a frown. "You appear unwell."

"No. I am . . . sorry." She turned to Julia and said hurriedly, "Forgive me. What were you saying?"

"Oh, I wondered if you would care to come on an excursion with me. We could visit the castle at Farleigh Hungerford, or we could even go to Wells. Jonathan would take us, wouldn't you, brother dear?"

Catherine noted his compressed lips, the way a reply didn't spring to his lips, and knew he did not want her company. Her heart panged again. "I . . . I think I would prefer we did not."

Mr. Carlew shot her a sharp look but said nothing. Julia pouted. "We could ask the general along, too, if you'd prefer."

Catherine studied her. She seemed restless, most unlike the Julia of last year she had known. Perhaps it was Julia who needed the excursion. "I do not want anyone to feel obliged —"

"Oh, but Jonathan won't mind." Julia's face lit again. "Please, Jon, you know I've always wanted to go and see the castle — it's said to be most romantic. And you *did* promise to take me one day."

His lips lifted in one corner. "I did, didn't I?"

"And you always keep your word, don't you?"

"I try." His smile faded. He half looked in her direction again. "But I do not want Miss Winthrop to grow fatigued."

"Oh, she won't, will you, Catherine? It's only nine miles away. We needn't go tomorrow, but one day soon?"

"You forget I return to London tomorrow."

"Oh." Julia's face fell. "But you will take us when you get back? Please say you will."

"Do not forget we have vouchers for the Wakefield ball," said Lady Harkness. "I understand you won't be attending, Miss Winthrop, but there is nothing like a masque for merriment, and I have always been partial to a chance to dress up."

"Imagine that," Aunt Drusilla said, *sotto voce.*

The green eyes glinted, before she gave a trace of a smile. "Please ensure whatever arrangements are made do not disturb our other plans."

"Certainly, Mother," Julia said, before turning to her brother. "But you *will* take us?"

His gaze finally found Catherine's again, his expression grave, no trace of a smile remaining in his eyes or on his lips. "I will."

Her skin prickled. Nothing could be plainer. He would take her, under sufferance, only to appease his sister.

A shadow passed over her heart, forcing her to once more pray away the burn in her eyes.

Jonathan walked into the coffee house, in an attempt to cure the restlessness that had plagued him since the visit to Gay Street that afternoon. This place would scarcely meet his need — heaven knew he had an early start tomorrow — but the questions circled incessantly.

He ordered and stood, leaning against the counter, listening to the hum of conversation soak into the wood-paneled walls. He needed to be out, to be distracted, unable to hear himself think. Home was too full of worries, that of his sister, his mother, his very own . . .

Had she guessed?

Jon winced internally at the thought. But something had made him stop by the flower stall, that same perverse impulse dragging him here tonight.

Would she accept flowers, if she knew they

were from him?

He groaned, loud enough for the proprietor to glance his way.

"Here 'tis," he said, pushing a cup of coffee in his direction. "No need to get upset, now."

"I wasn't —" Jon bit back the rest of the comment, fished out a coin. "Thank you."

The man's eyes widened. "I'll need to make change."

"Don't bother. It's yours."

"Well, I be right grateful, sir. Anything else you need? A private room, perhaps?"

"Thank you, no." To be amongst the living, that's what he needed. Not alone. Not with his thoughts.

He took his drink to a table near a quiet corner from which he could see most of the room. Conversation rumbled around him as he took a sip, enjoying the slight bite of the hot liquid sliding down his throat. He'd never been much of a drinker, not like Carmichael and Hale, and had not wanted to find solace in an inn. Coffee houses had long mixed business with socializing, and there were days like today when a man's thoughts turned too dark if he were alone.

At the table behind him the voices picked up volume. At the name "Winthrop" his ears pricked.

"They say he's old enough to be her grandfather!"

Jon stilled. No, surely not —

"We know what that means, eh?" A snigger. A snort. A guffaw.

Something white and hot slashed across his chest, followed by a fresh pang of pity for Catherine. How could strangers taint another's character so? He loathed to see the innocent suffer, even if the person in question had nigh on broken his heart. He shifted very casually, one arm stretched along the chair back beside him, glancing over as the three rumormongers continued.

"They say ol' Winthrop left nowt but debts!"

"Aye, spent it all on the tables."

"And on his fancy birds."

His breath constricted. He'd heard rumors of his predecessor's infidelity, but if these men had, too . . .

Jon leaned closer to where the men sat. "Forgive me, I could not help but overhear. Are you talking about Lord Winthrop?"

The gruff-voiced man nodded. "Aye. From Gloucestershire."

"Please excuse me. I'm new to town. Are you suggesting Winthrop was a gambler?"

"Not suggestin'. He was. A miserly, cheating gambler. Sure as I'm sitting here."

"But he did not leave debts." Jon had paid them — all he could find, anyway.

The red-bearded man scowled. " 'Ow can you know that?"

"I am acquainted with the family, and so naturally I am concerned when lies are being spread."

"You calling us liars?" The third man, a large man with fists like hams, flushed.

"I suppose I am."

"Roight!" He pushed to his feet. "Nobody calls Jock Robinson a liar and gets away with it."

The proprietor hurried over, wiping his hands on a towel. "Is there some kind of trouble?"

The big man nodded, jerked a thumb at Jon. "This Harry Who-knows is calling us liars."

"Is this so?" The proprietor glanced at Jon, his expression a mix of worry and pleading.

"I'm sure you can understand a man's objection to slander, especially when it concerns me."

"Concerns you?"

"Yes." Now Jon rose, meeting Jock Robinson eye to eye. "You see, I am Lord Winthrop."

"You?"

"Aye." Jon smiled thinly. "And I assure

369

you, I do not gamble, nor do I cheat people, and I've certainly never had any . . . fancy birds, I believe you said?" He raised an eyebrow at the gruff-voiced man.

"I . . . I —"

"I know it is unpardonable of me to eavesdrop, but I would be most appreciative if you could tell me the source of your information."

"Sir, I . . . well, er . . ."

"I see. Well perhaps when you choose to remember, you will kindly inform them that the former Lord Winthrop's debts were all discharged quite some time ago. If anyone should require further information, they are advised to enquire with my solicitors in London. Of course, one should perhaps ask the question of why such scurrilous accusations are being made . . ." He raised a questioning eyebrow.

The men glanced at each other as the proprietor gestured to Jon. "Anyone who calls this man a miser or a cheat can leave my establishment and not return."

"But —"

"That includes you, Jock Robinson. No —" He held up a hand at the man's protest. "I've had enough of your spreading gossip like a clutch of old crows."

"And perhaps you might desist from

spreading further wickedness about Miss Winthrop and the general," Jon continued. "Anyone who dares impugn her character will have me to deal with."

"And me," his loyal host said, crossing his arms.

"I hope we understand each other, gentlemen. Good evening."

With a nod of appreciation to the coffee house proprietor, Jon collected his cloak, victory marking his steps as he strode outside, where the crisp night air shocked sense back to his brain.

What had he done?

The perverse imp fell silent.

He groaned again. Had his words helped to clear Catherine's name, or simply provided more fuel for idle speculation?

Chapter Twenty-Three

Ten days later

The day for the excursion to the castle at Farleigh Hungerford eventuated on a fair Friday. From her vantage point at the drawing room window, Catherine noted the sunny conditions seemed to have melted the siblings' previous coolness. Julia seemed in fine spirits, the restlessness for once gone. Mr. Carlew, too, seemed more lighthearted, joking with his sister, smiling as they walked up and waited for the door to open.

Catherine herself felt buoyant. Today was a precious outing. And even if his company might prove awkward at times, without his company she would not receive this treat, so she was happy to endure this trial with no small measure of joy.

There was a murmur of voices in the hall. She wiped her gently perspiring hands down the skirt of her new riding dress, another gift from her aunt. This particular hue of purple became her well, adding a flush to her cheeks and a sparkle to her eyes, so Bess had kindly said earlier. But perhaps that was more to do with this thrumming anticipation —

"Miss Winthrop."

Her greeting with Julia was warm; with him cool.

"But where is the general?" Julia looked around, as if she expected him to pop up from behind the settee.

"He did not wish to come," Catherine said, sticking to the story they had arranged yesterday. The general had said a number of other things, but Julia did not look like she would appreciate a dissertation on the evils of long rides with old backs.

"We best be off, as it is a fair distance." Mr. Carlew bowed to her mother and aunt, and led the way.

Catherine gathered her skirt over one arm and followed.

Outside were three horses. "Oh! I did not know you had brought Ginger!"

"I brought Gulliver and Ginger on my return from London." He coughed. "I did not realize she was being housed by Hawkesbury at the Hall."

What could she say? That she didn't trust Frank? That she did not want him to feel any sense of obligation?

She hurried to the mare, crooning over her, laughing as Ginger nudged her face. She glanced over her shoulder and smiled. "Thank you. You cannot know how much I have longed to ride her. This is the first occasion I've had to go riding in months."

Mr. Carlew's brows knit. "You are not serious?"

"I'm afraid so."

"I hope you remember how to ride," Julia said.

Catherine chuckled. "I hope you remember to keep up."

What followed was one of the more remarkable days in recent memory. The chance to ride brought such a sense of freedom, the chance to escape the judgmental hilled township even more liberating.

Her smile felt as wide as the River Avon. Here was fresh air, speed, convivial company, and the wondrously pretty patchwork of hills and fields so representative of what made Somerset renowned for its beauty. Ginger responded well to Catherine's encouragement, seemingly equally pleased to have the chance to be put through her paces. They crested the hill, and came to a halt, as the glorious panorama stretched into the distance.

"Oh, this is wonderful!" she exclaimed, as they waited for Julia to catch up.

"I had forgotten how well you ride," Mr. Carlew said.

"I had forgotten how much I enjoy this."

She glanced across. Now she could look at him, she remembered how it felt to almost drown in his eyes. Blue, like a summer sky, filled with light, filled with promise. And when he smiled like that —

Her heart caught. She glanced away. A too-long glance only stirred up memories best forgotten. Their mutual "engagements" made everything safe now. Safe, but dangerous, for if she relaxed and let her guard down, she'd be fooled into thinking the past few years had never happened.

"I don't know why we thought this such a good idea," Julia grumbled, her hair windblown, falling from its chignon. "I think the two of you should just go on without me."

"Don't be silly," Catherine said, nudging Ginger closer. "This would not be nearly as fun without you."

"Oh, I don't know. You two seemed to be having a grand old time."

Catherine glanced at Mr. Carlew, surprised by the smile on his face.

"It is nice to ride with someone who doesn't always argue with everything I say,

375

poppet."

"Catherine! Never tell me you are letting him have his own way?"

"I will never tell you that, no, Julia."

He laughed, a deep rumble that triggered warmth in her chest. How well, too well, she remembered those days when she could make him smile.

Her smile faded, and she nudged Ginger into a canter, determined to shake off the shadows of the past. Today, this day, she *would* enjoy.

For the rest of the day she fought to stay relaxed, to revel in the freedom she remembered from years ago. Freedom to be herself, to not merely conform, but to smile and laugh as she had with Serena as children, freedom to not hide behind opinions not her own. So when Julia exclaimed over the greenness, wondering if Somersetshire was greener than the land surrounding Winthrop, she did not hesitate to disagree. When Mr. Carlew mused over what bird call it was, thinking aloud that it sounded like a meadow pipit, Catherine could quite happily contradict and call it a red-flanked bluetail, pleasure filling her at being proved right when they spotted the flash of red on its wings as it fluttered away.

The ruins of Farleigh Hungerford Castle

lived up to Julia's hopes, her delight at the ivy-clad rounded towers and Gothic exterior matched by her pleasure at the wild and windswept gardens. "Oh, isn't this romantic?"

Mr. Carlew glanced at Catherine before saying, "Rather, I'd say overgrown."

Catherine chuckled at Julia's crestfallen face. "Oh, don't mind him, Julia. You know your brother delights in being practical."

"I'm sure he does not possess a romantic bone in his body."

Catherine glanced away, fighting the fire flooding her cheeks. How well she knew Julia's assertion to be blatantly untrue. But she would *not* stir up such feelings. She took a step, two steps away, eyeing the surrounding landscape. "There seems to be something of a walled garden over there. Should we — ?"

"Oh, yes!" Julia scampered past, leaving Catherine to walk at a more sedate pace with Mr. Carlew. She dared glance up at him; was surprised by the red tingeing his cheeks under his tan. Surely he didn't remember — ? No. She shook her head at herself. That way heartache lay.

"Oh, Catherine . . ."

Julia's voice drew her through the archway, and she stopped on the mossy flagstones, drinking in the scene. The beds might be terribly overrun, but she could see how lovely the garden would have been, centered by something that looked like a mulberry tree. Rosemary peered through clumps of weeds, primroses clumped pale yellow, and old-fashioned flowers — spring snowflakes, and lungwort, and narcissus — gave promise of spring.

Catherine breathed in the surroundings, that oh-so-elusive happiness warming her at last. "Oh, this is beautiful."

Mr. Carlew drew near. "It has retained the beauty and charm of times past."

Catherine dared not look at him, his words reminding how she — unlike this lost garden — had kept neither beauty nor charm. She swallowed, and moved closer to Julia, whose initial look of pleasure had drooped to something more pensive. "Julia? Is something the matter? You seem a little sad."

Julia sighed, peeking over her shoulder to where her brother stood, several yards away. "This is so lovely. I just wish —" She bit her lip.

"You wish?"

"Tell me, Catherine," her voice dropped to a whisper, "have you seen anything of Major Hale in recent weeks?"

Catherine blinked, perplexity slowing her words. "Why, yes."

"And how did he appear to you? Was he well?"

"He appeared so, yes."

Julia opened her lips as if to say more, but closed them, as a cracked twig and her brother's approach sent her scurrying to the far end, where a stone seat curved into the wall. Catherine glanced up at Mr. Carlew, his nearness and the traces of what seemed to be a smile soon chasing all thought of Julia away.

"I am glad you could come today, Miss Winthrop." Warmth kindled within, mingled with surprise. "Julia enjoys your company."

Implying he did not? She forced down the hurt. "She was kind to include me."

"You did not think you could escape one of Julia's plans, did you?" His lips tweaked to one side. "Once she gets an idea in her head, she proves very difficult to dissuade."

"I understand this outing was a promise you had made her some time ago."

"One she would not let me forget."

His eyes seemed to search hers, as if trying to convey a deeper meaning, but what she did not know. She dropped her gaze, moving to where a purple sweet violet valiantly bloomed against the wall, noting with surprise that he kept in step. A tug of her glove and she caressed the flower. She peeked up, to see him watching her still, and released the stem, fumbling for something to say. What could she say that would be deemed innocuous?

"I always thought Winthrop could support a walled garden."

"There would be space were the yew hedge at the back removed."

"Oh, I wish it were! It's such an ugly, decrepit hedge that takes up far more space than it should. And a sunken garden located there —"

"Would receive the morning sun in winter —"

"And planted correctly could make a wonderfully cool retreat in summer."

"And walls would make it completely private."

"The perfect escape." She sighed. "Can you imagine how wonderful it would be?"

"Yes."

His smiling gaze connected with hers, and again she felt the tug of attraction. Oh, he was handsome. Oh, if only every day could be like this, sharing moments of perfect accord, and dreams for the future . . .

"Catherine? Jon? Why are you staring at each other in that funny way? Surely you must be as famished as I am."

"Y-yes." Catherine pulled her gaze away, sure her cheeks must be fiery red.

The rest of the day did not see the return of the earlier ease, but neither did it hold the cold tension of previous weeks. Instead, something akin to tentative steps towards renewed friendship was unfurling slowly in her heart, bolstered by Julia's banter over luncheon at the small coaching inn, and Catherine's small victories in the silly races they engaged in on the ride home. She felt almost . . . carefree.

Until they arrived back at Gay Street and stiff, sore legs refused a graceful descent from Ginger's back. She had no wish to be considered missish, but . . .

"Catherine? Are you quite all right?"

Her cheeks heated at Julia's words. "I think I'm too out of practice."

"May I assist?"

Seconds later, his hands were on her waist, holding, lifting, causing that familiar feeling of breathlessness. The heat of his closeness, his scent of bergamot and musk, assailed her senses, swirling emotion within, before she stepped from his clasp and schooled her expression to neutrality. "Th-thank you."

Hours later, she could still feel the pressure of his hands, could still smell his delicious scent, could still hear his laughter blending with hers. Emotions clashed within, a thousand renewed regrets swooping in like bats at midnight. She pushed them aside, focusing on the day's joy. And as she went to sleep that night, she knew she would forever look back on today as one of the golden days of her life.

Through the drawing room window Jonathan caught a glimpse of blue hills. His heart picked up pace as it had every time he thought back to that perfect day last week.

Her laughter. Shared smiles. The sense of years peeling back to younger days, to uninhibited innocence, to love. Had his reference to retained charm been too oblique? He'd never been one for an overly romantic turn of phrase, but she had always drawn such fancies from him, just as she'd drawn him to pocket the purple flower she had touched, even now hidden beneath the covers of his Bible upstairs.

He hated feeling this way. Hated how he dreamed of her. Hated his envy of the old general. Hated this feeling of duplicity, engaged to one, when his heart had always been engaged by another.

And now he had to see her. Offer felicitations for her birthday, as he might a mere acquaintance. His hands clenched.

A knock prefaced his butler's entry. "Excuse me, sir, but Lord Carmichael has arrived."

"Carmichael?"

"The one and only," said the viscount, gracefully pushing past the butler, who withdrew, closing the door.

"We were not expecting you. Is Major Hale with you?" asked Julia eagerly.

Carmichael glanced at Jon before returning his attention to Julia. "I'm afraid not, my dear."

Her face fell. "Have you spoken with him?"

"Not for some time now."

Julia's face darkened. "I bet we all know why that is." She shot Jon a look of fire and stormed from the room.

Carmichael eyed him with raised brows. "Don't ask."

"I'm not sure I need to. Poor petal. Has big brother proved a little overprotective?"

"She needs someone to keep her in line."

"I thought Bath was supposed to be doing that all by itself?"

"One would think a town filled with the gouty and half infirm would do that."

Carmichael chuckled, sinking elegantly

onto a sofa, only to immediately rise again as Mother walked into the room, hands outstretched.

"Dear Henry," Mother said, her smile widening as Carmichael kissed her hand like a medieval courtier. "Julia mentioned your arrival. To what do we owe this pleasure?"

"You need ask? It is always you, ma'am, who draws the bees as to the queen —"

"Says the drone."

"Now, Jonathan. You know I like a pretty compliment, and this young man can certainly deliver them."

"He certainly can," Jon muttered.

"Now what is wrong, old man?" Carmichael asked. "Have you got the sullens as well as your sister?"

"Of course not."

"Good, for I cannot abide staying with sullenly people."

"You're staying here, are you?" Jon asked.

"If you'll have me."

"Do I have a choice?"

"Not really. Especially when one has previously murmured the words 'open invitation' to such as myself."

"Did I do that?"

"If you didn't, you certainly should have," the viscount said with a grin. "Now tell me, is Miss Beauchamp in town?"

His defenses rose. "No."

"But that is a marvelous idea, Harry!" Mother said, clapping her hands. "We should invite sweet Lydia and her Mama to come stay, don't you agree, Jonathan?"

He couldn't very well say no, so he said nothing.

Fortunately Julia chose to return at that moment, wearing a green pelisse and carrying a small gold wrapped parcel. "Are we leaving now? I thought you wanted me to change, Mother."

"*I* don't want you to change, dear girl."

"Carmichael, stop embarrassing yourself."

"I don't know if that's possible, but I will try."

"Good, for we are going to Catherine's birthday tea, and you should be on your best behavior," said Julia.

"We are, are we?" Carmichael crooked a brow at Jon.

"Well, *we* have been invited."

"Oh. Well I'm sure they won't mind an extra, especially such a handsome, sophisticated extra as I endeavor to be."

"Not to mention modest," Jon added.

"No, we never mention modest."

Jon's reluctant amusement escaped in a chuckle, glad for the return of his friend whose spirits always boosted his own.

Carmichael grinned. "Well, I suppose if I'm to dazzle I should exchange these rags for something more apropos. My *dear* Lord Winthrop, will you kindly point me to my room?"

An hour later, having tamped down his impatience as he waited for Carmichael to get dressed then buy a gift — "for the uninvited should always bring something to render their presence slightly more agreeable" — Jon finally entered the Gay Street residence. After waiting for his mother and sister to greet its residents and the general, he could at last present his own salutations, and offer Catherine a bow.

"Many happy returns."

Something flickered in her eyes. Was it gladness? Disappointment? He studied her, and found himself falling into the fathomless depths of her dark eyes, remembering. His gaze slipped to her lips. Suddenly he wished his far more charming friend was not still waiting in the hall; wished the general far away. Wished he were free to say all he wanted to say —

"We brought you this." Julia thrust their gift into Catherine's hands to her murmured thanks. "But we also have a much larger surprise waiting outside."

"A larger surprise?" The dark eyes flashed to him.

"A surprise to us all," Jon muttered.

"The Viscount Carmichael," the butler announced.

Jon watched his friend's polished self-assurance on display as he greeted Lady Winthrop and was introduced to Catherine's aunt and the general. His geniality was such that he seemed set to become best friends with the general, when he turned to greet the room's other occupants.

"Good afternoon, Lord Carmichael."

He blinked. "Miss Winthrop?"

"The very same."

Carmichael shook his head and moved closer, grasping her hands. "No, not the same. Not at all!" He smiled, eliciting hers. "I must say, that color suits you admirably. I think you should make it your practice to never wear anything but lavender."

Catherine gave a delicious gurgle of laughter, and Jon was struck with envy. If only he could be so at ease with her. If only she were free —

"Carmichael?" Jon cleared his throat. "I don't believe I mentioned that Miss Winthrop has recently become betrothed to the general here."

"What?"

His friend's face wore such a look of comical dismay that Jon almost laughed. Almost.

"I'm sorry, where are my manners? Please, accept my felicitations." Carmichael bowed to both parties, but as he glanced at Jon, his brows rose so high Jon wondered if they might meet his carefully disarranged hair.

Catherine drew forward the other member of the party, who had until now remained near silent. "I don't believe you have met my younger sister. Lord Carmichael, this is Serena."

The pair exchanged bow and curtsy.

"Miss Serena Winthrop, a picture as soothing as her name. Why have I not met you before?"

The younger Miss Winthrop gazed at him disinterestedly. "I attend a nearby seminary. Miss Haverstock's."

"Ah, yes. An excellent facility I'm given to understand."

Jon bit back a smile. He would be willing to bet his last penny Carmichael had never heard of the place.

The cool-eyed sister seemed to agree, studying the viscount dispassionately before looking away, affecting interest in a vase of flowers. Jon smothered a chuckle at his friend's blink of surprise.

Julia moved to examine the arrangement,

too. "That is a pretty posy."

"It is from the general," Catherine said.

"No more mysterious bouquets?"

"None." Catherine smiled. "Perhaps I should sicken again, and we'll see if my unknown benefactor returns."

"What mystery is this?" Carmichael asked.

As Julia told him, Jon felt a trickle of unease.

"And what flowers were they? I should like to know, in case I should ever see a misplaced posy on a doorstep on our return."

"Violets."

"Violets, you say?" Carmichael turned. Jon met his gaze steadily. "Well, well . . ."

"I think it time we forget such things." Catherine's aunt eyed Jon with not a small amount of speculation. "Now, shall we have tea?"

Later, when they had returned home after dinner, Mrs. Villiers's unexpected hospitality extending to a meal, Carmichael's ponderings remained. "I cannot understand why she has accepted that old man. He might have a sterling reputation from the war, and possess a degree of wit, but he is *old.*"

"She is scarcely in her first bloom of youth," Mother snapped. "I would have thought her grateful to accept his suit."

"Yes, but is it a suit, or merely one of convenience? I detected nothing of the *amour* from either party."

A sick, tight feeling filled his stomach. Was Carmichael right?

"Perhaps he reminds her of her father," Julia said. "I know I still miss mine."

"He is nothing like her father," Jon muttered.

"When I was at the reading room today I overheard an old lady talking about them —"

"That is enough, Julia," Mother said imperiously. "Come, I think it time we went upstairs. Good night, Carmichael. Good night, Jonathan." She offered her cheek for a kiss that he performed obediently. She grasped his arm. "Do not let that man spend too long in idle speculation," she urged in a low voice.

He forced a smile, and she left the room, dragging a sullen Julia in her wake.

Jon offered further refreshment; Carmichael accepted, lounging gracefully on the settee whilst Jon prepared his drink. Jon himself had nothing. He felt too raw, too jittery.

"Tell me, does your dear *mater* object to my conversation in general, or merely to that involving the winsome Miss Winthrop?" Carmichael eyed him with a half smile. "I rather suspect the latter, though I can't for the life of me imagine why."

"I'm sure it's a challenge for you to imagine your conversation ever less than favorably received."

"Oh, you'd be surprised," Carmichael said, his features tightening for a moment. "And perhaps you did not notice the fair Miss Winthrop's equally fair sister give me what I imagine must be considered a cold shoulder?" He shuddered. "Thank goodness Miss Winthrop is not so unkind. She did look very pretty today, do you not agree, old man?"

He jerked a nod. Very pretty was an understatement.

"You will forgive my harping on the subject, but I cannot help wonder if your mother dislikes her. Why would that be?" Carmichael studied him, his air of insouciance at odds with those shrewd eyes. "You are being very quiet. No sardonic comments? No irony? Perhaps the new Lord Winthrop has been afflicted with a 'mysterious' disease?"

"Now you are being ridiculous. I wondered how long it would take to emerge."

"Ha! Yes, that's more like it."

To shift his friend's dangerous thoughts he talked of the masquerade set to take place the following evening. "Julia seems quite excited, which makes a nice change."

"Yes, she almost seemed a little fey tonight." Carmichael's brows pushed together. "I do not remember her as being quite so flighty."

"I admit, I feel uneasy. She has been quite moody of late, and talks of military men, and frequently mentions Hale. I cannot like it."

"No."

The patient ticking of the mantelpiece clock punctuated the room's quiet.

"If she does marry him for convenience's sake —"

"Julia?"

"No, Miss Winthrop, it is enough to make me wish I had been here so she might not have to resort to such desperate measures."

"You?"

"Why not?" His smile glinted. "There is no need to look at me with such daggers. I am a single man, and your fair cousin —"

"Third cousin," he growled.

"Your fair *third* cousin is quite fair these days. There is something about her lovely eyes . . ."

They pulled a man in. Made him want to

drown in their sparkly depths. Gave dusky promise of a thousand tomorrows.

"Old man, are you quite all right?"

"Yes," Jon grouched.

"Hmm. Well, I must say her looks have improved out of sight."

"Now you sound like Hale, judging on appearance alone."

"And you object why?"

He could say nothing.

"Old man, your attitude makes me think you a trifle envious."

"Of what?"

"I know the delectable Miss Beauchamp is yours, but I confess to having noticed a want of affection from your side at least, that rather puts me in mind of the general's. It is enough to make me think —"

"You do too much thinking, friend."

"Perhaps." Carmichael gazed at him steadily, until he could feel heat crawl up his neck. "Tell me, where does a man purchase violets at this time of year?"

Jon pushed to his feet and stalked from the room, closing the door against the sound of his friend's gently mocking laughter.

CHAPTER TWENTY-FOUR

Catherine threw the book on the bedcovers, disgruntlement muddling her thoughts, making her unable to fix her attention for longer than a minute. She shifted up against the pillows. Going to bed early tonight was a stupid idea. How was she supposed to read? How was she supposed to sleep? She couldn't. Not when everybody else was going to the masquerade.

Her desire to go to the ball had only increased after yesterday's conversation around her birthday meal. She'd managed to sit at the dining table, artificial smile in place, as everyone save Mama, Serena, and herself discussed costumes and dances and music. For even Aunt Drusilla had consented to attend, with the general as her escort. He'd asked if Catherine should mind his attendance without her; she couldn't very well say no, and he'd promised to go only for a short while, but still . . .

Perhaps ladies in mourning did not attend such things, but the initial flood of grief for her father was more an undercurrent of sadness now, sadness for her mother and sister, sadness for herself, even sadness for him. The rumors surrounding Papa had died down somewhat, but were enough to bring to mind the debts unpaid, the evenings of debauched laughter at the London house, her parents' rows over his unexplained absences. Could the whispers be true? How could she hurt Mama by asking?

She pushed aside the weighty memories. Pushed aside the heavy bedcovers. If only she could go tonight. If only she could have the chance to dress up, and dance, and perhaps see —

Oh, if only society did not dictate one's life quite so much!

A groan huffed out. Why did society insist on such burdensome rules anyway? Who had first decided what social customs designated right and wrong? What if that arbiter of society had been wrong? How could it hurt if she *did* attend? A masquerade meant she'd be disguised, nobody would recognize her, and if she could just have one chance to dance with him again, maybe he'd remember . . .

Catherine slipped from the bed and moved

to the window. Studied the pedestrians outside, the carriages, the street lamp giving occasional glimpses of feathers, diamonds, and other accoutrements that signaled their wearers were headed to the Assembly Rooms. If only —

No. This was foolishness. She couldn't go. Shouldn't go. She was acting almost like Julia, whose inner restlessness showed in eyes that brightened too quickly before dulling into despondency. Last night, Catherine had snatched brief conversations with the younger girl — enough to worry for her, pray for her — but any time she probed, Julia simply shrugged off concern with a careless laugh. Talk of the ball had seemed to light Julia from within, her anticipation making her almost thrum with excitement. And for once, Catherine could empathize.

She shifted from the window to her wardrobe. Studied the contents. Sighed. Even if she could go she had nothing suitable to wear. Her pulse quickened. But Aunt Drusilla may.

A diplomat's wife, Aunt Drusilla had spent time in Spain, her costume tonight simply an old-fashioned mantilla worn high on her head, a small concession to the masquerade. "For I am an older lady, and one does not want to appear dressed lamb-fashion."

"You will outshine them all," the general had said when he'd come to collect her, whilst Catherine had schooled her expression to not appear wistful as they departed.

Yes, Aunt Drusilla's wardrobe. Surely it wouldn't hurt to just look.

Catherine eased from her room, past the bedchamber of her mother, who had retired early, and hurried into her aunt's room. *Thank you, God.* There was no maid.

She opened the wardrobe doors. Searched through the carefully hung gowns. Yes, just as she remembered. Down one end was the *señorita* outfit she had borrowed nearly three years ago in London. Surely it wouldn't hurt to try it on, just to see if it still fit? Heart hammering, she snatched it up. Found the matching gloves. Added a black velvet domino. Remembered the mask. She hunted through the drawers. Nothing. Glanced at her aunt's dressing table. Saw the couple of masks neatly arranged, seized the red one, returned to her room. Changed. Studied her reflection in the looking glass. Bit her lips until they glowed pink. Added the diamond earbobs Papa had given her at her come out. The necklace of pearls and gold.

Yes.

Memories arose. A balmy spring evening in London. The thrill of new love, laughter, dancing. Oh, how she had loved to dance with him, their movements as easy as their conversation had always been. Perhaps she was not as slim as three years ago, there was more curve now, but surely the bodice was not *too* low. She bit her lip. There would be many ladies showing a great deal more skin. Besides, she'd be disguised . . .

If she went.

Her heart thudded painfully. She shouldn't. It would be a scandal to top all else if she were discovered.

But how could she waste this opportunity? How could she spend the rest of her life wondering, regretting? It might be the last time to remind him of who she once was, to remind him of what they once had. Wouldn't that be a good thing?

If she went.

She shouldn't. She couldn't! How could she get there, anyway?

Even if the general had not already departed, she could not have asked him. He might be willing to do many things for her, but he would not do that, being such a stickler for honor and appearances. Aunt Drusilla would have simply been horrified, and liable to make such a fuss. Mama would awaken, demand to know all, and banish Catherine back to Winthrop at once. Who else? Miss Pettigrew? Julia? Julia might sympathize, but her assistance would be limited, besides which her propensity for trouble would likely lead to much more than a simple passage to the Assembly Rooms . . .

But wait. One of the reasons Aunt Drusilla preferred Gay Street was its proximity to so many of Bath's chief attractions. The Assembly Rooms were only a few twists and turns away. Surely she could walk there, and there was no danger, not with the pedestrians still plying the street. And how could it hurt, especially if she wore the domino as disguise?

If she went.

She stared at her masked reflection, as wisps of memory taunted anew. His intake of breath at her appearance. His warm smile. His laughter. His hands, holding hers. The way they'd danced in perfect unison. His deep, deep voice as he'd whispered, "If ever any beauty I did see, which I desir'd, and got, 'twas but a dream of thee."

Her heart thumped. How could she forgo a final reminder of that dream?

Collecting a deep breath, she eased open her door, stole past her mother's silent bedchamber, down the central stairs. Snatches of laughter drifted from downstairs, the servants no doubt relishing an earlier night than usual. On the hall table, Dobson had left a candelabra burning, its light too bright, hurrying her movements. She slowly opened the front door. It squeaked gently, but nothing signaled that anyone had heard. Left unlocked, Catherine could easily reenter, her escapade unnoticed — provided she returned before Aunt Drusilla.

She stepped out into the darkness. The route to the Assembly Rooms was one she had walked many times before. A turn onto George Street, left onto Bartlett, then onto Alfred. She hastened her steps, a lone woman was not safe, even if some people thought Bath's chief inhabitants only feeble old men. Relief bloomed within at the sight of the glowing flambeaux lighting the entrance. Groups moved to the colonnaded great doors, through which spilled strains of merriment and music. Now to get inside . . .

Her heart sank. She had no voucher! Oh, why hadn't she thought this through?

A large party of revelers moved slowly to the entrance. She inched through the shadows to hover in the dim outskirts, avoiding eye contact as they laughed amongst themselves.

"Well, hello!"

She jumped. Glanced up to see a middle-aged man peering at her. Her brain scrambled for something to say. *"Hola."*

He laughed. "I didn't know we had a *señorita* in our midst."

"You do now, *señor,"* she said and smiled. Perhaps if she stayed in character, and spoke the little Spanish she remembered from Aunt Drusilla's lessons long ago, tonight might prove as successful as her last venture to a masque.

The older man who appeared in charge presented his vouchers, and she shuffled to the opposite side, glad the black domino didn't draw attention. Amid the bustle and bright chatter she inched forward, closer, closer to the door.

"Excuse me, miss."

The party began moving, so she walked quickly, without a backward glance.

"Miss!"

Catherine dashed inside, exhilaration pounding her chest as she threaded through another large crowd then hurried downstairs to the changing room, all the while marveling at the variety of costumes — and the fact that she was actually here. After removing the domino, she glanced at her costume. Smiled. It did look well, even if the neckline

401

felt a little low.

"Miss?"

She jumped. "Y-yes?"

A woman dressed as Columbine motioned to Catherine's hair. "Your comb is simply beautiful."

"Th-thank you." She had been unable to resist using Julia's gift, a seed pearl and gold comb, to prop up the black lace mantilla. But unlike Aunt Drusilla's, Catherine's veil did not hide all her hair. She offered the kind lady a compliment on her dress, and carefully retied the ribbons on her mask, before noticing the ample girth of Mrs. Lampscombe in the background. Her pulse spiked as she maneuvered around the kindly Columbine.

"Ah, a pretty *señorita.*" Mrs. Lampscombe eyed her dress. "There are a few of you here tonight."

"Si, señora."

"Hmm, well." Mrs. Lampscombe frowned, glanced at Catherine one more time, then bustled self-importantly away.

When Catherine's heart had resumed its regular beat, she moved back up the stairs to the ballroom. The trick as a single lady was to walk purposefully, to make it seem as if she was with a party. The mask provided confidence, her recent encounters giving assurance that while she might not go unnoticed, she could still pass undetected. Of course, if Aunt Drusilla saw her . . .

Her heart picked up pace again. But her aunt's recognition was unlikely, seeing as she much preferred conversation to dancing, and would likely spend the night with her cronies — and the general — in the Tea Room. She moved to stand near the fireplace, the flames warming her back as she stood partially obscured by the plumes waving from the headdresses of the older ladies sitting in front. Before her, a cavalcade of dancers performed a country-dance. Mrs. Lampscombe was correct. Catherine could see at least two other *señoritas* amongst the other costumes, which also included a shepherdess, a Cupid, several Grecian-inspired characters, as well as several from the Medieval and Elizabethan ages.

"Good evening." A man's voice breathed beside her.

She glanced up. Stiffened. Was that Lord Carmichael dressed as a chevalier? The viscount had never really noticed her; surely he would not recognize her now? She dipped a curtsy, lowered her eyes, lowered the pitch of her voice. *"Si, señor."*

"May I say you are the prettiest *señorita* here tonight?"

She held her fan close to her face, and peeked up. *"Si, señor."*

He grinned. "Tell me, can you say anything beyond those two words?"

"Si, señor." She glanced around. If she could get away . . .

Her heart thumped. Aunt Drusilla was walking toward her beside the general!

"Would you care to dance?"

If she danced, he might recognize her. But if she did not dance, Aunt Drusilla would definitely recognize her. *"Si, señor."*

He laughed, drawing her by the hand. It was another country-dance, one in which she need not mind her steps, as she had danced it many times before.

The general moved within her line of sight. He had not bothered to dress up, having said the previous day that his military coat should suffice, especially as he'd earned it the hard way, unlike the foolish dandies who hired theirs. She paced back. The general was turning, turning —

"Excuse me, sir." Leaving a nonplussed viscount, she rushed behind a man dressed in a Hindustani turban and robes, allowing his passage through the room to screen her, until she reached the relative sanctuary of the room's corner. There, people milled together, their figures alternately shielding her from view and affording glimpses of the dancing.

A pink *señorita* turned her head to stare. Catherine waved her fan to cool herself as she kept searching, searching. In another corner she recognized Julia, her fair hair dressed with flowers apropos of the Greek goddess Persephone, talking animatedly to a dark-haired man who, though his back be to her, reminded Catherine somewhat of Major Hale. In yet another she saw Lady Milton and Perry, neither of whom had bothered to dress up, chatting with Mrs. Lampscombe. The room twirled with color and magic and crystals, a plethora of the fanciful: soldiers, Greek gods and goddesses, comic and classical figures. Oh, where was — ?

There! Her heart threatened to escape the thin satin of her gown. How handsome he looked, dressed as a chevalier like his friend. For despite the black mask, the tall blond figure could never be disguised too effectively.

"Good evening."

Catherine froze. Turned. Recognized the green eyes glittering behind the diamond-encrusted silver mask. Recognized that only one matron could appear so modish simply by the addition of star-shaped diamonds embroidered onto a clinging black gown and nestled in the high black wig which covered the natural color of her hair. Her smile remained fixed as she curtsied. "G-good evening, *mi señora.*"

The emerald gaze scanned Catherine's costume before offering a tiny nod. "I see you are aware of me but, alas, I remain in the dark."

"But you are the night sky, are you not?"

For a moment the figure in black stilled, before a small chuckle came from behind the mask. "Well said, my dear."

As the scrutiny continued, Catherine lifted the fan to hide her face. How could she escape?

"I confess to admiring your earrings very much."

"Gracias, señora."

Her heart panged amidst the color and noise and the fear of discovery. Poor Papa, trying to buy her affection through expensive trinkets. She lowered her head, blinking away the burn in her eyes.

"Ah, now I see." At the purr in the voice she peeked up. "That is a very pretty comb."

Catherine's breath caught.

Lady Harkness chuckled. "You surprise me, my dear. I didn't think you had it in you."

She gasped. Lady Harkness had recognized her?

"Carlew, who is that divine creature in red talking to your mother?"

Jonathan watched the figure carefully, tiny sparks of half recognition flickering as she bent her head. "I am not sure."

"I managed half a dance with her before she ran away."

"Losing your charm, are you?"

"Never! She simply must not have known it was me."

"Which is rather the point of a masquerade, is it not?"

"Well, yes. But anyone with half an eye can tell it is you underneath that getup."

Jon shrugged. Dressed in a French cavalier style as Carmichael had insisted, the faint ridiculousness he'd felt at home had quickly worn off, surrounded as he was by others who looked far more foolish.

"I shall ask your mother to introduce me, and insist on finishing my dance with the pretty *señorita.*"

"As you wish."

Carmichael grinned and disappeared through the throng.

Good luck to him. Jon did not want to dance. He'd fulfilled his obligations by dancing with his sister and mother, but his feet might as well have lead in them.

"Excuse me, sir?" Mr. Donaldson, the master of ceremonies, bowed. "May I offer the hand of a Miss Galbraith, should you be seeking a partner?"

"Of course." It was ungentlemanly to refuse. Jon bowed to the young lady, whose smile suggested she'd despaired of finding a partner. "Good evening."

"Good evening, sir." The young blonde shepherdess curtsied, and he led her out to join the set that was just forming. As he waited for their turn, he scanned the room. With the advantage his height provided, he could see his mother and the *señorita* had disappeared, whilst Julia was in the next set, dancing with young Milton, a twist to her lips that suggested disgust. Carmichael he could not see. Had he found his mystery lady?

The music shifted, and he performed the movements mechanically. Dancing with such a quiet partner had benefit, as the lack of conversation allowed his thoughts to roam free. But perhaps it was not wise, as he could not help but compare tonight's masque with the last he had attended, three years ago.

Such foolish hope that had made his heart

and feet fly. Dancing with her had been a dream, holding her in his arms fueling visions for the future. Then when they moved outside —

Enough! He shook his head at himself. The music signaled the end of that dance, and he escorted his partner back to her grateful parents. Somehow he was caught in the rush to the floor for the next dance, one that allowed much exchanging of partners, as he danced with a parade of princesses, carnival characters, and those dressed in the costumes of nationalities ranging from a Scottish highlander to a Turkish sultana. Just as he was wishing he had refused to come, his partner twirled off and was replaced by a *señorita.* In red.

He held out his hand. She took it in her gloved one. "Good evening."

She glanced up. Gasped. "G-good evening, sir."

He led her through the first movement. Another shy debutante, dressed beautifully but too provocatively for her years. "There's no need to be frightened. I promise not to eat you."

A smile wisped across her lips as her eyes, half hidden behind the mask, met his again, dark, soulful, mysterious. "Promise?"

His heart thudded. No debutante would

dare make such a comment. No wonder Carmichael had been entranced.

He studied her carefully. The dark head was now bowed, a pearl comb holding a froth of lace in her hair. Small, perfectly shaped ears wore the only other ornamentation, save for her necklace and the spangles in her dress. "Are you enjoying yourself?"

"Si, señor," she replied in husky tones. "And you?"

"Oui," he said, joining in with her game. *"Parlez vous francais?"*

"Non." Her lips curved.

He echoed the motion, even as he felt a faint tug of recognition. She was definitely not the shy debutante he had initially thought. Who was she? They moved around the set, together, then apart. He noticed his mother studying them, her arms crossed, one hand flicking her lace fan back and forth, as if waiting for something to occur.

"My friend danced with you earlier." Jon nodded to where Carmichael now danced with Julia. "The chevalier there. He said you ran away. Will you run from me, too?"

"No, señor."

Their gazes connected, something tightened across his chest. Wisps of memory begged to be recalled. He exhaled. "Please, *señorita,* can you tell me if we have met

410

before?"

"No, señor."

"You cannot, or we have not?"

Her smile widened.

Before she could respond, the dance led her away to curtsy to the next man, during which Jon could appreciate her figure, her gown clinging to her curves —

"Lord, help me," he muttered, averting his eyes. He should not be entranced by the *señorita*. Miss Beauchamp was his intended and alone should occupy his thoughts.

But when he finished the dance, having released his partner to her chaperone, Jon could do nothing save search for the mysterious lady in red. He found her, half hidden behind a pillar, watching the dancing, a slight wistful droop to her lips. "Here you are."

"You are observant, *señor*." Her lips lifted in one corner.

He chuckled, and snagged the attention of a passing footman. "May I offer you some refreshment? A glass of punch, perhaps?"

"I would prefer lemonade, sir."

Jon stilled, peering closer at the *señorita*. He had known a young lady whose dislike of mixed drinks had led to many a whispered conversation and laughter — and almost to the altar. Her eyes were bright behind her mask, her lips, stained pink, held a quirk of mischief.

"Pardon, *señor,* is there a problem?"

"You . . . you remind me of someone."

"Me, *señor*? I am nothing but a poor girl." She stepped back, away from the candlelight spilling from the chandelier.

If it *was* her . . . His heartbeat quickened. "Tell me, what are your favorite flowers?"

A beat. "I do not know why this should concern you." She glanced away.

"I should think lilacs, or perhaps the lily?"

"No." Her smile flashed. She stepped away, her fan waving rapidly.

"Perhaps a rose? 'For a rose by any other name should smell so sweet.' I wonder at your name, *señorita.*"

The fan stopped waving. "*Señor,* please excuse —"

"Violets?"

Her gaze snapped to meet his.

His heart kicked. It *had* to be. He stepped closer. "Catherine?"

She shook her head. "Excuse me, sir."

And with a twirl of her skirts she was gone.

Jon moved to hurry after her, but a touch on his arm gave him pause.

"Leave her," Mama murmured.

He exhaled. "You know that was Miss Winthrop?"

"I certainly did not expect to see her. Nor, it must be said, did I expect to see her looking quite so . . ." She waved a hand dismissively.

Dashing? Intriguing? Beautiful? Any word would fit.

"Well," his mother continued, "you seemed to be having quite a time with her."

"I was not sure it was she."

"And if you were?" Her look was piercing.

He had no answer.

In some ways it had felt like coming home, a reversion to the ease and familiarity he remembered of years ago, where one would catch the unsaid, finish their sentences, laugh with the unspoken jest. In another, he felt a mix of dread and anticipation, the excitement of the unknown, the potential, the tremulous hope.

Why had she come?

His mother frowned. "I do not know quite what Julia sees in her. She's such an odd creature."

His soul burned in protest. He forced calmness into his voice. "Miss Winthrop is not odd, Mother."

She stared at him. "I meant Julia, dear boy."

The noise of the ballroom, the rush of people, filled his senses again. He pushed to his toes, but still the mysterious *señorita* remained elusive. His soul strained to find her, to speak with her again, to perhaps finally ascertain if the spark he'd sensed was simply his vain imaginings or something more. "Mother, please excuse —"

"Where is she?" Jon turned to see Carmichael attended by his sister. "Come, old man, I saw you talking with the lovely *señorita* but a few minutes ago."

"You mean Miss Winthrop?"

Carmichael's jaw sagged. "That was she?"

"Catherine was here?" Julia said. "Mother? Why didn't you tell me? Where is she?" She looked about eagerly.

"She has gone." Jon's voice sounded flat, even to his own ears.

"But how did she come? It was not with the general. He came with her aunt, and look" — Julia nodded to the exit — "they are now leaving."

His gaze tracked to the exiting duo. Duo, not trio.

Julia gasped, her eyes widening. "You don't think — ?"

His heart drummed loudly, as Carmichael chuckled, and said the words he didn't want to hear.

"The naughty minx! She's come alone."

■ ■ ■ ■

Catherine hastened through the Assembly Room's vestibule. She had set out to leave as soon as Aunt Drusilla had begun her farewells; experience said it would take another ten minutes before she retrieved her cloak. But in pausing for a final look at the dancing, Mr. Carlew had stopped her, and she'd reveled in the delight of old banter — making her late. She had to hurry. She pulled the hood of her domino lower and rushed down the front steps. Though some might have suspected, she still could not afford widespread recognition.

"Ahoy, there, lass. Dinnae be running away."

Catherine glanced to her right. A group of soldiers, their uniforms somewhat tattered, stood eyeing her. She shivered. Glanced to her left. Dim alleys beckoned.

"Come on, lass. We just want a word."

A bottle clanked. Footsteps scurried behind.

Lord, help me!

The footsteps picked up speed. Her pulse's tempo outpaced them. She hurried towards the darkness, her breath coming in gasps. *"Dear God!"*

415

"Excuse me, miss?"

The voice, vaguely recognized, made her slow. Glance up. Stop. "Major Hale?" She pulled her mask away for a better look. "Oh, it *is* you!"

"Miss Winthrop?" He blinked. "What the deuce are you doing here?"

"I . . ." she glanced over her shoulder, and shivered. The soldiers remained, watching, leering.

"My sister," Hale said loudly. "Foolish girl. Thought I'd gone home."

There was a chorus of grumbles and the men retreated.

Catherine released a deep breath. "Thank you, Major Hale."

"Don't mention it."

She glanced up at her protector. Upper room lights revealed the melancholy lining his face. "Sir, forgive me but you do not seem well."

"I . . ." He threw a hand through his hair. "How can I be? When all is . . ."

"When all is what, Mr. Hale?" The hopeless look on his face thickened her throat. "Sir, you seem troubled."

"Troubled? Oh, if it was merely that. I . . . I am in agony."

"Sir, you have friends." She placed a hand on his arm. "Mr. Carlew —"

"He is not my friend."

She drew back. "But . . . Julia?"

"What has she said?" he asked eagerly.

"Sh-she seems most concerned for you."

"She is an angel."

Major Hale and Julia? Oh, no.

"Did you see her tonight? Never has she looked lovelier. If it were not for that brother —"

That overprotective big brother.

Slow dread crept over her, prickling her skin. Something made her look up, look over her shoulder, back at the Assembly Rooms —

To see Mr. Carlew, the viscount, and Julia standing on the front steps, staring in their direction. Behind them stood Lady Milton.

Nausea slid through her stomach.

"Look at them, judging." He snorted. "Poor Julia doesn't have a chance."

"But, sir —"

"Come. Tie your mask back on. We should go."

Before she was caught, and had to explain. After asking her direction, Major Hale took her hand, and soon they were twisting through the back alleys to Gay Street. She glanced up, could see the general's coach turn at the corner.

Panic hurried her movements. She raced

417

up the steps, opened the door. Thank God it remained unlocked! "Th-thank you, sir."

"When may we speak?"

She had to get rid of him! The coach rumbled closer. "T-tomorrow morning? At Debenhams?"

"I'll be waiting."

She nodded, eased the front door shut, and hurried up the main stairs to her room. She closed and locked the door, stripped off the garments, and slipped into bed. Below she heard a soft murmur of voices. Moments later, she heard steps creak outside in the hall, waiting a long moment before creaking away again.

She huddled under her covers, heart racing, mind spinning with the events of the night: the music, the lights, the costumes, the dancing. Mr. Carlew, his soft words, the light in his eyes, his hand holding hers, the stirring of sweet memories. Conscious of so much.

Conscious of one thing.

She was now hostage to Hale's demands.

Chapter Twenty-Five

"How could she?"

Julia's white-faced question continued to haunt Jonathan, long after they had returned to Camden Place and she had rushed off to bed.

By mutual consent they had not told Mother about what they'd seen. He felt sure she would soon learn all; Lady Milton would see to that. He would tell Mother tomorrow, but right now could not find the words. For Julia's words echoed those in his heart. How *could* Catherine do such a scandalous thing? It was one thing to have thought a young lady might throw off the conventions of mourning to attend a masquerade; it was quite another to do so without proper chaperonage — to attend in the company of a known rake!

"I think we're both in need of some restoration," Carmichael said, picking up a decanter.

"Not for me." His brain felt too foggy already.

Carmichael poured himself two fingers of whiskey and sank into the seat opposite. A blissful kind of silence — or was it numbness? — filled the room, drowning out the clatter in his mind.

"Well! That was an eventful evening." The viscount gave a flash of a grin. "I have to say I no longer think a mouse is *quite* the right description for her."

Images of her sensual dress, her painted lips, her flirtatious manner arose, stirring desire, stirring confusion. Was it possible he had been fooled all this time? Were the rumors circulating around Bath concerning her fast ways that he'd dismissed as wickedness actually true?

"She was . . . nothing like I've known."

Except that wasn't really true. He'd known her like that. Had even once encouraged her in her self-assuredness. But how had this turned so badly? Leaving him feeling furious, frustrated, bereft?

"Well, I know its not the usual thing for a mourning miss, but I'm glad she got the chance to have a little fun. After all, she won't get much chance with the general."

"He seemed to be enjoying himself."

"But not with her." Carmichael swallowed

his drink and eyed him. "It's all a little messy, isn't it, old man?"

Jon inhaled, working to overcome the spike of anger prompted at his friend's words. Why did he have to look at a fellow quite so perceptively?

His mother returned, her wig off, now draped in a wrapper. "Julia seems a little down."

He bit back a sarcastic comment, thankful for his friend who mentioned something about the sad lack of dancers. "Perhaps that was the problem tonight, Lady Harkness."

"Perhaps." Her keen green eyes shifted to him. "And you, Jon? What reason might you give for your sister's shifting spirits?"

"I could not say." Would not say. He had unnerving suspicions but until he learned more he could say nothing. Yet. "She has been mercurial of late."

"True." She glanced between them. "Am I interrupting something? Is there perhaps more to this than I know?"

He swallowed a sigh. "Tomorrow, Mother. I will tell you tomorrow."

She frowned. "There is nothing of concern for tonight?"

Not so long as Julia remained in her room all night. "No. Go to sleep, Mother. Sweet dreams." He kissed her cheek, waited as she left the room, then resumed his slumped posture in the chair.

"I do not envy you, old man." Carmichael placed his glass on the side table. "What will you do?"

He could not answer as the worries whirled within. He must talk with Julia; must talk with Hale. Must speak with Catherine. His heart panged.

"She is your cousin, is she not? Sorry, *third* cousin. You are now the head of your family, so I suppose you must speak with her."

"I should go tonight."

"And do what? Demand to see her? Demand an explanation? How would that help?"

"At least I'd know she arrived home safely, and wouldn't be —" Cursed with anxiety, worried about threats to her virtue, imagining the worst, helpless in his fear.

Carmichael shook his head gently. "You cannot go. If it really was Miss Winthrop, then she has obviously slipped out without others knowing, and is most likely now tucked up in bed. And for all his reputation, you cannot really see Hale harming her in any way, can you?"

"Well . . ."

"And storming in there demanding to see her would only set you up as possessing an

422

interest far beyond that of a cousin, and might raise questions over your motives, old man." A beat. "Unless you truly do hold interest in her beyond that of a cousin."

"*Third* cousin."

At the sound of his friend's soft laughter Jon looked up. Met the too-perceptive gaze once more. Felt the tips of his ears burn. He hastened to say, "Perhaps the general —"

"She obviously did not care to seek his opinion, just as he did not seem too mindful of hers. You know, it really puts me in mind that perhaps they are not so attached as you suppose."

"Carmichael," he gritted out.

"Do you growl at your shareholders as you do your friends? It is a wonder you have any of either, the way you carry on sometimes. I am simply trying to be helpful."

"Or simply trying."

Carmichael laughed. "That's the spirit." His amusement faded, his eyes now shaded with something akin to understanding. "But you do need to speak with her. And find Hale."

"Where would he be?" Panic clawed up his throat, pushed him to his feet. "What if he leaves? What if he" — he swallowed bitterness — "compromises her?"

His friend's face softened with sympathy. "Tomorrow, old man."

Jon nodded, his heart weighted with dread. Tomorrow.

Too close, and yet too far away.

Catherine rose early, heavy-eyed, the lack of sleep making her movements slow, but she could not linger in bed and risk Bess discovering her nighttime activities. She lifted the Spanish gown, now dry, from where she'd hung it in front of the fire last night. She'd waited an age until she was sure Aunt Drusilla had gone to bed before commencing her ministrations, damping out the stains, cleaning the fan, the mask, and domino. They were now ready to be returned, but the gloves would have to wait for later. She would just hope Aunt Drusilla did not require her gloves any time soon.

She carefully laid the pieces under the bed, thankful the valance hid them from view — and that regular cleaning meant no dust motes lived there to give away her endeavors. She tiptoed to the door, unlocked it, and then crept back to bed, thinking over the previous evening.

What a wonderful dream! To know she still possessed that indefinable something that made him smile. She'd felt it. Seen the moment he had felt it also, when it seemed the years had rolled away and they were once more young and carefree. For a moment, she had gloried in knowing she was the one he sought. For a moment she had luxuriated in the memory of their long-ago kiss: the warmth, the passion, the heady joy of desire; the feeling of home found in his lips. For a moment she had even thought it possible he might truly smile at her, as if he'd never needed to forgive, and they could be happy, together at last.

But such wonderful dreams had slowly dissipated in the night, stalked by heavy shame.

Oh, she should never have gone! Should never have gone *alone.*

His mother knew, Lord Carmichael knew, Julia, Lady Milton — oh, the shame!

And *he* knew. Her heart caught, remembering afresh the moment he had realized who she truly was. Had made it obvious he'd known, shock and disgust writ large in his blue eyes.

Oh, she should never have gone!

The recriminations circled, the doubts, the worries pecking at her like a foul bird. What would people say when they discovered what she'd done? What would Mama? What would her aunt? The general? Now she truly *was* scandalous, a liar, a deceiver, brazen, and sunk far below respectability. Her heart clenched. *Lord, forgive me —*

A knock came at the door. "Miss?"

She dredged up a smile as Bess appeared. "Good morning."

"You're awake bright and early. I suppose extra sleep does help."

Guilt cramped her stomach. "It usually does."

"Oh, are these your gloves? I must have missed them yesterday evening."

"Um, they actually belong to my aunt. I . . . I borrowed them." That was not a lie at least.

"Shall I give them a clean? They look a little dirty."

"Th-thank you."

"Of course. Will there be anything else?"

Her cheeks heated. Bess could not see under the bed. "That will be all."

"Very well, miss."

Throughout the morning she was in a welter of nervous anticipation, waiting for Aunt Drusilla to leave her room, waiting for the maids to clear away, waiting to return the clothes, waiting for the knock at the door signaling the new gossip surrounding her. For she felt sure Lady Milton would feel it her duty to report to her neighbors just what she'd seen.

She shivered. And then there was the problem of Julia.

Coupled with her personal shame were other worries that had crept up in the night. What was Julia playing at? What did Hale want? Toward him she felt a mixture of gratitude and trepidation. He had come to her rescue in a most gentlemanly way. And he obviously cared for Julia . . . but why had he seemed so sad? Why was he angry with Mr. Carlew? Something had estranged them, but what? How could she meet the major today without knowing more of the facts? She couldn't.

Catherine sighed. She would have to forgo his visit until she made another.

She would have to visit Julia.

"I do not want to see her."

Jonathan eyed his half sister as she crossed her arms and sat on the drawing room settee. The servant's message that Miss Winthrop had called and wished to speak with Julia had taken them all by surprise. Julia's reaction had startled even more.

"But, Julia, she is your friend."

"No, Mother. I will return to my room should you continue to harangue me."

Mother looked anxiously at Jon. He could

only offer a small shrug.

"I will see her," said Carmichael. "I must compliment her on that gown she —"

"You will do no such thing. *I* will speak to her."

"Jonathan? You look so serious. Is something the matter with Miss Winthrop?"

"I hope to find out," he grated.

"Now I know it was a silly thing to do, going off to a masque, but I must admit to a degree of admiration," his mother said. "I did not think she possessed such . . ."

"Courage?" suggested Carmichael.

"Foolhardiness," Jon muttered.

"Gumption," Mother said with a nod. "Anyway, I'll wager she was not recognized by any but we."

"Lady Milton knows."

"What? How? Oh, that *is* unfortunate."

"Indeed." How to make a scandal worse: have Lady Milton as witness.

"Will your conversation require my presence? Sometimes an older lady's guidance can be helpful in such matters."

"Thank you, Mother, but that will *not* be necessary." He had a fair idea his mother's presence would prove more a hindrance than a help.

Carmichael shot him a quick look before turning to the ladies. "Lady Harkness, perhaps you can tell me your opinion on my arrangement of this neckcloth. I confess to having more faith in your opinion on such important matters than that of your son."

Jon glanced once more at his sister, whose burning eyes chilled him, then made his way to the study. "Miss Winthrop."

She turned as he entered the room. Her eyes were shadowed. "Mr. — Lord Winthrop."

Her sop to his title withered any sympathy within. "I see you are alone. Again."

She seemed to shrink in her chair. "S-sir, I know it was wrong —"

"Wrong? Wrong was going to a ball in the first place. Have you forgotten you are in mourning?"

Catherine flushed, shook her head.

"But to go to a masque, unaccompanied." He drew out the last word, making it seem more question than statement. Would she own to her relationship with Hale?

She said nothing, her dark eyes pleading.

"What were you thinking?" he barked.

He noticed her jump. Her eyes grow shiny with tears. He felt a moment's regret then hardened his heart. How would she ever learn until she felt so ashamed she would never dare again?

"I . . . I wanted to remember."

All at once his memories flooded in, sweet times, when they'd been so akin in every thought he'd grown so sure of his decision. Another ball, another masque, a night when hopes had blossomed into actuality — before true reality set in.

He bit back a groan, forced his attention to the present. "You should not have gone."

"You seemed glad that I did." Her voice was soft, cutting him to the quick.

Yes, he had enjoyed their interactions, had imagined if things were different . . . He shook his head, cleared away his doubts. Forced steel into his voice. "What about your intended?"

Catherine swallowed. "The general and I —"

"What about Hale?"

She blinked, as if taken aback at the bite in his voice. As was he. He forced his fingers to unclench — he had to calm down.

"I c-came to speak with you about him."

"Oh, you did?" Hale's words from Christmas rose again, stirring his anger. Hale had wooed her, obviously won her. How *could* she? "So this wasn't a visit of repentance."

"I . . . I beg your pardon?"

"You are not here, begging forgiveness for your misdemeanor?"

430

For a moment her lips parted, as if she were taken by surprise. Then her chin lifted. "I understand that my actions last night might have been misinterpreted —"

"You were seen, with Hale, running off in a dark alley to goodness knows where."

She blanched. "This is what you think?"

"Me. And Carmichael. And Julia. Oh, and let's not forget Lady Milton."

Her chin quivered, there was a distinct flash in her eyes, but she said nothing.

"Yes, Lady Milton. There's never a whiff of scandal that woman does not know about! And because of that, as head of the family —"

"It's a fine time for you to talk so well," she muttered.

"What?"

Her voice sharpened. "Talking as though you are responsible for all Winthrops when you are not even aware of what is happening under your nose."

"I beg your pardon?"

"Where is Julia? It is *Julia* I wished to see."

"She is with my mother. She does not wish to see you."

Her shoulders sagged. "Then she is angry with me, too. She does not understand —"

"Understand what?" Frustration, mingled with personal disappointment, urged his anger on. "That you are not the friend she thought? That you say one thing then do another? That you lead a man on only to laugh in his face?"

She gasped. "I did no such thing!"

"You did! Three years ago! You have not changed. You lead the poor old foolish general around on a string, when really he is your insurance while you have a little fling."

Her mouth fell open. "You are mistaken, both about the general, and about three years ago —"

"Am I?"

"And it seems I am sadly mistaken about you." She rose, eyes smoldering, hands trembling. She gripped the back of the chair, but still he could see her agitation. "Yes, I won't deny I attended the masque, that I went there alone. I know it was wrong; I knew it at the time. And neither will I deny that I saw Major Hale. He kindly offered his protection for my homeward journey."

Guilt stabbed. Something he should have done.

"He seemed most concerned about your sister —"

"Leave Julia out of it. You are not responsible for her."

"She is my cousin, and my friend, and as such, I *do* feel responsible for her." Her voice was soft, yet contained an iciness he'd never heard before, a coldness matching her glacial expression. "And if you take your responsibilities as head of your family seriously, might I suggest you start with those living under your roof!"

He clenched his fists. Inhaled. Forced his breath out slowly. "Are you quite finished, Miss Winthrop?"

"No. Your allegations against me are as baseless as any of Lady Milton's lies. I might have forgiven your behavior in the past —"

"*My* behavior?"

"But I cannot forget the words you have expressed just now that show how deep your hate for me truly is." Moisture trickled from her eye. She swiped it away. "I do not like you. I do not want to see you. You are too quick to believe falsehoods and not listen to fact. You are not the gentleman of honor I once lo—" She swallowed. "Thought."

His conscience pricked. "Miss Winthrop. Catherine —"

"I do not want to speak with you again. I am but your third cousin, so any sense of familial obligation is meager to say the least. So I remind you, *Lord* Winthrop, as far as my mother and I are concerned, you are

433

not responsible for us, not responsible for me at all!"

She turned, moving to the door.

He hastened around the desk to hold the door closed. "You return home?"

"Yes."

"I will send for the carriage." Her chin lifted. "Oh, pray do not be concerned. I do this simply to protect your reputation as a lady."

Her eyes narrowed. He stood so close he could hear her agitated breathing.

"Very well."

He barked commands at servants, whilst she moved to stand at the window, as far from him as possible, twisting the ribbons of her reticule until he could see they'd be destroyed, her back poker-straight with indignation. He'd never been more thankful than when the footman finally announced the coach's readiness.

The short journey was silent, her gaze averted, the air seething with resentment. He escorted her to the door, managed what he hoped was a pleasant expression for the butler, offered the startled aunt the excuse "Miss Winthrop went to visit my sister," then departed.

Upon arriving home he barked another order for his groom, then rushed upstairs to change into riding dress. He would need a long ride to rid himself of the heat of his words. The ice of hers. The hurt cramping his heart.

He was buttoning up his topcoat when a knock at the door caused him to turn.

Carmichael leaned against the doorframe, brow knotted. "Old man, are you quite all right? We heard shouting, then you were gone. And now you're back."

"Your powers of observation do you credit," he gritted out, picking up his hat and gloves.

"I sense violets shall remain unpicked?"

"Shut up, Carmichael!"

And he rushed down the stairs into freedom.

CHAPTER TWENTY-SIX

She should not have gone. She should not have gone either to the masquerade *or* to his house.

He despised her.

Water filled her eyes, pain gnawing hungrily across her chest, as it did every time she remembered the incident of three days ago. His words. His contempt. His fury. Sometimes the pain felt so intense she might almost buckle under its weight. How could she count *this* joy? How could everything have turned so badly so quickly? Somehow this felt even worse than his previous rejection. At least she'd been shielded by the impersonal nature of the letter. Now she had nobody, no shield, and no hope.

She studied her reflection in the mirror. Dark, dank hair scraped back into a simple chignon. Bess was too busy to attend to Catherine, so her toilette had simplified to the basics; dressing hair was not part of her regime. She peered closer. Shadows underscored her eyes, smudges that never went away, smears of weariness that highlighted the extreme pallor of her skin. Even her eyes, which he had once said were her best feature — as dark and mysterious as an enchanted wood — her eyes looked so tired, more haunted than a graveyard at midnight. She looked what she was: an old maid. Was it any wonder he preferred Miss Beauchamp to herself? Once upon a time he might have considered Catherine's looks appealing, had indeed encouraged her to liveliness, to hope and dream; now he only looked upon her to disapprove.

Despondency washed over her again, thick, weighty, bearing down on her soul as iron.

She breathed in. Out. Rose from her dressing table to make her way downstairs to the drawing room where Mama sat with her sister reading correspondence. Mama glanced at a letter before tossing it aside with a sniff and a dismissive "Solicitors. What would they know?" She eyed Catherine with a frown. "Catherine, you are not looking at all well."

Breathe in. Breathe out.

"Perhaps you should put on some rouge."

"No." Better to look dowdy than to look painted.

"Is something the matter? Do you need to see a doctor? I know Cornelia Milton swears that Dr. Janus is a godsend, and I'm prepared to overlook her patronage of the fellow if it would do you some good."

"Elvira, leave her. I'm sure Catherine is merely tired."

"Tired? I don't know what she has to be tired about. Save for that visit to Julia Carlew she hasn't gone out for days."

To avoid her mother's piercing gaze, Catherine picked up her tambour and stared at the needlepoint pattern. What should she say? She didn't want to lie. Was withholding all of the truth a lie? What if it was to protect someone else? If she exposed her suspicions about Julia, wasn't that merely contributing to more gossip, more speculation? How could she meet with the major? She'd said she would, and she hated not keeping her word. Fresh regrets clawed at her, like a thousand bats circled within. She rubbed her head. What was she to do?

A gasp drew her attention to her mother's shocked face. "Oh my!"

Oh no . . .

"Catherine! Can you explain this?" Her mother flapped a letter under her nose.

"Mother —"

"This . . . this baseless report, containing the most alarming allegation I have had the misfortune to read."

Catherine swallowed. Which allegation?

"Can you tell me why people are saying you were seen in the company of a certain man?"

She could. She chose not to. "The general is not my only friend, Mama," she hedged.

"But apart from Mr. Carlew, the only other is that young Carmichael man, and I cannot like you spending much time with him. He seems too smooth a man."

Memories rose of his unexpected visit in this very room. "I think Serena agrees with you."

"Oh, Serena!" Her mother groaned. "That girl is an enigma to me. She always has been, with those cool looks of hers."

As her mother and aunt discussed the difficulties of Serena, Catherine thanked God for her sister's unwitting role in turning Mama's attention from her elder daughter. Her thoughts returned to her other problems. How could she speak with Hale? She'd been prevented three days ago, their meeting aborted first by her thwarted visit to Julia, then by her mother's scolding upon Catherine's distressed return. But she *must* speak with Hale. He should not carry on in this secretive manner with Julia.

Her heart snarled some more. How could she make things right with Julia? She *had* to know her actions were wrong, falling for a man her family deemed unsuitable. But how to speak to her . . . Catherine's scrawled note yesterday had been returned, un-opened. She would do almost anything, but — risk his censure, risk his condemnation? That she simply could not do. Her eyes blurred. No. God would have to provide the opportunity because she would never darken *his* front steps or speak to him again.

Ever.

God seemed to have heard her prayer for the next day, on her visit to the circulating library, Catherine saw her. Julia saw her, whitened, turned away. Catherine hurried after her. "I must speak with you."

Julia moved as though to go. Catherine touched her arm. "About Hale."

She stopped. Turned. Her eyes were like shards of blue ice. "I do not wish to speak with you of him."

"Please, Julia. I assure you, he does not care for me, and only wishes to see you."

The younger girl's face contorted like she might cry.

440

Catherine's heart writhed. How well she understood such agony. "Julia." She swallowed. "I . . . I wish to explain, but we cannot speak here." There were too many curious faces, too many hushed whispers.

Julia blinked rapidly, her gaze dropping to study the toe of her slipper, peeping from the flounce of her skirt. "Perhaps . . . I could persuade Mother of the benefits of a stroll near the rotunda in Sydney Gardens this afternoon. Around three?"

Relief rushed through Catherine's chest. "I will await you."

Doubt shadowed her decision for the following hours. Was she right? Should she try to speak with Lady Harkness again? Lord Winthrop? What if Julia's apparent *amour* for Major Hale was nothing more than a young girl's foolish imaginings? But what if it were not? Would Catherine prove the fool for getting involved?

With a prayer for wisdom, she made her way out onto the gravel path near the rotunda. Julia hurried toward her. "Quickly! My maid is nearby, but I do not wish for her to see you." The younger girl clutched Catherine's arm, leading her to a narrow path behind a hedge of hawthorn. "I'm sure she will only tattle to Mother or worse, my brother. He has forbidden my seeing you."

Catherine's heart wrenched. "Perhaps we should not —"

"But I am *glad* to have defied him. For now I know all is as it should be. I should never have doubted you, Catherine." She tugged her down onto the bench next to her. "You won't speak a word to anyone?"

"You . . . you are not in any trouble, are you?"

Her blue eyes opened wide. "Of course not!"

"Then why must such things be kept quiet?"

"My brother is a tyrant! He does not wish for my happiness."

Words refused to form. Tyrannical . . . yes, she could understand.

"You *know* I am right. I heard him the other day, yelling at you like you were a doxy."

She gasped. "Julia!"

"No. He was very wrong in his manner toward you. Lord Carmichael and I could not think how he could behave so appallingly. Even Mama agreed."

Emotions clashed within her chest. She bit her lip. How to explain why she had gone . . .

"Catherine, I know you only have my best

interests at heart."

"As does your brother."

"No. He refuses to listen. He is stubborn beyond anyone I've ever met."

"But —"

"Dearest Catherine, you cannot know what he is truly like. He takes a prejudice against someone and refuses to see their side."

She nodded reluctantly. Hadn't this proved true in her own experience?

"He took a pet against my Hale, and now refuses to countenance him, even refuses Carmichael to speak of him."

"And you do not know why?"

"He refuses to say."

"And you and Hale?"

Julia blushed, her eyes downcast. "He . . . he wishes to marry me."

Catherine's mouth sagged. Envy streaked hot and cruelly through her. Oh, to have a man she loved wish to marry her! She swallowed. "I . . . I was not aware you knew him so well."

"We've known him some time. He's been friends with Jon for years. Then he came to Winthrop, and later we met in London. Oh, Catherine, I know others cannot see it, but truly, he is all that is gentlemanly and good!"

Catherine said carefully, "People have

443

said . . . he is s-something of a rake.”

Julia's eyes flashed, and she tossed her curls impatiently over a shoulder. “That was before he met me.”

A bird chirruped from a nearby elm. The Avon's quiet burble ascended from below. The breeze pricked coolness around her cheeks. What could she say to Julia that would be heard?

“Does your mother know of your regard?”

“Mother? She spends more time worrying over marrying off Jon than she does thinking about me.”

The words stung, as did Julia's obvious bitterness. *Lord God, give me wisdom . . .*

“Please, Catherine. Just meet him. You will see he has been falsely represented.”

Meeting Hale again could not hurt, could it? After all, he'd helped her before.

She sighed. “Very well.”

“Miss Winthrop, I cannot thank you enough for agreeing to see me.”

She nodded, thankful cloudy skies meant this path alongside the Avon was not busy. Her reputation could scarcely take more prying eyes. Yet meeting a gentleman was not easy; she had needed to request the general's help once again. When she'd murmured something about taking a walk in Sydney Gardens — apparently a favorite meeting place for Julia and the major — he had been quick to agree. When they had "accidentally" met the major, he had been all booming cheer.

"Hale! Well met, old fellow. You have been missed these past weeks."

Hale's tired glance at Catherine held questions he could only ask when the major had run into another acquaintance, allowing them to hurry ahead. "You have spoken with Julia?"

She nodded. "She says you wish to marry her."

"You are surprised." His eyes were watchful, drawing truth from within.

"I did not think you so serious about *one* young lady," she confessed.

He snorted. "He has poisoned you against me, hasn't he?"

"Mr. Carlew?" At his nod she shook her head. "We have never spoken of you."

He frowned. "So you judge me — ?"

"On what I have seen, and I have not seen you pay attention to one lady before." She gave a small smile. "But that is not to say you cannot."

He sighed. "Carlew thinks my past determines my future, that my reputation bars me from finding happiness with Julia."

"He is not quick to forget," she murmured, before adding wryly, "but I am the last person in Bath to think one's reputation is always based on fact."

"I knew you would understand!" He stopped and grasped her hands. "Please, Miss Winthrop, help me find happiness with my Julia."

"But how?"

"Invite her to walk with you again. Then if I should happen to meet you, as happened so fortuitously today, then we might speak, and you will know our love is sincere."

She bit her lip. The general's booming voice was calling her. She turned, gave him a small wave. What should she do?

"Lord Winthrop has forbidden her to see me."

"Yet we both know his decisions are not always correct?"

She looked sharply at him.

"Miss Winthrop, please do not tell me you do not wish the past were different?"

Fear trickled through her. What did he know?

He smiled, and again she was struck by his charm. "I met Carlew in India, y'know. He never was one for the ladies, even though they flocked to him. I asked him about it once, and he said a girl had nigh on broke his heart."

Her mouth dried. She stared at him, disbelieving. No, no, he had broken hers . . .

"You do not credit it? If you could but have seen him."

She shook her head. "I do not know what you have heard, but you . . . you must be mistaken."

He eyed her for a moment before inclining his head. "I do not wish to argue with you, Miss Winthrop. But can I ask this: do you not sometimes wish the past were different?"

Sometimes? Try all the time. "But wishing cannot change things."

"Exactly. The past cannot be changed. But our future . . ." He sighed heavily. "It is our choices that shape our future."

She thought on his words as they neared the general. The past could never be changed, but God could help shake off the shadows to embrace the future. Her prayer from earlier bubbled up again. *Lord, give me wisdom . . .*

"I will endeavor to speak with her."

And write another note to Lady Harkness and her son.

Catherine eyed the envelope. That of another note returned, unopened. She bent her head to her stitching again. Mama and Aunt Drusilla's conversation rippled around her, but she could only think of her dilemma. Her attempt to speak with Lady Harkness at the Pump Room this morning had been thwarted by *his* sudden presence, forcing Catherine away. Anxiety and frustration expanded in her chest. She had yet to meet Julia again, but could not doubt Julia's exasperation with a brother who seemed so controlling.

How could she have been so blinded to not see this about his character? His accusations had opened her eyes, and she now realized his imperfections — yes, he was stubborn, inclined to quick judgment and an overbearing manner. But neither was she perfect; stubborn pride could not be held only at his door, and she was inclined to self-pity as well as less than charitable thoughts about her mother.

These realizations had prompted another: that her love for him might be bruised and battered, but still could not die — would never truly die. It thrummed deep within, marking her soul just as the Avon had carved through the local landscape. He might be overbearing at times, and she might not like all his actions — his words of accusation still caused tears to spring to her eyes — but his intentions had nearly always proved him honorable, stemming from consideration of others. Was it possible what looked like control was really misplaced concern?

Her hand trembled with the needle as she sat, attempting interest in her mother and aunt's conversation, as the questions bubbled away. What should she do? What would be truly best for Julia? *Heavenly Father, what do you want me to do?*

"Lord Winthrop, my ladies."

Before she could manufacture an excuse to leave he was there, tall and imposing in her aunt's drawing room. She could not look at him so she studied her needlepoint, carefully stitching as his deep-voiced greeting grated on her worn-thin nerves.

"Catherine?" Mama said. "You are aware we have a guest?"

"Of course."

"Perhaps that could be left for another time."

She clenched her teeth, placed the fabric down, and looked up, careful to not look higher than his neckcloth. Perhaps it was childish, but she could not bear to see the contempt she knew lived in his eyes. Could not bear to see his disappointment in her — which so mirrored her own.

Catherine blinked away the moisture. Pushed her cheeks into a smile. Pretended to listen like she cared as her mother and aunt exchanged social inanities with him, while she wondered how poor Miss Beauchamp would cope with his intimidating ways. Her heart panged; she pressed past the emotion. Julia. She needed to speak with him about Julia! But how could she? She dare not expose Julia by voicing such things in front of Mama and Aunt Drusilla. And had he not returned her notes and made his disdain for her concern so very plain? Nausea slid through her midsection. What should she do? *Lord, what should I do?*

"I return to London, and so wish you all well."

He rose, took her aunt's hand, then her mother's, and offered a farewell.

"Goodbye, Miss Winthrop." He did not seek her hand; she did not give it.

Her gaze lifted as far as his lips, frustration stirring again, heating her chest. How could such innocuous words come from a mouth that had spouted such vitriol? How could he pretend all was well between them, when his words still had the power to dampen her pillow at night? How could those lips have kissed hers, those lips that once pledged undying love, only to treat her

450

with such scorn and disregard? How could he ignore her concerns about his sister? She pressed down a whimper, pressed down the pain.

She nodded, he bowed, and was gone.

London

Dinner at the Beauchamps was everything good and proper. Candlelight flickered, conversation simmered, silverware glinted. But though he smiled and conversed, inside he felt hollow, his thoughts a hundred miles away in Bath.

Catherine had not looked at him. Had not spoken to him. He knew he was in the right, but her determination to ignore him still . . . stung. The only good thing from the awful events stemming from the masque was that Julia suddenly seemed calmer, less volatile. She'd even given him a big hug before he'd left, murmuring something about being glad he was her brother. That at least had brought a smile to his soul, at a time when he sorely needed some joy.

"Lord Winthrop? Tell me, what do you think best?"

His mind scrambled. What had they been speaking of? "I'm sorry, Miss Beauchamp, could you repeat the question?"

Lydia's father narrowed his gaze. Jon

forced himself to pay attention, but soon his thoughts were drifting again. He'd been like this ever since that horrible day in his study. Unable to focus, unable to feel, to the point that today's meeting with the shareholders had only narrowly avoided being a complete disaster thanks to the quick wits of his financial officer, who had stepped in when Jon could not answer a question. Jon had spent the rest of the session working to gratify and assure his shareholders, the success of which he was still not entirely sure.

He glanced across at his hostess, her daughter. Managed a weak smile. He knew about attempting to please. Mrs. Beauchamp and Lydia were well disposed to be pleased; Lydia's father not so much. Jon's time in London was not only to attend to his monthly business duties, but also to assure himself he was not making a mistake. He rather doubted he had ever occupied much of Miss Beauchamp's heart, just as she could never fully occupy his. But she was pliable, willing, and sweet, not spoiled by a history of pain. Like *she* was.

Like he was.

Nausea swirled within. Catherine, always Catherine. Why must he always think of her? Why couldn't he care more about the sweet girl sitting opposite?

How had it come to this?

Was he truly as dishonorable as Catherine believed?

Chapter Twenty-Seven

One week later

Catherine turned the page of the romance Lavinia had given her, a kind gesture from a kind friend. Lady Milton's wicked tongue meant even visiting the circulating library was now a strain.

Lavinia's visit this past week had helped quell some of the rumors. The obvious attentions of the Countess of Hawkesbury, sitting next to Catherine at services, and during concerts, and at an exclusive dinner which the earl's cousin attended along with the true notables of the town, had lent added respectability, as well as bolstered Catherine's spirits for a time. Lavinia's little daughter was extremely sweet, drawing forth Catherine's latent maternal longings.

Such activity meant she had seen very little of Julia, and had almost forgot the troubles concerning Julia and the major, indeed nearly forgot the general, whose attentions still continued. At times she wondered if she might as well give her hand to the general for real, except for vague suspicions he would rather give it to another . . .

She turned another page. Carriage wheels clattered on the cobblestoned street. Catherine ignored it. No visitors came for her, and Mama and Aunt Drusilla were out visiting Miss Pettigrew. She concentrated on her novel. If she could not live happily ever after, then she would try to be content reading about the happy endings of others.

There was a knock at her bedchamber door. Bess entered, curtsied. "Miss Winthrop, you are required downstairs."

"I beg your pardon?"

"It is Lady Harkness."

Her chest thudded. Was this finally her chance to talk about Julia? Catherine rose from her window seat and descended the stairs, straightening her morning dress as she silently murmured a prayer.

"Good afternoon, Lady Harkness." She curtsied. "I'm so glad you have come. I have wished to speak with —"

"Oh my dear! Tell me she is with you!"

"I beg your pardon?" A sense of foreboding filled her as she noticed her ladyship's reddened eyes. "Do you refer to Julia? Is she not at home?"

"No! She has disappeared."

Breath caught. "I beg your pardon?"

"I had the headache, and did not realize until luncheon that she had not come down earlier. It appears she did not sleep in her bed last night at all." Her voice broke, she wiped her eyes. "I had hoped you might know something."

Guilt arrowed across her heart. "I . . . I understood she and . . . Major Hale were close."

"I beg your pardon?"

"I b-believe they are sweethearts."

"No!" The green eyes widened with shock. "You think she is with him?"

"Julia once said . . . h-he wanted to marry her."

The older lady's face blanched. "You think they have eloped?"

Catherine said carefully, "I . . . I could not say."

"No! Not my sweet Julia. She could never do such a disgraceful thing!" She sank into a seat, covered her face with her hands, her shoulders heaving.

Catherine stood silent, awkwardness preventing movement. Lady Harkness never seemed to welcome affection, but surely she would appreciate a sign of sympathy now? She took a step, then hesitated as the older lady looked up accusingly.

"Why did you not tell me this?"

"I . . . I was not privy to their plans."

"But you knew of their mutual affection!"

"Of which I wrote you several notes."

"What? I never saw them." Lady Harkness groaned. "Oh, but where could they be? Oh, what should I do?" Her eyes seemed to plead with Catherine, as though she truly desired an answer.

"H-have you written to your son?"

"I sent a letter, but he is in London, and by the time he receives it, it will be too late."

Catherine moved to sit beside Lady Harkness and grasped her cold hand. "We could make enquiries at the local inns. Perhaps the general could help."

"Oh, yes. Yes."

"Shall I write a note to him now? Something discreet of course."

"Oh, would you?"

"Yes, of course."

Within minutes Catherine had scrawled a request for the general to visit at his earliest convenience. She handed the note to the footman, and requested tea. A short time later they were sipping tea, the drink as restorative to Lady Harkness's nerves as Catherine's missive seemed to have been.

"Oh, I knew you were sensible." Lady

Harkness sighed. "If only I had realized how serious things were."

"Julia is old enough to know the consequences of her actions."

"But she could not realize how dire it is to lose one's reputation!"

"Perhaps she truly loves him," Catherine ventured.

"Loves him?" There came a snort, followed by a litany of reasons why this elopement most certainly did not involve love.

Verses from her morning devotions rose to mind as Catherine listened, sensing a yearning behind the reproach and blame. "Perhaps," she interposed, "perhaps this will prove opportunity for them both to learn more about what love means. Love that 'beareth all things, believeth all things, hopeth all things, endureth all things,' " Catherine quoted softly. "Love that never fails."

Lady Harkness was quiet for a long moment before shaking her head. "Oh, if only I had known."

"I . . . I tried to tell your son."

"Jonathan? He never mentioned it." Her brow wrinkled. "Was that the day you argued?"

Catherine nodded, focused on her tea, unable to face the scrutiny sure to be in that green gaze.

"Oh, my dear, I never like to question him when he's in one of those moods. You mean you told him back then?"

"I tried to tell him my suspicions back then," she said cautiously.

"And he did not listen? He gets that from his father. His real father. The Winthrop one. He could never abide being told he was wrong. I was ever so glad when he died. Not that my son needs ever know that."

At her sigh, Catherine peeked up. Lady Harkness's pretty face sagged wistfully. "I was so fortunate to meet Harold Carlew, that he was prepared to take on a widow and babe. He was truly a good man. I've always hoped Jonathan would end up more like him, and to a great extent he has. Apart from this wretched stubbornness, of course."

They sat quietly for a while, Catherine marveling at her ladyship deigning to confide. Somehow she doubted such confidences would occur in Mama's presence.

"Tell me, Miss Winthrop, would you satisfy an old woman's curiosity?"

"You are not old, my lady."

"I am, but thank you, that is kind." She twisted the rings on her hands, as if nervous. "Please forgive a mother's natural interest, but would you mind telling me what happened between you and Jonathan three years ago?"

Catherine stilled. Her chest tightened. Nausea swirled.

"I understand you may not wish to," Lady Harkness rushed on. "And you do not need to oblige me. But I cannot help but wonder what caused him to want to leave so quickly. And to India of all places! It almost broke my heart."

She swallowed. Well she knew the pain of a broken heart. So she explained, as succinctly and without blame as she could.

"Oh, my dear!" Lady Harkness put a hand on her mouth. "I . . . I did not know. I always gathered from the little that he did say that you rejected him."

"Reject him? How could I? I loved him."

Lady Harkness was silent a long time.

Catherine forced herself to remain seated, to blink past the tears, to breathe past the rawness clogging her throat, filling the room. What did Lady Harkness want from her? How much more of her heart must she expose? Oh, if only the general would hurry, or Mama and Aunt Drusilla return.

"Is that why you went to the masquerade?"

Catherine's gaze lifted to meet the green

eyes once again, now filled with something akin to sympathy. "I just wanted to see" — she swallowed — "to see . . ."

"If there was a chance?"

She nodded.

"I understand," Lady Harkness said gently. "And Hale?"

"H-he helped me get home safely."

"Which my son misunderstood." She sighed. "Poor Jon."

And suddenly Catherine could feel a pang of sympathy for him, too. Tainted by the scandals around him, yet determined to be honorable, to do right, he had once given Catherine his heart only to be burned by her supposed rejection. No wonder he was so quick to hold her apparent misdemeanors to account again. But . . . why would he have thought she rejected him?

"Catherine?"

She looked up, heart twisting at the older lady's serious expression.

"Could you find it in your heart to love him again?"

Memories sweetly stirred. But they were dust, echoes of long ago. "He is engaged to Miss Beauchamp. I do not think he wishes —"

"My dear" — her voice was gentle — "that is not what I asked."

461

And risk further rejection? Risk further censure? How could she bare the truth within her soul? She shook her head, lifted her eyes to meet the green ones. "I cannot say."

London
Four days later
Day after day of fruitless searching had made him a desperate man. Where was she? How could she have been so foolish? Every night when he finally crashed into bed, body exhausted, still his mind circled endlessly. Had he been too hard? Was this Hale's revenge? What could he do? Where was Julia?

Mother's letter three days ago had galvanized him into action. He had enquired with those acquainted with the major, had employed half a dozen enquiry agents to search every London posting inn and those on London's major roads, had even taken Carmichael, Hawkesbury, and a couple of other close associates into his confidence, for he could not publicly spread the word of his sister's disappearance. But heaven knew it would only be a matter of time before the polite world had yet another scandal to titter about over their cups of tea.

He glanced at the scrawled note. Beauchamp requested an audience with him at his earliest convenience. Jonathan grimaced. Might as well get this unpleasant duty dealt with, too.

An hour later he sat listening as the older man mumbled something about whispers concerning Julia. Beauchamp stuttered his excuses, but his dear Lydia had had a change of heart and could not possibly, etcetera, etcetera.

Jon schooled his features to indifference. "I quite understand." How many others would pull back from furthering connections with him? How many other ladies would refuse to accept his less-than-innocent family members? A kind of gnawing pain filled his heart. If only . . .

He swallowed. Pushed aside regret. Eyed the man he would not be calling father-in-law. "I will send the notice to the newspaper."

The older man grunted. "Seems the other was only placed a week ago."

A month, actually. But it should not have been sent at all.

Mr. Beauchamp sighed, slouched deeper in his chair. "Well, I'll say this for you, Winthrop. You've a pretty head for business, even if you can't control that sister of yours."

Jon eyed him. Did the man expect him to

thank him?

Beauchamp chuckled. "Never mind. You and Lydia would never have suited. She's a good girl, but prone to be flighty, always giggling over her latest fashions and furbelows." He smiled indulgently. "I've a good mind to keep her close this next little while, until . . ." He harrumphed. "Well, I, er, I suspect you need a young lady with a decent head on her shoulders."

Like the one he'd accused and misjudged and railed against.

Like the one who had tried to warn him of his sister's carrying on.

Chapter Twenty-Eight

"Miss, I hope you don't mind, but the only available coach is quite a meager thing, just a driver really, and he's from Kingswood way."

"I suppose that won't matter greatly. As long as he's prepared to leave immediately."

"Yes, miss. Shall I tell him to come now, then?"

"Yes, please."

She handed Dobson the folded note together with her letter for Mrs. Jones and watched him leave. It didn't matter where the coachman was from as long as he removed them from Bath as soon as possible. And Kingswood was in the same general direction as St. Hampton Heath. North, at least.

"Catherine, my dear." She turned to see her aunt approach. "Are you sure this is the best idea?"

"It is if you are not to suffer from this latest scandal."

Aunt Drusilla sighed. "I do not want you worrying about me."

"Well, I *shall* concern myself with Mama's well-being. She does not need the whispers of Papa's sordid affairs reaching her ears."

"That she does not." Her aunt's face grew grim. She grasped Catherine's hand. "But my dear, will you manage?"

"Of course I will." Catherine gave a wry smile. No choice but to consider this next trial as pure joy. She moved upstairs to supervise the last of the packing before assisting Bess with Mama's belongings. For such a relatively short amount of time, she had amassed a great deal of possessions. In one of the more excruciating moments of Catherine's life, she had returned what she could early this morning, items she was sure would not be missed and would fetch fair recompense. Was it any wonder Mr. Whittington had been concerned?

"But why, Catherine?" Mama complained yet again, wringing her hands. "I do not understand the rush to leave."

She would if she knew what people were whispering about Papa's female friends. And she would if she had properly read the solicitor's letter rather than leaving it for Catherine to attend to. "Mama, I *strongly* feel we would be better off back in the cottage." At least there they would not be tempted to spend funds they didn't have.

"Yes, but *why*?"

Catherine drew in a deep breath. "I have grown so weary of Bath, Mama. It is a very pleasant town, to be sure, but I fear I cannot face the constant whispers anymore." Especially with this new scandal about to break forth.

"But have you not been facing such speculation already? I thought you were made of stronger stuff."

She swallowed. Breathed in. Exhaled. "Mama, I want to return home. Back to Winthrop."

"That is not our home anymore."

"And neither is Aunt Drusilla's. Mama, our cottage will suffice. It will be summer soon, and bound to be warmer. And we can be of comfort to Lady Harkness at this distressing time —"

"I have no desire to comfort *that* woman."

"But I do. How would you feel if Serena or I ran away? Would you not be grieved? Can you not understand how few people she can draw on at this time?"

Mama sniffed. "I did not think you so magnanimous in your feelings towards her."

"I did not understand her." Until recently.

467

"So I wish to return."

"But —"

"I think it a good plan, Elvira," her aunt stated from the door. "Many of the best people have already gone to London, and I fear good society will be thin on the ground."

Catherine caught her aunt's significant look. Yes, the doors to social events would be firmly closed once news got out.

Mama made a face like a pouting little girl. "You sound as though you would like to be rid of us."

Another look, weighty with resignation. "Well, to be frank, it has been a trifle longer than what I first expected."

"Well!" Mama drew herself up. Catherine silently applauded her aunt's heavy-handed tactics. "If that is the case, we shall no longer intrude upon your time."

Catherine's wry amusement faded as she helped Bess carefully fold Mama's gowns and place them in silver paper. The events of recent days continually pressed upon her soul. Julia's elopement had provided plenty of fuel for the gossips, leading to a virtual closeting of Lady Harkness inside her Camden Place abode, before she had fled to Winthrop yesterday. But it was Mr. Whittington's letter that had proved impetus for their own urgent departure.

They had no funds. Mama had spent nearly all her allowance, and Catherine's own settlement was well and truly squandered. Such news was almost laughable. How *had* Mama accessed such funds? It was a mystery. Catherine could only thank God once again that Serena's school fees had been paid in advance, and hope that Serena being cloistered away with her studies would protect her from the worst of tittle-tattle. Catherine was thankful she still had a meager amount of cash in her reticule, enough to return home. Once there they would have the cottage . . . and fewer expenses.

Her thoughts turned to future provision. Perhaps Mama might be agreeable to disposing — for a large sum — several of the large Winthrop paintings she could not hang due to the limits of the cottage walls. They might even manage a stay at Avebury, to save something in the way of expenses. Heaven knows so many of Papa's relatives had been more than willing to abuse his hospitality over the years with their month-long stays. Perhaps it was time to return the favor.

Because what was the alternative? The only person who could help was Lord Winthrop, and she was not going to ask him, not even if she be forced to eat gruel for the rest of her days. She would *never* ask for his assistance, nor ever let him know the depths of this new shame.

A sound of clattering hooves drew her attention to the window. "I believe our carriage has arrived."

She hoped Mama would consent to ride in such a thing. It was somewhat dilapidated looking, and possessed no footmen, only a coachman, but it was all they could afford.

"Good. I am anxious to depart as soon as possible."

Catherine bit back a smile. Aunt Drusilla's tactics might be drastic, but they worked.

Minutes later they were farewelling Aunt Drusilla and the general, whose appearance she put down to her aunt's hurried instruction to a footman.

"My dear girl, what can I say?" The general clasped her in a fatherly hug. "This has been an immense pleasure making your acquaintance."

"And yours, sir. I will never forget your kindness in helping protect my reputation."

"You are welcome, even though I fear your departure means I will be the one whose reputation suffers. Jilted by such a pretty young thing."

She laughed before saying, in as innocent a manner as she could, "Perhaps you and my aunt shall find consolation together."

He blinked. Harrumphed. Blushed. Glanced at her aunt whose cheeks wore a similar hue.

Catherine's smile widened. So she *had* been correct . . .

Mama bustled forward, her expression such that she seemed ignorant of any byplay. "Thank you, Drusilla, for condescending to accommodate us so much longer than you wished."

"Now, Elvira —"

"I see now that our presence has been a burden —"

"Mama, don't be so discourteous! Aunt Drusilla has been marvelous." Catherine gave her aunt a warm hug. "Thank you, for everything."

"Are you sure you don't mind?" her aunt whispered as she held her near.

"I am very pleased for you both, even though I shall be seen as the pitiful spinster who lost out to her aunt."

"I meant about the other."

Which other? The loss of money? The loss of Father's reputation? Her own? The loss of love? There were so many unpleasant elements to her life she could scarcely count them.

She drew back. Forced a smile. "Apparently I have much joy to consider."

"Joy?" Mama said. "How this can be thought joyous I don't know."

They exited to the curtsies and bows of the staff, Mama's inward hiss of disapprobation audible as they entered the coach. Catherine waved farewell as Mama started faultfinding.

"Why must we travel like this? It is not as though we are complete nobodies."

"It is less expensive this way, Mama."

"Well, I call it repugnant. We would certainly have never traveled like this when your dear Papa was alive."

"No." But perhaps if they had occasionally, they would not need to flee Bath under such ignominious circumstances.

"That sister of mine seems to hold her regard for us quite cheap."

"I don't know how you can say that! She has been more than generous with her house, her servants, her time, her money. Mama, shall I tell you why we need to leave Bath? It is because of Papa. Did you know about his gambling debts?"

Her mother stared wide-eyed.

"Did you know we have no money? Those

gowns you kept buying? I had to return some of them this morning because we cannot afford to pay for them. We can no longer impose upon Aunt Drusilla's generosity, as we have troubled her so much already. And we cannot stay in Bath because people will start whispering about how poor we really are. Is that what you want?"

"But —"

"Mama, it is *true.* Aunt Drusilla knows it. And soon all Bath will know it, too."

Mama seemed to wilt before her eyes.

For several long minutes there was no sound save the whinnying of horses and various creaks as the carriage struggled up the hill. Outside the clouds massed darker, the sky grew dim.

"How do you know this?" Mama's voice was quiet, worried.

"The letter from Mr. Whittington."

"I should have . . ."

"Yes."

Another long silence descended, while Catherine struggled to get her emotions in check. This seemed no adventure now, it was hard to count this as joy. The future seemed much like this journey: long, desperate, in the dark.

"I did not think things quite so bad," Mama finally said. "Nothing was said after the funeral, so I thought Walter's debts paid."

"Mr. Whittington believes they were. And hushed up. By Mr. Carlew."

"That man."

"Yes, that man."

Her heart twisted. As much as she still writhed internally over his words, deeper down she was cognizant of a sense of obligation to him. His discharging of Father's debts had proved him generous to her family, once upon a time. Just as he had loved her, once upon a time. She blinked back the burn in her eyes.

The coach slowed, then stopped at the inn, where they had a quick bite to eat while the horses were exchanged.

Mr. Nicholls, their coachman, a man of few words, jerked a thumb to the carriage. "Best be getting in. We've got a way to go over the heath, and I don't much like the look of that there storm."

Catherine glanced in the direction he was facing. Angry dark clouds billowed high into the sky. The scent of rain was in the air. No, she didn't much like it either.

"Come on, Mama. We best start moving."

Half an hour later, the heavens opened, and the coach slowed again. At the knock on the window Catherine slid open the glass to hear the shout. "Miss Winthrop, I be needing to take a detour. The bridge ahead is washed out."

"Very well!" she called, before ramming up the wooden window sash.

Rain pelted the glass as the coach turned and rolled down the hill. The stretch of road was bumpy, involving several slow passages as they moved through rain-soaked sludge.

"I do not like this, Catherine."

"Come, Mama. We do not need to be afraid."

"But it feels like a place where highwaymen might lurk."

Catherine pushed a smile past the shiver of fear. "I think you have read too much Gothic nonsense. I'm sure Mr. Nicholls is a careful driver."

"But he could scarcely outrun a highwayman. I've heard they like to dwell in such places."

"And what if they do? We have so little it would not be worth their while. Besides, the coach is scarcely one they would pay attention to, seeing as it's so little and old."

"I suppose that is some comfort."

But her mother's words wormed inside, and Catherine could not help but taste the fear. The next hour was spent offering encouragement and distraction, while her faith struggled against growing unease. *Lord God,* she prayed, *thank You for being with us. Help us to return home safely —*

A sharp crack sizzling with light was immediately followed by a thundering boom.

Mama shrieked. At the same moment the horses bolted, jolting them from side to side. "Catherine!"

"Mama, do not worry!"

Another lightning bolt pierced the darkness. Another ominous rumble. The horses' whinnying became frantic. She could hear the coachman's shouts, somewhat muffled by the storm raging outside.

She clasped her mother's hand. "We will be all right. We'll soon be home —"

A great splintering sound crackled above them and the carriage veered up, first on one wheel, then the other. Mama's moans became cries as she was flung against the corner. Catherine gripped the leather strap, but she too hit the side as the carriage turned sharply once again.

Then they were tipping, toppling, the carriage bending, buckling, her last conscious thought how the horses' screaming sounded so much like theirs.

Bath Road

Jonathan prodded Gulliver onwards through

the mud, his hopes dropping with every squelching step. Where was she? The hopelessness within doubled each night she remained lost. How could she disappear? Did she have no care for her family? Did she have no compunction, no shame?

His time in London had proved a complete failure. Nobody had seen either of them, his discreet enquiries probably doing more harm than good as speculation mounted as to why he should be seeking his sister's whereabouts. He'd begged Carmichael to remain vigilant in London for any word, whilst he followed the second option: seeking news in Bristol.

He'd arrived in Bristol two days ago. Enquiries at the coaching inns had similarly proved useless, until a chance conversation with a hostler had mentioned a young lady fitting that description who, just over a week ago, had boarded a ship to Liverpool. The young lady had seemed a little anxious, but as the soldierly gentleman had paid handsomely, nobody had liked to enquire too closely.

Liverpool. His stomach tensed. They could only be seeking the Scottish border. An unusual route, to be sure, but by now they would have arrived, or would soon. Regardless, Julia's reputation was irretrievably lost. And now he needed to return to face his mother with his failure.

He nudged Gulliver towards Bath. Thank God he only had a few miles to go. He was already behind time, his journey interrupted just after midday when he was forced to seek shelter at an inn as the worst storm in a decade had thundered overhead, and played havoc on the roads, before massing to attack the hills to the north and east. He glanced to his left. Even now they remained shrouded in darkness, hidden by heavy rain. He could scarcely wait until this filthy mud was removed from both his person and poor Gulliver, caked in it up to his hocks. God pity any other poor travelers caught up in the storm.

Ahead, the leaden clouds parted, shafting thin rays of late afternoon sunlight on the golden-stoned buildings edging the hillside. He crossed the Avon, hurrying Gulliver homewards, conscious of the pointed fingers, the barely concealed guffaws. His jaw clenched. Yes, he was a pitiful sight. And doubtless the good folk of Bath would have heard his distressing news . . .

He arrived in Camden Place, beyond ready to be clean. He issued orders to the footman for his horse to be cared for, adding, "And tell my mother I have returned and will speak to her momentarily."

"Of course, but sir —"

"Don't. I cannot take another excuse today. Just do what I ask."

And without waiting to hear anything more, he raced up the stairs, washed, and was soon changed.

He returned to find his servants glancing at each other in the hallway. "Well, what is it?"

"It is your mother, sir. Lady Harkness has returned to Winthrop."

"What?"

"She, er, felt it better than remaining here. Her departure being so sudden she insisted some of us remain to close up the house," the footman added in an apologetic tone.

Jon bit back a word, pushed a hand through his hair. "So I need to return to Winthrop."

"Sir, I would suggest something to eat might be in order."

He turned, closed his eyes, drew in a breath. Forced out, "Very well."

"Of course, my lord."

He exhaled, opened his eyes, moved to the study. Perhaps Mother had left a note?

He read it. Nearly cursed. Sank into a seat, and remained there even when the footman informed him that a nourishing repast had been prepared.

What should he do? Where could he go? He should return to Winthrop, but leaving Bath like this felt so unfinished, merely compounding his failure. What if, however unlikely, Julia were to return?

He eventually pushed to his feet, moved to the dining room to eat his food, the brain so quick at unraveling the mysteries of finance now dulled to such a slowness he could barely discern what he ate. What should he do? *Lord, what should I do?*

Nothing settled, his spirit remained restless, thoughts churning ever ceaseless.

Weariness begged him to find his bed, to try to sleep. But rest? He shook his head, pushed back his chair. He couldn't rest. He needed to find out, now. And he suddenly remembered just who might know some of those answers.

He hurried out into the damp evening, walking with quick steps the path to Gay Street he had trodden so many times before. The walk through sodden streets would do him good, neither did he wish to inflict further suffering on poor Gulliver. Besides, it might even help curb the worst of his temper by the time he saw her.

A turn here, a corner there, and he arrived. Knocked on the door. Waited. Spoke to a footman. "Oh, but sir —"

"Who is it at this time of night?" a male voice grumbled.

Jon frowned. The general was here? At this late hour? He pushed past the open-mouthed footman and moved to the drawing room.

"Mr. Carlew!"

"Mrs. Villiers, General Whitby." He glanced between them. "This is a surprise."

"As is your visit, sir."

Embarrassment heated his cheeks. "I apologize for my unexpected appearance, but I won't keep you long. May I please speak with Miss Winthrop?"

They glanced at each other. "I'm afraid that is impossible."

"I understand she might not wish to speak with me, but it is imperative —"

"She is not here, sir."

"Oh. Is she out?" One head nodded, the other shook from side to side. He frowned.

"Does this concern your sister?"

"I suppose the news is all over Bath."

"I'm afraid so." Catherine's aunt gestured to a seat.

He sank into the opposite sofa heavily. "I am sorry for interrupting like this. I have just returned from Bristol, after London proved devoid of any information. It seems likely they are on their way to Scotland."

"You will not chase them?"

"I will, after I see my mother. I just learned that she left for Winthrop a few days ago." He kneaded his forehead. What a disaster his actions had led to. He'd need to travel to Scotland, force Julia to return. Dear God! Would he have to duel Hale?

"I'm terribly sorry, Lord Winthrop," Catherine's aunt said, her dark eyes so like those of her niece.

His eyes burned. He swallowed, willed his voice to be steady. "I . . . I had hoped Miss Winthrop might know something."

"My sister and niece have returned to the Dower House."

"What? Why?"

"There was nothing keeping them here."

He frowned. His gaze sharpened. A mantelpiece clock ticked off the seconds. He studied the general. Glanced at Catherine's aunt. Returned his attention to the older man. Long ago suspicions resurfaced, swirled, solidified. "You were not engaged."

"No."

"Then . . . why?"

"I was a friend when she had few."

Unlike him. Gnawing hopelessness pushed his head into his hands. He should have been the one protecting her, helping her.

Instead, he'd been so blinded by bitterness he'd virtually ignored her, then become even more resentful when her independence led her further away.

"My lord?"

He lifted his head to encounter her aunt's relentless gaze. "I have always loved her."

She nodded. "I had wondered."

"What?" The hollowness within threatened to overwhelm. "How? Why?"

She told of Catherine's tears and anguish, both those from three years ago and those more recent.

His soul twisted more deeply. "I . . . I cannot believe she would think that of me."

Her eyes narrowed. "Catherine said she wrote you a letter."

"I never received a letter." His heart wrenched afresh. Poor Catherine. No wonder she'd held him in aversion. For if she thought that . . .

"Perhaps her father somehow learned of her attachment and suppressed it."

Guilt writhed within. Of course he knew. "She did not wish me to, but I spoke to her father. He said he would never countenance such a union between his daughter and a 'cit,' that she was destined for someone far more titled. He said I'd been a fool to imagine Catherine cared for me, that she was merely leading me on. I could not bring myself to disclose her actions, yet his words made me doubt. He . . . he demanded I write to break off any attachment. Foolishly I obeyed."

A groan escaped. If only he hadn't! "When I saw her next she seemed so cold and distant, I could never bring myself to speak to her again. So I left for India." And in leaving, had left not only a wounded sweetheart but a broken mother, while his own soul pulsed with bitterness.

"I am such a fool." An axe to the heart could not wound so deep. "Her father lied. Both to her and to me."

"He was always an unscrupulous man." She told him of Lord Winthrop's debts.

"I sought to pay all those of which I knew."

"On my sister's behalf, I thank you."

Her words and the approval lining her eyes were small concession to the swirling recriminations. How had he, honest, industrious he, been brought this low? He'd failed his sister, failed his mother, failed his Catherine, failed his intended —

"Dear God! And to think I almost married another!"

"Nobody forced your hand, sir."

He swallowed. Nodded. "I cannot blame anyone but myself."

"Wait, you said almost?"

He offered a ghost of a grin. "My sister's cursed attachment seems to have saved me from mine."

"Well, that is one thing for which to be thankful."

Not that it could help him now. Catherine would never want to see him again. Not after his last words to her. *Lord, help her forgive me.*

He rose, offered his hand. "I wish you well, General. My felicitations to you both."

"Thank you, my boy."

They accompanied him to the door. "We shall continue to hold your sister in our prayers."

Jon thanked them, the weight burdening his heart seeming only to increase.

Mrs. Villiers wished him safe travels, before adding, "Elvira and Catherine left earlier today. You might see them tomorrow."

"I appreciate your concern, but I fear it is too late."

"May I offer you a word of advice?"

"Of course." He braced for another sharp-tongued reprimand.

"You are a good man. Do not lose hope. Remember, trials are merely opportunities for faith to grow."

His eyes burned. He nodded stiffly, walked home slowly, fears nipping at his heels like a pack of dogs, swarming from every side. *God forgive me. Help Catherine to forgive me. Somehow save us from this mire.*

CHAPTER TWENTY-NINE

A steady pulsing sound filled her ears. A burning sensation streaked along her elbow.

Catherine cracked open an eye. Darkness. How long had she been unconscious? A smudge of white drew her attention, focused her vision. "Mama?"

Her voice sounded cracked. She swallowed. Tasted rawness, blood. She slid her tongue around her teeth; they all seemed there. "Mama?"

A groan. Another, louder now. "My shoulder. Oh, Catherine . . ."

She pushed to a sitting position, rocking the carriage.

"Stop moving!"

"But I must." She winced as her hip protested the sudden shift.

Now she was semi-upright, and she could hear above the rain a desperate whinnying and snorts from outside. The horses sounded pained . . . Oh no! Poor Mr. Nicholls!

She crawled over scattered boxes and belongings to reach her mother's side. "Mama, are you hurt anywhere else apart from your shoulder?"

Her mother gingerly moved. "I don't believe so."

Thank you, Lord. "Mama, I need to check on Mr. Nicholls. I cannot hear him at all."

"This wretched rain."

"I'll be back in a moment."

"Hurry."

Her mother's groans accompanied her as she shoved open the door. Water pelted her from the dark sky. The carriage lay on its side, and she scrambled out, catching her gown and scraping her legs as she scrambled down. A hysteria-laden giggle pushed out. Good thing Mama couldn't see her now. The impropriety of a daughter with a gown hitched up to her ears as she clambered around in her stockings would be enough to injure her sensibilities far worse than any shoulder.

She pulled her dress into order and stumbled to the front. Sputtering light from the carriage lamp showed the driver's seat lay crushed as one horse lay still, the other twitching, snorting, moving desperately as if to free itself. "Mr. Nicholls!"

Catherine wrenched the damaged lantern free and hurried to the prone form. In the evening dimness and the rain she could just make out his face. She sank to her knees, leaned over him. "Lord God, please let him be alive."

Fingers beneath his nostrils felt slight huffs of warmth. He was breathing. She peered over his face. "Mr. Nicholls!"

No stirring.

She leaned back on her heels, eyeing his twisted leg. She grimaced. It seemed worse than the leg she'd seen Jem Foley break several years back whilst escaping a bull. That had taken months to mend, and even today, years after the incident, he still walked with a small limp. This seemed much worse.

"Mr. Nicholls, we need to get you help."

But where was that to come from? She glanced around as desperation edged up her throat. "Lord God, please help!"

The words comforted somewhat, her voice seeming to soothe the horse's cries. She moved to it. Its partner was dead, and she suspected this one would be also before too much longer. Her eyes blurred. She smoothed a hand over its nose. "I'm so sorry."

Tears trickled from her eyes, joining the moisture on her face from the rain.

"Catherine!" her mother's voice called weakly.

She inhaled deeply, limped back to the carriage. "Mama, we need help. Mr. Nicholls is not responding, and the horses are either dead or dying. I" — she braced herself — "I shall have to get someone to come."

"But how? It is nighttime. You cannot leave me here."

"I will walk, and you will need to stay here. You will be warm and protected inside."

"But what about Mr. Nicholls?"

Catherine sighed. "I would prefer him to be inside also but I don't have the strength to move him."

"I don't mean that! What if he wakes and I am all alone with only him —"

"Mama, he is in no position to attack you, if that is what concerns you."

"You don't need to take that tone with me. I am frightened! What if a wild animal should come?"

"Like what? A tiger?" Catherine bit down her frustration. "Mama, I am scared too, but if I don't leave soon I'm worried that Mr. Nicholls will die. What would you prefer? Me to stay, in the hopes someone will come along this track, or for me to" — try to, she added silently — "get some help?"

"I . . ."

She climbed up, in, found blankets, spread one over her mother, collected and placed within reach the basket of food Aunt Drusilla had given them earlier. "Now see if you can sleep. I am sure it will be some hours before I can return."

"You will leave me the lamp, at least?"

"No, Mama. I will need it."

"But —"

"Mama, I need you to be brave. And pray. For Mr. Nicholls as well as me. Now I will see you soon."

Catherine climbed back out, jumping down into squelching mud, her feet sinking up to her ankles. She tugged down the second blanket, caught on the door, and moved to cover Mr. Nicholls. His driving coat would protect him from the elements, but the blanket would help also. "Mr. Nicholls?"

Still no response. "God, protect him."

Staggering to her feet, she peered through the rain. They appeared to have slid down an embankment, the carriage lodged against a tree. She would have to scramble up the slope to find a track. The rain continued to pelt down, soaking her. She should retrieve her heavy woolen cloak, but it was in their luggage strapped to the back of the carriage — which, judging from its current position, meant she could probably retrieve it now.

She hurried to the back and found the trunk, forced open the lock with the mud-encrusted heel of her boot, and hunted through its contents until she found what she needed and wrapped it securely around her.

"Catherine? What are you doing?"

"Just getting my cloak."

"I thought you'd gone and come back."

She closed her eyes, breathed in. Out. "I'll be back soon, Mama. Don't worry. Just pray."

Before her mother could continue her indictments, Catherine slithered up the steep slope, carefully holding the lantern as she grasped branches and tree trunks to haul her way to the top. The track was barely discernible, the grooves in the road the only clue in knowing where to walk.

"God help me," she murmured, casting a last look at the broken mess before setting off to what must be west. There was no point returning from whence they came; she recalled few signs of habitation along the way. She held the lantern before her, working by its feeble light to step on what looked like firmer ground, and not the heavy mud that threatened to steal her boots and balance. Count her trials all joy? A broken laugh escaped. But at least she did have a lamp, though its light be fickle, and might not last much longer. And at least she wasn't injured, and could hopefully find help. *Please, God.*

The track was boggy, her progress slow. She tugged her cloak against the chill of predawn air, fighting the desire to cry, the longing to give up. Her legs ached with the effort of staying upright, her arms ached from holding the carriage lamp. Perhaps attempting such a feat was foolish, and it would have been better to wait for daylight. But by then poor Mr. Nicholls would surely have worsened, if not be —

She swallowed. *Lord, protect him.* Fighting to remember God's promises from the Psalms, she trudged on.

The charcoal of night slowly merged to ash, enough to dimly see by. She glanced at the lantern. How long since the flame had died? She cast it away, then jumped at the loud clatter. Ahead, the forked road demanded decision. Already hopelessly lost, she veered to the right, and the track that seemed less muddied.

Light was stealing over the hills to the east by the time she spotted a cow. Her heart lifted. Surely if there was a cow there must be a farm, and people who would help. The twitter of early morning birdsong encouraged her as she plodded on. Her skirts were caked in mud, her cloak now sodden. The slight breeze chilled, her feet were rubbed raw. Thank God it had ceased raining. Thank God for those days deprived of Ginger's company. Those long walks along Bath's steep streets had helped improve her stamina. She could surely not have walked this far without practice.

"Step along now."

Mists parted, revealing a tall figure, with a long stick. Salvation at last!

She hurried toward him. "Excuse me!"

The figure turned, his mouth gaped.

"Hello. I know I look a sight but I need your help."

He paced back. Took another step away.

"There has been an accident!" She moved forward. "Please, sir. Would you help me?"

He stared at her as though he saw a ghost. Then, without a word, he turned and ran away.

"No!" She hurried after him. Tripped. Her hands landed in something greenish brown, something that looked and smelled like . . . bovine excrement.

"No!"

Her chest grew tight. She wiped her hands, pushed to her knees, as frustration crashed over disappointment. Tears welled. She forced them back. They leaked anyway. Soon she was sobbing loudly in the field as the cows watched her placidly. "God, help me!"

Could He feel any further away?

Her hair fell in her face. She pushed it back. Wonderful. Now she would have cow excrement in her hair. She stumbled to her feet. The farmhand had long disappeared. She could chase him, but rather suspected he might chase her off with a pitchfork. She trudged back to the cart tracks and forced one foot in front of the other.

By the time the sun had reached the tops of trees she could see a building. Probably an outbuilding, a barn or suchlike, but nonetheless it signified habitation. She stumbled to it. A barn. Empty. She shook her head, trudged on. Another building drew her attention. It was two-storied, wider. A house. She hurried toward it. Banged on the door. Inside, the sounds of early morning bustle ceased.

"Hello?" She banged again.

The door opened. A swarthy man stared at her, his dark eyes widening, as he looked her up and down. A leer curled his lips. "Well, look what we have here."

"Please, sir, I need your help."

"You look like you do, miss. And I'm just the man to help you." He hitched up his breeches, eyeing her with an expression that sent shards of fear to her stomach.

"I don't think you understand —"

"No, I don't think you do. Come 'ere, you." He swung a meaty hand and tried to grasp her arm. She backed away. " 'Ere, what's this mud?" He sniffed his hand. Swore. "Smells like dung!"

She turned and ran away, as he cried, "I don't want no dealings with a dirty trollop!"

Her legs were pumping, her lungs were on fire, her skirts hampering her as she ran, so she picked them up. *God, keep me safe!*

She stumbled back to the track, struggling to breathe. In the distance was another large building, like a type of inn. She rushed towards it. Banged on the heavy wooden door. "Help! Help me!"

The door opened. A sharp-featured man stood there, frowning. "What is it?"

"Please, sir, there is a man chasing me!" She gasped, sucking in air, willing the dizziness to cease.

He stepped outside, closing the door on safety, and the delectable scent of baking bread. "I don't see no such man."

"Oh, but he was!"

He turned, eyed her dispassionately. "Well he ain't now. So be off with you."

"But, sir, I need your help!" Her breathing slowly steadied, regaining normalcy.

"I already told you, miss, there is no man chasing you. Now be gone. We don't serve the likes of you around here."

"The likes of . . . ?" She drew herself up as she'd seen Mama do. "I fear you do not understand. I would appreciate if I might speak to the mistress of this establishment." Perhaps a woman might take pity . . .

"Would yer listen to 'er, then. Hoity toity!"

"Please, sir! I am Miss Winthrop of Winthrop Manor. My mother and I have had a carriage accident and our coachman is severely injured. I need help!"

He eyed her incredulously. "I don't believe —"

"Desmond? What is all this racket?" A large, round woman, her face as wide and dimpled as an apple pie, waddled close. "Lord 'ave mercy, miss! You look a dreadful sight."

"Please, ma'am, have pity. My mother and

I are traveling from Bath to St. Hampton Heath —"

"That's an awful long way from 'ere," the man said.

"And we were forced to detour because a bridge was out, but our carriage overturned, and Mama and the coachman are hurt, so I had to walk, and I'm so dreadfully tired, and . . ." Tears came to her eyes. She wiped at them, smearing dirt across her face.

"There, there. Come on in. We'll get you fixed up."

"But Mama —"

"Desmond will see to that, won't you, Des?" The woman drew her forward. "He might be my 'usband for nigh on twenty years, but I only let 'im think he rules the roost. Now, where did you say your carriage might be?"

Catherine pushed against the headache forming in her forehead. Where had it occurred? "We could not cross the bridge because it had washed out, so we came down the hill around a bend, and the lightning startled the horses, and we toppled down an embankment."

"Ah, Darley's corner. I know where you mean. Well, you come along with me —"

"Please, I think my mother would prefer to see me and know I was all right."

"You'd rather go back than get cleaned up? You *are* an unusual sort."

"My mother can get anxious." Although the sight of Catherine in all her muddied glory . . . "Perhaps if I may quickly wash off the worst?"

"Of course, miss."

A few minutes later, face and hands at least clean, stomach clenching in pleasure as she nibbled a slice of fresh bread, Catherine was encouraged outside by her benefactress, a Mrs. Nabtree.

"Hop along with Des, then." She grinned. "Perhaps your smell will encourage him to not spare the horses."

"Th-thank you."

And thank God. He had helped them once again.

Winthrop

Jonathan rushed into the drawing room, relief ballooning in his chest at the sight of the person sitting on the settee. "Mother!"

"Oh, my dear!"

He sat beside her, drew her near, felt her tears soak his shoulder. The struggles of his long ride home, thwarted by landslips and numerous detours, seemed to fade as he gently patted her back. "How are you bearing up?"

In answer she handed him a letter, post-marked Carlisle. "It arrived today."

He scanned Julia's handwriting, his heart sinking as his fears were confirmed. "So by now they are likely married." *Please, God.*

"Oh, Jonathan!" Her bottom lip trembled. "I have failed her."

"No, I did. I did not trouble myself to consider her feelings. I was too harsh with her, too unkind to him. If I had just listened —"

"You cannot blame yourself. She is old enough to take responsibility, so I was told."

"Who dared tell you such things?" He found a small smile. "I must congratulate them."

"Miss Winthrop."

He blinked. "You spoke with her?"

"Yes, back in Bath. She offered comfort when I needed a friend."

"She was friendly?"

"Of course." Her green eyes glinted. "She was most generous in choosing to . . . to overlook some of our family faults, shall we say."

He shook his head. "I was too hasty. I judged her too quickly."

"And I was dismissive, when really I should have seen . . ." She bit her lip.

"Seen what, Mother?"

"Seen that her avoidance derived from hurt, not a misplaced sense of family pride."

His heart felt raw, exposed. "You know?"

"Catherine told me. You know also?"

"Her aunt."

"Oh, Jonathan. Could this not be a chance to redeem the past?"

"I fear she will never want to speak with me again. I was so harsh the last time we talked. I blamed her when she was blameless."

"And yet, my dear, love always forgives, always trusts, always hopes."

Surprise curled round his churning emotions. His mother knew the Bible?

"Don't look so shocked, my dear. I have recently been reminded about such wisdom, and have derived much comfort in the Scriptures at this time."

"I am glad. Who — ?"

"Catherine."

He exhaled. Catherine, always Catherine. The person who might hold the keys to finding his sister. The person who had always held his heart. His lost love. His lost future. Catherine had spoken of such things? Hope flickered against the hurt. "You think she loves me still?" he asked in a low voice.

"Do you love her?"

"I never stopped."

"Then if one heart can hold such tender feelings for so long, perhaps the other can, too."

But if she did not . . .

His mother squeezed his hand. "You will not know unless you speak with her."

"Have you spoken with her since their return?" Perhaps if he could gauge where her affections might lie.

"They have returned? I did not know. But you should go and see her. Find out if she feels the same."

"After all I've said and done, I can only hope."

"Hope is what we need."

He hugged her again, his spirits lifting. Even with Julia, hope — and a great deal of prayer — was what was needed.

Dower House

"What do you mean they have not returned?"

Mrs. Jones lifted her hands. "The letter told me to expect them yesterday. But I've not seen hide nor hair of them."

"Perhaps they visited elsewhere on the way," he said, trying to stifle the alarm within.

"I don't think so. That road is straightforward enough. And Miss Catherine is pretty reliable at letting me know when plans change."

He rubbed a hand through his hair. "You think they might have had an accident?"

"I don't rightly know what I think. Except they ain't here, and I've got another meal going to waste."

"Perhaps you should not cook any more until you are certain of their arrival," he said, sure the meal had not been completely wasted, at least as far as Mrs. Jones was concerned.

"P'raps. And p'raps you will go find the mistress and Miss Catherine, if you don't mind me saying so."

"I do not mind. And there is no perhaps. I *will* find them, of that you can be sure."

He hurried away, back to the Manor to gain what resources he needed. His heart cramped with fears. Where could they be?

Chapter Thirty

Wickwar, South Gloucestershire
Five days later

"Thank ye, miss."

Catherine nodded, pushing out a smile as she cleared up from her pitiful attempt to help. It wasn't Mr. Nicholls's fault he lay unable to move. Their coachman's broken leg was so painful she thought him incredibly brave to put up with her ineffectual nursing. More than once she had heard his hiss as she'd attempted to clean the wound as the doctor had shown her.

She closed the door, and slumped against the wall. How long until the doctor returned? She'd sent the boy several days ago, with messages for both the doctor and Mrs. Jones at the cottage. But nothing, no reply. Had they even got through?

Stifling the resurging fears, she hurried down two flights of stairs to the kitchen and deposited the latest bundle of bloodied bandages in the fire. Washed her hands. Collected the tea things for Mama. The doctor had diagnosed a sprained shoulder, which apparently necessitated Mama's inability to do anything more than lie in bed like a queen, giving orders to Catherine. Not that there was anything remotely stately about their accommodations. Mr. Nabtree had put them in very narrow, very drafty top rooms, tucked under the high, pitched roof, where Catherine knocked her head on the beams a half dozen times each day. Their lodging in rooms seemingly more suitable for dwarf-sized servants had been the cause of dissension between the innkeeper and his wife, evidenced in an overheard squabble.

"You can't stick 'em up there!" Mrs. Nabtree had protested. "They're Quality!"

"Quality who can't pay."

Catherine sighed anew. He was right. They were living on their host's good grace. The food was palatable, their cramped quarters in the rafters at least allowing for a bed for Mama and a pallet on the floor for Catherine. She could not permit poor Mr. Nicholls to suffer the indignities of rooming above the stables, and had given him her room. Mrs. Nabtree — bless her — had taken pity last night and provided opportunity for them to bathe and wash their hair, opportunity for Catherine to retrieve from their luggage the special soap Aunt Drusilla had bestowed upon her, and relish its aroma and the delight of being clean.

But she was weary. *So* weary. She forced herself to mount the steps: ten steps, a turn at the landing, then another ten. The past days of worry and arguments with Mr. Nabtree and his staff, combined with caring for two at times cantankerous patients, had worn her patience and emotional fortitude thinner than a gossamer handkerchief. She was bone-crushingly tired, so tired her left eye had developed a twitch and her hands a tremor. But what could she do? She'd begged the innkeeper for assistance but he turned a deaf ear. She possessed enough coin in her reticule to pay their "shot," as Mr. Nabtree called it, for another day at most, but when the doctor came — if the doctor came — she would have to beg for his mercy.

"Catherine!"

She clutched the tray. Held herself still. Reminded herself to breathe. She *could* do this.

"Catherine!" Her mother's voice called again through the slightly opened door. "How much longer must I wait?"

Her hands shook, causing the tea tray to

wobble. Just breathe. God was with her, giving her strength.

"Catherine?"

The deep voice drew her gaze to the dim stairwell. Beneath the banister, on the landing below, stood Mr. Carlew. Her grasp on the tea tray slackened, resulting in an almighty crash.

"Oh!" She winced as the burning liquid seeped through her clothes.

"Catherine? What is that noise?" Her mother's querulous voice came again as Mr. Carlew pounded up the stairs to her side. He was here, he was close, his hand on her arm —

"Miss Winthrop, please forgive me. I did not mean to startle you. Are you hurt?"

She shook off his hand. "I am not injured, thank you."

"Catherine? What is it? What is going on?"

"Nothing Mama. I spilled the tray, that is all."

"Always such a clumsy girl."

Cheeks scorching, Catherine bent to pick up the broken china.

Mr. Carlew stepped closer. "You are not well. Allow me to take care of this." He moved to the banister. "Hello? Hello there!"

Within seconds a maid appeared and was issued with instructions. Within a minute she returned with a small pot of goose grease and a bucket and broom. As the maid commenced cleaning, Catherine surveyed the reddened skin on her forearm, and gently rubbed in the salve.

"Miss Winthrop, please." She lifted her gaze to meet his, darkly blue. "Please permit me to send for a doctor."

She uttered a mirthless laugh. "You can send for a doctor, but it doesn't mean he will come."

He frowned. "I do not understand."

"Catherine? Catherine! To whom are you speaking?"

She bit back the sigh, pushed open the door, forced a smile in the direction of the bedridden figure. "Lord Winthrop is here, Mama."

"Who?"

"Lord Winthrop, our cousin," she added, for the benefit of the maid. A swift glance saw her recommence cleaning.

"What is that man doing here?"

Catherine turned, raising her brows.

He half smiled, moving to stand beside her in the doorway.

She closed her eyes for a few seconds, savoring his nearness, savoring his scent. If only she did not feel this wretched light-headedness, this feeling like she might topple at any moment.

"I have come to enquire of your welfare, ma'am."

"Welfare? What does it look like? Oh, stop standing in the hall. I've no mind that all might know my business."

He followed Catherine into the room, closing the door behind them. "Forgive the intrusion, ma'am, but your failure to arrive at Winthrop caused no small alarm. I have spent the past five days searching, until a small village boy recalled seeing a group arrive at this, er, establishment."

"We remain hardly by choice!"

"Naturally, ma'am." He glanced at Catherine, a questioning look in his eyes.

"Mr. Nicholls has broken his leg and cannot be moved," she said softly.

"Mr. Nicholls?"

"Our coachman. He was injured in the accident."

His eyes widened, compelling her to explain. "We were returning from Bath when the horses were startled in the storm and the carriage overturned, injuring both poor Mama and Mr. Nicholls. We have been here since, unable to relocate, although we have sent word of our predicament."

He turned to her mother. "Ma'am, I trust you are not severely injured."

"No, but . . ."

When Mama's complaints finally wound to a halt, Catherine insisted she rest. She closed the door and continued her story in the hall. "The doctor has been once, but has not returned."

"So who has been caring — ? Surely not you."

She drew herself up. "Is that so hard to believe?"

"Of course not. Again, please forgive me." His lips twisted. "At times I do not express what I mean to say, I'm afraid."

"Well, what do you mean to say?" She winced at her snappish tone. Had exhaustion eaten away all semblance of politeness?

He opened his mouth, closed it. Drew her to one side as the maid finished wiping down the mess and placed the broken china in a wooden pail. "We were concerned when you failed to return as indicated by your letter. Then when we could not find you —"

"I sent word."

"None appeared."

Frustration tightened her chest. The little scamp must have run off with her money! She pressed her lips together, hiding her gaze by examining the stain marring her skirt.

"Miss Winthrop, do you need to change

your gown?"

That would require reentering her mother's room. She shook her head no.

"Then may I suggest you go downstairs to the private parlor?"

"But the innkeeper —"

"Knows I have reserved it. You will be safe from prying eyes."

Her fingers clenched, as again that ball of frustration tightened across her chest. How had *he* managed to do what she could not?

He glanced at her hands, offered a rueful looking smile and his arm, and escorted her downstairs to a comfortably furnished room. He closed the door, leaving her alone, but not before she heard him order two meals to be brought directly.

She sank onto the chair, feeling her body relax for the first time in days. Her head sank to her hands, elbows propped up on the table, careless of the impropriety. Nobody could be as tired as she. She closed her eyes, half wishing she could fall asleep, yet a new skein of tension wound thick in her chest. For while Mr. Carlew had proved all that was kind, his solicitude also served to remind her that this was only for the briefest of interludes; his heart belonged to another.

But . . . oh, to be so cared for, looked

after. Her eyes filled with tears.

The door opened and the aroma of rich beef stew preceded the maid's entrance. Mr. Carlew followed immediately. She hurriedly wiped her eyes, and sat up, pushing her hair behind her ears. No doubt she looked a mess, but without a looking glass she could not know — not that such things mattered, anyway.

"Please eat," he said.

So she did.

He watched her for a moment then ate, too. The room was silent for all but the scrape of metalware against bowls. Eventually he placed his fork down, his gaze so piercing she could only look up.

"You said you sent word?"

"I . . . I gave a note to a post boy, but I gather he did not deliver it."

He frowned.

Her stomach twisted. Did he doubt her?

"And you've been run off your feet." He shook his head. "I spoke to the coachman. It seems the horses took fright and took you far away from the main road. It's only by the merest chance I came here."

"Or the good Lord," she murmured.

His strained features suddenly softened as he laughed. "That, too." His smile faded. "I still wish you had thought to tell me. Why did you not send word again? Or hire another hack to get you home?"

She swallowed. Swallowed again. How to explain her lack of finances? "I . . . I thought I could manage."

"For how much longer? You're exhausted as it is."

Her eyes blurred again. She bit her bottom lip to stop the tremble, shifting her gaze to hide her tears as she massaged another layer of goose grease onto her forearm.

He sighed. "Forgive me. Perhaps it is best if I leave you to finish your meal in solitude."

Catherine nodded. Turned so she could see the lower part of his face, but not his eyes.

"I should not speak so harshly." His lips turned wry. "I suppose this is what you wished to avoid?"

She dipped her head in acquiescence.

"Very well. I shall speak with your mother and then the coachman. You shall not be disturbed by my presence any longer."

He departed quickly, before the protest on her lips could be uttered. She did not find his presence disturbing, rather the opposite. His appearance had immediately eased some of the burden from her shoulders, for she knew he would do all in his power to comfort and protect her.

Even if only from a sense of duty.

A rawness refilled her eyes, filled her throat. She pushed away the half-eaten bowl. Propped her head in her hands. Closed her eyes, locking in the moisture.

If only he did not still despise her.

After hurried interviews with both Lady Winthrop and the coachman, during which Jon soon learned the depth of their indebtedness to Catherine's quick thinking and strenuous efforts, and was duly horrified to realize she was sleeping on a pallet in her mother's room, he visited the innkeeper, who assured him he had offered them his best care.

The large woman frowned at her husband. "Do you take 'im for a fool? Anyone can see what kind of establishment this is."

"I cannot think how you thought it permissible for a baron's wife and daughter to be forced to endure such rough conditions."

The man's eyes rounded. "Baron's daughter, did you say?"

He sighed. Trust Catherine's modesty to not shout her antecedents.

"I don't know no baron who can't afford to pay for better accommodation."

"Cannot afford?"

Suddenly it all made sense. Fresh guilt

washed over him. If only he'd arrived sooner, if only he hadn't been so stubborn, if only . . . "Unfortunately it is too late to remove them today, so they will need to remain another night. As will I." He groaned, envisaging the flea-ridden night ahead of him. "I shall need a bedchamber."

Jon left and returned to the room, a parlor in name only. He knocked then pushed open the door. His heart thudded loudly at the sight. "Catherine!" He rushed to where she sat, her head resting on one arm splayed across the table.

He bent closer, gently shook her shoulder. "Catherine?" She was sleeping, a deep slumber no words, no shaking could disturb.

His heart softened. Shadows lined her eyes, her hair curling in tiny tendrils around her small, perfect ear. Her hands were chapped, smudged with dirt, her displaced sleeve showing the red mark on her wrist from the earlier burn. Exhaustion might hold her, but he minded not. She was beautiful.

His gaze tracked to her lips, slightly parted. Were they as soft as he remembered?

His heart thudded. He leaned close —

The door squealed opened. "Oh! Excuse me, sir. I came for the plates."

Jon shifted away, aware of the speculation

in the maid's eyes as she collected the bowls and utensils. He moved to the window. In the distance the hills smudged blue on the horizon.

"Sir, your bedchamber is ready. It's just down the hall."

"Thank you."

The maid shot him a wide-eyed look and then pulled the door closed.

Jon moved back to the table. Tried shaking her awake, to no avail. "Catherine?"

He could not leave her here. And he could not in all good conscience let her sleep on that pathetic pallet. She would not sleep effectively, especially at the beck and call of her mother, and it was obvious she craved rest. Perhaps . . .

Moving close, he wrapped one arm around her shoulder and one around the back of her knees and gingerly lifted her. She sighed. His heart thudded painfully. She smelled clean, with that subtle sweetness he associated wholly as her own. He carried her to his bedchamber, pushed open the door, laid her on the bed.

The door opened wider. "Sir, I — oh!" The maid blushed, retreated. "I came to see if you needed anything —"

"Will you please look after Miss Winthrop? I . . . I should not be here, but I feel

sure she would rest better here than upstairs."

"Of course, sir."

"Perhaps another room can be found for
me?"

"I will find out, sir."

So he retreated to the parlor, and sank
into the seat Catherine vacated, telling
himself not to stir up memories. But she
had felt so good in his arms again, like she
belonged, her scent curling desire, fueling
dreams . . .

He groaned and flung his head in his
hands.

CHAPTER THIRTY-ONE

Catherine sighed. Rolled over to the other side of the bed. The soft, comfortable bed. She opened her eyes. Studied the unfamiliar room, the unfamiliar bedstead, the male clothing atop the corded trunk in the corner. She gasped, panic banding her chest as she studied the bed's left side. The covers appeared undisturbed but . . .

What had she done?

A knock preceded the maid's entrance. "Good afternoon, miss. You slept the day away."

Afternoon? Catherine shifted up in the bed, noticed she still wore her gown from yesterday. The heat of embarrassment flushed her skin. What must everyone think of her? She could not meet the maid's gaze. "What day is it?"

"Thursday, miss. There is a fresh gown here for you. Shall I help you into it?"

She nodded. Where had this helpfulness

come from?

The maid was swift in her ministrations. "Would you be requiring something to eat now?"

"Th-thank you." Just the thought made her stomach growl.

"If you'll go into the parlor next door, I'll be in shortly."

Catherine entered the room and sat at the table. She should probably check on her mother, but at the thought of all those stairs, a fresh wave of weariness washed over her.

"Miss Winthrop?" The deep voice compelled her attention to the door. "I trust you slept well."

She felt a deep blush heat her skin. "Th-thank you, I did." She could not look at him. What must he think of her? But she had to know. "That was your room."

"Yes."

"Where did you sleep?"

"I arranged for your pallet to be shifted to Mr. Nicholls's room." Relief filled her as he continued. "I assure you, nothing untoward occurred. I would not have you think me ungentlemanly."

"It is only that I have known myself to be" — she swallowed — "l-less than maidenly at times."

"You?"

She looked up. Saw his incredulous expression. She bit her lip.

"When have you ever been less than what you ought?"

Surely he would not make her say it.

"I know what I accused you of back in Bath, but that was spoken from frustration and wounded pride. I am so very sorry, and beg your forgiveness for being such a fool."

"You are forgiven, sir." She dropped her gaze. "But that was not what I referred to."

Floorboards creaked as he stepped closer. "Tell me what you mean."

Her gaze could only ascend as high as his waistcoat, a serviceable navy color, one she remembered as bringing out the depths of his eyes. "I refer back to that time in London, when I," she swallowed, "when I . . . kissed you."

"When you kissed me?" The astonishment in his voice made her meet his eyes. His entrancing blue-gray eyes. "I thought I kissed you."

Oh . . .

"I thought my actions had given you such an aversion to me that you complained to your father and that was why he drove me away."

"No! Of c-course not. Did you not receive

my letter?"

"No."

He hadn't? Breath hitched. Had Papa discovered it, and withheld it, and thus forced her to believe a lie?

"He told me you were leading me on, that you did not care."

"No." How could her father have said that? He truly *had* lied. "I-I thought you horrified by my abandonment of propriety."

"How could I be horrified? Not when that was the sweetest moment of my life." He smiled, the action coiling heat deep within.

For a moment she was transported back, back to when he used to smile at her like so, when the world felt so full of possibility. But — her gaze faltered — they could not go back. He was engaged. To a perfectly lovely young lady, who would make him a perfectly lovely young wife. Her heart wrenched.

"Miss Winthrop? You frown. Have I said something to upset you?"

She shook her head, trying desperately to think of a way to get this conversation back to neutral territory. But something niggled. What had he said? "Wait — you said my father warned you away? I did not know you spoke to him."

"I know you did not wish me to, and I

should have bowed to your wisdom. But I did not want to continue seeing you without his blessing." His lips pushed to one side, his expression wry. "Needless to say, I did not get it."

For some reason, his confession brought liquid to her eyes, and she blinked rapidly to remove the moisture. Her heart gave a tiny spurt of anger towards her father. Her devious, dishonest father. How could he pretend to love her? No wonder he'd tried buying her affection with gigs and earbobs. He must have realized the magnitude of his deceit.

She sighed. Poor Mr. Carlew. He *had* been blameless. He *had* loved her. But there was no point reminiscing. He was engaged to another. They should not linger in such memories. "Sir, I —"

"I almost think we would have been better following Julia's example and running away, instead of asking permission to pay my addresses to you." He stepped closer.

Catherine swallowed, attempting to clear the ball of emotion lodged in her throat. "Y-you don't mean that, surely."

"You don't know how many times I wished exactly that. But I could never do something to hurt your reputation — or your chances at a better match."

She could dwell in the past no longer! What had they been speaking of before recalling too-sweet memories of their yesterdays? She peeked up at him again. "Y-you gave up your room for me, for which I am very thankful."

His lips twisted in a rueful expression. "It was apparent you would not sleep well whilst staying with your mother, and this so-called inn had no other rooms. How you managed any rest on that thing I don't know."

"I am sorry you were not comfortable —"

"I think only of you!"

His words hung in the room. She stared at him, wide-eyed.

He continued. "My comfort does not matter. And I'll gladly relinquish that room for your use as long as necessary. Although I cannot help but wonder why you didn't avail yourselves of it to begin with."

"We were not made aware we had a choice."

"What?" He looked thunderstruck. "I cannot believe —"

"In Mr. Nabtree's defense, we were somewhat bedraggled, and did not present as though we had means —"

"That is no excuse! Surely the laws of hospitality should have — Did your mother not say who you are?"

"I'm afraid Mother's complaints have been so numerous, Mr. Nabtree was not particularly mindful," she said wryly.

His lips pursed. "And you, being meek and humble, did not wish to force the issue."

Meek and humble, or weak and helpless? It did not matter now.

He was silent for a long moment. When next he spoke his voice seemed deeper, huskier, somehow. "You cannot have any idea what trials we've been going through, wondering where you were, what had happened."

"After the inn costs, I could not afford to send word again."

"But surely you would have known I would reimburse at the end."

"They demanded funds beforehand. And I . . . I could not presume."

"Presume? Do you think me some kind of monster who would deny you? I cannot stand that after all these months you still think so poorly of me."

The guilty knot in her stomach twisted more tightly. "I do not — that is, I —"

"We have been worried sick. I . . . I have failed to protect my sister, a fact that grieves me deeply, knowing I could have prevented

it. And then when you did not return —"
His hand reached to touch hers, the simple caress hitching breath in her chest. "Oh, Catherine, I could not stand it if anything should happen to . . ."

You.

The word hovered between them unsaid, but the look in his eyes and the way his fingers gently tightened on her hand told her everything he could not say.

Her chest constricted, her cheeks grew fiery. She opened her mouth —

A knock came at the door. "Excuse me, sir, miss."

The maid gave them a shrewd glance, which removed his hand from hers and caused her to say, "Hello, Sarah. My *cousin* has come to take us home. Is that not good news?"

"If you say so, miss." She deposited the plate of food and left again.

Catherine met the blue-gray gaze, finding his eyes filled with something indiscernible. Was he embarrassed at being found in a compromising position, or had he not liked her insistence on their cousinly connection?

"Eat, before your food grows cold."

She obeyed, conscious of his intense gaze, of the depth of feeling between them, filled with unspoken things. Eventually she finished and pushed her plate away. He moved closer, sat opposite. Leaned near. "I would be glad to take you home."

That deep look in his eyes . . . Her breath caught. She swallowed. Swallowed again. "I said I did not want you to be responsible for me."

"You can say such things, but it will not change the fact that I will always feel responsible for you." He smiled. "How can I not, when you have always, and will always, live within my heart?"

Oh . . . Her heart tugged to believe, for her dreams to run free. "You don't mean that, surely."

"Yes, I do."

"But . . . but Miss Beauchamp?"

"We are not betrothed."

Breath suspended. She stared at him, the hope for so long feeble and weak suddenly leaping into flame. "You . . . you are free?"

"I believe she cared more for the match than the man. And I," he shrugged, "I cared for nothing when I thought you betrothed to the general."

Her cheeks heated. "I was wrong to agree to such a plan."

"We were both wrong. But now I hope things can be made right."

The years unraveled between them as he

spoke in a low voice something of his feelings in past weeks. His plea for forgiveness interspersed with something of his hopes, his desires, his dreams, his wish to fulfill all her dreams and desires.

His love.

His *love!*

How truly wonderful.

It took another day of arrangements — and another uncomfortable night on the pallet trying not to dream — before they could begin the journey home. Jonathan oversaw Mr. Nicholls's transportation back to Kingswood and to his grateful wife; paid the innkeepers, who still seemed somewhat bemused by the fact a Lord, a Lady, and a Miss Winthrop had stayed; then arranged a carriage to transport the ladies back to Winthrop.

Gulliver was forced to trot alongside while Jon claimed the carriage seat opposite Catherine, despite desiring to sit beside her. At least here he could watch her, and allow his spirits to rise and fall with every flicker of smile she gave when her mother was not watching.

Jon studied her, the shadows as the carriage passed through a grove of trees by turns shading then revealing her features, her usually serene face seemed more light-filled, her eyes first entreating and then calm, leaving him wondering if it was his imagination or just a trick of the light. Did she forgive him all his trespasses, or only the more recent? Would her mother hinder or help his suit?

Lady Winthrop turned from her perusal outside. "Mr. Carlew, I cannot thank you enough for taking us from that awful place." She gave a visible shudder and then fixed him with one of her more stately expressions. "You have proved yourself most gentlemanly, and I thank you."

He fought a smile, catching the flash of amusement in Catherine's eyes before gravely returning her nod. "I am always glad to be of service, ma'am."

"Hmm. Well, if that be the case, then I might ask you to remedy a few things upon our return. You are aware, are you not, of the gross insufficiencies of the cottage we are forc— that we dwell in now. Perhaps, when you can spare the time, you might venture across and we could discuss what needs to be done."

"Mama!" Catherine whispered, red staining her cheeks. "Lord Winthrop need not —"

"I am very happy to assist as much as possible to ensure your comfort, and that of your daughters" — he smiled at Catherine — "is all what it should be."

"Well, that is good, then." She settled back in her seat, and to his astonishment — and Catherine's, evidenced by her widened eyes — proceeded to make small talk with him for the next hour.

After the first inn stop he noticed Catherine's eyes grow heavier, her blinks longer. Lady Winthrop seemed somewhat restive, cramped in the incommodious carriage. It was the first available means of transport and thus would return them home the most quickly, though the journey was not nearly as comfortable as he had wished.

The carriage swerved around another bend, jolting Catherine into her mother's shoulder. Lady Winthrop winced, but said nothing.

"Ma'am, might I impose upon your goodness and suggest Miss Winthrop move to this side? It would allow more room for you, and she need not fear bumping your injuries."

"Of course." She gave a queenly nod.

Catherine met his gaze, her cheeks tingeing pink. He smiled, held out his hand, and helped her across, settling her beside him, then ensuring the blanket was tucked securely around her. "Are you quite comfortable?"

"Yes, thank you."

He now was not. Now she was so near it was all he could do not to grasp her hand, to draw her tight to his side. Seated so close he was infinitely aware of her, aware of the length of her lashes, the whorl of her ear, the way her breathing slowed as the motion of the carriage eased her to sleep. Her head jerked, he shifted fractionally, and soon her head rested against his shoulder.

Warmth ballooned within his chest. This was how he wanted it to be. He glanced down, his heart tugging a smile to his lips. If only she could always feel such ease with him.

"Ahem." He glanced up. Met the speculation in Lady Winthrop's eyes. "So that's the way of it, then."

"It is the way it has always been, ma'am."

"Then that piece of fluff?"

"Miss Beauchamp?"

She nodded.

"I regret my actions concerning her. I admit I was too proud and bitter when I first returned, although it didn't take long to once again appreciate Catherine's inestimable qualities. But her heart seemed set against me."

She had the grace to look shamefaced. "Well, I, er, didn't exactly encourage her."

"And I, to my shame, did not pursue her. Miss Beauchamp was only ever my second choice, one I felt I had to make when it seemed I had no other option."

"You refer to General Whitby?"

"Yes."

"How you could believe such foolishness I don't know, but I will give you this. You seem an honest man, and if experience teaches us anything, it's that honesty trumps intelligence every time." Her gaze sharpened. "You are not engaged?"

"My sister's elopement scandalized the Beauchamps into rejection."

She nodded, and he felt a wild streak of panic. Were Julia's sins enough for Lady Winthrop to object also?

"That only proves how ridiculously prejudiced some people can be. I'm glad I'm not so easily persuaded to overlook a gentleman's good heart because of a relation's folly."

His heart thumped with hope. "Then I, then we . . . ?"

"Have my blessing? Yes."

He grinned, and gently wrapped an arm around Catherine's shoulders, allowing her to rest more comfortably. Lady Winthrop smiled back, and — miracle of miracles — he found himself thinking he might get on with his future mother-in-law quite well after all.

CHAPTER THIRTY-TWO

Catherine awoke from a very pleasant dream to find it true. He was holding her, and her mother was looking on approvingly. She blinked, glanced up, met his smiling blue gaze. Upon realizing she leaned against him, she blushed, pushing away to a more upright position. "I'm so sorry."

"For being exhausted? That *is* a crime worth apologizing for."

She chuckled; he echoed it softly, the sound filling her heart with warmth.

"Ladies, as we are almost there, I had best confess that in your absence, I engaged some men to complete a small amount of work around the Dower House. I hope you will not find it too presumptuous but will take it in the spirit in which it was given, as it is something I should have attended to before I allowed you to remove there."

As her mother murmured — surprisingly — something of an admittance that the previous Lord Winthrop should have attended to things better, he slanted Catherine an inscrutable look.

No . . . She tamped down her irrepressible imaginings. No, she dared not hope for more.

The carriage turned into the laneway leading to the cottage, the wooden fence now standing more upright than a line of militia. The fields beyond were freshly cut, so fresh, the pleasant tang of grass still hung in the air. The drive held none of the bumps of their exiting journey; the holes having been filled. But it was only when the carriage came to a standstill and they were handed outside that Lord Winthrop's forewarning drew gasps.

The cottage was transformed. Gone was the broken shutter, now fixed and freshly painted, to match the repainted windowsills and door likewise refurbished.

"The roof!"

"There were a great many tiles that needed replacing. I trust you will be not bothered in the next rain shower."

"How did you know?" Catherine asked. "It wasn't obvious from outside."

"Your servant was, ahem, somewhat informative on particular deficiencies, shall we say?"

She dragged her gaze away. Oh, why had she and Mama been quite so vocal in their faultfinding? She studied the front garden, as remorse continued to churn. "I see you managed to persuade the flowers to bloom, too."

He chuckled again, a low, warm sound that wrapped gladness round her heart. "I'm afraid I cannot take the credit, as they managed to flower all by themselves."

She smiled, and picked a pale pink lilac blossom, before following Mama inside, only to be forced to halt by Mama's exclamation.

"You painted inside!"

"I didn't personally, and please forgive me if these are not the colors you would have chosen. But it seemed an opportune time to do so, without occupants who might be bothered by the odor and chaos that generally results from such actions."

"It will do very well," her mother pronounced with a nod.

Catherine smiled, glancing over her shoulder to see a similar expression on their benefactor's face, which melded to something sweeter when he caught her eye.

All of a sudden she was conscious of how near he was, that he could easily take her hand, that the hall, though freshly painted, still retained something of its former dimness. She glanced away, forced herself to breathe.

"Ah, Tilly, Mrs. Jones. How are you?"

As her mother spoke with the servants, Catherine tilted up a glance and said in a low voice, "Thank you, sir, for all this. You are very good."

His lips pushed to one side. "If only that were true."

"You are!" She placed her hand on his arm. "You have been exceedingly kind, when . . . when we have often been anything but. I'm sorry."

"Sorry for my kindness?" His smile flashed. "If you prefer, I'll ask the men to retrieve those cracked tiles —"

"No!" She smothered her laughter. "You know exactly what I mean, sir."

His smile grew wistful. "If only that were true."

She experienced another jolt of wonder, peering at him more closely to determine his meaning when Mama's throat-clearing drew her attention to the speculative looks of the servants. Catherine stepped away, found a smile, and said, "Well, this is all wonderful, is it not, Mama?" She grasped her mother's arm. "Shall we see what more awaits us?"

Mrs. Jones guided them to the kitchen, and then Tilly showed them upstairs. Everywhere was improved, mended, and freshly painted. While Mama supervised the unpacking of luggage, Catherine wandered outside, finding their benefactor beside the stables.

She hurried toward him. "Oh, Mr. Carlew," she breathed, the name falling unconsciously from her lips. "I cannot thank you enough."

His look was almost apologetic. "So you approve?"

"I don't know why you wish for my approval, sir."

"I don't know why you do not." He picked up her hand. "Miss Winthrop —"

"Hello, Miss Cathy," Jack burst forward, tailed by Frank who also offered a greeting, before touching his forehead. "Oh, my lord, I didnae see you."

"I am usually not so easy to miss," he murmured, releasing a sigh as the groom insisted on showing her the recent refurbishments, all the while exclaiming about his new assistant's way with animals.

When Frank finally paused for a breath she glanced up at the tall man beside her. "Is this more of your doing, sir?"

"Jack spends much of his time working

with Wilson up at the Manor, with a regular day a week working here. Wilson is extremely pleased with Jack's skills, and Jack's wage is, of course, being covered by myself." Lord Winthrop's brow furrowed. "I hope you do not mind."

"How could I mind?" She smiled up at him, warmth filling her at the look of pleasure in his gaze. She tugged her gaze away, happy to be led on a short tour of the stables, which could now accommodate several horses as well as her gig. She was happier still to be reunited with her pet. "Ginger!"

Lord Winthrop nodded. "You never did explain why she was being housed at the Hall." His eyes twinkled. "But I gather it had something to do with not wanting to have a sense of obligation?"

She ducked her head, thankful Frank and Jack had moved away. "I don't know what to say."

"You could have asked me. I would have helped."

"I'm sorry."

"There's nothing to forgive. Just tell me if you approve."

"Oh, I do! But why?"

He tugged at his neckcloth, not meeting her eyes. "I . . . I was unaware just how things were situated, until I came to visit."

"When was that, sir?"

"After Christmas. Mrs. Jones was so good as to list a variety of shortcomings regarding the cottage, including the poor stables, and the kitchen stove she mentioned several times."

Well she remembered the early days as Mama and she bemoaned the cottage's cramped conditions. "I'm afraid things were a little difficult for us to adjust to."

"Naturally they were. I'm only sorry that you did not see fit to mention such things before such a drastic move away became necessary."

She could not look at him. How many times had Mama declared she would not ask *that man* for anything? "You could have visited and learned this for yourself."

"I did attempt to visit, at the beginning, but received such a cold welcome that I realized my company was neither sought nor welcome."

She studied her feet, remembering Mama's crowing at having sent away the imposter in no uncertain terms. "I am sorry, sir."

"I also regret things were not as they ought to have been, especially for such a lady as your mother."

"I suppose it is good to attend to matters

now, so your Mama . . ." Her voice trailed away. How ridiculous to think his mother would be forced to live in the cottage. How many houses did she own?

"I think we may safely assume your mother's concerns and wishes concerning the Dower House will be the only ones to be considered," he said drily.

"Oh." Her brow furrowed. But what about her wishes? Did he have no thought for her?

He smiled. "Miss Winthrop, I hope you and your mother will come to dinner tomorrow night. We should like to celebrate your return."

"Of course. We would be delighted."

He bowed, picked up her hand, and gently pressed it with a kiss. "Until tomorrow?"

"Until tomorrow." And her heart fluttered with anticipation.

Next day

"Ah, dear Lady Winthrop, and dearest Catherine. How wonderful to see you again."

"And to see you, Lady Harkness," Mama said, offering a nod. "I felicitate you on your daughter's marriage. I trust she is well?"

A shadow crossed her face before Lady Harkness replied, "Yes, thank you. Julia writes that she is extremely happy, and

540

apologizes for their haste. I, of course, have no wish to see that man again, but should my dear daughter wish to visit from the wilds of Scotland I would have no hesitation in welcoming her here."

Something tight in Catherine's chest eased. Thank God Julia was safe, was even happy. Did this mean Jonathan would not need to chase his sister beyond the border?

A quick glance at him revealed his pensive look. He met Catherine's gaze. "She has made her choice. We will pray and hope that God will guide their way."

She nodded. How important to remember God's promises in times of hardship, that hope could be found in trusting Him.

Lady Harkness smiled. "Perhaps Jonathan, you might wish to show Catherine the gardens? They are very pretty at this time of evening, with the birds and such."

"Of course. Miss Winthrop?" He offered his arm, which she accepted, and led her outside to the terraced garden where the fountain now tinkled water.

It was a beautiful evening: mild, no breeze, the day's sun tinting everything with a golden glow. As promised, the sparrows danced and flitted in the water, sprinkling tiny diamond droplets.

She smiled up at him. "I am so glad you

fixed the fountain. It was always one of my favorite things about this garden when I was a child."

"So Geoffreys said."

"You asked him?"

"I did not want anything spoiled that you held dear. When Mother called in the redecorators, I did not let them touch your room, nor that of your mother and father."

"But why?"

He smiled gently. "Surely you can guess."

Breath caught. She tried to tamp down the throbbing of her heart. Her guesses had proved erroneous in the past.

"I hope you approve?"

"How can I not? Everything is as it was, only better now, as it should be." Had Papa had the money to fix things. The old pang hit her, but not like before. Instead of intense pain it held something more bitter-sweet. Poor Papa.

"I am glad, for . . ." He glanced away.

The moment suddenly took on a weight, a significance, an importance. It felt like her moment to ask, to push the conversation into honesty demanded by things of eternal consequence.

"For . . . ?"

His attention returned to her, resolve written on his face. "For I wish my wife to enjoy living here as much as I do."

"Y-your wife?" She stepped back. No, surely she had not misread the situation. Surely he harbored feelings no longer for Miss Beauchamp.

His lips widened, as he gave a low chuckle. "Don't look at me like that, dearest Catherine. You must know my feelings by now."

She shook her head. "I . . . I have been wrong before."

"You were not wrong before. You never *were* wrong. You have always been all that is good, and true, matchless and beyond compare." He reached down, plucked a handful of sweet violets and presented them to her. She drank in the sweet, subtle scent, heart thrilling, heat filling her cheeks until she was sure they held a similar hue to the dusky pink shawl she wore. "I remember you once told me what violets symbolized."

He did?

"I have always thought them so appropriate for you, so sweet, so modest and unassuming, yet ever faithful, ever lovely."

He had?

"I just wish I'd never given you cause to doubt." His eyes shadowed. "I can never forgive myself for that time."

"Oh, please" — she placed a hand on his

arm — "please don't hold on to that any-more."

"I won't, if you . . ." He picked up her hand, examined it. She could see the gold in his long lashes as his perusal continued. Breath caught in her throat as he lifted her hand and kissed it. He shifted closer so she was forced to look up. From this near posi-tion she could see the bronze hairs on his chin, the lips tweaked into pensiveness, the eyes so clear and blue holding a promise. "Dearest Catherine, say you'll forgive me."

Her heart sang at his nearness, at his endearment. "Of course I forgive you."

"You are so kind, so generous, when often I have not been." He shook his head. "I was an angry fool, embittered by your father's refusal, then I came here, saw your sweet-ness hadn't changed, only matured, but I was convinced you could never love me again —"

"I never stopped."

"Really?" His eyes glowed with tender-ness. "Then I have been twice the imbecile, for I was a jealous fool when I saw you in Bath."

"The general was but a kind friend, someone who paid me compliments while I tried to convince myself I would not die if you married Miss Beauchamp."

He laughed, low and husky. "She came at a time when I was at my lowest, my weakest, when I was sure you could never hold me in affection again."

She winced internally. Oh, if only she had been quicker to forgive, to understand his good nature had never changed. If only she had been brave enough to show her true feelings, how many months might they have already had together?

He shook his head. "It is true she tickled my heart, but she could never dwell there, making life lovely and worthwhile, not like you always have."

Oh-h-h . . .

He released her hand to gesture at the gardens. "All of this, the cottage, everything was all for you. There has never been anyone but you. My dearest Catherine, I love only *you*."

Happiness broke over her as a wave. "Oh, Jonathan." His name tasted like honey. "I love you, too."

His smile could light a thousand night skies. "Dearest, sweetest Catherine, say you'll make me the happiest of men and be my wife."

"I will."

His fingers slid across her cheek, his eyes darkened, before dropping to her lips. She closed her eyes, her nerves tightening in expectation, and in a moment both sweetly reminiscent and shamelessly eager, she felt his breath caress her skin before his lips closed over hers.

A stab of wild joy pulsed deep within, and she leaned close, closer, savoring his fingers framing her face, holding her as tenderly, as possessively, as his kiss.

This moment — made of memories, sustained by dreams — this delight cherished, once thought lost forever, now rekindled, sweeter than ever.

How truly wonderful.

EPILOGUE

Winthrop
May 1817

"I congratulate you, Lord Winthrop, on your wisest investment yet."

Jonathan smiled down at the pert Countess of Hawkesbury. "She is a treasure not easily won."

"And yet you have won her, which says as much about her ability to appreciate a person of quality and character as it does yours."

"Thank you."

She grinned. "Now I know about protocol — Nicholas is forever having to tell me what social customs must be followed — but I simply insist you escort your betrothed instead of me."

"But —"

"Come now. Do you wish to suffer the disapproval of an earl's wife?"

"Not at all." The dinner gong sounded.

"So go. Collect her now."

He did, much to the surprise of the other guests, but they didn't mind, and neither did he, for there was no one else he'd rather speak with, gaze upon, than his lovely Catherine.

"You are so lovely, my dear."

Her cheeks flushed, making her eyes seem ever more starry. Mourning had been put off, she wore a simple cream gown with slightly puffed sleeves, from which slipped her elegant arms. Around her neck was the ruby necklet Harold Carlew had once given Mother. She had happily bequeathed it to Catherine. "Of course she should have it! It never suited my coloring, anyway. Besides, I much prefer emeralds."

The dinner passed in a surfeit of dishes, but he was barely aware of what he ate, of what was said, save that he was happier than he ever dreamed. Here, seated at the head of Winthrop's table, surrounded by the people who wished them best, next to the woman soon to be his wife. Was it possible a man could die of happiness?

Clothilde leaned past Drusilla to gain his attention. "Did I mention Avebury's fortunes have improved?"

A few times, yes. He listened anyway, glad more for Peter's sake than anything else.

Peter at least seemed to have derived joy from his archaeological diggings, telling stories of his time at the coast in a manner sure to bore a few guests very soon.

He turned to Catherine, seated at his right, and met her smile. Her lips beckoned him nearer, her eyes deep pools of mystery that the candlelight only enhanced. How long until they wed?

"Excuse me, old man, but please remember there are other guests here."

Jon blinked, his reverie broken, and said to the viscount, seated next to Catherine, "Unfortunately, some of my guests do not let themselves be forgotten."

Carmichael grinned, before saying to Catherine, "I think he is entranced by your beauty, Miss Winthrop. You are lovelier than I have ever seen, if I may be permitted to say so."

"You may," Catherine said, her eyes, her smile fixed on Jon.

Jon's heart swelled. How good, how right this was. How *blessed* he was by God.

"Why must you?" Serena Winthrop asked from opposite Carmichael.

"I beg your pardon?" the viscount asked.

"It is not *my* pardon you should beg. It's Catherine's, and Jonathan's, for flirting with his intended."

"Serena!" hissed her mother. "Do not bother the viscount."

"Mama, I rather doubt he's ever bothered by anything one says, but feels instead a sense of superior amusement."

"Serena!"

Jon laughed at his friend's dumbstruck expression. He sipped his wine and murmured, "I do believe she has your measure, young man."

Carmichael's look of surprise melded into something approaching rueful. He turned more fully in his seat as he studied Catherine's sister. "What an extraordinary young lady you are."

"Thank you." Serena gave him one of her cool looks, as Catherine called them, before returning her attention to her plate. For a young lady of eighteen she possessed a poise and self-assurance worthy of a duchess three times her age. Her words could be quite cutting, though her countenance remained as tranquil as her name.

Jon raised his brows at Carmichael, who still seemed at a loss, before smiling at his wife-to-be. Thank God he had learned to push past Catherine's aloofness, to understand her depths. If he hadn't . . .

"Well, I suppose you'll all be relieved to learn I shall soon return to London." Amid the sounds of protest, his mother smiled. "No, it is time."

He saw her smile slip a little, and he felt a similar shadow. His sister's fate hung over them like a silent weight. No word apart from that one letter to say they were married. While that assured somewhat, he remained concerned that the enquiry agents he'd employed had failed to locate her or Hale. Where was she? *God, protect her...*

"You shall be missed, Lady Harkness," Catherine said, with a tender look.

"Perhaps. But that might be because there will be so much less to talk about in my absence."

Amid the ripple of laughter came Lady Winthrop's voice, "You do not feature in *every* conversation, Clarinda."

"And that is as it should be. For tonight we should focus on my wonderful son's marvelous engagement to a simply wonderful girl, whom I am very proud to welcome as a daughter."

Catherine's cheeks pinked. She glanced to the side, held his gaze. "Wonderful."

He smiled. Wonderful. And awe-inspiring, how God transformed two pained hearts with such surprising grace. He clasped her hand. Words from a long-ago poet leapt to mind: "If our two loves be one, or thou and

I love so alike that none do slacken, none can die."

Their love, their hopes, once thought lost, but found again: stronger, deeper, forever.

AUTHOR'S NOTE

In 1816, England (and much of the Northern Hemisphere) experienced what became known as "The Year Without a Summer" when global temperatures dropped, and rain and unseasonable coolness led to harvest failures and food shortages. This is believed to be the result of the Mt. Tambora eruption in April 1815 in the Dutch East Indies, which saw the release of microscopic particles into the air that led to magnificent sunsets in England, such as those painted by J. M. W. Turner and witnessed by Clara in *The Dishonorable Miss DeLancey.*

I was blessed in 2015 with the opportunity to visit the United Kingdom and see my sister who was living there at the time. During my stay, we had the joy of visiting Bath, made famous as the place of Roman-era thermal springs and as the setting of several novels by two of my favorite authors, Jane Austen and Georgette Heyer, including my favorite novel of all time, Jane Austen's *Persuasion*. If ever you get the chance to visit Bath, do so. It is a World Heritage Site lined with stunning eighteenth-century architecture, and to visit the Pump Room to "take the waters" (not as vile as often portrayed!), or to visit the magnificent Abbey, or to see the Assembly Rooms much as they were in the Regency period is a real privilege. This Aussie author loved the opportunity to step back in time and walk around historic places made famous in books and films — so different from my part of the world.

For photos and more information about my trip to Bath, and to check out the book club discussion guide and other behind-the-book details, please visit www.carolynmiller author.com.

ACKNOWLEDGMENTS

Thank You, God, for giving this gift of creativity and the amazing opportunity to express it. Thank You for patiently loving us and offering us hope through Jesus Christ.

Thank you, Joshua, for your love and encouragement. I appreciate your willingness to read my stories, and all the support you give in so many ways. I love you!

Thank you, Caitlin, Jackson, Asher, and Tim. I love you, I'm proud of you, and I'm so grateful you understand why I spend so much time in imaginary worlds.

To my family, church family, and friends — whose support, encouragement, and prayers I value and have needed — thank you. Big thanks to Roslyn and Jacqueline for being patient in reading through so many of my manuscripts and for offering suggestions to make my stories sing.

Thank you, Tamela Hancock Murray, my agent, for helping this little Australian negotiate the big wide Ameri

Thank you to the authors
who have endorsed, and enco
opened doors along the way: you
ing!

Thanks to my Aussie writer frie
Australasian Christian Writers, C
Writers Downunder, and Omega W
appreciate you.

To the Ladies of Influence, your su
and encouragement are gold!

To the fabulous team at Kregel, thank
for believing in me and for making *M*
Winthrop shine.

Finally, thank you to my readers. I treasur
your kind messages of support and lovely
reviews. I hope you enjoyed Catherine's
story.

God bless you.

ABOUT THE AUTHOR

Carolyn Miller lives in New South Wales, Australia, with her husband and four children. A longtime lover of Regency romance, Carolyn's novels have won a number of RWA and ACFW contests. She is a member of American Christian Fiction Writers and Australasian Christian Writers.